GUARDIAN

ZHEN HUN

GUARDIAN

ZHEN HUN

WRITTEN BY

priest

ILLUSTRATED BY

Ying

COVER ILLUSTRATION BY

Marmaladica

TRANSLATED BY

Yuka, Shry, amixy

Seven Seas Entertainment

GUARDIAN: ZHEN HUN VOL. 2

Published originally under the title of 《镇魂》 (Zhen Hun)
Author © priest
English edition rights under license granted by 北京晋江原创网络科技有限公司
(Beijing Jinjiang Original Network Technology Co., Ltd.)

Cover Art by Marmaladica
Interior Art by Ying

Seven Seas press and purchase enquiries can be sent
to Marketing Manager Lauren Hill at press@gomanga.com.
Information regarding the distribution and purchase of digital editions is available
from Digital Manager CK Russell at digital@gomanga.com.

Follow Seven Seas Entertainment online at
sevenseasentertainment.com.

TRANSLATION: Yuka, Shry, amixy
ADAPTATION: Ealasaid Weaver
COVER DESIGN: M. A. Lewife
INTERIOR DESIGN & LAYOUT: Clay Gardner
COPY EDITOR: Jehanne Bell
PROOFREADER: Jade Gardner, Pengie
EDITOR: Laurel Ashgrove
PREPRESS TECHNICIAN: Melanie Ujimori, Jules Valera
MANAGING EDITOR: Alyssa Scavetta
EDITOR-IN-CHIEF: Julie Davis
PUBLISHER: Lianne Sentar
VICE PRESIDENT: Adam Arnold
PRESIDENT: Jason DeAngelis

ISBN: 978-1-63858-940-2
Printed in Canada
First Printing: March 2024
10 9 8 7 6 5 4 3 2 1

TABLE OF CONTENTS

ARC 3: MERIT BRUSH

APPENDIXES

ARC 3

MERIT BRUSH

CHAPTER 1

NIGHT HAD ALREADY FALLEN when Guo Changcheng left the Group Home for Autistic Children. Fresh snow covered Dragon City, and the roads were treacherous. He had to drive at a snail's pace, hoping to reach the post office before it closed for the day. His dumpy little car was packed with all kinds of books—textbooks, exercise books, and children's literature, to name a few. They were all wrapped in craft paper and plastic, and he planned to mail them to the elementary school he sponsored before the end of the year.

Between Guo Changcheng's timidity and his mediocre driving skills, he navigated the wet, slippery road as if his car were a large turtle. But it might simply have been an inauspicious day for traveling, because he nearly hit someone despite his cautious driving. A person in gray dashed out in front of him and fell, landing practically under the wheels of his car.

Several cars skidded to a stop. Only the fact that everyone was driving very slowly due to the snow and slick roads prevented utter pandemonium.

Cursing, a man with an explosive temper rolled down his window to yell, "What's your problem?! If you're trying to scam someone, can't you at least do it someplace with less traffic?!"

Guo Changcheng was already scrambling out of his car. "A-are you okay? I'm so sorry! I really am."

The person who'd fallen was incredibly skinny, barely more than skin and bones. His withered face was half-hidden by the brim of his hat, and what skin Guo Changcheng could see was a waxy yellow. A black aura seemed to cling to the man, but perhaps that was just his imagination.

The incensed bystander was still raging. "Why are you bothering with him? Why didn't you just run him over?!"

Guo Changcheng, conflicted, waved apologetically at Mr. Road Rage before trying to reach out and help the fallen man up. "Can you stand? C-can I take you to the hospital...?"

The man on the ground responded to Guo Changcheng's kindness by slapping his hand away. Then, he pulled himself up and walked away.

But as he did, their gazes just so happened to meet. Startled, Guo Changcheng found himself staring into horrifyingly empty eyes, devoid of any spark of life. As the man brushed past, Guo Changcheng then glimpsed something below his ear: a pitch-black mark shaped like a fingerprint.

"Are you sure you're all right?" Guo Changcheng yelled after him. "Do you want my contact information? If anything comes up, you can call me! My name is..."

But the man in the hat had already turned and disappeared down a little side street.

The driver who'd been yelling left as well, but not without leaving a parting shot in the middle of the street in the frigid wind for Guo Changcheng. He spat, "What kind of dumbass are you, bro?"

Guo Dumbass sighed, turned, and opened his car door. But as he was about to get in, he suddenly saw a reflection in the car window.

The guy in the hat had reappeared, his profile just visible around the corner. Somehow, he looked as if he were up to no good.

Just then, two women walked past the lurking man. As they crossed his path, his mouth suddenly gaped open and his tongue, nearly fifteen centimeters long, protruded. Watching them go, he inhaled deeply.

One of the women abruptly staggered, as if her blood sugar had just crashed. She seemed to be on the verge of passing out, but her companion was able to steady her—and then something floated out of her body and straight into the man's mouth!

Guo Changcheng whirled around, but there was nothing to be seen other than the snowy street bustling with pedestrians.

He stumbled into his car, heart pounding thunderously. Quickly taking the little baton Zhao Yunlan had given him out of his bag, he tucked it into his jacket's inner chest pocket. He gave it a firm pat, as if it were a source of courage, and inched his car back onto the road.

When Guo Changcheng arrived at work the next day, he was greeted by Zhu Hong's meal card flying toward his face. "Xiao-Guo, jie wants beef pancakes today—the kind that've been fried to a crisp! And bring me a cup of yogurt while you're at it!"

Guo Changcheng was accustomed to being bossed around, so he simply set down his bag, made a noise of agreement, and left for the cafeteria. He reached the doorway just as Chu Shuzhi arrived with half a jianbing in his mouth. Guo Changcheng snapped to attention. "Good morning, Chu-ge!"

"Mhm." Chu-ge barely raised an eyelid to give him a once over, as if not wanting to be bothered with him, and kept walking.

But after only a couple of steps, Chu Shuzhi abruptly reversed course. He grabbed Guo Changcheng by the collar and dragged him back before the kid could leave the office. "Hold it. What filthy thing did you run into?"

Guo Changcheng gave him a blank stare.

Chu Shuzhi's jianbing-scented hands seemed to grab something from Guo Changcheng's shoulders, then spun him around. After briskly swatting at Guo Changcheng's back and both sides of his waist, Chu Shuzhi took out a napkin and wiped his hands before giving Guo Changcheng a shove. "You had bad luck all over you. I cleaned you up, so you can go now."

Red-faced from all the swatting, Guo Changcheng darted off, running with tiny steps. Munching on the thin crisps inside the jianbing, Chu Shuzhi asked, "What is this kid cultivating for? He's so rich with merits that he's practically dripping fat."

Zhu Hong, who still hadn't had breakfast, found her mouth watering as if he were describing a succulent pig nearly ready for slaughter.

"Hey, is there food?" Zhao Yunlan came dashing through the criminal investigation unit's door. Catching sight of Chu Shuzhi, Zhao Yunlan gave him a quick pat-down without another word. When his search turned up a hard-boiled egg in Chu Shuzhi's coat pocket, he unceremoniously claimed it for himself.

Chu Shuzhi was outraged, but as Zhao Yunlan's subordinate, he didn't have the guts to protest.

Next, Zhao Yunlan grabbed a carton of milk from the fridge, ripped it open, and guzzled it down.

"That's mine!" Daqing yowled. "You're even stealing cat food?! Have you no shame?!"

Zhu Hong asked, "Why don't you go to the cafeteria?"

"I'm in a hurry." Mouth full of milk and egg, Zhao Yunlan strode off purposefully...straight into a wall.

At that very moment, Guo Changcheng happened to return with the beef pancakes. Before he had a chance to register the shock, he saw his boss vanish through the wall.

"Okay, close your mouth." Zhu Hong took her breakfast from him. "There's an invisible door there. It leads to the library. You're a mortal who doesn't have enough cultivation to understand anything in there even if you could enter, so naturally, you can't see the door."

Despite having just finished his jianbing, Chu Shuzhi didn't feel quite full without an egg to follow it. He quickly snagged a piece of the beef pancake out of Zhu Hong's hands. "I can see it, but I can't go in. I'm barred from the library."

"H-how come?" Guo Changcheng asked.

Chu Shuzhi answered with a somewhat ominous smile. "Because I have a record."

Guo Changcheng bit his tongue. Unsurprisingly, he was still afraid of Chu-ge.

Five minutes later, Zhao Yunlan burst back out from the wall, now holding an old, tattered book. He tossed the eggshell and milk carton into Guo Changcheng's garbage can, then grabbed a tissue from Zhu Hong's desk. Without a word to anyone, he left so quickly that wind seemed to rise in his wake.

That was the last they saw of him for the day.

It had already been half a month since they'd returned from the snowy mountain. In the blink of an eye, New Year's had come and gone. The temperatures in Dragon City had plummeted with the arrival of a huge windstorm that blew everyone, living and dead alike, into the Lunar New Year.

The approach of the Lunar New Year found Director Zhao so busy that he could barely remember his own name. Between humans, ghosts, yao, and monsters, he had endless social obligations. All day, every day, his work phone rang like a hotline. The desk calendars in each department had already been changed to new ones. In the depths of winter, darkness came early, so the "night shift" staff were out and about even before the end of the workday.

On this particular day, Sangzan floated into the criminal investigation unit.

Comrade Sangzan didn't have it easy. In life, he had been a ruthless conspirator. After his death, he'd been stuck in the Mountain-River Awl. Days, then years, then centuries had all run together while the outside world carried on without him. And now that he was free and reformed, ready to be a new person—a new ghost, rather—he faced a harsh realization. Once a cunning conspirator, he was now too ignorant to understand anything anyone said.

The only person left in the world who could communicate with him was Wang Zheng, and while the Hanga language was her mother tongue, the plain fact was that she'd stopped speaking it by the time she was twenty. In the three hundred years since then, she'd been fully immersed in Mandarin. So when Sangzan realized it was easier for Wang Zheng to communicate with the outside people and ghosts than with him, he decided to knuckle down and learn Mandarin as well.

Sangzan was a ruthless person. As evidenced by the fact that he'd once poisoned his own wife and offspring, he would stop at absolutely nothing to achieve a goal. So for half a month now, he'd been muttering random syllables in Wang Zheng's ear practically nonstop, driving her halfway to a nervous breakdown.

But by this point, he was slowly starting to grasp Mandarin pronunciation and could now mimic others somewhat. He could even hold simple conversations.

Working hard to shape each syllable, one slow word at a time, Sangzan relayed the Mandarin message he'd been entrusted with the best he could. "Gelan says...besides the yeely 'bomus,' there is a benedict fee. She... She wants emryone to prepare their wheat."

He hadn't memorized the message very well. He understood only half of what he was saying and was parroting the sounds.

"Amitabha, why are we preparing wheat?" Lin Jing asked. "Are we making buns for the Lunar New Year's Eve dinner?"

Gesturing, Sangzan said, "Not buns. 'Wheat.' It's batter if it's 'transformation fee'..."

"Director Zhao said that on top of our year-end bonuses, everyone will receive an extra 5,000 yuan as a benefit. Come to my office and get it before this weekend. Next week, give me all your receipts, especially the ones for transportation costs. Labor insurance receipts are acceptable too." Wang Zheng hastily floated down from upstairs, shooting a glare at Sangzan. "Can't even learn to speak properly."

Sangzan's usually stern and fierce expression turned tender at the sight of her. With a love-struck smile, he went over and tugged carefully on her hand.

"Don't mess around. I'm busy," Wang Zheng scolded quietly before addressing the room. "Who did Director Zhao go to meet up with? I have an urgent document that needs his signature."

Sangzan said, "I-I'll take it..."

Wang Zheng raised a hand to block him and ducked out of his way. "You? You'll scare his drinking buddies."

Sangzan didn't get angry about being rejected. He just tagged along behind her like a large dog, watching as she hurried through the darkened hallways, flustered and busy. Occasionally, she'd stop and say something to him in a language no one else understood, bringing a peaceful, satisfied smile to his face.

"I fucking hate people who flaunt their love in front of everyone. Especially in a foreign language," Zhu Hong complained. "The public nuisance finally stopped flirting with everything that moves, but now these two are trying to blind me with their sappy displays!"

"May Buddha have mercy," Lin Jing intoned. "Unwed Benefactor, be free of envy, jealousy, and hatred."

Zhu Hong was about to give him a smack when the phone on her desk rang. She took the call instead. "Hello? Oh? Where?"

She gestured sharply, preventing anyone from leaving. Everybody watched as she tore a sticky note free and began to scribble on it. "Mm-hmm. Go on... 26...Yellow Cliff Road. Yellow Cliff Temple Hospital, right? Okay, I'll let them know. Oh, and when you have time tonight, come by the office. Wang Zheng has a bunch of stuff for you to sign."

It was clearly Zhao Yunlan on the line.

Zhu Hong hung up and said, "In keeping with our department's tradition of doing nothing all day and then racking up overtime at night, it's five minutes past time to clock out and our fucking boss has just dumped a pile of work in our lap."

Hearing that, Lin Jing bolted out the door before anyone else could react. As he vanished into the night, he cried, "Not listening, not listening! I'm not listening!"

Zhu Hong stuck the note with the address to the wall, wrapped her scarf over her face, and followed right behind him. "I'm a cold-blooded animal; I'm afraid of the cold! Goodbye!"

Daqing slipped out as the door shut. "My winter coat hasn't even come in yet!"

And just like that, the only ones left in the office were Chu Shuzhi, who hadn't had time to react, and the fool Guo Changcheng.

"Fuck," said Chu Shuzhi.

Ten minutes later, Chu Shuzhi was a passenger in Guo Changcheng's car, and the pair were on their way to Yellow Cliff Temple Hospital.

Chapter 2

OUT OF ALL THE PEOPLE Guo Changcheng feared the most, Chu Shuzhi topped the list. Even Zhao Yunlan had to move aside. While Zhao Yunlan was powerful, he also tended to be kind. He cracked jokes and messed around like any normal person might. At most, he was intimidating in the way a father or brother might be.

Chu Shuzhi was different. To Guo Changcheng, he always seemed to have a cold, mysterious aura, like some sort of unapproachable sage.

Guo Changcheng, carrying his ever-present little notebook, followed Chu Shuzhi into the hospital. He didn't dare utter even a single unnecessary word.

A young police officer was waiting by the door. After checking his ID and showing him theirs, they headed for the patient's room.

As they walked, the officer, xiao-Wang, said, "Our boss is in there too. He just got off the phone with Director Zhao. The situation is pretty grim. Somebody out there is selling poisoned food. The hospital still hasn't been able to figure out what the victim in here was actually poisoned with."

"Poisoned food?" Chu Shuzhi asked. "What did he eat?"

"Some fruit," xiao-Wang said. "According to the family, the victim bought an orange at the roadside and ate it. The second he finished it, he collapsed. They immediately rushed him to the hospital and called the police."

As he spoke, xiao-Wang opened the door to the patient's room. They were greeted by an agonized, chilling scream. Startled, Guo Changcheng stood on tiptoe to peek from behind Chu Shuzhi.

On the bed lay a man who might have been thirty or forty years old, writhing and struggling against the group of doctors and nurses trying to hold him down. A sobbing woman, perhaps a family member, stood beside him.

The man had a death grip on one doctor's hand as he howled and gave shrill cries. "My leg! My leg's broken! Aaaaah, my leg! Aaaaah!"

"His leg?" Chu Shuzhi turned to xiao-Wang. "Didn't you say it was poisoned food?"

"Thing is, his leg's fine," xiao-Wang said. "Not even a bruise. Nothing shows up on the X-rays either. None of it makes any sense."

Chu Shuzhi approached the bedside and patted a nurse on the shoulder, asking her to make room for him. He pulled back the man's eyelids and examined his pupils. After also checking behind the man's ears, he chanted under his breath. Then he reached out with a grabbing motion and pressed down hard against the man's chest with a clenched fist.

The struggling patient was suddenly calm.

"Does it still hurt?" Chu Shuzhi asked.

The man, finally able to catch his breath, gave him a grateful look and shook his head.

The doctors and nurses, on the other hand, were all giving Chu Shuzhi strange, judgmental looks. It was very possible that they all suddenly suspected there was a cult involved somehow.

When Chu Shuzhi let go, the man instantly resumed his desperate screaming, rolling around on the bed. Chu Shuzhi ignored him, turned to Guo Changcheng, and snapped his fingers. "We're done here. Let's go. We've gotta get back and write a report."

Guo Changcheng gaped. Done? How could this count as being done? What had even happened, exactly?

After Shen Wei concluded his last class, he waited until the students had left before packing up his own things and returning to his home in the Mortal Realm. On the way, he couldn't help repeatedly looking at his phone, even though the device had only three functions: calling, texting, and displaying the time.

Shen Wei wasn't a fan of technology. He was a slow-tempered, antiquated man who still found writing letters more convenient. If something was urgent, he could write a quick note. If not, he could take his time writing, and so what if it ran a little long? And as for phone calls, well, you paid for those by the minute, which gave him the horribly uncomfortable sense that someone was scrutinizing him as he spoke.

All of that aside, there was a sense of happiness and anticipation in the act of opening a letter, especially if the person who'd written it was special to him. Every single word was full of life, and letters could be kept forever.

Alas, Zhao Yunlan never wrote. He couldn't even be bothered with all the strokes it took to write his own name when signing for packages, so he'd draw a circle and leave it at that.

Shen Wei's phone still held every text Zhao Yunlan had ever sent him. He couldn't bear to delete a single one.

In the time since they'd returned from the snowy mountain, Zhao Yunlan hadn't pestered him even once.

Perhaps Zhao Yunlan still felt uncomfortable—and why wouldn't he? Who *wouldn't* be made uncomfortable by someone as inauspicious as the Soul-Executing Emissary?

It was just as well, Shen Wei told himself. At most, a mortal might live a few dozen years—barely the blink of an eye. When death arrived, a human life would be extinguished like a candle, and this life would be no exception. In dying, Zhao Yunlan would once again forget him and this awkward interlude.

The door to Shen Wei's bedroom was always closed. He pushed it open, and the lights inside turned on automatically, revealing a room devoid of furnishings. Instead, there were portraits on the wall, with framing and mounting that betrayed their great age.

The paintings were all of the same man: his front, his profile, his back. His clothes changed with the times, but the man himself was always the same, down to the subtlest expression of his brows. Life after life after life, never changing.

Old paintings gave way to an array of photographs of all sizes. Here the man was still a child; there he had grown up. There were photos of him laughing and photos where his brows were drawn in concern, photos of him fooling around or engaged in conversation. There was even one immortalizing a moment when a cat had jumped onto his head.

Each and every one was of Zhao Yunlan.

It's fine if I'm the only one to know. It's fine if only I remember, Shen Wei thought. When the time came, he too would simply disappear. Nobody would notice.

It wasn't as if he should ever have existed in the first place.

Until that day came, the only liberties Shen Wei allowed himself were a few extra glances when Zhao Yunlan didn't notice. He occasionally slipped into Zhao Yunlan's home at night but never dared stay for long. Zhao Yunlan was very alert.

But in a stroke of good fortune, Zhao Yunlan recently had many dinners to attend, and he would arrive home half-drunk. Only at such times could Shen Wei risk drawing a little closer.

Shen Wei had done everything imaginable to protect this one person—the one person he could never touch. And yet those people *dared...*

Cold fury flashed across Shen Wei's face. He vanished in a cloud of black mist.

The Soul-Executing Emissary sped past the Huangquan Road, alerting the Netherworld. Trembling, the Head Magistrate brought the Heibai Wuchang[1] and a crowd of reapers to welcome him at the foot of the Naihe Bridge. When Shen Wei arrived, the Magistrate offered him the utmost respect. "I didn't know my lord would be gracing us with his presence."

The Emissary didn't react. He only said, "The Mountain-River Awl has appeared and is now in my hands. The Merit Brush shouldn't be far off."

The Magistrate's close observation suggested that the Emissary was in a foul mood. Smiling, he said carefully, "Yes, my lord's methods are certainly..."

The Emissary cut him off with an icy glance. "I've come to tell you something. Whether or not you believe me, *I* am the protector of the Great Seal. I won't miss a single one of the Four Hallowed Artifacts. I will carry out my duty. And if I ever

---

1 *Heibai Wuchang (黑白无常) are two deities, one dressed in black and one in white, who lead the souls of the dead to the Netherworld.*

wished to break my vow, nothing could stop me—not even if you reawakened Kunlun-jun or restored the primordial gods to life. Stop your dirty tricks. You do not want to anger me."

The Magistrate bowed his head very low. "I fear my lord may have misunderstood. Connecting the *Book of Merits* to the *Book of Life and Death* was the Guardian's idea. That's why we rushed to make it and give it to him. We never imagined it could betray my lord's identity. We greatly regret not considering things more fully..."

There was a trace of a sneer in the Emissary's voice. "For your sake, I hope that's true. Mind your actions. I'll take my leave."

On his final words, the Emissary was already disappearing into a cloud of black mist. Eventually the air of cold and wrath that accompanied him dissipated, and the reapers could finally let out a breath of relief. The Magistrate wiped sweat from his brow with a sleeve.

"My lord," whispered a reaper, stepping forward. "The Emissary has a point. The Four Hallowed Artifacts are divided between him and the Chaos King of the Gui, and he is the protector of the Great Seal. Even if Kunlun-jun did awaken, he's just a mortal now. What could he do? I say we might as well relax and have faith in the Emissary."

"If the Great Seal were to break, do you know what kind of price would be required of its protector?" the Magistrate asked quietly. "All the primordial gods had to sacrifice themselves, never mind *him*, a demigod. It took hundreds of tribulations and lifetimes for him to cultivate a physical form for himself from the vicious darkness. Do you really think he could throw away tens of thousands of years of effort and sacrifice himself for the Great Seal?"

The reaper shivered, worried and anxious once more.

Voice still low, the Magistrate continued, "It's best for the doer to undo his own handiwork. It was Kunlun-jun who appointed the Soul-Executing Emissary as the Great Seal's protector. At this point, our only choice is to reawaken him."

"But Kunlun-jun's immortal spirit has been reincarnated over thousands of years. He's just a mortal now! Almost none of his divinity remains..."

"Yes. *Almost* none." The Magistrate looked up. "Have you heard of the Heavenly Eye?"

"When we conduct a field investigation, we need to write a routine report upon our return. I'm a slow typer, so you do it." Chu Shuzhi poured a cup of tea and settled leisurely into a chair. "I'll dictate."

Guo Changcheng sat upright in front of the computer. At this hour, there were no "people" left in the Special Investigations Department, only souls floating around. In the darkness, the sole light came from the criminal investigation unit.

It wasn't long after the pair had sat down that there was a knock at the door. After Chu Shuzhi called out in response, a steaming hot tray flew in. The tray held two sets of utensils, four different dishes and a soup, and two large bowls of rice. The headless ghost's feet didn't touch the floor. It lightly floated over to them and just as lightly set everything out on the table. It even got out a bag of cat food and filled Daqing's bowl.

Daqing gave a reserved nod. "Many thanks. Add some whole milk for this venerable one."

By now, Guo Changcheng was accustomed to the environment at 4 Bright Avenue. He'd gradually come to realize there wasn't much difference between humans and ghosts. Some ghosts were quite kind, like this headless fellow who always thoughtfully brought a large warm meal when someone had to work overtime to write a report. This gesture made Guo Changcheng, who only had 20 yuan to his name after visiting the post office the day before, feel a springlike warmth.

"That's pretty much it," Chu Shuzhi said. "To get the format right, just work off an older report. Tighten up your language a little. The victim wasn't poisoned at all. They were cursed by a resentful spirit—you know, as in 'resentful energy.' His leg was in excruciating pain, so the spirit who cursed him most likely died of an external injury. Also, the victim's forehead was ashen, and his eyes were red. He had a karmic line under the lower eyelid, but not very deep. There was also a black merit mark behind his ear, but it was faint. Odds are he isn't directly related to the person setting down the curse and doesn't deserve this level of retribution.

"Initial assessment: this deceased spirit has almost certainly committed serious crimes..."

Guo Changcheng's paws lay flat on the keyboard. His head was swimming, and he couldn't follow Chu Shuzhi at all.

Chu Shuzhi sighed. "What do you not understand?"

"What's a 'karmic line'?"

Daqing's head snapped up, revealing a fresh milk mustache on his black fur. Furious, he demanded, "What is wrong with Zhao Yunlan? These days he's always either in a daze or letting himself think with the wrong head. Does he do a shred of actual work anymore? Has he still not trained the newcomer? Why doesn't this kid know anything?!"

Chu Shuzhi couldn't sit there and let a cat insult his boss. He bestirred himself and pointed out, "Lately, Director Zhao's been busy getting things in order to move the office. If he can get everything nailed down, next year we'll move into a space with a large garden. You'll get to have a big cat house hanging in a tree where you can keep an eye on the birds' nests."

The Cat Lord paused, and his anger began to cool. After a moment, thanks to the prospect of the big bird-watching cat house, he decided he could forgive Zhao Yunlan.

His whiskers twitched disdainfully as he addressed Guo Changcheng. "The 'karmic line' has to do with karma, duh. Actions and consequences. Let's say you're walking down the street and a mugger jumps and kills you for no reason. You didn't do anything to cause that to happen, so it's an undeserved catastrophe. However, if you're in a mugger's way when he comes running out, and he stabs you because you were in his way, then you died as a result of being in his way. Now, that's bad timing and inevitable fate, so even though it's a reach, it *can* be considered a case of cause and effect. But the resulting karmic line would be so light that you could probably brush it off with your hand."

The cat continued, "Now suppose a mugger came running down the street, recognized you as the guy his wife cheated on him with, and killed you in a rage. You wouldn't be able to wipe away the karmic line that resulted, but it also wouldn't be too dark. That indicates that there is a connection, but the consequence is disproportionate to the crime, so the cause and effect aren't equal. But if a mugger comes running..."

Guo Changcheng, having now been offed by a mugger multiple times, couldn't help asking, "And that mugger realizes I'm his greatest enemy, whom he'd been planning to kill, and he stabs me to death, the karmic line would be pretty deep, right?"

Daqing bobbed his head approvingly. "The boy can be taught."

"Then...what's a merit mark?" Guo Changcheng asked.

"People who've accrued merits or sins have a mark behind their ears," Chu Shuzhi said. "For example, if someone secretly killed someone else, that act would leave a black mark behind their ear even if no one else ever found out and they never faced legal consequences. People used to talk about 'damaging one's merits,' and that's what they were referring to. Of course, a normal person with no cultivation won't be able to see it."

Chu Shuzhi glanced at Guo Changcheng. He could see a clear white mark behind Guo Changcheng's ear. The intense yet gentle light radiating from it was invisible to most people. Even someone whose third eye was open would still have to concentrate hard to see it.

Guo Changcheng didn't notice. Deep in thought, he asked, "Is the black mark like a fingerprint stained with soot?"

Freezing, Chu Shuzhi asked, "You've seen it?"

With a nod, Guo Changcheng recounted his experience of the previous night.

Daqing listened and snorted. "If even a mortal passerby could see it with just a glance, that guy's probably due to be struck by lightning any moment now."

Seeing that Guo Changcheng was lost again, Chu Shuzhi explained, "Merits are usually invisible to the naked eye. The thing you ran into probably wasn't human. Yao who cultivate don't dare harm humans at random. The consequences of gaining or losing merits are what guide their behavior. Once a merit mark is dark enough, it will draw divine retribution. Having the Heavens smite you is no joke, and if it reaches that point, the guilty creature won't be the only one to suffer. If there are lesser yao in the area and they're not careful, they'll be affected too. So to keep innocents from harm, and to prevent bad apples like those from appearing, the yao carefully tally everyone's merits at the Yao Banquet at the end of each year. If anyone's too out of line, they'll take care of it internally first."

Guo Changcheng only half understood. "Then will humans also be struck by lightning if they do too many bad things?"

"No." Tail up, Daqing jumped to the ground and curled into a huge ball of fur by the computer's air vent, enjoying the warmth. "Have you ever heard the saying 'Those who repair bridges and mend roads go blind, while those who commit murder and arson have many sons'? The Mortal Realm has its own laws and regulations. Most people have only this single fleeting life, and it's over before karma even has time to work. When each life is no more significant than an ant, the Heavens can't be bothered. Often there's not much point to a mortal cultivating their merits, but if you do enough good deeds, it might someday bring you good luck, though there's no guarantee. Look at you—you possess a remarkable number of merits, but you're still a poor little cabbage with a hard life."

Guo Changcheng had been quite young when he lost his parents. He was an orphan with a soft nature and no particular talents. Even though Zhao Yunlan liked to joke that his presence brought random good luck, the reality was that Guo Changcheng didn't actually have such deep or abundant good fortune. He had the look of someone doomed to a hard life.

"Really? I have merits?" Guo Changcheng was boggled at Daqing's description. "I have a hard life? I don't, though! My life is pretty great. I'm just kind of useless, that's all."

He thought he had no skills or talents. In fact, ever since he was a child, his aunts and uncles had all pitied him. They would rather give their own children a bit less rather than let him go without. Although his family situation was better than those of his peers, he still grew up to be but a useless piece of kindling—and yet his uncle had ushered him into such a good workplace. His boss and colleagues didn't look down on him for it; rather, they'd allowed him to stay, and they all took care of him. How could all of that not be considered good fortune?

The black cat's eyelids had been growing heavy, but at Guo Changcheng's protest, he opened them wide again and took another close look. A golden light flashed through those deep green eyes. But before Daqing could comment, Zhao Yunlan walked in, accompanied by chilly air and the smell of booze.

Hoarsely, Zhao Yunlan asked, "How's the report going?"

"Oh," Guo Changcheng began. But before he could offer an update, Zhao Yunlan cut him off with a wave and stumbled into the bathroom to throw up.

Chu Shuzhi and Guo Changcheng hurried after him. Daqing tutted, then leisurely stretched out his fat paws and followed, swaying as he walked. "Dumbass human."

The dumbass human in question was clutching his stomach and slumped in a corner of the bathroom, face pale. He seemed unable to stand up. Chu Shuzhi patted his back. "How did you let yourself get this drunk?" he asked, before issuing an order to Guo Changcheng. "Xiao-Guo, get him a cup of warm water."

Zhao Yunlan accepted the water and rinsed away the taste of vomit before finally rising to his feet unsteadily. "A bunch of assholes kept forcing drinks on me. What was I supposed to do?"

"Don't give me that shit," Chu Shuzhi said. "If you honestly didn't want to drink, who'd be able to force you?"

Using the wall for support, Zhao Yunlan walked out, avoiding eye contact. In a muffled voice, he said, "I've just lost my love. Can't a man drown his sorrows?"

"Aiyou, Professor Shen still doesn't want you? Seems the people's teacher isn't blind after all. The crowd is delighted by this news."

Daqing brushed against Zhao Yunlan's leg as he passed. "Hey, you didn't drink and drive, did you? The cops are quite vigilant this time of year. Drinking and driving will land you in jail."

"Fuck off!" Zhao Yunlan growled.

He found a chair to sink into. Dispirited and eyes downcast, he said, "Xiao-Guo, go get Wang Zheng. Tell her to bring all the stuff I need to sign. Lao-Chu, get me up to speed."

The situation was straightforward, so Chu Shuzhi's explanation was brief. Zhao Yunlan listened with half an ear, eyes downcast. It was impossible to know if his brain was even still working. Having been filled in, he said, still a little drunk, "You're sure this case falls under our jurisdiction, right? How about this. Hurry and get the report done tonight. I'll wait here until you're finished, and then I can just stamp it, scan it, and upload it. Hopefully we'll hear back tomorrow and won't have to waste another day."

That was fine by Chu Shuzhi. After all, he wasn't the one who'd just puked up his gallbladder. Wang Zheng came downstairs with a cup of honeyed water. She spread a stack of documents in front of Zhao Yunlan, who barely gave them a glance. He was having too much trouble keeping his eyes open. He scrawled haphazard signatures on everything and then waved Wang Zheng and her shadow away. "Don't flaunt your love in front of this poor single man. Hurry up and fuck off!"

By the time Chu Shuzhi and Guo Changcheng had the preliminary investigation report ready for him to sign and stamp, Zhao Yunlan was sound asleep, head on the table. Daqing woke him with a furious punch in the back. "I forgot to ask. How's my super-luxurious cat house in the trees coming along?"

Dazed, Zhao Yunlan said, "You stupid big fatty, I'll kill and eat you."

Daqing jumped onto his shoulder and yowled into his ear. “Meow! Where’s my luxury cat house?!”

Zhao Yunlan picked up the honeyed water, which had long since gone cold, and drank it in a single gulp. Then he grabbed the fat cat by his short neck and tossed him aside. “It’s all but confirmed. If it’s quick, we can move in next fall.”

Hearing that, the black cat immediately changed his tune. His aggressive attitude vanished as he rubbed against Zhao Yunlan’s hand and sucked up to him. “As always, our boss is so competent. Um...if the nest beside the cat house had eggs in it, that would be perfect...”

Zhao Yunlan flicked Daqing’s head away and wiped his hands on the desk.

“Damn cat,” he said coldly. “You’re getting fur all over my hand.”

Then, before Daqing could explode, Zhao Yunlan speedily signed the report and stood up. “That’s it for me. Good work today, you two.”

“Wait,” Chu Shuzhi said. “How did you get here?”

“Taxi,” Zhao Yunlan replied. “I’ll get another one back.”

“It’s so late and cold,” said Guo Changcheng kindly. “You might not be able to get a taxi here. Why don’t I drive—ow!”

Chu Shuzhi had stomped on Guo Changcheng’s foot ferociously under the table. Then, this busybody shot up out of his chair, pushed Zhao Yunlan back down, and took his phone from his pocket, all before the man could react. “Shen-laoshi’s already on winter break. I’ll get him to come pick you up.”

Speechless, Zhao Yunlan tried to grab his phone back, but Chu Shuzhi nimbly evaded him, addressing Guo Changcheng and Daqing. “Hurry and hold him down. *Hold him down!* Look how drunk he is.” He turned to Zhao Yunlan and said, “Listen to me. The way Shen-laoshi looks at you says it all. I don’t believe for a second that he doesn't feel anything for you. He must just be deep in the closet. As your coworker, I'll help you out this one time."

Zhao Yunlan was being restrained by Guo Changcheng and Daqing, who only wanted more chaos in the world. The cat had gone so far as to sit on Zhao Yunlan's stomach, nearly crushing the air out of him and making him keel over on the spot. "Please show some mercy!" Zhao Yunlan yelped. "I have enough trouble without your help!"

Shen Wei's voice came from the phone. "What is it?"

Chu Shuzhi waggled his eyebrows at Zhao Yunlan. Shen Wei had picked up on the very first ring. That was a level of attentiveness one couldn't even get from their own father. *This* was what Zhao Yunlan called heartbreak?

"This is Shen-laoshi, right? Um, I'm Zhao Yunlan's coworker. Our boss drank way too much, and now he's here hugging everyone he can get his hands on. He's throwing the whole office into disarray. I was just scrolling through his phone, trying to figure out who to contact, so I took the liberty of calling you. Could I, uh, trouble you to pick him up?"

Zhao Yunlan grabbed a pen holder and hurled it at Chu Shuzhi's head. Chu Shuzhi dodged while continuing to talk on the phone. "No, no, it's fine. He's just drunk and throwing things. Mm-hmm. Okay. Okay, we'll take care of him. Please hurry. 4 Bright Avenue, the criminal investigation unit on the second floor. See you soon!"

Chu Shuzhi hung up and struck a salacious pose, blowing a kiss at Zhao Yunlan. "He's at your beck and call. You've got this in the bag. Don't forget my matchmaker's feast."

Zhao Yunlan jabbed a trembling finger at him. "Y-you *bitch*."

To no one's surprise, Shen Wei arrived promptly.

He had only knocked once before the door to the criminal investigation unit opened from within and a person was shoved out without warning. Shen Wei caught him, and Zhao Yunlan fell headfirst into his arms.

But even if he couldn't stand up straight, Zhao Yunlan still had some fight in him. He pointed back into the office at Chu Shuzhi. "Just you wait, you little bitch."

Chu Shuzhi squeezed a smile out of his bitter melon face. "Aiyou, I'm so afraid."

Shen Wei didn't know whether to laugh or cry. He nudged Zhao Yunlan's shaking hand down. "That's enough."

"If I don't deal with you right now, you'll never know your place!" Zhao Yunlan raged.

He tore free of Shen Wei's hold, throwing himself toward Chu Shuzhi.

Shen Wei sighed. He slung one arm around Zhao Yunlan's waist and grabbed Zhao Yunlan's wrist with his other hand, effectively disarming him.

He gave a nod to the onlookers inside and said, "I apologize for the disturbance. I'll take him home now."

With that, he dragged Zhao Yunlan away.

Chapter 4

HAVING TRULY GOTTEN HIMSELF good and hammered, the stumble in Zhao Yunlan's step was genuine, but a visit to the porcelain god and a good nap had dealt with the worst of the booze's effects. By now, his mind had already cleared up. But being alone with Shen Wei—with the *Soul-Executing Emissary*—was excruciatingly awkward. Since Chu Shuzhi had said he was too drunk to see straight, Zhao Yunlan decided to just roll with it.

Shen Wei had left the car running to keep it warm as he went upstairs to collect him. Zhao Yunlan noticed it as soon as he got in, and the gesture warmed his heart. He slumped against the seat, hiding by pretending to be asleep.

Shen Wei gave him a light nudge. "Wait until you're home to sleep, all right? It's easy to catch a cold outside."

Zhao Yunlan played dead.

Giving up on waking him, Shen Wei leaned over and buckled Zhao Yunlan's seat belt. At such close range, Shen Wei's scent filled his nostrils. In sharp contrast to the frigid smell that surrounded the Emissary, Shen Wei's scent was refreshing, like the lingering hint of soap on fresh laundry. Beneath the Emissary's black cloak, a symbol of terror for humans and ghosts alike, was someone pristine and gentle.

There was a rustling noise off to the side. Shen Wei took out a bottle of water, filled a little cup, and then swirled the cup twice in his hand. The chilly water started to steam. "At least take a sip," he said, holding the cup to Zhao Yunlan's lips.

Zhao Yunlan cracked his eyes open. In the darkness of the car, the only light seemed to come from Shen Wei's eyes. That light was exactly right—not too dim, but not blinding. Zhao Yunlan's heart thudded heavily in his chest. He drained the cup while Shen Wei held it, then let Shen Wei get a throw blanket from beneath the seat and drape it over him. Finally, Shen Wei turned up the heat and began to drive, pulling smoothly out onto the road.

As he drove, Shen Wei used one hand to tuck the blanket under him. He gave a faint sigh and then, barely audible, Shen Wei murmured, "Why are you so appallingly bad at taking care of yourself?"

Zhao Yunlan was just resting his eyes, but as he listened to the winter wind outside the car window, he found himself comfortably curling his hands and feet. It had been a long, long time since he'd felt such warmth on a cold night.

In the two weeks since getting back from the snowy mountain, he hadn't contacted Shen Wei even once.

People around Zhao Yunlan came and went. When he was single, he was happy to walk the blurry line between romance and friendship to preserve his confidence. He'd pursued Shen Wei the same way he'd pursued plenty of others, but somehow, ever since the hope of romance between them seemed to wither on the vine rather than blossoming, everyone else he met seemed dull and uninteresting.

He had become a celibate old monk overnight.

But recently, in the darkest hours of the night, when dreams left him dazed and disoriented, his thoughts would return to that day when his stomach had acted up and he'd forced Shen Wei to stay with him at home—how he'd slept nestled deep in his blankets as Shen Wei quietly read and watched over him, while delicious smells wafted from the kitchen.

In that moment, Shen Wei had struck him in the heart, fierce and unerring.

Deep down, Zhao Yunlan had always yearned for a certain kind of life: a life two people shared companionably, where they could even enjoy silence together. Neither would find the other annoying or hound them or try to pick fights. They would make space for one another, but there would always be warmth between them. Like they had always lived together, existing in their own private world, needing nothing but each other.

And then there had been that moment in the dilapidated little hut on the mountain, when he'd jolted awake at midnight to find Shen Wei's eyes burning into his.

You always want what you can't have, right? Zhao Yunlan pressed his face into the blanket, a self-deprecating, bitter smile twisting his lips. What kind of masochist was he, unable to let any of that go?

Zhao Yunlan lived quite close to 4 Bright Avenue. He was still tangled in his messy thoughts when they arrived. Shen Wei helped him up to his apartment and out of his coat, then hung the coat up, laid him down on the bed, and disappeared into the bathroom in search of a damp cloth.

Even though Zhao Yunlan gave every sign of being blackout drunk, Shen Wei was the picture of propriety. He wiped Zhao Yunlan's face, hands, and feet carefully, not touching him anywhere else, and tucked him in. After that, out of habit, Shen Wei began tidying the room. He even made sure to take away the half-full cup of water on the bedside table in case Zhao Yunlan tossed and turned in the night and knocked it over.

It was clear to Zhao Yunlan that he held a special place in Shen Wei's heart. He felt as though all his life, people—other than his parents and cat, that is—had always either needed something from him or depended on him. No one had ever placed him at the tip of their heart like this before. Listening to Shen Wei puttering around so carefully and quietly, his own heart was in utter disarray.

Once Shen Wei had finished tidying up, he looked over to where Zhao Yunlan lay motionless. He seemed so quiet. Shen Wei hesitated, torn, and found he couldn't bear to leave. He allowed himself to go stand by the bed, feasting on the sight of Zhao Yunlan.

Dear god, Zhao Yunlan thought, desperately maintaining his pretense of sleep. The tension threatened to crush his heart. *I'm begging you, stop looking! If you're planning to leave, hurry up. This is going to be the death of me.*

Shen Wei didn't hear his thoughts. Nor did any god. Some time passed, and then, as though bewitched, Shen Wei slowly bent down, leaning in close enough to feel Zhao Yunlan's breathing.

On the brink of losing his mind, Zhao Yunlan, through sheer force of will, managed to keep playing dead.

It was more than Shen Wei could possibly stand. Pressing his hands to the bed on either side of Zhao Yunlan, he let their lips brush together, soft as a dragonfly dipping its tail into the water. It lasted only a moment. His eyes were closed, as though he had taken immeasurable comfort from that most fleeting contact. His heart thundered inside his chest, offering the illusion of mortality. For just a second, Shen Wei almost felt human.

There in the dim light, he'd stolen a kiss from the love of his life. His heart soared with elation and sweetness. Even if he had died then and there, he wouldn't have uttered a word of complaint.

Zhao Yunlan's mind, however, was perfectly empty. Inside his heart, it felt as though a single strand of hair bore a weight of thousands of pounds. That strand had been stretched past endurance, and now it finally snapped without a sound.

Shen Wei had supposed that the tiniest of stolen kisses would go unnoticed, but before he could straighten back up, the apparent "corpse" on the bed animated, grabbing him with both arms.

Shocked and caught wholly off guard, Shen Wei was dragged down. Zhao Yunlan aggressively flipped them both over, pressing their bodies together.

The scent of alcohol still lingered on Zhao Yunlan's breath, but his gaze was clear. Peering into Shen Wei's eyes, he asked quietly, "My lord, what are you doing?"

Shen Wei's mouth opened, but he was too panicked to speak.

Zhao Yunlan stared at him for a while, complex feelings passing through his eyes. Then he suddenly took hold of Shen Wei's chin. "And here I always thought my lord was a gentleman. I never imagined you were the type to go around stealing kisses in the dead of night. Such an unprofessional kiss, at that."

Shen Wei was at a loss for words. "I..."

Even when Zhao Yunlan's kiss landed on his lips, Shen Wei was still stupefied. He was certain that he was having an absurd but beautiful dream. Helplessly, he reached out and hugged Zhao Yunlan close. The kiss was both exquisitely skilled and playful, threatening to effortlessly peel back Shen Wei's defenses and leave him at Zhao Yunlan's mercy.

Nose to nose, Zhao Yunlan said lightly, "Now *that* is what an expert kiss should be like."

The soft bed, warm from Zhao Yunlan's body, ensnared Shen Wei like a web. He was securely trapped and unable to utter a word. Zhao Yunlan's top two buttons were undone, exposing narrow, beautiful collarbones that still smelled faintly of cologne. A single whiff nearly stopped Shen Wei's breath, sealing his mouth. He was no longer sure which of them was intoxicated.

Zhao Yunlan brushed the stray hairs on Shen Wei's forehead back. Mouth at Shen Wei's ear, he said, "Let me ask you something. You've been avoiding me for ages, and yet you've never just completely stayed away. Did you do something terrible to me once, or...are you afraid of falling into my trap? What are you so worried about? Humans and ghosts not belonging together?"

The last bit of flushed color drained from his face as Shen Wei recoiled. His hands curled into fists on either side of Zhao Yunlan, then he reached out to push him away.

Grabbing Shen Wei's hand, Zhao Yunlan forced his fist open finger by finger. "Stop trying to fight me and stop trying to fight yourself. Shen Wei, whatever you are—the Soul-Executing Emissary or something else—I'm brave enough to say I'm into you. What about you? Do you have the balls to admit it?"

Shen Wei squeezed two words from between his teeth. "Let go!"

Zhao Yunlan ignored him. "No. I'm just a mortal." He forced his fingers between Shen Wei's, intertwining them and then gripping tight. Their hands were locked together as if they were grappling, knuckles turning blue. "A mortal's life is just like an ant's. The seasons blur together and then it's over, just like that. Death and farewells are written in our fates. I'm not afraid of destiny or being struck down by lightning, and I'm not afraid of you. I don't know how long my life will be. I could die tomorrow, and I don't want—"

Shen Wei clapped a hand over Zhao Yunlan's mouth, cutting off that inauspicious sentence.

The two looked at each other for a long time. Finally, Shen Wei shook his head very, very slowly.

Zhao Yunlan's tense shoulders sagged. With a disappointed look, he released Shen Wei and got up. "Forget it, then."

He spoke as if he were perfectly clearheaded, but as soon as his feet hit the floor, he lost his balance. His legs gave out, sending him to his knees; the alcohol still sloshing around in his belly slammed into his skull. He moaned in pain, clutching his head.

Shen Wei hurried to help him up. "I thought you weren't drunk?"

Zhao Yunlan was in a peculiar state where he could reason clearly but couldn't walk in a straight line. It left him blunter and more forward than he might otherwise have been. Unsteadily, he waved Shen Wei's hand away and opened the bottom drawer of the bedside table. He pulled out a plastic document holder and slapped it down in front of Shen Wei. "Open it," he ordered, words slurring together.

After a moment's hesitation, Shen Wei took it and flipped it open. He found himself looking at a property deed for a residence with a garden. The address placed it near DCU's University Road.

Zhao Yunlan slumped against the bedside table and stretched his long legs out in front of him. He took a cigarette from his pants pocket, only managing to light it after three or four tries.

He smoked the entire cigarette before speaking again. Voice low, he said, "I bought it before we went to the mountains. The SID office is going to be relocating, so I've been looking all over for a new place. I passed by this neighborhood and decided to check this one out, and it just felt...*right*, somehow. I got carried away and bought it, even though it wiped out my savings.

"Then I started thinking about how good the transportation options are in that area and how close it is to DCU. I thought, if you were willing to be with me, you wouldn't need to drive to work anymore and you could sleep a little later in the mornings. I know it's pretty big—definitely more than two people need, but that means you can have a large study...and I want to get a dog, one that's not too bright. Once in a while we could stage a Great Battle of the Cat and Dog or something, like some special New Year's entertainment..."

An uncontrollable tremor overtook Shen Wei's hands. The file folder crinkled as he trembled.

"But then, surprise! Coming back from the great northwest, it turned out that you can just teleport from one side of the city to the other. Driving? Getting up early?" Zhao Yunlan chuckled. "Mm... But obviously none of that was the point. I was mostly out looking because we need a new office, not because of you. I just... thought about that stuff while I was at it."

Shen Wei slowly met Zhao Yunlan's gaze. It seemed much the same as always, but with the teasing stripped away, what remained was the gentleness Zhao Yunlan ordinarily kept deeply hidden. Catching just a glimpse of that rare sight was enough to compel one to drown in it.

For Shen Wei, it felt like being torn in two. Half of him was nearly swept away with joy. The other half had plummeted into the depths of the Huangquan.

He was on the verge of losing his mind entirely.

Millennia of loneliness and desolation had failed to drive him to insanity, but a few offhand sentences passing through the lips of this one man were enough to send his emotions careening out of control. The ancient line was painfully true: *For love, the living may die, and the dead may live again. Could those unwilling to die or those unwilling to live again even profess to feel love?*[2]

When your very soul was being turned inside out, how could you even be sure if you were in the present moment or a day in the distant past?

Unattainable hope was like a gossamer thread sustaining him. Shen Wei had believed that Zhao Yunlan would never know he was the sole reason for Shen Wei's existence, or that he alone was why Shen Wei had made it this far.

The most determined of hearts could never be broken by winds that might cut you to ribbons, or by frost that pierced you like a sword. That power belonged to the open hand extended to you during a long journey, or to the tender voice saying "come home" in your ear.

For a second, Shen Wei was gripped by the desire to interrogate the Heavens themselves. Why did *he* have to be the Soul-Executing Emissary? Ants, which perished almost as soon as they were born, were permitted to pair off under the sunlight and rain; birds, which lived out in the open, were allowed to find safe harbor surrounded by branches. Among all things that existed between the earth and sky, he had been born peerless and lonely, but there wasn't even the tiniest fragment of space meant for him. Everyone feared him, offered him deference, plotted against him, or even schemed incessantly to bring about his death.

Having been born from brutality, mercilessness, and Chaos itself, it was inevitable that he was sometimes unable to rein in the violence within his heart. His desire to kill was like the tides. He yearned to cut down every last one of those people. But he

---

2 *From the Ming Dynasty opera* The Peony Pavilion (牡丹亭) *by Tang Xianzu, an epic romance that transcends the bounds of mortality.*

was held back by a sworn oath known only to himself. Thousands of years had passed, and yet Shen Wei dared not betray that oath in even the most minuscule way. It was his last remaining connection to that person.

Shen Wei's eyes were so red that they seemed to brim with blood. "My very existence is inauspicious," he said. "I can only bring you harm."

A corner of Zhao Yunlan's lips quirked, revealing two shallow dimples on his cheeks. "I guess we'll see if my health bar can outlast your attacks then, huh?"

Shen Wei, not realizing he was joking, did not reply. He pinched his own palm and had nearly torn his flesh open when he finally burst out, "H-how can you force me this way?"

Zhao Yunlan sighed as his smile faded. He stubbed his cigarette out in the ashtray.

The very first time he'd laid eyes on Shen Wei, he'd known he liked him. He'd initially thought it was just because Shen Wei was so perfectly his type and had let himself gloss over how natural the instant familiarity between them felt. Zhao Yunlan had yet to look into the Soul-Executing Emissary's past, but seeing Shen Wei like this, how could he possibly ask him directly? There was always the sense that some tremendous anguish was locked away in Shen Wei's heart. Why else did he bring such coldness with him every time he appeared in those black robes?

Didn't he feel cold?

"Sorry," Zhao Yunlan said. He gently eased Shen Wei's clenched hand open, holding it in his own. Then he leaned down and placed a soft kiss on the back of Shen Wei's hand, casually tossing the incredibly expensive property deed aside. "If this is too much for you, just pretend I never said a word."

Shen Wei closed his eyes, overwhelmed by his own shamelessness. If he'd wanted to hide, why couldn't he have just behaved himself and stayed beneath the Huangquan? If he had, Zhao Yunlan could have lived dozens of lives without even the slightest chance that the two of them would meet. Zhao Yunlan would never have even known of his existence.

But he'd been unable to help himself, unable to resist. Without a hint of shame, he'd put himself on a street corner, only to suddenly act chaste and hard to get when someone took notice.

He had always despised himself, but this was a new pinnacle of self-loathing.

Zhao Yunlan massaged his temples lightly. In a barely audible voice, he said, "I have plenty of assets, but I doubt they'd appeal to you. All I really have to offer is my heart. But if you won't accept it, then just forget about this."

The words smashed into Shen Wei's heart like a stone, unearthing an ancient memory of a voice right by his ear, speaking in the exact same offhand way. "I hold all the world's famous mountains and rivers in my hand, but what of it? They're nothing but a bunch of rocks and wild waters. Of all that I am, the only part worth anything may be my heart. If you want it, it's yours."

The man before him was the same as always, as if the past had come back to life.

Shen Wei abruptly wrapped his arms around Zhao Yunlan, holding on with what seemed like every ounce of his strength. He squeezed until the man's bones cracked from the force as he buried his face against Zhao Yunlan's neck. Then he leaned past Zhao Yunlan's shoulder and bit into his own wrist, tearing into it so brutally that the bone was nearly exposed.

The crushing weight of thousands of zhang of the Netherworld bore down on him. He was unable to weep, but in the throes of such pain, perhaps he could only shed blood in lieu of tears.

The scent of blood immediately told Zhao Yunlan that something was very wrong. "Shen Wei! What are you doing?! Let go!"

Shen Wei only clutched him even tighter.

A human life lasted only a few dozen years. It came and went like a shimmer of light on water. A single thought filled Shen Wei's mind: was he not worthy of even this tiny, fleeting fragment of time?

"Shen Wei!" Taking advantage of Shen Wei's daze, Zhao Yunlan finally struggled out of his grip, only to find the bedsheets stained crimson. "Is your head full of holes?! It's not like I abducted you in broad daylight to make you mine. When you shook your head, did I say anything? Did I push? Did you need to start spilling blood just to deter me?"

Cursing and fuming, he jumped up to get his first aid kit, but Shen Wei suddenly grabbed hold of him again.

"I accept," Shen Wei said quietly.

Zhao Yunlan froze for a second, but Shen Wei smiled, sounding almost calm as he repeated, "I accept. In this lifetime, whether dead or alive, I won't let you go again. Even if one day you've had enough or tire of me, even if you want to leave me, I'll never let you go."

It was another few frozen moments before Zhao Yunlan processed that Shen Wei was telling him how he felt. There was no room for relief; mostly he just felt exhausted.

Wasn't being in a relationship all about the give and take of flirtation? Romance? Flowers under the full moon? Why was it about blood when it came to him?

It suddenly struck him that Shen Wei was probably the type of person who'd made "watch out for the quiet ones" such a cliché: he was ordinarily meek, with no sign of a temper, but his silence hid twisted things, and his honest appearance masked his perversion. When everything came bubbling up to the surface, it was like a nuclear explosion.

Wordlessly, Zhao Yunlan retrieved the first aid kit from under his bed and took out a disinfecting wipe. He sat on the edge of the bed, brow furrowed, and tugged Shen Wei's wounded wrist toward himself to wipe it clean. The blood was as cold as its owner.

Shen Wei's eyes were still locked on him. "If you must die, it must be in my arms and by my hand."

"*Please* shut up." Zhao Yunlan applied heavy pressure to Shen Wei's wrist. "Why do you go insane at the drop of a hat?"

After ministering to Shen Wei's wound, Zhao Yunlan was completely worn out, mentally and physically. He was out like a light the second his head hit the pillow, this time with no pretense.

Shen Wei looked at the tight, neat bandage wrapped around his wrist. Holding his breath, he eased himself under the blankets and lay down, feather light, on the empty half of the bed Zhao Yunlan had left for him. After a long moment, he took Zhao Yunlan's hand in his and held it against his chest, closing his eyes.

It was a rare peaceful night of sleep.

Early the next morning, a bizarre assortment of smells coming from the kitchen brought Shen Wei out of his slumber. He lay still as a stone for half a minute before remembering where he was. As he looked at the incriminating evidence on his wrist, a hint of red tinted his usually pale face.

What had he said and done the night before? How had things gone so far?

Just then, a thick and muddy voice said, "Morning."

Shen Wei trembled as he hastily looked up to see Zhao Yunlan with a pair of chopsticks in his mouth and a plastic board in his hands. The board was at least a meter long, with a row of five indentations on top, each one just big enough to hold a large bowl or a medium-sized plate.

Five places. If there weren't many people eating, it was just enough to carry the standard four dishes and a soup all at once. How lazy must someone have been to invent such a magical object?

The marvel in Zhao Yunlan's hands held more wonders: five bowls of cup noodles in a neat row, all still steaming. The combined aroma verged on indescribable.

Shen Wei could only stare.

Zhao Yunlan boldly plopped himself onto his sofa. With the confidence of a leader addressing a country, he said, "From left to right, we have braised beef noodles made with water; aged, pickled cabbage noodles made with milk; mushroom and chicken noodles made in the microwave with some water and butter; seafood noodles—though I thought they were a little bland, so I added a spoonful of sweet bean sauce; and finally, bacon cream noodles made with hot coffee. That one should be quite good. Pick whichever one you'd like to have."

A touch of embarrassment set in after he reached the end of the list. "Um... I don't really know how to make anything else. But since you finally visited, I thought only two cup noodles wouldn't be enough."

So he'd made five. How...generous?

Shen Wei's gaze swept across the five steaming cup noodles. He was at an utter loss as to how Zhao Yunlan hadn't died of food poisoning yet.

But if it was something Zhao Yunlan had made, even if it were a bowl of rat poison, Shen Wei was still willing to eat it all without the tiniest change in expression—though he made sure to choose the most normal cup noodles offered. He also allowed himself a subtle comment. "Processed foods like these aren't good for the body. You shouldn't eat too much of them."

With total honesty, Zhao Yunlan said, "Money's been tight recently. If my year-end bonus doesn't come soon, I'll have to go beg for food at my parents' place—unless you want to sponsor me? I can warm your bed."

Shen Wei choked on a mouthful of slightly spicy soup. He turned and started coughing violently.

Zhao Yunlan laughed, then casually said, "By the way, the end of the year is coming up. Almost time to tally up everyone's merits. There've been more thieves than usual in the Mortal Realm lately, while the yao and ghost cultivators have all started making last-minute efforts to do better."

Shen Wei cautiously sat up. Primly, he said, "Doing good for the sake of doing good only results in shallow karma. How could merits be gained so easily?"

"Mm." Perhaps Zhao Yunlan had temporarily disabled his taste buds, as he was drinking the magical mix of coffee and cup noodle soup without batting an eye. "You know, someone out there is still committing crimes despite the pressure."

The first of the Four Hallowed Artifacts was the Reincarnation Dial, the second was the Mountain-River Awl, and the third was the Merit Brush. Two of the four had already appeared in the world, and Shen Wei couldn't help being a little sensitive to the word "merit." He was about to ask for more details when Zhao Yunlan's phone, which had been thrown to the side, suddenly rang.

Zhao Yunlan set down his cup noodles and checked the caller ID. "Speak of the devil. Here they come again."

Only a single night had passed, but two more people had been hospitalized.

Like the first, they weren't ill or injured, nor had they suffered an accident. They just clutched their legs, writhing on the floor in pain. The patients' families had called the police at 5 a.m.

Poisoning cases had a tremendous negative impact on local law and order. The situation was worsening, right at the end of the year when the government was working hard to maintain stability. With absolutely no idea what else to do, the District Bureau higher-ups could only keep harassing Zhao Yunlan.

Chu Shuzhi and the others were already sure the case would fall into the Special Investigation Department's lap sooner or later. In the morning, as soon as the workday started, they would submit their report. Having no other choice, Zhao Yunlan agreed to go to the hospital and see the situation for himself.

Chapter 5

Once notified, Guo Changcheng didn't dare make Zhao Yunlan wait. Scared of being caught in the morning rush hour traffic, he opted to go to the hospital by subway. As a result, he was out waiting in front of the hospital for over half an hour, suffering in the bitterly cold wind. He was dangerously close to becoming an ice sculpture by the time Zhao Yunlan arrived...with Shen Wei in tow.

Guo Changcheng was frozen to the point that his tongue was stiff. "D-D-D-D-Director Zhao." A trail of snot crept down his face. He sniffled it back up, which did nothing to improve his image, and sneaked a confused glance at Shen Wei. *Why did Director Zhao bring "family" along on a case? Maybe Shen-laoshi is sick?*

Despite his curiosity as he watched Shen Wei and Zhao Yunlan speaking quietly to each other, Guo Changcheng didn't have the nerve to intrude by getting any closer. He only dared to follow a few steps behind, shoulders and head bowed, like a little eunuch trailing along in their wake.

Flu season was in full swing in Dragon City, so the hospital was bursting with patients. Lagging behind, Guo Changcheng was swept aside by the crowd. As he struggled to break free of the current of people, he stood on tiptoes, trying to locate the pair, but by the time he managed to break free, Zhao Yunlan and Shen Wei had disappeared.

Fortunately, he'd been there once before and knew where to go. When he couldn't find Zhao Yunlan, he headed up to the inpatient department on the sixth floor. Just as he arrived, a group of doctors and nurses rushed past him with a patient.

As he scrambled out of their way, Guo Changcheng happened to catch a glimpse of someone outside the window—the *sixth-floor* window!

What he was seeing was clearly impossible. Every instinct Guo Changcheng possessed told him that something was off; his pulse raced. But human nature being what it was, fear robbed him of the ability to look away.

It was a man outside the window: skinny and hunched, wearing a ragged knit hat that revealed frostbitten ears and a shock of white hair. He was bundled in a large cotton jacket...and he was floating in midair, entirely lacking his legs!

Guo Changcheng could see that the man's legs had been chopped off just below the pelvic joint. The hacked stumps were plainly visible, with short lengths of bone jutting out from the rotting, bloody flesh. Blood seeped inside the building through the window frame, dripping and pooling on the floor. It seemed as though the bleeding would never stop.

Yet not a single passing doctor or nurse noticed a thing. It was like no one could see the man silently staring into the inpatient area.

Half of his face was caked with dirt and blood. His eyes bugged out as if he were a terrifying wax figure. He just kept staring coldly at all the people coming and going, one corner of his cracked lips tugging upward. His expression was indescribably resentful.

郭长诚

Without warning, a hand clapped down on Guo Changcheng's shoulder. By then, his fear had escalated enough to freeze even his ability to scream. Instead, he shot up into the air without a sound, heart lurching and thumping within his chest.

Seeing Guo Changcheng pale with terror and doubled over, with his legs squeezed together so tightly, Zhao Yunlan said, "What's up with you?"

Guo Changcheng's mind went blank. He had temporarily forgotten all human language and was unable to speak a single word. Instead, he raised a shaky hand and pointed at the window at the end of the hallway.

Zhao Yunlan's confused gaze followed Guo Changcheng's finger and simply saw a window—a window no one would call pristine, but it was far from filthy. There was nothing of note other than dust and a little bit of frost.

Baffled, Zhao Yunlan asked, "What did you see?"

In a bit of a panic, Guo Changcheng looked back to the window and saw...nothing at all. He scratched his head and checked that the coast was clear. Keeping his voice low, he described what he'd seen, tripping over his words.

Zhao Yunlan's brow creased as he studied his underling. Nothing of what he knew about Guo Changcheng suggested that the little dumbass had the intellect and balls to successfully lie to his boss's face, so he probably wasn't bullshitting. Zhao Yunlan went over to the window and extended his hand. When Clarity didn't react, he swiped his hand over the windowsill and cracked open the rusting window. Bitingly cold northwest winds surged inside, but that was all. He felt nothing but the chill.

A nurse rushed over. "Excuse me, sir, but can you close the

window? If you want some fresh air, please go outside. We have patients here who need to stay warm."

Zhao Yunlan quickly closed the window and turned to her with an apologetic smile. The young nurse, confronted with a high-caliber hottie, flushed red. Muttering a half-serious complaint under her breath, she scurried away.

At some point, Shen Wei had come up beside him. With a small cough, he deliberately positioned himself between Zhao Yunlan and the retreating young woman, who was sneaking a peek back at him. Zhao Yunlan glanced at him with a hint of a smile. He gave Shen Wei's scarf a tug and leaned in close. Lips almost brushing Shen Wei's ear, voice pitched so no one else could hear, he asked, "Did you catch a cold? What are you coughing for?"

Shen Wei took an alarmed step back. If he'd been wearing a long robe, he probably would have gathered his sleeves, lowered his head, and said, "Two men mustn't openly touch in broad daylight."[3]

Zhao Yunlan couldn't help but laugh quietly.

The tips of Shen Wei's ears reddened, and he abruptly changed the subject. "What are you looking at?"

After a sweeping glance at Guo Changcheng, who was standing a bit away from them, Zhao Yunlan briefly summarized what he'd been told.

Shen Wei listened, then thought for a moment before answering seriously. "His third eye hasn't been opened, but there's something quite unusual about him. I feel as though he's able to see echoes of the past through reflective surfaces."

---

3 *A play on a common saying, "There cannot be direct contact between men and women," which refers to strict rules from a bygone era regarding bodily contact between unmarried men and women.*

Zhao Yunlan's eyebrow shot up. "What do you mean?"

"Think back to when we first met at Dragon City University, when I suddenly arrived and interrupted your investigation," Shen Wei said. "The night before, when I heard that an accident had taken place at the school, I suspected it might have something to do with the escaped Hunger Ghost. I sent a puppet to investigate the victim's dorm room. The puppet left before daybreak, but later, when this young man climbed into the window, a fascinating connection sprang to life between him and my puppet. I felt him looking through the glass and seeing my puppet climbing out the window the previous night. That's why I came. At the time, I didn't realize you were there."

To be precise, he'd been unaware because the shit-stirring Chaos King of the Gui had purposefully interfered with his ability to sense Zhao Yunlan's location.

When Guo Changcheng had written his report about the incident, he *had* mentioned seeing a skull in the window, and something about there being a person cloaked in black in the skull's eyes. But since most of the report had been useless bullshit, Zhao Yunlan had dismissed it and used the paper as a coaster.

"So you think there may actually have been some legless person—or ghost—peeping through this window?" Zhao Yunlan asked. "Not now, maybe at some point last night or even before?"

"Mm-hmm. Didn't you say that the two new poisoning victims were sent here at midnight? If I'd hurt someone, I might also want to come and see for myself exactly what happened to them."

Zhao Yunlan smirked. "You? Hurt someone? You can't even kiss except in secret."

Shen Wei was far too much of a gentleman to bear even whispering to each other about such intimate things in public. His ears felt as if they were on fire. In a slightly louder whisper, he scolded, "Don't talk nonsense!"

Zhao Yunlan shut his mouth but not his eyes. As the saying went, beauties had bright eyes, and those eyes could speak volumes. Director Zhao's eyes went a step further and conveyed pure lechery. Shen Wei, unable to endure that gaze languidly caressing him from head to toe, turned and escaped to the patients' room.

When the three of them arrived, they were greeted by an officer with a worry-worn face. After showing each other their IDs, the officer who had introduced himself as xiao-Li grabbed hold of Zhao Yunlan's arm and his expression turned bitter. "It's a relief you're finally here. I've been waiting for you all morning."

Zhao Yunlan glanced into the room. "Aren't there three victims? Why is one missing?"

"The one who came in yesterday isn't doing so great," Officer Li said. "He's in the ICU. I think these two will be joining him there soon."

"What makes you say that?" asked Zhao Yunlan.

"At first, the patient couldn't stop yelling about how his legs hurt," said Officer Li. "He was in so much pain that he was just rolling around on the bed. Once he finally quieted down, he was like a fish out of water. His eyes were open, but he was unable to speak, and he completely ignored everyone. Every so often he would twitch and seemed to lose all feeling in his legs. He eventually went into shock. Is this really poison? I've worked this job for many years, and I've never heard of any poison causing symptoms like these."

"You're right. It might not be poisoning." The look Zhao Yunlan directed at him seemed deep and cold, as if his words had some hidden meaning.

Officer Li shivered.

Zhao Yunlan patted him on the shoulder. "Anyway, the hospital hasn't reached any conclusions yet. Anything is possible. Let me see the victims."

The doctors, nurses, and patients' families were asked to temporarily clear the room. Once only the two profoundly afflicted patients were left, wailing and screaming in a chorus of agony, Zhao Yunlan swept his eyes over them both. He then briskly knocked one unconscious and turned his attention to Guo Changcheng. "Did you bring your notebook?"

Guo Changcheng nodded hurriedly.

"Take notes." Zhao Yunlan bent down and addressed the victim who was still awake. "Ma'am, do your legs hurt?"

The victim was a middle-aged woman who was in too much pain to lie still. The hospital staff had had no choice but to restrain her to the bed. She nodded, eyes shimmering with tears.

Next, Zhao Yunlan got out his wallet—a "wallet" that held no cards or money. He opened it, revealing a thick stack of yellow paper talismans. He leafed through them, explaining to Guo Changcheng as he went. "Paper talismans are very important tools. Ideally, you'd store them in some sort of order so you aren't scrambling to find the right one when you need it. Of course, learning to use them is an art all its own..."

Unbelievably, this unpredictable boss was settling in to deliver a leisurely lecture while the victim cried out like a pig at slaughter. Guo Changcheng lacked the mental strength for it. With more than half of his attention taken by the screaming woman, it made him feel particularly restless.

"Now, for situations like hers..." Zhao Yunlan folded the middle-aged woman's ear forward so that they could see behind it.

"Your third eye hasn't been opened, so you can't see merits, but you can check it with the help of a very basic talisman."

He pulled out a paper talisman and held it out to Guo Changcheng. "This one will open your third eye."

Guo Changcheng was about to close his fingers on the talisman when Zhao Yunlan's hand snapped up and stuck it unerringly on his brow. "Like this," Zhao Yunlan said.

Completely unprepared, Guo Changcheng felt an indescribable iciness from the talisman. There was somehow a weight to it, piercing him like a sharp knife. His vision blurred and the world changed right before his eyes...but in a way he couldn't quite identify.

"Come take a look." Zhao Yunlan beckoned him closer.

Guo Changcheng hastily looked down and was shocked to see that the victim on the bed was now shrouded in a layer of black mist. Her face, which had only looked slightly haggard before, now appeared very strange indeed. A faint aura of death radiated from her, as if she already had one foot in the grave. Her legs had looked just fine before but were now completely encased by the black mist, creating the illusion that there were only two uneven stumps.

Finally, he looked at her ear again and saw a large mark behind it: a grayish sort of color, not very dark, that nearly covered her entire neck. It might have been an unusual birthmark.

"A darkness like this behind someone's ear indicates that they are lacking in merits," Shen Wei explained. "*The Book of Life and Death* records all the merits of a person's life. Every time a person commits evil, the handprint of a little ghoul marks the back of their ear. The darker the color, the more heinous the crime. The print we see here isn't dark, but it covers a substantial area, indicating that while she has never caused any grievous harm, she is likely very selfish and has committed an endless stream of petty sins."

Shen Wei paused, then added, "Of course, her evils don't warrant death. Hurting her this severely is taking things a little too far."

Guo Changcheng nodded timidly and hurried to make a note. But before he'd finished writing, it struck him that something was very strange about all this. His head snapped around, and he stared at Shen Wei in shock.

"What are you looking at?" Zhao Yunlan pushed his head back. "*He's* the real master. It just took me a while to recognize what was right in front of me."

As he spoke, he pulled out another talisman. This one was also placed in front of Guo Changcheng for him to study. "This is a simple talisman for dispelling evil. It's fairly basic, so it doesn't always work. That's fine if it doesn't. It'll help us gauge the strength of what we're up against."

Guo Changcheng was silent, unable to imagine how hearing that might have made the woman on the bed feel.

Zhao Yunlan slapped the yellow paper talisman down onto her, causing a massive ball of black gas to spew from her body. It shot up like a menacing geyser, only to be knocked partway back when it hit the ceiling. A contorted face took shape in midair, mouth wide open as it howled hysterically at them.

It all happened in a flash. One moment Zhao Yunlan had been delivering a lecture on theory and now they were in a haunted house. Guo Changcheng screamed and bolted for the door. But Director Zhao, as though he had eyes in the back of his head, dragged Guo Changcheng back by the collar.

Keeping a firm hand on Guo Changcheng, Zhao Yunlan studied the black mist. “Weird,” he murmured. “Why is there so much resentment?”

“Ghost!” yelped Guo Changcheng. “Ghost, ghost, ghost!”

Zhao Yunlan snorted. “Like you’ve never seen a ghost before? Why would I have ordered you to join me if I wasn’t expecting any?”

A powerful bolt of electricity burst from Guo Changcheng’s pocket. With the wisdom of experience, Zhao Yunlan immediately let go and backed out of the way. The black shadow hanging in the air met the same fate as the huge knife in the Hanga tribe’s secret tunnel.

“We hadn’t asked it anything yet! No one told you to kill it!” Zhao Yunlan slapped the back of Guo Changcheng’s head.

Guo Changcheng was on the brink of tears. “I-I’m scared...”

“Can’t you hold it in for a while?” Zhao Yunlan demanded.

From day one, Guo Changcheng had both feared and respected his boss. Even if Zhao Yunlan unleashed a toxic fart, he would treat it as a divine utterance and think the boss had made an excellent point. So upon hearing this, Guo Changcheng made an immediate attempt to obediently contain his terror.

He tried until his face was beet red, but he couldn’t stop trembling with fear. Voice thin as a mosquito’s buzz, he said, “I...really can’t hold it in.”

The pointed side-eye Zhao Yunlan gave him lasted until Guo Changcheng was shaking badly enough that there was a real risk of another 10,000-volt discharge. And then, unexpectedly, his heartless boss laughed. “You sure do keep things interesting.”

Guo Changcheng only blinked. It seemed like a strange compliment.

"Don't bully him," scolded Shen Wei.

Meanwhile, the stricken woman finally managed to do more than gawk at them. Moving with great difficulty, she knelt on the bed and bowed to Guo Changcheng. "Thank you, Immortal. Thank you, young Immortal!"

Overcome with embarrassment, he stammered, "No, no, no, I... I-I-I..."

He was utterly tongue-tied, face and ears ablaze. A crackle from his pocket was the only warning before his stun baton generated a fireball that nearly ignited Zhao Yunlan's jacket.

"Okay, please stop bowing to him. If you're not careful, he's gonna blow." Zhao Yunlan gestured to the woman, keeping two meters between himself and Guo Changcheng. "I just want to ask you a few things. I hope you'll cooperate."

When she eagerly nodded, he asked, "Yesterday, were you hospitalized after you ate an orange you bought on the roadside?"

"Yes," she said. "It was already dark by then. I'd gone to the supermarket to buy a few things, and when I came out, I happened to see someone selling oranges by the side of the road."

Zhao Yunlan interrupted. "Did you notice the fruit seller on your way into the store?"

She thought about it, then hesitantly said, "I...don't think so? No, I'm sure. I was keeping an eye out for fruit vendors along the way. So I would've noticed him before going in."

So the fruit seller had been deliberately waiting for her.

"What did this person look like?"

"Uh...a man. He was awfully skinny, and he had such a ratty knitted hat... I think maybe he was wearing a cotton coat? Gray, maybe?"

"What about his legs?"

"His legs?" She froze for a second before the memory came back to her. "Oh, right! I remember! Something seemed wrong with his legs. He walked with a limp. If you hadn't mentioned it, I wouldn't have remembered. I sure hope he isn't a cripple with a prosthetic leg."

Without waiting for a response, she began to ramble. "Let me tell you, O Great Immortal, people like that are all messed up. Cripples, mutes, whatever kind of disability they have, it doesn't matter. Their hearts are all twisted up because they're missing part of their body! Of course someone like that would go around poisoning people! If you ask me, everyone like *that* should be rounded up in one place so someone can keep an eye on them. It's not like they can do anything but disrupt society, after all."

It was becoming clear to Zhao Yunlan how this woman had wound up with that handprint-sized mark behind her ear. Some people just plain lacked one of the five virtues from the day they were born, and as a result, tiny but aggressive evils seeped from their very pores. None of them were deadly, but every one of them had a vicious bite.

The diatribe continued. "For example, there's a deaf man living near me. He can't find a wife, so he got a stupid dog. Every time his door opened you could hear that damn dog barking. And of course he couldn't hear it, being deaf and all, so he never did a damn thing about all that yapping. I can't believe I waited so long to buy that rat poison. I should've killed the thing sooner..."

Zhao Yunlan ran out of patience. He stared straight into the woman's eyes and mercilessly overpowered her mind. She finally fell silent, blank eyes rolling back in her skull, and went down, headfirst. Speaking flatly into her ear, the stone-faced Zhao Yunlan said, "Something you ate disagreed with you, so you just went to the bathroom. It's all out of your system now, but you slipped and stepped in your own shit. You won't be able to get that stink out of your nose for at least a month."

As Zhao Yunlan's words grew ever worse, Shen Wei gave a pointed cough.

"The hot policemen who came by this afternoon were following normal procedure. They asked about the person selling the poisoned oranges, and while they were at it, they educated certain citizens a little..."

"Ahem!" Shen Wei cleared his throat.

"That's all. Take some time and reflect on that."

After he was finally finished with her, Zhao Yunlan was the last one to leave the room. From the doorway, he looked back with an evil smile. "Have a nice nightmare, ma'am."

Shen Wei, afraid he might launch into a full-on reenactment of *The Ring* in the woman's ear, dragged him out.

"She doesn't know the person who poisoned her." As soon as he was out of the room, Zhao Yunlan snapped straight back into training Guo Changcheng. "The karmic line under her eyelid isn't very deep. Presumably she wasn't poisoned by the dog she offed. In circumstances like these, the most likely scenario is that the person doing the poisoning is just harming people for no reason."

Guo Changcheng's pen flew furiously as he scribbled in his little notebook. Zhao Yunlan slowed his speech and let him catch up a bit before continuing. "If that woman had had a direct connection with the culprit—for example, if she'd killed someone and they came back for revenge, that would be none of our business. Laws in the Mortal Realm don't allow for revenge, but once a person crosses the threshold of yin and yang, the law of an eye for an eye and a tooth for a tooth is as natural as night and day."

Guo Changcheng nodded continuously as he listened.

"But the fruit seller was a stranger to her. That and the faint karmic line mean there was only the shallowest of connections between them—like one of them might have stepped on the other's foot or something small like that. So if a violent ghost is deliberately harming people for some reason, we have the authority not only to arrest it but to take care of it on the spot."

Guo Changcheng subconsciously patted the jacket pocket holding his stun baton. The corner of Zhao Yunlan's lips twitched. "Call Zhu Hong and tell her to get the higher-ups to expedite our paperwork. I want full authority in this situation by tonight, so get a move on!"

Chapter 6

A LITTLE PAST FOUR O'CLOCK in the afternoon, just as dusk was setting in, Zhu Hong hurriedly arrived at the hospital with the proper authorizations for a joint operation.

"The people from the District Bureau just left," Zhu Hong said. "I ran into them downstairs. They said they wanted to treat us to dinner sometime, so..." At the sight of Shen Wei approaching, she abruptly cut herself off. After taking a moment to rephrase what she was saying for an outsider's ears, she finished, "So the case is entirely ours now."

Noticing her hesitation, Shen Wei quickly handed the drinks he'd just bought to Zhao Yunlan. In an understanding tone, he said, "Please do your work, everyone. I'll just—"

"You're not going anywhere," Zhao Yunlan cut off both his words and his retreat. "I'm not about to let you have second thoughts and disappear."

The hospital hallways were always full of people. Between being tall, full of physical grace, and an overall hottie, Zhao Yunlan generally drew attention to begin with, but publicly touching and grabbing hold of another man quickly drew curious stares from all around.

Shen Wei swiftly assessed the situation. "We're in public," he said softly. "Have some discretion, please."

Zhao Yunlan responded by turning to glare at the onlookers. "What are you looking at?" he asked, unfazed. "Never seen a couple of hot gay guys before?"

Shen Wei and Zhu Hong were both stunned speechless for a moment, and then they spoke almost at the same time. "It's not appropriate for me to be here while you work," Shen Wei said.

More quietly, Zhu Hong said, "That's right, Director Zhao. Our internal regulations..."

"*I'm* the one who set the regulations," Zhao Yunlan interrupted her. "If I'm unhappy with them, I can change them any time I want. Besides, what they say is that we need to keep outsiders from witnessing or participating in our investigations. He's not an outsider."

Shen Wei froze, momentarily sure that Zhao Yunlan was about to reveal his identity. But instead, Zhao Yunlan lowered his voice so that he sounded like an annoying brat. "He's not an outsider— he's my partner."

Dumbfounded, Zhu Hong turned away and looked blankly out the window. She had the feeling that she'd just seen the lord of incompetence claim his throne.

She sent a quick text to the criminal investigation unit back at 4 Bright Avenue: *Hurry, come see the public nuisance at Yellow Cliff Temple Hospital. Don't make me suffer alone.*

The group answered her summons and swarmed the hospital before dark. But rather than getting to witness anything, they were pressed into service by Zhao Yunlan.

"Lao-Chu, go to the roof and set down two layers of one-way nets in case he makes a break for it. Make sure that once he enters, he can't leave. Xiao-Guo, go observe, then write me a report of what you've learned after we wrap things up here. Zhu Hong, set up a surveillance bell on every single door and window in the inpatient department, then section off the space here and establish your own domain. Don't let any random bystanders wander in. Make it neat—Daqing!"

Daqing and Lin Jing had been busy whispering to each other. "Look at Shen-laoshi's wrist," Lin Jing was saying. "You can see a glimpse of gauze. Our boss is such a beast."

Daqing's eyes went incredibly wide, and his imagination had just started to run wild when he suddenly heard his name. Every molecule of his fat started quivering.

"What are you doing, slacking off?" Zhao Yunlan side-eyed him. "Go help, you damn fatty!"

Shen Wei's hearing transcended that of any mortal. Having overheard the discussion, he stiffly tugged his sleeve down.

"As for you..." Zhao Yunlan rounded on Lin Jing and pulled a small bottle from his pocket. Lin Jing gulped, gripped by a sudden bad feeling. Zhao Yunlan gave him an evil smile. "Here's some resentment I scraped off one of the victims."

In the simplest terms possible, Chu Shuzhi explained it to the rookie who didn't understand shit. "Violent spirits are all born from resentment. Picture the spirit like the body of an octopus. It reaches out and curses other people with that resentment, which then acts like the octopus's arms—the spirit can feel each of those people through it."

Guo Changcheng had been trailing around after Zhao Yunlan for some time by then and hadn't yet had a chance to eat supper. Thanks to Chu Shuzhi's explanation, he couldn't help thinking about takoyaki. His mouth watered and his stomach rumbled noticeably.

This bizarre reaction wasn't at all what Chu Shuzhi had expected.

Zhao Yunlan tossed the bottle to Lin Jing. "I'm worried that he won't fall for it tonight, so here's what you're gonna do: as soon as it gets dark, get out there, destroy the resentment inside the bottle, and lure the violent spirit into Zhu Hong's domain."

Silently, Lin Jing looked at Zhao Yunlan and then at the bottle in his own hand. Realizing that he was being baited into becoming a tank to pull aggro, he said, "You did this on purpose."

Zhao Yunlan didn't bat an eye. "Yeah, and?"

Lin Jing swept his eyes over the others. The black cat wore a crafty sneer, and everyone else's expression was unsympathetic and indifferent. He let himself wallow in sorrow for a moment before wheeling around and flinging himself at Shen Wei, who was leaning unobtrusively against the wall. "My liege wishes to sacrifice this humble monk before the flag of battle!" he cried. "Noble consort, I beg you, intercede on my behalf!"

Shen Wei didn't have the first clue how to respond. As the Soul-Executing Emissary, he was accustomed to people reacting to him like rats spotting a cat. Having never been on the receiving end of teasing like this, he was at a complete loss. He turned to Zhao Yunlan as though asking for help.

Zhao Yunlan, on the other hand, was delighted by this high-quality display of ass-kissing. He averted his eyes, showing no interest in intervening.

After considering his options, Shen Wei held out his hand for the bottle. "I'll go in your place, then."

He hadn't even finished speaking before an ominous stare pierced Lin Jing's spine. Even if Lin Jing had been ten times braver, he wouldn't have dared use the "noble consort" as bait.

The fake monk managed a dry chuckle and tucked the bottle into his own breast pocket. "Amitabha. Our duty is to encourage goodness, eradicate evil, and protect people's lives and possessions. How could I foist this honorable and arduous calling off on someone else? Off I go!" With those words, he darted off at the speed of light.

"Then how can I help?" Shen Wei asked.

Zhao Yunlan replied, "I know a restaurant a bit south of here that's pretty good. Come eat with me."

Once again, Shen Wei had no idea how to react.

Zhu Hong ground her teeth. "I'm angry, but I have to bite my tongue."

Chu Shuzhi fixed his eyes on the ground. "Yup, biting my tongue."

Daqing simply meowed.

Shen-laoshi, however, had a conscience. "We can't do that. How about this: you stay here and give orders, and I'll go hold the Gate of Life for you. Then, if need be, I can assist."

Everyone went dead silent at his words. Zhu Hong's brow furrowed, and Chu Shuzhi's face turned pensive. But Guo Changcheng, the only one confused, piped up. "What's a Gate of Life?"

Chu Shuzhi ignored the question. Expression serious, he asked, "How did Shen-laoshi know what kind of array I'll be putting down?"

"Two layers with four gates each, anything that enters is unable to exit. I could extrapolate as much from seeing the places Yunlan pointed out just now for monitoring. However, if the violent spirit's resentment is too thick and heavy, he could tear through the temporary net. At that point, if the Gate of Life becomes a Gate of Death, it'll be hard to control. I'll guard the eye of the array just in case."

Chu Shuzhi looked him up and down. "Shen-laoshi knows all of this even though you're just a university professor?"

"I've picked up a few things." Shen Wei nodded politely at everyone, then addressed Zhao Yunlan. "I'll be going, then. You be careful."

With a feeling of deep satisfaction, Zhao Yunlan watched him leave.

Zhu Hong and Chu Shuzhi turned toward Zhao Yunlan in unison, faces full of confusion. Daqing stood up on a chair by the window on his hind legs to watch as Shen Wei walked out of the hospital and unerringly took his position on the Gate of Life. As though feeling the cat's gaze, Shen Wei looked up and smiled at him.

Daqing's eyes flashed. "A master."

Very quietly, Zhu Hong asked, "Director Zhao, who exactly is Shen-laoshi?"

Zhao Yunlan, now in an excellent mood, half-jokingly said, "You don't want me to answer that."

Daqing's dark green gaze shifted to him. "Does that mean you know what you're doing?"

Zhao Yunlan leaned back lazily in his chair. "When have I ever not?"

"I just think it's weird," said Zhu Hong. "First, when the Reincarnation Dial appeared, he was there. And then with the Mountain-River Awl, we just *happened* to run into him when we were heading to the mountains. Dragon City is so big that I don't even know all my neighbors! I can't believe that was all coincidental. Doesn't it seem planned to you, Director Zhao?"

"To be honest, yes, there's a story behind it all." Zhao Yunlan chose his words carefully. "But I don't think he'd want anyone else to know, so I'm afraid I can't say more than that right now."

An icy weight settled on Zhu Hong's chest. If Shen Wei were some ordinary person, she, Lin Jing, and the others could amuse themselves and kill time gossiping about him and Zhao Yunlan. She could even tease and laugh at their boss, or go as far as writing smutty scenarios about him on Weibo. But the revelation that Shen Wei's nature was more aligned with theirs made her uncomfortable, as if she'd suddenly been stabbed in the heart with a long, thin needle. The blood dripping from that wound reeked of jealousy.

"What is Shen-laoshi a master of? Making arrays?" Chu Shuzhi was curious. "When he's free, can we have a chat?"

Daqing's tail flicked up. A little worried, he said, "You're getting yourself tangled up with someone who isn't an ordinary human. Even if you don't want to go into detail, could you at least tell us which side your friend is on?"

With the three of them grilling him, it was as if Zhao Yunlan had found a sugar daddy, not a partner. His fleeting patience finally evaporated. With an impatient wave, he said, "What's with the interrogation? Did I say this was a press conference? Get to work!"

Zhu Hong wanted to say more, but Daqing had already jumped down from the chair and meowed at her from a few steps away. She could only sigh in resignation as her fist, hidden in her sleeve, clenched even tighter. She caught up with Daqing without another word.

Zhao Yunlan noticed the subtle hostility radiating from her, but that didn't strike him as strange. Zhu Hong had always been careful and meticulous, and he'd brought Shen Wei, a complete stranger, into their little circle without warning or explanation. Of course she'd be uneasy.

To show her that he understood, Zhao Yunlan called after her. "Hey, wait."

Zhu Hong's footsteps paused.

"I want to respect Shen Wei's wishes," he explained, "so I really can't say much. But there's no need to be concerned about him, so don't worry. Just treat him exactly like you'd treat me."

Treat him exactly the same, my ass. Zhu Hong stalked out without replying, thinking about how badly she wanted to slap a certain jackass named Zhao.

Chapter 7

AT LAST, darkness fell over the city.

High up on the roof, the wind whistled strongly. It had made a mess of Chu Shuzhi's hair. He was so tremendously thin that he resembled human jerky, as though he'd be a stringy mouthful if you took a bite. Unable to shake the feeling that Chu Shuzhi might be blown off the roof at any moment, Guo Changcheng kept glancing over to check on him.

Guo Changcheng himself was immobilized with fear. There was cinnabar all over the rooftop beneath his feet; Chu Shuzhi had used the cinnabar to turn the rooftop into a gigantic talisman, drawing on its surface as if it were a huge piece of yellow paper, and then pinned down the eight positions with black stones.

From where he stood at the center of the giant talisman, Guo Changcheng immediately felt the atmosphere shift. The night wind carried a particular smell, one he couldn't quite describe. It was sticky and wet, but not unpleasant, despite the tang of mud and blood. A barely perceptible thread of bitterness wound through it.

Guo Changcheng took a whiff, feeling a little lost. "Chu-ge?"

"That's the smell of a resentful spirit." Chu Shuzhi didn't look up. Within the wide net that had been set up, the light color of Shen Wei's coat was starkly visible. He was standing precisely in the net-closing position. "Who did Director Zhao manage to ensnare this time?" Chu Shuzhi murmured. "Shen… I've never heard of anyone by that name."

Shen Wei seemed to look up, but it was too dark for Chu Shuzhi to see his face. A moment later he vanished from sight, and Chu Shuzhi's expression turned serious. "It's here."

"Huh?" said Guo Changcheng.

"This isn't the time for 'Huh?'" Chu Shuzhi stalked over and stuck a yellow paper talisman to Guo Changcheng's face. "Shut your mouth and keep quiet."

The distinctive pungent smell intensified. Down on the ground, in the northeast corner, Lin Jing stuffed his phone back into his pocket and twisted open the little bottle expressionlessly. A cloud of putrid black smoke rose into the air. Lin Jing looked up and made a vajra seal with his hands; the look on his face was intensely focused, almost divine.

However, despite Zhao Yunlan's instructions, he didn't immediately kill it. Instead, he began quietly chanting scriptures that would grant the soul transcendence. After all, it was a soul that had once been born and raised by the Heavens and Earth. It had been born into existence from the essence of all things. It might have only experienced a few lives so far, or it might have already been through countless reincarnations. Lin Jing didn't have it in him to uphold the law with the same violent efficiency as Zhao Yunlan.

But the low chanting of scriptures was like casting pearls before swine. The resentment had grievances to address. How could it bear to listen to such tedious nagging? It responded by swelling and expanding monstrously in the air until it blotted out the moon and stars. It roared at the sky.

Just then, three gunshots shattered the quiet of the night. They shredded the flimsy strand of resentment, and it faded away.

A window on the sixth floor had been pushed open from inside; Lin Jing spotted the flicker of a flame.

It was all too easy to envision Zhao Yunlan's furrowed brow and commanding expression as he holstered his gun and grumbled, "All those scriptures have rotted your brain."

But it wasn't over.

The wind carried a distant roar of fury to their ears. Lin Jing pressed his hands together with a silent "Amitabha," then backflipped up into the naked branches of a nearby tree.

A huge black cloud of smoke struck the spot where he'd just been standing, shattering the tidy tiles and thrusting the shards into the air. A massive figure appeared within the reeking wind. It was at least four or five meters tall and appeared human—but only the top half. A bit of protruding bone was all that remained of its legs. Blackish blood trailed behind the figure as it approached; the ground sizzled and melted wherever the blood touched.

The being seemed ready to destroy all who stood in its way, even God or Buddha himself.

Lin Jing laughed dryly, but his steps never faltered. He leapt up and grabbed the ledge of a second-floor window. Like a gigantic spider, he raced up the side of the building, using the jutting window ledges and tiny handholds in the wall. He ascended faster than an elevator, with the black shadow close behind him.

When he reached the sixth floor, Lin Jing yelled to the black cat at the window. "Catch it!"

Daqing pounced. Six bells, each hanging in its own window, began to toll in perfect unison. Zhu Hong cried out and an immense python slithered out into the fray, curling its tongue and swallowing a cloud of the black smoke.

The shadow pursuing Lin Jing battered indiscriminately at everything in reach. The ringing of the bells came faster and faster as the python continued drawing the black smoke from the resentful spirit into its mouth. Bit by bit, the shadow shrank.

Eventually the shadow hanging in the air was almost completely gone, and the man hidden within was revealed. It was the person Guo Changcheng had seen outside the hospital window, with salt-and-pepper hair and red eyes.

Zhao Yunlan abruptly stubbed out his cigarette on the windowsill. "Zhu Hong! Move!"

The moment he spoke, the six clanging bells stilled and fell silent. Every window on the sixth floor had been blown out entirely. The tremendous python settled to the floor and was a woman once more while the maimed man immediately grew dramatically. Zhao Yunlan leaned over and grabbed Zhu Hong, only two or three meters from the resentful spirit floating outside.

"Soul-Guarding Order." Zhao Yunlan narrowed his eyes. In a voice like ice, he said, "After your death, you didn't go find a place to reincarnate. Instead, you emerged during New Year's to poison people. Why?"

The words "New Year's" seemed to set the resentful spirit off. One huge, smoke-shrouded hand made a grab for Zhao Yunlan's neck.

The Soul-Guarding Order transmuted into a whip like a live vine. It lashed out from Zhao Yunlan's sleeve and coiled around that huge hand, leaving human and ghost deadlocked on a pile of shattered glass.

Zhu Hong gave Lin Jing a forceful shove. "Are you blind? Go help!"

Lin Jing hadn't caught his breath after his Spider-Man impression, and his fingers hurt from all the climbing. "Help? Help...

Help how? Look at the size of that thing! You have way too much confidence in me. What can I do?"

"Ring the bell!" Zhu Hong snapped. "You have to ring the bell every day. That's what monks must do, right?!"

Her yelling made Lin Jing's ears ring. "Miss Benefactor, can you please calm down?" he pleaded. "I'm just an uninitiated monk! Have you ever seen an uninitiated monk ring the bell every day? Besides, my Buddha may be merciful, but he has dominion over occult things. That spirit was human before he died, so the bell can only affect him so much. You think it can deal with resentful energy that even you couldn't swallow?"

"I don't care!" she said. "Just hurry and think of something!"

Lin Jing glanced in Zhao Yunlan's direction and gave a deep, helpless sigh. "Why didn't Buddha, in his infinite mercy, make this disciple just a little bit hotter too?"

Then he reached into his pocket and pulled out a small, palm-sized vessel shaped like a teapot. When he lifted the lid, the aroma of fragrant oil wafted out. Lin Jing peered inside, clearly reluctant. But just as he was about to pour it, Zhao Yunlan waved at him. It was like the boss had eyes in the side of his head. "Save your lamp oil. You're not needed here."

He'd barely spoken when the resentful spirit managed to struggle free of the Soul-Guarding Whip. The whip rose high, wavered, and then silently withdrew back into Zhao Yunlan's sleeve.

Roaring, the resentful spirit tore through the window frames and began to squeeze its way into the hospital hallway. The opening of the window seemed about to burst at any moment.

In response, Zhao Yunlan took a single step back. He extended both arms in front of himself, parallel to the floor with his palms facing out, fingers spread. With a short knife in his right hand, he silently sliced across his left palm. Fresh blood flowed into the groove of the blade and immediately congealed.

Off to the side, Daqing saw what was happening. Fur bristling, he sprang into Zhu Hong's arms. The smile that spread across Zhao Yunlan's face bore no resemblance to his normal smile. In that moment, his eyes seemed unusually deep; his warm gaze had turned cold. His tall nose cast a shadow across his face in the darkness. There was an eerie, indescribable malice in the curl of his lips.

"Netherworld realms, heed my command." The resounding and faintly hoarse voice that emerged didn't sound like Zhao Yunlan's either. Hearing it felt rather like being grated by a dull saw might. "With blood sworn and cold iron as witness, three thousand ghost soldiers I call. Perish, foes, though mortal or god; any may fall by their blades—"

There was a perceptible pause after each syllable as he spoke the last few words. The congealed blood on the blade turned black, and countless armored soldiers began to pour from the pale white wall behind him. Mounted on warhorses of white bone and dragging rotting weapons, they surged forth like an indomitable force of nature. With a great battle cry, they clashed with the massive resentful spirit.

All the strength seemed to have drained out of Zhao Yunlan. He stumbled back and leaned on the wall behind him, ignoring everyone's terrified gaze. He shook his still-bleeding hand and said, short of breath, "I still got a little blood on my sleeve. Will dry cleaning get it out?"

Very carefully, Daqing asked, "Yunlan?"

Zhao Yunlan raised a brow. "Hmm?"

That expression was all too familiar. This was the Zhao Yunlan who was always in need of a good swipe. With no further hesitation, Daqing reached out and smacked him. "What the fuck was that?! I never taught you this kind of sorcery!"

Zhao Yunlan said smugly, "Humans can read, dumb cat."

Daqing jumped to stand on Zhao Yunlan's thighs, forepaws on the human's shoulders. Right in Zhao Yunlan's face, he bellowed, "What *exactly* did you take out of the library?!"

Zhao Yunlan patted the cat's head with his good hand and scratched his chin. Daqing reflexively closed his eyes and started to purr.

"Soul Book," Zhao Yunlan said. "Don't worry, I'm not studying sorcery. I was researching something else and stumbled on this. The urgency of the situation made me think of it just now. I wasn't planning on doing anything. Don't you have any faith in my good character?"

Cursing his kitty instincts, the black cat gave his head a forceful shake to dislodge Zhao Yunlan's hand. "Good character? Do you even possess such a thing?!" Cat spit sprayed Zhao Yunlan's face.

But having said that, Daqing jumped down to the floor with a huff, grudgingly accepting the explanation. He trusted Zhao Yunlan to not go too far, but he wasn't happy about it. "If you want your ugly mugshot to show up on the Netherworld's wanted list for everyone to see, then I have nothing to say."

He hadn't fully gotten the sentence out before Zhao Yunlan grabbed him from behind and pinned him to the floor. "Whose picture is ugly? You neckless fat cat!"

That was when Chu Shuzhi phoned from the roof. He'd been all too happy to watch the chaos unfold and was vibrating from head to toe with uncharacteristic excitement. "Was that the Ghost Army just now? Who summoned them? Are they crazy? That was so fucking hot!"

That was more than Zhu Hong could take. She hung up on him.

Finally catching his breath, Lin Jing butted in. "Is the Ghost Army summoned with blood?"

"Blood and iron are both mediums." Zhao Yunlan straightened up, dusting himself off. "What's actually doing the summoning is malice. Since malice is so sinister, I think it's a form of fighting fire with fire."

Zhu Hong hesitated for a moment, then edged closer. "You have malice in your heart?"

"What, am I not human?" Zhao Yunlan chuckled and answered readily. "Of course I do—loads of it. To be honest, I don't think the Ghost Army Summons should count as sorcery at all. It's great stuff, like mental yoga—gives you a good detox and leaves your whole body relaxed."

Zhu Hong was too stunned to reply, but Daqing jumped onto Zhao Yunlan's shoulder and punched him in the nose.

"Damn fatty!" Zhao Yunlan hollered.

The Ghost Army had driven the resentful spirit into a corner. Realizing he wouldn't be able to get anything out of the situation, he decided that escape was the best course of action.

The array Chu Shuzhi had set up outside activated at once. A bolt of lightning that had been waiting in the skies all that time was suddenly unleashed. The Ghost Army chasing the spirit disappeared at the same moment, leaving the resentful spirit pinned in place by the lightning. He began to struggle violently in a giant net of electricity. Quakes rocked the ground beneath the hospital.

From the roof, Chu Shuzhi yelled, "Don't let him get away!"

Shen Wei, who had vanished some time ago, reappeared out of nowhere behind the resentful spirit. He reached out and closed a hand around thin air. It was as if an invisible hand was tightening around the spirit's neck. The black miasma dispersed little by little, revealing a legless man staring in Shen Wei's direction with utter hatred.

Unmoved, Shen Wei tightened his fingers. The spirit crumpled like a piece of paper in his hand and was gone.

CHAPTER 8

WITH THEIR TARGET APPREHENDED, the domain Zhu Hong had established automatically faded away. The glass shards on the floor reassembled themselves into intact windows. Inside the hospital, there was still an endless stream of nurses making the nightly rounds and patients coming to the emergency room. The street vendor outside the entrance had already packed up their wares. The occasional taxi hurried past, clearly not on the lookout for customers.

The peacefulness of the night might have never been broken at all.

Shen Wei raced up to the sixth floor, arriving at the same moment as Chu Shuzhi, who was coming down from the roof.

Chu Shuzhi's arrogance was rooted in his confidence in his abilities. He was civil enough with people he knew but rarely bothered paying attention to strangers. Now, though, he addressed Shen Wei warmly. "You did a beautiful job of holding the eye of the array."

Shen Wei offered a hurried nod of greeting, but his expression was even more tense than someone about to be operated on for acute appendicitis. He took out a small bottle and gave it to Chu Shuzhi. "The spirit is in here. Keep a close eye on it."

Then his attention turned to Zhao Yunlan. "Come with me. We need to talk."

He dragged Zhao Yunlan into a bathroom and locked the door. Staring at Zhao Yunlan in the dim light, he quietly asked, "Was that the Ghost Army just now?"

"Yeah."

"Was it you?"

Zhao Yunlan nodded, not even trying to deny it. "Who else?"

Shen Wei's lips set into a sharp, straight line. "Who taught you the Ghost Army Summons?"

Again, Zhao Yunlan's answer was forthright. "I happened to read it in a book in the Soul-Guarding Order library."

Shen Wei wordlessly raised a hand and aimed it at Zhao Yunlan's face, but couldn't bear to actually strike him. His hand stopped dangerously close, his palm near Zhao Yunlan's ear.

Zhao Yunlan froze. "Shen Wei?"

"Don't talk to me!" Shen Wei was pale with fury. His hand, still held in midair, trembled. "'Perish, foes, though mortal or god; any may fall by their blades'? The Guardian's power must defy description! What mad arrogance! Don't... Don't you fear punishment from the Heavens?"

Zhao Yunlan had rarely seen Shen Wei or the Soul-Executing Emissary show true anger. He quickly caught hold of Shen Wei's ice-cold hands and apologized first, the rest be damned. "You're absolutely right. I was wrong. If you want to hit me, go ahead. Don't be mad, okay? Don't be mad."

Shen Wei shook him off. "Do you think this is a joke? Are you somehow unaware that gathering souls with the Ghost Army Summons is utterly forbidden sorcery? Do you even understand what sorcery is? Do you imagine the Three Realms are beneath you? With such disregard for the Heavens, will nothing satisfy you but to tear the sky asunder?! When that happens, you...y-you'll..."

He broke off abruptly. When he could finally speak again, he took half a step back. "When that happens, what am I to do?" he asked, voice shaking.

Zhao Yunlan's heart ached for him. He reached out to pull Shen Wei into his arms. "I was wrong, babe. I'm sorry."

He thought his apology was appropriately sincere, but the words triggered something in Shen Wei. Shen Wei shoved him away, pinning him against the door with one hand and grabbing his collar brutally with the other. "Don't try to fool me the same way you've fooled who knows how many others."

"Okay." Zhao Yunlan gave a helpless sigh. "I'll just stop talking, then."

With no more warning than that, he leaned in to ambush Shen Wei's icy lips.

Caught off guard, Shen Wei instinctively pulled back, but warm hands came up to cradle his face. Zhao Yunlan seized the opportunity to force his lips open. Shen Wei was overwhelmed by a refreshing scent of mint. His anger and reason crumbled; all he could see was a chaotic swirl. He couldn't even process it when Zhao Yunlan ended the kiss.

Zhao Yunlan calmly removed Shen Wei's hand from his collar before Shen Wei regained the ability to think. Shen Wei stared blankly at him, face completely red. "You..."

Eyes crinkling, Zhao Yunlan gave him a smile. He reached up and mimed zipping his own mouth closed to indicate that he wasn't talking. Looking down at Shen Wei, he then swiped his thumb across his lips and licked it lightly.

Shen Wei was too embarrassed to know where to look.

Swinging Shen Wei's hand with his own injured one, Zhao Yunlan drew Shen Wei's attention to how the cut on his palm was already starting to scab over. The shocking crimson of it made Shen Wei's eyes sting. He carefully lifted Zhao Yunlan's hand. Bright white light covered and sank into the wounded palm, and the cut began to close. In an instant, the skin was perfect and unbroken.

Shen Wei hauled him to the sink to rinse the blood away. "Does it hurt?"

Zhao Yunlan didn't say anything.

Left with no other choice, Shen Wei said, "You can speak."

"It does hurt," said Zhao Yunlan.

Shen Wei's brows furrowed as Zhao Yunlan continued, "My back hurts. So does my chest. You actually got angry at me! You're the soul of courtesy to everyone else, but you got *angry* at me! You won't even let me talk! How could you make me so sad?" His words were punctuated with a pout.

Shen Wei, not realizing Zhao Yunlan was trying to be cute, mumbled, "I… I didn't mean to…"

Zhao Yunlan looked up at him expressionlessly. Just as Shen Wei was starting to panic a little, Zhao Yunlan reached up and tapped his own lips. "Kiss me again. Coax your forgiveness from your lord's lips."

Shen Wei's face went blank, and his ears turned scarlet. He immediately turned to leave. "How shameless!"

But he looked back upon reaching the door, realizing that Zhao Yunlan hadn't followed him, or indeed, moved at all. Zhao Yunlan was still right where Shen Wei had left him: leaning against the wall, looking at him with something that might have been a smile.

Shen Wei was already touching the lock on the door, but after another moment's hesitation, he seemed to accept his fate. He returned and kissed Zhao Yunlan, hands on Zhao Yunlan's waist.

If he was already so thoroughly wrapped around Zhao Yunlan's little finger, how would he fare in the future?

When the team returned to 4 Bright Avenue, Chu Shuzhi set up an escape-proof net outside the interrogation room. Only once the place was bristling with yellow paper talismans strung up like Tibetan prayer flags did he go inside and lock the door, open the little bottle, and release the resentful spirit.

Zhao Yunlan got a chair for Shen Wei and lit a cigarette before lazily addressing the spirit. "You have the right to remain silent. Every word you say from here on out will be used as evidence in court, so think carefully before you open your mouth."

Three spirit talismans ensured that the legless resentful spirit couldn't leave the ground. The look on his face was sinister as he asked, "Evidence in court? What court? What evidence?"

"You testify to all your merits and sins before the Yanluo Courts, which are fair and just," Chu Shuzhi snapped. "Enough bullshit. Speak only when spoken to!"

The spirit gave a cold laugh.

Chu Shuzhi shot a sidelong glance at Guo Changcheng, who immediately sat up straight and looked down at his palm, which he'd turned into a cheat sheet by writing all over it. As though reciting from a book, he began, "N-name, age, time of death, cause of death."

The resentful spirit's gaze fell on Guo Changcheng, eliciting another shiver of fright. Chu Shuzhi put a hand on Guo Changcheng's shoulder.

Lin Jing slammed his hands down on the table. "What are you looking at?" he demanded viciously. "Hurry up and answer!"

"Wang Xiangyang, age 62. I died last year on the 29th day of the twelfth lunar month when I was hit by a car."

Guo Changcheng gave Chu Shuzhi a careful glance, then looked back down at his cheat sheet when Chu Shuzhi nodded. Chu Shuzhi, brimming with curiosity, followed his gaze. The text crammed onto Guo Changcheng's hand read, "Oh, xxx (name), if your cause of death was xxx (cause of death), why did you harm innocent people?"

Stammering, Guo Changcheng began, "O-oh, Wang Xiangyang, your cause of death was actually the 29th day of the twelfth lunar month—I-I mean, a car. Why did you harm innocent people?"

Chu Shuzhi barely managed to contain his laughter by turning aside and coughing dryly into his hand.

"Innocent?" Wang Xiangyang's voice was just above a whisper. "Who's innocent? How about you tell me, little brat. Who's innocent? Them? Are *you* innocent?"

The culprit got to ask questions too?! Guo Changcheng wasn't remotely prepared for this development. He could only sit there in bewilderment.

Fortunately, the kind Shen-laoshi cut in and came to his rescue. "Can you describe the accident?" When Wang Xiangyang only eyed him silently, he continued, "How are the people you cursed connected? What does it have to do with selling oranges?"

"I was just a peddler before I died," Wang Xiangyang answered eventually. "I lived in a village on the outskirts of Dragon City. Every day, I brought seasonal fruits into the city to sell. My entire family depended on that income. My wife had uremia, so she couldn't work. Our son was almost 30, but he couldn't find a wife and I couldn't afford to buy him a house in the city. Since you had to ask, I don't mind sharing."

The corners of Wang Xiangyang's mouth pulled up into a sneer. When he lowered his head, he looked no different from any ordinary human at a quick glance.

"I love those few days just before and after the Lunar New Year. All those who've moved to the city return to their hometowns for the holiday, so the city gets nice and quiet. And since people have nowhere to shop and everything in the stores is so expensive, business is always a little better than usual for me. Ah—the 29th day of the last lunar month is always such a wonderful day.

"Last year, the final lunar month was only twenty-nine days long, so Lunar New Year's Eve fell on that day. The city had lifted the ban on firecrackers and fireworks. There were these two boys... maybe around ten. Ha! Rich kids in their expensive clothes, with no discipline at all. They had firecrackers stuffed in their pockets and were throwing them into the road, under people's feet. They nearly burst one of my tires. I was so cold I wasn't thinking straight, so I caved and scolded them a little. One of the brats threw firecrackers at me while the other one snuck behind me and pushed my cart over. All my oranges and apples went rolling everywhere.

"That cart of fruit was supposed to get my family through the New Year. I panicked and tried to pick it all up. It was the middle of the day. Lots of people were passing by. I kept saying, 'Please be kind, help me out,' but one guy picked up an orange and peeled it without even looking at me. He just ate it, and he said, 'Your stuff's all covered in dirt now, so who's going to buy it? Why bother picking it up? Just share it with the rest of us.'

"And he wasn't the only one. A bunch of people saw and simply grabbed what they wanted. Some even brought bags. I said, 'You can't do this. You have to pay. You can't just take my fruit.'

But they all ignored me and left with it. When I tried to chase after them, I was hit by a taxi.

"It was snowing heavily that day, and there was ice on the road, so the taxi couldn't stop in time. The driver slammed on the brakes, but it skidded several meters and rolled right over me. My upper body rolled along with the wheels, leaving my legs behind. And in the last second of my life, a stray orange hit me in the face.

"Well? Don't you think I died unjustly?"

A dead silence filled the interrogation room.

"Should I not take my revenge?" Wang Xiangyang asked. "Is it right of you to arrest me? Even if I go to the Netherworld, how should the Yanluo Courts judge me?"

No wonder each victim's karmic line was so faint.

Wang Xiangyang looked quite frightening as he leaned back in his chair. "When I was alive, I had no clue that there were people like you specifically in charge of stuff like this. If it's your job to deal with injustice, why am I in here, not them?"

Guo Changcheng read over the hint he'd written for himself: *Family, friends.* "Won't you at least think of your descendants?" he blurted. "Don't you want to accumulate some merits for your son, your grandson, and your wife, who's sick right now?"

Indifferently, Wang Xiangyang replied, "My son didn't marry, so I don't have grandchildren. Anyway, they're both dead already. The Wang family is finished. What son of a bitch should I collect merits for?"

Guo Changcheng went utterly still. "Dead? How did they die...?"

"I killed them. My house is out in the country and doesn't have heating, so we had to keep the little stove going for warmth. I floated back home in the middle of the night and covered the fire in the coal stove so it couldn't ventilate. They died in their sleep." Wang Xiangyang paused, then added, "It was painless. Now they're on their merry way to their next life. How nice."

"How... How could you do that?"

The look Wang Xiangyang gave him was calm. "I think living is more painful than death. Wouldn't you agree?"

Why hadn't Lin Jing been able to help Wang Xiangyang let go of his resentment? Because he had never done anything evil when he was alive. He'd spent half of his life working diligently only to meet a tragic and absurd end.

If someone was absolutely filled with hatred, there was no room left in their heart for any tenderness at all. Once he had personally severed his only connection to this world, nothing remained that could call forth even a trace of longing or kindness in him.

If he were still alive, perhaps the passage of time and wisdom gained along the way could have lessened the hatred in his heart. Perhaps new comforts would have allowed him to live out the rest of his days. But he was already dead and, having lost his life, he no longer cared for anything. His soul was forever stuck in that moment when he lost his life under the wheels and gave in to obsession.

To Zhao Yunlan's mind, it wasn't an easy situation. On the one hand, pocketing some fruit on the roadside was immoral, but did those who did it deserve to die? Even being caught stealing someone else's wallet would, at most, result in a thief being sent to a holding cell. They couldn't just be shot on the spot.

On the other hand, those people's greed had caused the death of this good, honest man who'd been looking forward to going home for the New Year. Why shouldn't he hate them? Why shouldn't he exact revenge?

It was Shen Wei who spoke first. "Those who seize what they want without permission are thieves, whether it's gold and silver or a handful of fruit. Theft is theft. And to cause another person to lose their life in the course of it? I believe they are as guilty as someone committing murder for personal gain."

As soon as Shen Wei had opened his mouth, it was too late for Zhao Yunlan to stop him. However he appeared at the moment, he was still the Soul-Executing Emissary. Legend said that the Soul-Executing Blade had come into existence even before the Reincarnation Cycle was established. Now that he had spoken, not even the Yanluo Courts could overturn his verdict. With those few words, Shen Wei had essentially sanctioned Wang Xiangyang's revenge.

As Shen Wei spoke, Wang Xiangyang felt the power restraining him melt away.

"However," Shen Wei continued, "even if you were to let them go, the consequences of their evil would catch up with them down the road. If they died before that happened, justice might come in their next life instead. You were once simply a mortal soul, but having lost yourself in hatred, you've become a resentful spirit. You've committed heinous acts, such as killing your wife and son. Even if I give you leave to seek revenge, you might ultimately still be imprisoned in the Eighteen Levels of Hell. Are you certain you'll have no regrets?"

Other than Zhao Yunlan, Wang Xiangyang was the first to recognize that Shen Wei was unlike everyone else present. After studying Shen Wei for a while, he said decisively, "I won't."

Shen Wei turned to Zhao Yunlan, feigning earnestness. "How should he be dealt with, then?"

You've already dealt with it! What are you asking me for? Zhao Yunlan glared at him, then coughed lightly. He still had to help Shen Wei maintain his cover, so he took a Soul-Guarding

Order from his pocket, slapped it down on the interrogation table, and slid it in front of Wang Xiangyang. "Before daybreak, a reaper will come collect you. Give them this and tell them to take you to the Yanluo Courts for a travel pass."

Wang Xiangyang accepted the Soul-Guarding Order with both hands.

"Let me just reiterate what he said," Zhao Yunlan added. "With the travel pass, you'll be able to indulge your hatred for a while, but you will be punished many times over in the future. Before you act, make sure you think things through."

"You don't need to remind me. I've already killed more than ten people. There's no turning back." Wang Xiangyang shook his head, then smiled bitterly. "I never imagined that even after death, there would still be a place for me to plead my case. Thank you."

Everyone in the room was shocked. "Wait," Zhu Hong said. "More than ten people? You're sure? They're all definitely dead?"

"Of course they are," Wang Xiangyang replied frankly. "Gruesome deaths for all of them, and not a single one will ever be able to reincarnate."

Zhu Hong gave Zhao Yunlan a shocked and uncertain look. Thanks to the exploding population and hectic pace of society, it wouldn't be surprising for them to miss a death here and there if evil spirits wreaked havoc in the Mortal Realm. But as soon as it was more than one or two, it wasn't only the Soul-Guarding Order that should have noticed. Even individual mortal sects in the city with just a trace of cultivation should have picked up on the escalating evil.

But they hadn't.

If Wang Xiangyang hadn't volunteered the information, not a single one of them would have known he already had the blood of more than ten souls on his hands.

Shen Wei immediately thought of the Merit Brush. "Did you make use of some method to alter your merits?"

"Of course," Wang Xiangyang admitted without hesitation. "Right after I poisoned my wife and son and was about to go after my first target, someone found me and offered me a deal."

"What deal was that?"

"He said that if I just started killing without reservation, I'd quickly be noticed by those who maintain order between the Mortal Realm and the Netherworld. So he sold me a charm. He said if I wore it around my neck, you guys wouldn't be able to detect me. In exchange, he wanted the souls of the people I killed," explained Wang Xiangyang. "I have no use for the souls, and I'm already dead, so he had nothing to gain from tricking me. I agreed and found out he'd told me the truth. No one bothered me at all. Those people all thought they had some weird illness."

Zhao Yunlan asked, "Did you see if there was anything written or drawn on the charm?"

"Yes," Wang Xiangyang said. "My name and birth chart. At first, the ink from his brush was black, and then it became red. The black words were written on the inside, then circled in red."

As he spoke, he lifted a small octagonal yellow paper talisman hanging around his neck. "This is it here. Feel free to take a look."

Chu Shuzhi took it and opened it up. As Wang Xiangyang had said, it contained a line of words circled in red. But before anyone could take a closer look, the talisman burst into flames and turned to ash.

Shen Wei's one quick glance wasn't enough for him to be sure whose handwriting it was, but from Wang Xiangyang's description, it was almost certainly the Merit Brush. One's wrongdoings were recorded in black, while red ink recorded good deeds. No matter if you were tremendously kind or horrifically evil, or if you were a corrupt traitor or unshakably loyal, a single stroke of the brush could wipe it all away.

Legend said that the Merit Brush's handle had been carved from the roots of a tree growing out of the Huangquan. The wood was incredibly hard, difficult to cut even with a steel knife, but the tree had no branches or leaves, no flowers or fruit. It was known as "the Ancient Merit Tree."

Shen Wei sometimes thought that this tree that was "dead but not yet born" mocked the so-called merit system of the Three Realms, where people did good out of a desire to accrue merits and forsook evil only to avoid punishment. If everyone was ultimately driven by self-interest, what was the point in differentiating between good and evil?

"What did this person look like?" Zhao Yunlan asked. "Where did you encounter him?"

Wang Xiangyang gave it some thought. "He just looked...ordinary. It's strange—now that you're asking, I suddenly can't remember. As for where..."

He paused, pinching his brow. "My memory's gone all hazy, but it must've been near my house. I lived in West Plum Village, ten kilometers west of the city. You can check it out if you wish."

Shen Wei stood up and nodded at him. "Many thanks."

Calmly, Wang Xiangyang said, "I should be thanking all of you. I have nothing to hide about those murders. Talking about them is fine. Ask all the questions you like."

Shen Wei left the interrogation room ahead of anyone else.

Zhao Yunlan gave Lin Jing's shoulder a quick pat. "Tell the reaper to come, and when they get here, explain the situation. The Netherworld will know how to handle it."

Having said that, he followed Shen Wei out.

Shen Wei was waiting at the end of the hallway. They went into Zhao Yunlan's office, and Zhao Yunlan closed the door behind them before asking, "What, you think it's the Merit Brush?"

"I can't be entirely certain," Shen Wei said, "but it's very likely. Even if it proves to be a fake, it must have been made by someone who knows the Four Hallowed Artifacts like the back of their hand."

"Mm." Zhao Yunlan rubbed his chin.

"What are you thinking?" asked Shen Wei.

Zhao Yunlan was about to reply when the shadow of a skeleton puppet flickered outside the window. He went over to the window and opened it to let the puppet in. The puppet lowered its skull to him in an awkward bow, then went straight to Shen Wei's side, where it transformed into a note and gently came to rest in Shen Wei's hand.

Still by the window, Zhao Yunlan glanced up at the impenetrable and distant night sky. He had the unsettling feeling that there were eyes watching him from out in the darkness.

Shen Wei's expression went dark as his gaze swept across the paper.

"Something came up?" Zhao Yunlan asked.

"Yes, urgent business. I have to go." In a heartbeat, the refined university professor became the Soul-Executing Emissary, enveloped from head to toe in an icy chill. As he hurried out the window, he made sure to tell Zhao Yunlan, "You absolutely cannot go alone to that West Plum Village he mentioned. No matter what, wait for my return."

When Zhao Yunlan didn't respond, Shen Wei turned back to look at him, only to find him leaning lazily against the wall. Half-seriously, Zhao Yunlan grumbled, "This is horrible. I finally managed to gain a little ground with my lord, so I thought maybe I could get you to put out a little tonight. Now I'll be spending the night lonely and unsatisfied." He sighed as he added, "Tomorrow I'll be coming to work with dark circles under my eyes."

Speechless, Shen Wei passed through the window without another word and disappeared into a cloud of black mist.

Zhao Yunlan tucked a cigarette between his lips and lit up. He sat quietly in deep thought for a while, surrounded by the swirling smoke. Eventually, once he was sure Shen Wei was well and truly far away, he opened a desk drawer and loaded the gun he kept hidden under his pant leg. He then took out the wallet filled with yellow paper talismans.

"Urgent business suddenly coming up *now*?" He stubbed out his cigarette and snorted. "If I stay put, all the effort they put into luring you away will be wasted."

Zhao Yunlan put on a jacket and headed out of the city, driving straight for West Plum Village.

In the dead of night, there was no traffic to speak of. It took him less than two hours to reach the village Wang Xiangyang had mentioned. This far outside the city, the air was silent, aside from a dog's occasional bark. Zhao Yunlan circled the village and finally, at the west side, he found a cluster of large pagoda trees. Every one of these trees had a trunk that was too thick for even a grown man to wrap his arms around.

Zhao Yunlan parked the car and got out, then walked around the giant pagoda trees a few times. Among them, something peculiar caught his eye.

Back when the yao's great trial had befallen them, they had used the same trick: planting pagoda trees in the same formation as the

Big Dipper. The curve of the spoon gathered yin energy, while the handle of the spoon extended to the west, symbolizing a bridge between the yin and the yang. Once enough yin was gathered, it was possible to find the entrance at the eye of the array.

And here, coincidentally, there were untended graves scattered on the mountain across from these pagoda trees—an overgrown, cold hillside with graves everywhere.

Chapter 9

THE NOTE SHEN WEI had received said, *Something is wrong with the Great Seal. Return at once.*

He rushed down through the Huangquan. Wandering souls made way before him, subconsciously parting like duckweed pushed aside by the waves. How long the descent took was impossible to say, but he finally reached the bottom of the Huangquan. Gradually, the water grew darker and darker, and the black mist around him thickened. And below that, there was no water at all, only a deathly, silent blackness.

To walk through that blackness was to lose all sense of time and space. For those within, all that remained was the utter desolation of feeling like the one person left in all the world. It was impossible to see where you had come from or where you were going. The cold defied description.

Here, thousands of chi below the Huangquan, in this vast emptiness where one's senses encountered nothing at all, lay the Great Seal. But just now, a violent stench of blood flooded the tranquil darkness. Something was quickly approaching.

Shen Wei went down on one knee, pressing a hand against the ground. "Show yourselves!"

He was immediately surrounded by seven or eight youchu, all of them roaring as they threw themselves at him.

"How naive," he scoffed.

In all likelihood, the youchu were appearing outside the Great Seal due to Zhao Yunlan's summoning of the Ghost Army. What Zhao Yunlan didn't know was that the "ghosts" of the Ghost Army weren't ghosts in the traditional sense. When folktales spoke of a "ghost army," they referred to powerless earthbound spirits under the Netherworld's command. Such spirits had been ordinary mortals in life, and in death they remained unremarkable, with little power. How could they dare answer the staggeringly arrogant call of "Perish, foes, though mortal or god; any may fall by their blades—"?

No, what the Ghost Army Summons brought forth were things from a place devoid of light that was deeper than the Huangquan and darker than Hell: "The lightless land that held the prison of the Great Disrespect."

Back when Pangu had split apart the sky and earth, separating the clear from the muddied, the "muddied" was Earth. Everything had its natural order; Chaos was divided. After that, the muck that was Earth passed through an eon of sedimentation, and this place had come into existence to contain the filth—a place outside Heaven and Earth.

Unfortunately, when Nüwa had created people from mud, she'd rushed the job. She didn't wait until the filth in the ground had fully settled to the bottom before hastily shaping the mud into people. Thus, from the very beginning, humans were born with original sin. Humanity's lust for tyranny and destruction was rooted within it. The sages called the lightless place the "Great Disrespect." They separated it and locked it away by force, creating the Great Seal.

This Ghost Army came from beneath the Great Seal. They had no form of their own. The metal armor and the horses of bone were simply reflections of the summoner's overactive imagination.

If Zhao Yunlan hadn't used blood and iron as mediums, even if these things had crawled up out of the ground, anyone else would have seen only ranks of youchu.

The Ghost Army Summons was an incredibly dangerous piece of sorcery. If the caster wasn't careful, it could easily backfire on them. Zhao Yunlan had pulled it off for two reasons: one, he was talented, and two, he was lucky. With Shen Wei keeping watch downstairs, the things Zhao Yunlan had called forth hadn't dared cross the line. But by summoning the Ghost Army, it was as if Zhao Yunlan, the gifted troublemaker, had drawn a vial of blood from the Great Seal, which was already crumbling. The emergence of *these* youchu was a side effect.

Shen Wei handily dealt with the youchu who dared to approach, then flew toward the Great Seal.

The Chaos King of the Gui, who had once been sealed here, had made his escape and was now running amok in the world. More and more youchu were escaping into the Mortal Realm as the crack in the Great Seal spread. Shen Wei again knelt down as he silently chanted the Sealing spell, temporarily fortifying the decaying seal.

Slowly, the shaking calmed, but his expression remained deadly serious. How long could this peace be maintained?

By the time he returned to the Mortal Realm, it was almost light out. When he arrived at Zhao Yunlan's small apartment, he made sure to move quietly, thinking Zhao Yunlan would be resting. But as he entered, his expression turned grave. He switched on all the lights with a wave of his hand...and found the apartment empty. The blanket he had folded that morning was still at the head of the bed, undisturbed. Zhao Yunlan hadn't come back home!

Meanwhile, at 4 Bright Avenue, Wang Zheng was busy scolding her colleague.

"Chu Shuzhi, we've been over this. Once you're done with all these paper talismans, clean them up. When the cleaning lady comes tomorrow, what do you expect her to do about them?"

Guo Changcheng darted over. "I'll do it, I'll do it!"

Without a word, Daqing walked straight into the wall that wasn't a wall in the criminal investigation unit office. Inside was a totally different world. It contained endless rows of hardwood shelves, so tall they seemed to run straight into the ceiling. The ladder for accessing them looked very old. The room's walls were inlaid with large sea dragon pearls that kept the space as bright as day while not harming the souls who could be hurt by sunlight.

The scent of ancient books drifted from the shelves—the fragrance of ink that had settled for many years mixed with the musty smell of pages that had gone unopened for a long, long time.

When Sangzan had arrived, he'd been put in charge of keeping the library in order. The collection included books in both traditional and simplified Chinese, neither of which he could actually read. All he could do was meticulously compare the characters on the books' spines to the labels on the shelves. He was extremely slow, but diligent and never made a mistake.

This was the first dignified job he had ever had. He was no longer a slave being beaten and cursed at, treated like an animal, nor was he the faithless leader whose only goal was the destruction of the people who looked up to him. Now he could live quietly and freely with the person he cared for most—exactly what he'd hoped and schemed for all his life but had never been able to attain. He treasured this new existence beyond measure.

Seeing Daqing enter, Sangzan greeted him earnestly. "Henlo, cat."

"Henlo, stutterer," the cat replied.

Sangzan stopped dead. Wang Zheng was a quiet, refined girl who would never teach him insults, so the term wasn't familiar to him. With perfect sincerity, he asked, "What i-is a slutterer?"

Daqing stepped over the wooden shelves. Thoroughly preoccupied, he gave a careless lie in response. "It means 'good bro.'"

Sangzan nodded in understanding, then enthusiastically gave it a try. "Oh, henlo, cat slutterer!"

When Daqing didn't reply, Sangzan continued, "Cat slutterer, wart…what do you went to read?"

Daqing lay down on the shelf above Sangzan's head. "Zhao Yunlan, Director Zhao—did he return the book he took out a few days ago? Let me see it."

It was as if Sangzan were taking a foreign-language listening test. He attentively tilted his head, then patiently asked Daqing to repeat the request three times. Finally, he got the gist. Beaming with accomplishment, he pulled a book that was waiting to be reshelved off the little cart. "Th-thus won."

The cover was already ragged, and there was a coffee stain on the corner—no need to say which heathen was to blame for that. The simple title *Soul Book* was written forebodingly on the cover. It had been slightly ripped, making it look even more tattered.

Daqing jumped down from the bookshelf to the little cart. He flipped through the book with a paw, only to find its pages blank. There was nothing at all to see.

His heart sank—his cultivation was inadequate.

For whatever reason, Daqing's current power was less than a tenth of what it had once been. In fact, it was even hard for him to transform. But he was still an old cat yao who had lived tens of thousands of years. Would he lose to Zhao Yunlan, a mortal?

If *his* cultivation wasn't up to the task, how had Zhao Yunlan done it?

"I've never seen this book before." Daqing patted the book, unconsciously turning in circles on the spot and chasing his own tail with anxiety. "Where did it come from?"

Who had put the book there? Why was Zhao Yunlan the one who'd come across it?

Of course, if Daqing didn't know the book's origin, there was no way Sangzan would. The black cat and ghost stared at each other until, finally, the cat lowered his head and leaped to the floor, feeling uneasy. As he left, he found he wasn't even in the mood to eat his favorite food: jerky soaked in milk.

Zhao Yunlan was doing well for himself. He had food, shelter, and more—he even had some spare time to think about love and lust. Things were going smoothly for him. The black cat was lazy by nature, and many human concerns were beyond him, but seeing Zhao Yunlan simply be a dumbass youngster with many joys in his life was very gratifying for Daqing. This wasn't a boat he wanted to see rocked.

And yet...

Zhao Yunlan, who had been out all night, wrapped his coat more tightly around himself as he stood in front of the grave-covered hill.

Back when they'd been wrapping up the Reincarnation Dial case, he had followed the Soul-Executing Emissary to Li Qian's home. Up on the roof, he had accidentally overheard something: that the creature's master had gone "to the effort of having him brought before you."

What did that mean?

Before Shen Wei's identity had been revealed, he'd kept avoiding Zhao Yunlan. Thinking back on it now, someone had orchestrated their meeting, putting him right in Shen Wei's path.

Was it the ghost-faced figure? Why would that person try so hard to steer Shen Wei toward him?

And then there was the black notebook that the Netherworld had sent to him via a reaper. That book had confirmed Shen Wei's identity. Had that been the Netherworld's goal when giving it to him? Why?

Zhao Yunlan felt as if he were standing over a massive vortex. There was more going on in it than he could see, with innumerable hands reaching out of it—some trying to shove him away, others trying to drag him in. Each one seemed to have its own agenda; every face was shrouded in mist.

Looking at the hill, he saw a haunting wisp of light, a ghost fire, halfway up the slope. The cold light seemed to stare at him from a close distance, like dangerous eyes in the night. He quickly realized that the ghost fire was moving with him, stopping dead when he stopped. It seemed to be guiding his way...or luring him.

Zhao Yunlan decided to follow its lead, which meant slowly walking out among the untended graves outside the village.

The air around him thickened with fog. The fog rapidly grew heavier, until it was impossible to see more than a meter ahead. He and the ghost fire, its edges blurring in the fog, might have been the only things in the world. Ice-cold water droplets occasionally landed on his face as moisture gathered in the air.

Now and then, there came a sigh right beside his ear, as if countless souls were also picking their way through the woods on the slope. Zhao Yunlan didn't look at them. These ordinary souls might not seek to harm the living, but that didn't make them kind. They wandered the Mortal Realm, refusing to enter the Reincarnation Cycle. Every voice was weeping. Everyone felt that they had been wronged.

In all the world, how many people went willingly to their death?

Zhao Yunlan kept walking. The white mist and the hands reaching out of the graves all avoided the wide hem of his dark gray coat. Not a single wandering ghost dared approach him.

When the sound of crying began to come from all around him, Zhao Yunlan stopped among the graves and spread his palms, revealing the bright flame of a burning yellow paper talisman. Sobs turned into screams, and countless blurry shadows raced one another to escape. The thick fog must have been flammable, as the flame in Zhao Yunlan's hand burst up from his palm like a fiery dragon and incinerated every trace of white mist in the graveyard.

"If you want to wail about how horribly you've been wronged, go to the Yanluo Courts and bang on the drums there to voice your grievances," Zhao Yunlan said, his face stern. "What are you crying at me for?"

He looked up and saw that the ghost fire that had guided him had disappeared.

The night was as cool as water now, the starry sky as clear as if it had been scrubbed.

A third-quarter moon hung in the sky, and the now-dry wind scraped at his exposed skin like a blade. Zhao Yunlan pulled his scarf up to cover half of his face.

At that moment, a noise came from beside him—its sound swinging from near to far. It was a gruff voice, and it was singing.

"Three-quarter moon, forgotten grave mounds,

Ghost fire leads, and resentment abounds.
Wind through the trees, the bone flute's song,
foxes in human skin laugh along.
Ah, noble guest! Hearken unto this old man:
One head of living for fine sterling,
whole skin of a beauty for gleaming gold,
fat of a hundred-day infant, two or three pounds,
for half a lifetime's riches be sold.
And if you offer your souls, seven and three,
I promise ashes to ashes, dust to dust..."

The voice was like nails on a chalkboard. It made one's scalp crawl.

Zhao Yunlan's voice, in turn, was frigid. "Legend says that when an antagonist's opening monologue is too long, they pay for it with their lives."

He could hear rustling within the woods, as though countless small footsteps were passing through. Zhao Yunlan flicked his lighter and held the tiny flame up high, creating a small halo of light.

His head snapped around as a small, short shadow darted behind him, leaving the echo of a laugh like a Mourning Bird's cry in its wake.

Gripping a paper talisman, Zhao Yunlan silently stood his ground. The creature seemed afraid of him. It kept flying in circles, testing the waters, but never dared approach.

A long whip uncoiled from his hand, quick enough to create a breeze. Lashing out at an incredibly cunning angle, it curled around the thing's waist. With a flick of Zhao Yunlan's wrist, the whip slammed toward the ground, pulling a scream out of the thing's throat.

Taking his first good look, Zhao Yunlan saw that what he'd

brought down was a...person? About a meter tall. The person's face was crammed full of wrinkles, and his jutting nose took up almost half of his face, shoving his other features into what little space was left. With nowhere to go, they huddled together awkwardly.

Upon first glance, he looked like a giant inauspicious bird. His bean-sized eyes were murky enough to obscure their whites, and being caught in his gaze was rather creepy. He let out a sudden laugh, revealing a mouthful of large, crooked yellow teeth.

Half squatting, Zhao Yunlan rudely asked, "What the hell are you?"

The bird person gave him a dark stare. In a voice like a cracked gong, he said, "Brat, don't act so cocky. You're in deeper waters than you can imagine."

Zhao Yunlan snorted. "Please educate me, then, if you know so much. Exactly how deep are they?"

He took out a cigarette and deftly set it between his lips. His lighter twirled between his fingers as its flame sparked to life. There was a sharp click, followed by faintly minty smoke that set the bird person reeling and coughing.

Zhao Yunlan kept a firm grasp on the Soul-Guarding Whip, not giving an iota of slack. "You were the peddler just now?"

The bird person scoffed. "That's me. Is there something you'd like to sell?"

Ignoring the question, Zhao Yunlan narrowed his eyes and asked, "I guess that means you're the one going around with the Merit Brush, then?"

This time there was no answer. Tiny, sneaky eyes just stared at Zhao Yunlan like a venomous snake.

Zhao Yunlan flicked the ash from his cigarette, grabbed the bird person's collar, and dragged him up so they were eye to eye. "Except the Four Hallowed Artifacts aren't things you can buy just anywhere and get a free gift with purchase. You expect me to believe *you* have the Merit Brush? Come on, now. Who sent you? Who told you to lure me out here with some knockoff?"

The bird person had been exposed, but he didn't panic. A malicious smile crossed his face, further heightening his avian appearance. "Someone you wouldn't dare offend," he rasped.

"The only people I don't dare offend are my mother and my wife. Which of them are you fit to run errands for?" Zhao Yunlan flung him back to the ground. "I'm out of fucking patience. Push your luck too far and I'll kill you. So hurry and spit it out already!"

The bird person gave him a strange look, then croaked, "'West-northwest of the Western Sea, north-northwest of the Northern Sea, one hundred and thirty thousand li[4,5] from the shore. Surrounded by unpassable waters… Push open the Heavenly Gates to enter the Heavenly Palace.'[6] What power! What greatness! Do you remember it still?"

Zhao Yunlan gave him a blank stare. "No. Even as a kid, I always failed my language arts classes."

The bird person started to laugh. Moving one deformed arm with difficulty, he reached into his clothes and took out a tiny golden bell. "Then do you not remember this either?"

The mere sight of bells had always given Zhao Yunlan goosebumps. Bells could serve as a medium, and generally had the ability to summon souls and gather spirits…and in the absence of a soul fire on his left shoulder, his ethereal and corporeal souls weren't as stable as other people's.

As a result, he struck without hesitation, stomping on the bird

---

4 *From* Hainei Shizhou Ji (海内十洲记) *or* Record of Ten Lands within the Seas *is a collection of strange legends and tales compiled during the Han Dynasty, with author unknown.*

5 *One li (里) is an ancient unit of length equal to about five hundred meters.*

6 *From* The Huainanzi *(淮南子), a collection of essays from the early Han Dynasty based on a series of debates in the court of Liu An, Prince of Huainan.*

man's arm and shattering it. Then he bent over to pick up the golden bell.

But that palm-sized bell seemed to weigh half a ton, so heavy that the attempt to move it hurt his wrist.

The bird man guffawed. "The great... Can't even pick up a bell! Ha ha ha ha ha! Is there anything more absurd? You really *are* just a mortal!"

A sinister wind kicked up around them. The bell, still hanging from the bird man's broken limb, rang faintly a single time. Zhao Yunlan's nerves went taut, and the Soul-Guarding Whip lashed out, sending a huge ball of ghost fire flying. The ghost fire struck the top of a large tree with a trunk almost too thick to see around. The tree immediately started to visibly wither and blacken. In but a moment, it was reduced to dead and desiccated wood.

The wind rapidly blew clump after clump of ghost fire in Zhao Yunlan's direction. His whip cracked again and again as he backed up more than twenty meters.

White bone claws reached out from the grave mounds on the mountainside, crawling up from underground. The bird man Zhao Yunlan had stomped on just seconds ago floated slowly into the air before a dense backdrop of ghost fire. The little golden bell dangling from the bird man's broken limb swayed gently with the breeze, chiming almost inaudibly. It was as if it had woken up all the yin energy in the mountain. White mist began billowing from the top of the dead tree. The crow nesting there let out a long cry, then shot up into the deep, endless night sky lit by a moon that had turned a brilliant, hazy-edged scarlet.

It had become clear to Zhao Yunlan that this night probably wasn't going to end well for him, and he knew when to call it quits. Running toward the edge of the woods, he called, "Hey, don't skip straight to a fight out of nowhere! You haven't even told me why you lured me here. It can't just be because you're bored and wanted to fight me, right? I sit in an office all day long and barely exercise. It won't be a fair fight. We can find a more civilized way to resolve this, don't you think?"

After stomping on someone's arm and breaking their bones, he was asking them for a truce? The bird man just smirked at him.

The ghost fires pursuing Zhao Yunlan were relentless. Just as they were about to set his back ablaze, he grabbed the branch of a large tree, quickly pulled himself up, and then swung through the air and backflipped to the ground.

The ghost fires just barely missed him.

"Animating the dead, moving bones, commanding ghost fire—are you a ghost cultivator, or an immortal on earth? To the best of my knowledge, ghost cultivators fear encountering living humans, in case it ruins their forms of pure yin or reminds them of when they were alive—needless distractions that could manifest as internal demons. What does that leave, my lord? Are you some sort of Netherworld bureaucrat? Kindly enlighten me as to your department and position."

Furious, the bird person sneered, "Screw the Netherworld! I'd never stoop to taking orders from them!"

"Ah." Zhao Yunlan nodded. "I see how it is. You're one of the yao, right? Which tribe?"

Realizing he'd let too much slip in just a few short sentences, the bird person snapped his mouth shut.

Zhao Yunlan's eyes gleamed as things fell into place. Hints of dimples appeared on his face. "No, no, don't tell me. Judging by your appearance, you're from the Black Crow tribe, right? Those who 'hear the voices of the dead'? I'll have to have a chat with your tribe's esteemed elders later. I've always had a pretty solid relationship with the yao. We may not be all buddy-buddy, but we're at least cordial with each other. So, what's the meaning of all this?"

It was clearly a bad idea to let Zhao Yunlan continue guessing. The bird person started to ring the golden bell, only for Zhao Yunlan to suddenly brandish his hands after hiding them behind his back. At some point, during everything that happened, he had cut his own finger and used the blood to draw a complicated motif across two paper talismans, half on each one.

Now, as he brought the pair together, they were flawlessly aligned and had already burned more than halfway. One pointed to the sky and the other pointed to the ground.

Zhao Yunlan abruptly let go. A thunderous explosion arose out of nowhere as a dragon of fire took shape. In an instant of flashing lightning and flying sparks, the entire hillside of graves was scorched black. Countless ghost fires were silently swept up in it; the huge flame ignited the hem of the Crow tribe member's shirt.

But the short, ugly crow didn't even flinch. Though he was gaunt and slight of stature, for a moment, an awe-inspiring sternness showed on his unpleasant face.

In spite of himself, Zhao Yunlan paused and stared.

Within the fierce flames, the crow's face was split between human and bird. Pitch-black feathers appeared on his body. His shriveled, deformed wings spread and immediately caught fire—an ugly, pitiful sight on his back. With a scream up to the sky, he transformed into a cloud of black mist within the fire and disappeared into the golden bell.

The color of the firelight surrounding the bell suddenly changed, as though thousands of spotlights had converged. Zhao Yunlan closed his eyes at once, but it was already too late. Molten pain seared his eyeballs. Holding his arms in front of himself, he swiftly backed away, unable to see a thing.

The sound of bells rang out, as if hunting down his soul. It was like a nail being driven right into his ear.

In his daze, it seemed as though he could hear the sound of mountains collapsing. The center of a huge pillar that reached all the way to the sky fractured, and from someplace up high, an endless stream of boulders tumbled down. They rumbled and roared as if the sky itself were on the verge of falling.

And from somewhere far away, at the edge of the world, a booming voice seemed to call out. *"KUNLUN—"*

It was like the toll of a giant bell, pleasing to the ear, yet solemn.

A flood of blurry images flowed into Zhao Yunlan's head all at once, but before he could make any sense of them, he suddenly felt a new presence behind him—someone who had been spying on the fight for who knew how long, only now coming forward to snatch up the loot.

Whoever it was reached out to grab Zhao Yunlan's shoulder. Zhao Yunlan managed to sidestep diagonally, fighting dizziness, and cracked the Soul-Guarding Whip in the other person's direction. There was a small noise, followed by a tremendous yank from the other end of the whip that seemed to be trying to pull him over.

There was no time for regrets over the whip. Almost instantaneously, Zhao Yunlan let go but was still unable to dodge in time.

Phantom-silent, a hand touched the back of his neck. The world went black as Zhao Yunlan lost consciousness.

The person who had knocked him out caught him as he fell, revealing himself to be the ghost-faced figure Zhao Yunlan had seen at the sacrificial altar below the Mountain-River Awl.

The ghost-faced figure's wide sleeves fell upon the smoldering remains of the fire, snuffing it out in an instant. Even the thunder calmed. Holding Zhao Yunlan effortlessly, he bent to pick up that little bell that was as heavy as the Monkey King's staff.[7] He lifted it with but two fingers, holding the object up to study it for a while. With a sudden snort, he tucked it away in his sleeve as he turned to leave.

Having come up empty at the apartment, Shen Wei next raced to 4 Bright Avenue, just to find the building dark. The only ones working were a diligent group of ghosts.

Half-mad with worry, Shen Wei stood in the courtyard and took several deep breaths. Having calmed himself as much as possible, he cast his senses out to feel for Zhao Yunlan's whereabouts... only to discover with a shock that Zhao Yunlan was heading right for him.

Shen Wei whipped his head back to see someone familiar hovering high up in the air. Gentle, refined Shen-laoshi's expression changed instantly.

The ghost-faced figure—the Chaos King of the Gui—calmly took hold of the Soul-Executing Blade, which was presently pointed at his chin. Wholly unafraid, he glanced down and smoothed out Zhao Yunlan's clothing, which had been blown about haphazardly in the wind. He gave a light chuckle. "Seeing you, he'll stop at nothing to get into your good graces; he can't even be chased away. Seeing me, he attacked with that whip of his without a second thought. What a biased man."

"Let go." Shen Wei practically gritted each word out between his teeth. "Don't you dare touch him with your filthy hands."

"Filthy hands?" Ghost Face laughed. "Are yours so clean, then?"

Shen Wei's expression turned to ice.

---

7 *The Monkey King's staff, Ruyi Jingu Bang (如意金箍棒), was said to grow or shrink at will and is described as weighing about eight metric tons in Journey to the West.*

As Ghost Face tossed Zhao Yunlan over, Shen Wei hurriedly banished his blade to keep from injuring him, then caught him steadily.

"He's fine," Ghost Face continued. "Someone tried to forcibly awaken the one hidden within his souls. As for why, I'm certain you can figure it out. The Netherworld has never accepted you as one of their own. I do hope you'll give some careful thought to who's better to you, and whether or not those irrelevant people are worth ruining yourself for."

His gaze fell upon Zhao Yunlan as he continued. "Consider who you are. You could have anyone you want. Even if... Do you really need to fear loss so badly that it keeps you from attaining what you want most? Even I pity you."

Still cold as ice, Shen Wei said, "Your concern is noted."

An uncanny smile appeared on Ghost Face's mask. "Well then, don't regret it."

Then Ghost Face turned, his wide cape curling up high behind him, and vanished into the night.

CHAPTER 10

ZHAO YUNLAN was a little roughed up, but he didn't seem to have any serious injuries. He had redness on the back of his neck, perhaps due to a blow there, but beyond that, Shen Wei couldn't tell if there was anything else wrong. All he could do was sit uneasily at the head of Zhao Yunlan's bed, waiting for him to wake up.

He slept until noon the next day, not waking even when his phone rang over and over again. The sun was due south by the time his fingers suddenly twitched. Shen Wei, who had started to get anxious, took hold of his hand. "Yunlan?"

Before even opening his eyes, Zhao Yunlan grabbed the back of his neck. "Ngh, what fucking asshole..."

The fact that he had the energy to curse someone out went a long way in reassuring Shen Wei...until Zhao Yunlan said his name in a strangely muffled voice.

Shen Wei answered immediately. "Yes? What is it?"

Zhao Yunlan seemed a little confused. "What time is it? How come you're still up?"

Shen Wei froze, then glanced out the window. The sun was high in the sky, making it almost blindingly bright in the apartment.

Heart sinking, he waved a hand right in front of Zhao Yunlan's eyes, which upon close inspection looked faintly lost and unfocused.

There was no reaction.

When Shen Wei didn't respond, Zhao Yunlan knew something was wrong. He subconsciously turned an ear toward him. "Shen Wei?"

As Shen Wei was about to answer, Zhao Yunlan reached out with unerring precision and caught Shen Wei's hand in front of his face. It was cold as ceramic. Zhao Yunlan fell silent, then eventually said, "Oh. Something's wrong with my eyes, huh?"

Shen Wei's free hand clenched into a tight fist as he desperately attempted to control his own voice. "I'm taking you to the hospital right now."

Zhao Yunlan was abnormally quiet on the drive, as if preoccupied. Upon getting out of the car, there were moments when he seemed a bit lost as they walked; understandably, it would take time to adjust to sudden vision loss. He found that he almost didn't know which foot to step with and couldn't help wanting to grab at everything within reach, even with Shen Wei holding his hand.

To Shen Wei, Zhao Yunlan's face looked unusually pale. Perhaps Ghost Face had used excessive force. Shen Wei's own gaze darkened, coming dangerously close to betraying the suppressed evil underneath. The hospital staff he handed Zhao Yunlan off to nearly trembled with fright. To them, his vibe came across as some low-key mobster in a movie—someone who could somehow be a vegetarian and a devout Buddhist and yet also a stone-cold killer.

Unsurprisingly, tests revealed nothing wrong with Zhao Yunlan's eyes. The doctors were bewildered. There were no injuries or abnormalities, but the patient couldn't see a thing. After over half a day of poking and prodding, one doctor delicately suggested that the problem might be psychological, not physical, and recommended consulting a psychologist.

By the time they left the hospital, Zhao Yunlan, like some sort of unkillable cockroach, had adjusted to his blindness. He made a grab at the air, then said, "It's dark out, right?"

It made Shen Wei nervous when Zhao Yunlan kept his thoughts to himself, so he tried to keep him talking. "How did you know?"

"The air feels a little moister and colder. I figured that meant the sun's gone down."

When they reached the car, Shen Wei opened the door and used one hand to guide Zhao Yunlan and the other to make sure he didn't hit his head. After fastening Zhao Yunlan's seat belt, Shen Wei looked over and saw him smiling. "What are you smiling about?"

"I was just thinking that if I'm old and senile someday, I'd like it if you still took care of me like this."

Shen Wei's heart stirred, and his expression softened.

Zhao Yunlan continued, "If I start calling you 'Dad' because I don't recognize anyone anymore, don't you dare answer to it. You're not allowed to boss me around and take advantage of me when I'm senile."

Exasperated, Shen Wei said, "Things would certainly be easier if you were senile."

"What?" Zhao Yunlan made a show of being frightened and shocked. Grabbing his own collar, he said, "What do you have planned for me? Do you want to lock me up and force me to be yours?"

Shen Wei was struck speechless.

After half a day of being withdrawn while adjusting to his new blindness, Zhao Yunlan was blossoming again. As he got settled in the car, he began messing with the seat controls. First, he made it lie down flat, then he put it back up. Next, he explored the entire car with his hands. "Hey, I just realized that the passenger seat is indented. How come I never noticed it when I could see? Turns out there are some fun things about being blind. Did you know there's a darkness experience exhibit downtown? The tickets cost 40 yuan, so really, I'm saving 40 yuan."

This kind of revolutionary optimism was beyond Shen Wei's comprehension, and he could only manage a faint semblance of a smile in response.

As he dropped Zhao Yunlan off right outside his building, Shen Wei told him to stay put. But after parking, he came back only to find that Zhao Yunlan had already made his way to the curb alone and was practicing walking in a straight line, though he was about to fling himself into the embrace of a utility pole.

Shen Wei rushed over and grabbed Zhao Yunlan around the waist before he could knock himself out. Suddenly being lifted into the air was an exciting experience while blind; Zhao Yunlan actually let out a delighted whistle, as if wanting Shen Wei to do it again.

Patting his arm, Shen Wei leaned forward. "There are stairs up ahead. I'll carry you on my back."

Zhao Yunlan responded by stroking Shen Wei's back and smiling, but he made no move to obey.

Gently, Shen Wei asked, "What is it? Get on."

Feeling around for Shen Wei's hand, Zhao Yunlan bent down to kiss the back of it. "How could I bear to let you carry me? What if I crush you with my weight?"

He began slowly walking forward. If he hadn't bumped the first stair with his foot, Shen Wei might almost have believed his eyesight had returned. His pace was steady, and his steps were even. When he reached the elevator, he felt around for the buttons and pressed the right one. Then he turned slightly, waiting for Shen Wei.

Shen Wei made sure to step heavily. "How did you know where the elevator was?"

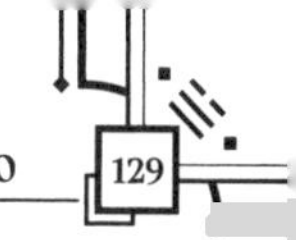

Without a trace of shame, Zhao Yunlan boasted, “With how observant I am, did you think I’m not familiar with my own place of residence? I don’t need eyes to know the number of stairs or how many paces the stairs are from the elevator.”

That was, of course, absolute bullshit. Forget the number of paces—Zhao Yunlan was the kind of rough, careless person who couldn’t even find his own teacup and slippers without scrambling around first.

The truth, as Shen Wei knew perfectly well, was that he must have been silently counting while being led downstairs that afternoon. Perhaps it was simply his personality, but somehow, no matter the circumstances, Zhao Yunlan always gave off an impression of “it’s no big deal.” Sometimes, even when whatever was happening *was* a big deal, people around him couldn’t help being affected by his attitude.

Zhao Yunlan calmly opened the door to his apartment and was just about to cross the threshold when a voice piped up from around his feet. “If you dare step on this lord’s tail, you’re fucking dead.”

He stopped, then bent down to feel around. “Daqing?”

It was immediately clear to the cat that something was wrong. He climbed up Zhao Yunlan’s arm. “What’s wrong with your eyes?”

Zhao Yunlan felt around as he entered the apartment. “Oh,” he said carelessly, “that feature’s been temporarily deactivated.”

Shen Wei grabbed him just before he collided with the doorframe. “Be careful.”

Shocked, Daqing jumped down onto the sofa. “What happened?!” He shot an accusatory glance at Shen Wei.

Without a moment’s hesitation, Shen Wei said, “It’s my fault.”

Zhao Yunlan didn’t know whether to laugh or cry. “And how’s that, now?”

He reached out a hand but didn't manage to touch anything. Daqing looked at that hand hanging in midair. With a disgusted expression that said "this lordly cat only deigns to humor you because you look pitiful," the cat tilted his head and rubbed against Zhao Yunlan's palm.

Zhao Yunlan laughed. "Don't worry. Good luck and misfortune usually come hand in hand."

Feeling around, he sat on the sofa and pulled a cigarette from his pocket. Gesturing arrogantly toward Daqing, he said, "I can't see. Light it for me!"

Daqing silently curled up into a ball of fluff, turned his back, and completely ignored Zhao Yunlan.

It was Shen Wei who took Zhao Yunlan's hand, lit the cigarette with a flick, and then pushed the ashtray in front of him.

"Last night, I met a little crow." Zhao Yunlan gave it a moment's thought and decided to redact some details of the previous night's events. "He said something like... Something-something, Western Sea somewhere, Northern Sea somewhere, some distance from the shore. I didn't understand the rest of it. He was probably talking about some mountain."

Daqing froze, so it was Shen Wei who reacted first. A shadow fell over his face. "Let's set that aside for now. How did you hurt your eyes?"

"Ugh, don't even ask." Zhao Yunlan waved dismissively. "It was all because of that damn bell..."

Daqing abruptly got to his feet. "What kind of bell?"

"I have it," Shen Wei offered, pulling a little golden bell covered in dust from his pocket. "Are you talking about this?"

Daqing's pupils constricted. "Why do you have it?"

"What is it?" Zhao Yunlan asked.

Daqing circled Shen Wei's hand a few times, focused intently on the little bell. Finally, in a very low voice, he said, "That's mine." He stole a glance at Zhao Yunlan.

"My...first master...tied that around my neck himself. Centuries ago. There was an accident... I lost it."

Zhao Yunlan extended a hand. "Let me see."

Instead, Shen Wei moved the bell out of reach. "I'm afraid you won't be able to pick it up."

Recalling what had happened the night before, Zhao Yunlan gloomily blew a smoke ring.

Daqing ducked his head and grabbed the bell from Shen Wei, then left through the window without another word. It was rare for this steady tank of a cat to be so obviously weighed down by his thoughts.

Zhao Yunlan tilted his head, listening. "Daqing?"

"He left." Shen Wei closed the window, leaned down, and slowly caressed the corner of Zhao Yunlan's eye. "I'll figure out a way to fix your eyes."

As though something had just occurred to him, Zhao Yunlan gave a sudden smile and said, "Actually, there's no rush."

Instinct told Shen Wei that the next words out of Zhao Yunlan's mouth would be indecent—and his instinct was absolutely correct. Even blindness wasn't enough to put a damper on Zhao Yunlan's perverted streak.

"Not being able to see is awfully inconvenient. Can you help me shower tonight?"

Shaking off the grubby paw that had mysteriously begun to grope his butt, Shen Wei went into the kitchen without a word.

Zhao Yunlan's smile faded as he closed his eyes and leaned back against the sofa, listening to the sounds coming from the kitchen.

In the darkness, a rare peace descended on him. This particular moment was almost enjoyable.

As his mind and body relaxed, Zhao Yunlan had the abrupt sense that there were weird shadows in front of him.

His eyes shot open, but he still couldn't see anything, and the shadows were gone.

Concentrating now, he closed his eyes again and began counting his breaths as he collected his thoughts and emotions. After some time, the shadowy shapes reappeared. He could "see" a ball of green by his left hand, emitting a dim light. It was very pale, but the flow of the light was ethereally beautiful...and the shape looked familiar, somehow.

What was to his left? The windowsill. And on the windowsill... a plant a friend had given him.

Could this possibly be the mythical "Heavenly Eye"...?

In the Mortal Realm, the Heavenly Eye, or the "Divine Eye," was often confused with the third eye, but in reality, it was something else entirely. The Heavenly Eye was said to be the eye of the soul. The soul relied on and was trapped within the physical body. Unless it was like the natural-born third eye of Erlang Shen,[8] ordinary people's Heavenly Eyes were always closed.

Zhao Yunlan never would have imagined that going blind would bring him the fortune of forcing his Heavenly Eye open.

As Zhao Yunlan tried to concentrate on the spot between his eyebrows, his surroundings came into focus. More and more things became perceptible: first, it was the flowers on the windowsill, the cat fur on the sofa, the ancient texts on his bookshelf... and an antique painting hanging on his wall.

---

8 *Erlang Shen (二郎神) was a powerful martial god from Chinese mythology, portrayed as the nephew of the Jade Emperor in Investiture of the Gods and Journey to the West, and known for his third eye and faithful dog.*

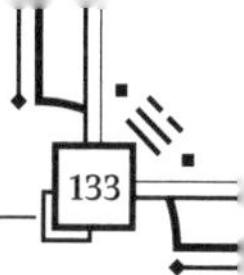

The Heavenly Eye seemed to only be able to see things that had life or spirit. He was still unable to see the sofa, the coffee table, or any of the things made in modern times that had no spirit to them.

Zhao Yunlan "looked" down at his own body and saw white light coursing through him. His left shoulder was empty, but on his right shoulder was a bright ball, radiant with beautiful light and colors—that must be his soul fire.

Something about the light of his soul fire was…familiar. He felt sure he had seen it somewhere before.

A sudden realization made him spring to his feet. His knees slammed into the coffee table, but he didn't even take the time to grimace as he stumbled into the kitchen. He could hear the sound of vegetables being chopped, but Shen Wei was invisible to him, perfectly blending in with the darkness—or maybe not so perfectly. A moment's study showed him to be even darker than the surrounding blackness. The only light about him came from the tiny pendant around his neck. The ball of fire in the pendant was identical to the sphere of light on Zhao Yunlan's right shoulder.

Shen Wei was prepping a head of cabbage. At the sound of movement, he glanced at Zhao Yunlan. "It's too chaotic in here. Don't come in."

Zhao Yunlan ignored him. Following Shen Wei's voice, he walked in carefully, then slowly reached out and hugged Shen Wei from behind. Resting his chin on Shen Wei's shoulder, he shut his eyes and tried to look at the cutting board with his newly acquired Heavenly Eye. But—perhaps because those vegetables had lost their vitality while being uprooted and frozen—he didn't "see" anything. There was only the faint scent of vegetable juices.

Then he looked down at Shen Wei, who was in his arms.

From the moment he'd embraced Shen Wei, a bright blood red had begun spilling outward from Shen Wei's heart. It flowed throughout the absolute blackness of Shen Wei's silhouette like molten lava, outlining a slim, graceful figure in Zhao Yunlan's ink-black vision.

It was as if life had suddenly burst into existence.

Zhao Yunlan silently took this in for a while. When he finally spoke, it was to casually grumble, "What are you chopping? I don't eat this. I want meat. I'm not a rabbit. As an injured person, I am petitioning for an improvement to my meals."

Shen Wei chuckled indulgently and lifted the lid of a small pot beside him. A hearty aroma of meat wafted out. "Don't be picky."

As he said it, the fiery colors on his body softened. The bright flow of crimson took on a strikingly warm orange hue, like the first glimpse of the sun after the break of dawn.

Shen Wei let himself be hugged, and Zhao Yunlan moved along with him, swaying from side to side and listening to the sound of the knife on the cutting board. His eyes were dark. When he looked down, they didn't seem dull, only unspeakably deep.

After another stretch of silence, Zhao Yunlan leaned in closer and asked, "Do you think I'm hot?"

Shen Wei's hands paused. "Do you have something proper to say or not? Stop messing around."

"It's perfectly proper!" Zhao Yunlan cleared his throat. "Comrade Shen Wei, consider this man beside you: an intellectual giant, a pioneer in his work, and a public servant who thinks only of the people, never himself. Do you think he's hot?"

Shen Wei was momentarily speechless, but then he laughed quietly. Looking down, he carefully cut the cabbage into strips.

In his hands, this simple task seemed like something to enjoy wholeheartedly, without a spare thought for anything else. "Whether or not you're hot is irrelevant to me. You could be a hulking giant with a head covered in scabs and feet covered with sores. You could be hideous and repulsive and still hold the exact same place in my heart."

"Next thing I know, you'll be proposing to me," teased Zhao Yunlan.

Even though it was just the two of them at home, the kitchen was no place for intimate behavior, so Shen Wei was still somewhat shy. He nudged Zhao Yunlan with his shoulder. "Get out of the way. I'm about to stir-fry, so go sit somewhere."

Zhao Yunlan obediently let go and took a step back, bumping up against the chilly metal of the sink. Almost casually, he asked, "Would you ever lie to me?"

Shen Wei paused, back still to him.

"Would you?" Zhao Yunlan persisted.

Shen Wei kept facing away. After a moment, voice low, he said, "I will not lie to you, nor will I ever harm you."

Zhao Yunlan observed Shen Wei's back with his Heavenly Eye. As he watched, the light flowing through Shen Wei slowly dimmed, like a firework burning out. It had happened in just the time it took him to say a few sentences. An inexplicable sadness welled up in his heart. "Okay, I believe you," he blurted out.

Shen Wei suddenly turned. "With no proof but my words?"

Zhao Yunlan smiled. "If it's you, I'll believe anything you say."

After saying that, he couldn't bear to "look" at the light rising and falling on Shen Wei. He turned away, acting as though what he'd said was just idle chatter. He started rummaging through the kitchen shelves. "Where's my beef jerky?" he mumbled. "I remember there being a bag of beef jerky here..."

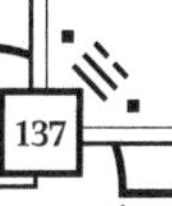

He was so flustered that he knocked over a plastic broom in the corner, stepped on it, and nearly fell on his face.

Shen Wei's hands were wet from handling the cabbage. Afraid of getting cabbage juice all over Zhao Yunlan, all he could do was extend an arm to break his fall. Zhao Yunlan fell heavily against his chest.

The apartment wasn't very big, so the kitchen was *very* small. It was just barely suitable for one person, let alone two grown men. Shen Wei was obliged to stay in that position and circle his arms around in front of Zhao Yunlan to rinse them under the faucet. His chin rested naturally on Zhao Yunlan's shoulder.

Zhao Yunlan was suddenly still and silent.

Once his hands were clean, Shen Wei let his arms hover around Zhao Yunlan as he steered him toward the door. "Even if you have jerky, it's long since expired by now. Stop looking. I put some snacks on the table earlier. Eat those if you're hungry, but don't eat too much. Food's almost ready."

Lowering his gaze, Zhao Yunlan smiled. "I'm starving, but not for food."

"Hmm?" Shen Wei paused. "What do you want to eat, then?"

Zhao Yunlan tilted his head and felt around for Shen Wei's chin. Once he'd touched it, he lightly ran a fingertip from Shen Wei's jaw to his ear, then leaned in. "You," he murmured. "I want to eat you."

As he was saying this, he happened to "look" directly at Shen Wei's face. Zhao Yunlan's eyes were very deep set, and when they were half-closed, the shadow of his eyelashes fell on the tall bridge of his nose. Even though Shen Wei was fully aware that Zhao Yunlan couldn't see anything, it still gave the illusion of being gazed at with deep affection.

Under that gaze, Shen Wei felt like his very soul was trembling.

Zhao Yunlan smiled and moved even closer, breathing in the light fragrance of Shen Wei's shampoo. "Why so nervous? You can try me out. I'm very gentle."

Without a word, Shen Wei dumped him on the sofa and ran away.

Zhao Yunlan stretched out his legs and lounged on the sofa like a lord, contemplating the idea of ordering a pair of red candles. He could light them at the head of the bed in the middle of the night, creating a romantic wedding-night atmosphere. That might be what it would take to coax a certain gentleman out of his clothes.

Well into the evening, Zhao Yunlan's heart remained antsy with *want*. Shen Wei, afraid he might be bored and restless from being unable to see, leaned against the headboard before bed and began reading a book to him. Shen Wei's voice was gentle and soft, with a perfect deep resonance. As Zhao Yunlan listened, ensconced in this intellectual atmosphere, it wasn't an appreciation for culture that rose within him. It was his most primal urge.

Something suddenly caught Shen Wei's attention. He broke off mid-sentence, turning toward the window. With no warning, Zhao Yunlan rolled on top of him, catching him in a hug and pressing him down on the bed. "Don't look," he whispered, lips against Shen Wei's ear. "Turn off the lights."

The room plunged into darkness.

Zhao Yunlan slipped a hand under Shen Wei's shirt, sending shivers through the entire length of his body. Shen Wei seized Zhao Yunlan's wrist, holding his hand in place. Zhao Yunlan lowered his head further and nibbled at Shen Wei's collarbones. His tone was downright oily as he said, "Mmm, it just takes one touch to get you hard? You miss me that much?"

Shen Wei was so perturbed that he could barely spare a thought for whoever was outside the window.

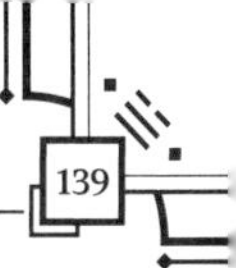

The wind carried a new sound, barely audible: the dageng woodblock. Zhao Yunlan's fingers, which were busily trailing fire everywhere they touched Shen Wei, suddenly spelled out a message on his skin. *Don't move.*

Yanking the blanket up to completely cover Shen Wei, Zhao Yunlan sat halfway up. His shirt was unbuttoned almost all the way to his waist, nearly falling off entirely, but his voice was full of cold steel. "If I were alone, I'd gladly welcome you. But as it stands, three's a crowd. I'm sure you understand."

There was a light cough outside the window. "The Magistrate heard that the Guardian's eyes were injured. He dispatched this lowly one to check on you. If I've disturbed you in any way, then I'm truly..."

"The Magistrate?" Zhao Yunlan raised an eyebrow, giving a meaningful laugh. "News sure reaches him quickly. I was only at the hospital today, and it's not even midnight yet, but here you are already. Well, I'm fine, my lord. You may go back and thank him for thinking of me."

"Yes, of course," the person at the window replied quietly. The intense yin energy outside disappeared.

Zhao Yunlan groped around on the bed. Shen Wei grabbed his hand and said, "That was a reaper? What..."

"Think about it, you dummy." Zhao Yunlan sighed. His fingers found Shen Wei's hair and gently smoothed it. Keeping his voice low, he said, "They're trying all sorts of ways to trick you. Some people in the Netherworld know who 'Shen Wei' is, right?"

Shen Wei hesitated, then nodded. He'd been hanging around the Mortal Realm for decades in human guise. The fact that he did it to watch over someone might be too embarrassing for him to spread around, but the Soul-Executing Emissary lingering in the

Mortal Realm was rather a big deal. He had to have at least notified the Ten Kings of the Yanluo Courts.

"Your status is high enough that you didn't need to ever get involved with the other side," said Zhao Yunlan. "They have their own concerns and priorities. When it comes to mortal or ghostly matters, everyone has their own agenda. And you..."

"Are you worried for me?" Shen Wei asked quietly.

Zhao Yunlan lowered his head, following Shen Wei's voice. "What do you think?"

Shen Wei's grip tightened, and Zhao Yunlan found himself wrapped in a fierce embrace, with Shen Wei's face buried in the crook of his neck. The embrace continued for an eternity, and Shen Wei was incredibly strong. Zhao Yunlan had planned to take advantage of the mood and get up to a little bit more, but there was no breaking out of Shen Wei's hold. Shen Wei just kept holding him possessively, as though he had no intention of letting go until daybreak.

Zhao Yunlan made a few futile attempts to free himself, but exhaustion caught up with him. With it came the realization that he had no choice but to fall asleep unsatisfied, letting his mind run wild with horny thoughts. He prepared himself for the most frustrating sleep of his life, so fired up that he felt on the verge of a nosebleed.

Perhaps because Shen Wei was holding him too tightly—it really was a little uncomfortable—when Zhao Yunlan did drift off to sleep, he started to dream.

He dreamed that he was in a cloudy, misty place, walking in circles. He was surrounded by ruins and debris, and there were countless people praying toward the sky. He spared them a glance and kept walking, eventually arriving at a place that was utterly dark and desolate.

For some reason, he felt a surge of annoyance. He snapped his fingers to summon fire, but the fire went out before it could catch.

Someone sighed deeply by his ear. "Why did you have to go through all this effort over an offhand comment?"

The voice was difficult to describe. It seemed to bypass his ears entirely and pierce right through his heart. Zhao Yunlan gave a violent shudder, and then he was awake.

It seemed like the sun must already be high in the sky. Shen Wei wasn't beside him anymore. He'd probably stepped out to buy something.

Zhao Yunlan saw darkness when he opened his eyes, and darkness when he closed them. His heart beat like thunder, cold sweat beading on his back.

Who had been speaking in the dream...?

Why did it sound like his own voice?

Chapter 11

AFTER HASTILY MAKING himself presentable, Zhao Yunlan felt around on the coffee table for the bandages and medicine that they'd brought back from the hospital. He casually wound the bandages around his head a few times to cover his eyes. With a bit more feeling around, he found paper and a pen on the bedside table. Without worrying about what the paper was, he scrawled "GONE TO 4 BRIGHT AVENUE." That done, he left the apartment, counting his steps.

No longer in the dream, his heart rate gradually slowed to normal. By the time the elevator opened on the ground floor, Zhao Yunlan had also gotten his breathing under control. Focusing on the Heavenly Eye between his eyebrows, he strode out into the world.

He "saw" crowds of people on the street and quickly learned to discern between humans and ghosts: there was a soft blurriness around some figures, and those were living people.

At first, he couldn't see very clearly at all. Everything was just a haze. But as he walked out of the neighborhood, it seemed as though he was adjusting to this way of "looking" at the world. The fuzzy edges of people's silhouettes started to sharpen. He began to see the three treasures gathered on the top of each person's head.

As someone passed by him, it suddenly clicked: the soft ring around each living person was a filmy layer that covered them from head to toe, with weird patterns on its surface.

At the intersection, Zhao Yunlan reached out to hail a taxi. Since he couldn't see, his only real option was to keep his hand extended and rely on luck. It was ten minutes or so before an empty car pulled up.

Feeling his way inside, he realized that the "patterns" on each person were actually text—text that was very small and densely packed and in constant flux. For a few seconds, Zhao Yunlan couldn't help but stare at the driver. It wasn't until the driver prompted him that he came back to himself.

"Sorry. 4 Bright Avenue. You can just drop me off at the entrance."

The taxi driver glanced curiously at his bandaged eyes. "Young man, what's wrong with your eyes?"

"Got hit while playing basketball," Zhao Yunlan lied casually.

The driver asked, "Aiyou, can you still see?"

"There's medicine in my eyes, so I can't open them," Zhao Yunlan said. "I'll just have to be blind for a few days, that's all."

The two chatted idly during the drive. When they arrived, the taxi stopped at the side of the road. Zhao Yunlan thought for a moment, then pulled his wallet from his pocket and handed it directly to the driver. "I can't see. Please just take whatever I owe you."

The driver was taken aback. "Huh? That's very trusting of you."

Zhao Yunlan chuckled. "There's not much cash in there anyway. Please take what you see fit."

The driver hesitated a second longer, then printed a receipt and rifled through the wallet. Zhao Yunlan spent those seconds staring closely at the ever-changing words on the driver's body and listening to the rustling sound of him flipping through his wallet. The driver seemed to take something out, hesitate, and stuff it back in.

A moment later he took out a different bill, got change from his pocket, and then tucked the change and receipt into the wallet together.

A corner of Zhao Yunlan's mouth lifted. As his vision grew clearer, he found he could make out the color of the text he was seeing: black and red. The instant the driver put the change into the wallet, Zhao Yunlan saw a row of tiny red text flash across the man's body.

So that's what it means. Zhao Yunlan thanked the driver, declining the offer to help him inside. *The tiny text records someone's deeds. Red for merits, black for sins. I guess he didn't take advantage of a blind man.*

Zhao Yunlan could unmistakably feel that something was rapidly awakening within him. What was unclear was whether it was good or bad.

Everything seemed to have started with the earthquake not long ago—the quake that revealed the Hanga tribe's Mountain-River Awl.

Had that earthquake really been caused by natural shifting of the Earth's crust?

The doorman who enjoyed carving bones saw him coming and set down the file he was working with. "Director Zhao!" he called cheerfully. "Oh, hey! What happened to your eyes?"

"An accident," Zhao Yunlan said, perfectly calm. "Li-shu, come give me a hand."

But before Li-shu could step out of the gatehouse, someone else came dashing up. Shen Wei grabbed Zhao Yunlan's extended hand, just barely keeping his grip and voice in check. "Couldn't you wait for me before wandering off? I came back from buying breakfast, and you were gone. You scared me half to death. If you do that again... If you do that again, I'll..."

Zhao Yunlan turned toward him. The perception granted by his Heavenly Eye just kept getting clearer and brighter, and now, through it, he gazed at Shen Wei.

What he saw was row after row of the bright red text that represented Shen Wei's merits. Those crimson characters flashed into existence repeatedly...yet none of them lasted. They appeared with the swiftness of the tide, only to be washed away by vast waves of darkness, as ephemeral as marks in the sand.

Zhao Yunlan's eyes suddenly stung as an emotion crashed over him, surging up from someplace he couldn't identify. It was as though some memory had been buried deep for hundreds of thousands of years, and a hurricane had just passed through and blown away the deep layers of dust covering it. What was revealed was some naked, inescapable truth that stabbed into the heart, setting off cascading waves of pain.

"I knew you'd come after me right away," Zhao Yunlan said smoothly. He was almost able to keep the tremble out of his voice. "It's good that you're here now. Come inside with me."

The whole SID office went into a frenzy at Zhao Yunlan's sudden arrival. Daqing had run off somewhere to be melodramatic. The people of the Special Investigations Department only now realized that, rather than going off to fool around someplace, their boss had gotten into an accident.

Zhu Hong unwound his bandages with trembling hands. When she saw his eyes, still bright but not quite able to focus, her own eyes reddened.

Zhao Yunlan's fingers twitched, but he remembered he couldn't see and shouldn't grope blindly toward his female employees. A tad embarrassed, he lowered his hand again. "Which of us is blind here? I haven't shed a single tear, so what are you getting emotional for?"

She flung the bandages at his face. "You, cry? If you knew how to cry, we wouldn't be here! There's nowhere you wouldn't dare set foot, no one you wouldn't dare cross, right?! You think you're second only to the Heavens, don't you? Fucking dumbass!"

After a moment of silence, Zhao Yunlan said, "Okay, this dumbass has heard you."

Zhu Hong rounded on Shen Wei instead. "Don't you like him?" she demanded. "Aren't you very powerful? Where were you when this happened to him?"

Chu Shuzhi and Lin Jing exchanged a glance. Something about this scene seemed not quite right.

Of course, Zhao Yunlan felt it too. He took a stab at smoothing things over with a joke. He tugged on Shen Wei's sleeve, deploying his most mischievous grin. "You like me? How come you've never mentioned it? Shen-laoshi, I think you have a very serious problem. If you like me, why would you tell her about it and not me?"

Zhu Hong had no use for his olive branch. "You shut up!"

His smile vanished as easily as it had appeared. "That's enough. I got into an accident while dealing with a private matter. What does it have to do with him? Do the two of us have to be tied together every second of the day? When the three-legged race becomes an official Olympic sport, let me know!"

Hurt crept into Zhu Hong's fierce gaze. Shen Wei finally had to speak up. "I should have..."

Brow furrowed, Zhao Yunlan gave a dismissive wave. "I don't want to talk about this right now. We can save these trivial matters for later. Right now, all of you shut up."

He took a Soul-Guarding Order from his pocket. As it began to burn, Zhao Yunlan quietly said, "Daqing, come here for a second."

In response, a collar bell jingled, and Daqing crept out of the library from beyond the wall. The black cat jumped onto Zhao Yunlan's leg silently and studied his eyes, then hopped up on the table. "I skimmed a few books, and I think I sort of understand what's wrong with your eyes. You said the earth flames you triggered set that little crow on fire, and then he sacrificed himself to the golden bell, right? I suspect what happened is that the spiritual chime and earth fire collided, resulting in too much yin energy. Since you were right in the middle of it, your eyes were injured. That's why you've temporarily lost your sight."

Zhao Yunlan nodded nonchalantly, but Shen Wei immediately latched onto the key point. "Temporarily?"

Daqing made an affirmative sound but glanced at Zhao Yunlan. He had the sudden suspicion that Zhao Yunlan knew something.

But Shen Wei was too worried to think straight and didn't notice. He barreled on to his next question. "How long will it take him to recover? What medicines does he need? Where can they be found?"

One look at Shen Wei told Daqing that he was genuinely worried. The cat sighed to himself and continued. "The Flower Yao tribe, who mostly keep to themselves, have something very precious that they call the 'Nectar of a Thousand Essences.' Legend says they make it from the best parts of the stamens from ninety-nine varieties of flowers—thirty-three each from the Mortal Realm, the Heavens, and the Netherworld. It's an effective antidote for hundreds of poisons, and gentle and nourishing to boot, so it's perfect for eye injuries. The best place to find them is probably—"

"At the year-end Yao Market," Zhao Yunlan said, finishing his sentence.

Daqing stilled. "How did you know?"

Zhao Yunlan didn't answer right away. He sat and petted the cat's head, turning something over in his mind. Finally, he said, "If you're done, there's something I need to say. First, from now on, any communication of *any* kind with the Netherworld needs to be put in writing so that I'll have a copy. Don't leave out a single word.

Second, no outsiders are allowed on the premises here. If anyone drops by with New Year's gifts, receive them at the gatehouse. Third, spread the word outside our office that we're entering the year-end wrap-up period. Try not to accept any new cases unless the order comes from the minister himself. And fourth, if anyone under the jurisdiction of the Soul-Guarding Order needs to come in late or needs a day off, you must have me sign off on it. I need to know where you all are at all times."

"Then the Yao Market..." Zhu Hong began.

"That's not a big deal. Shen Wei can accompany me," said Zhao Yunlan. "And that reminds me—Zhu Hong, I've told them to set up a private room for you on the third floor. For now, when you can't transform easily and need to rest, stay there. Don't take any leave."

His orders given, Zhao Yunlan stood up using the support of the table and began to make his way toward the library beyond the wall without waiting for anyone's response. "I have something I need to discuss with Sangzan. Shen Wei, wait for me for a bit. Everyone else, tell the other units what I just said."

The library was brightly lit. Seeing Zhao Yunlan, Sangzan greeted him cheerfully. "Henlo, Deeractor Zhao slutterer!"

"What the hell?" Zhao Yunlan paused. "Who taught you that?"

"Cat slutterer." Sangzan was fully aware that his pronunciation wasn't good, so he made a determined effort to correct himself. "Deeractor... Director... Director Zhao slutterer!"

Zhao Yunlan chuckled and didn't bother asking any further. Opening his Heavenly Eye, he realized he could see the outlines of most of the books. He glanced around, then turned back to Sangzan. "Find me that book I read the other day."

Sangzan retrieved *Soul Book* without hesitation. It was genuinely impressive that despite being illiterate, he could remember the precise location of each and every book.

The title on the book's cover was plainly visible to the Heavenly Eye. The book flipped itself open before he even had a chance to touch it. He noticed something at once that hadn't been so apparent the last time he'd read it: a page had clearly been ripped out. To his Heavenly Eye, the torn page seemed to seep a purplish-black blood.

Zhao Yunlan snapped the book closed. Sangzan observed his expression carefully.

After a few moments, Zhao Yunlan quietly asked, "Do you believe there are perfect coincidences in this world?"

Sangzan chewed over the question, working hard to figure out what "coincidence" meant. Thanks to the language barrier, he always seemed a little stupid; it was often all too easy for the others to forget that he had been a slave who'd turned the fate of an entire tribe. Only when he was silent did his innate spirit and zeal show through.

Sangzan shook his head. In a rare instance of perfect pronunciation, he said, "I don't."

"Neither do I," Zhao Yunlan said slowly. "As the one possessing the Soul-Guarding Order, all I wanted was to fulfill my duty of watching over the Mortal Realm, but some people just don't want to let me live in peace."

The sentence was too complicated, with all its nouns. Sangzan didn't completely follow, but Zhao Yunlan's intentions were plain in his expression. "Whet can I do to help?"

Zhao Yunlan looked down. "Pass me a piece of paper."

Working from memory, he wrote down what the crow yao had said to him that night. Zhao Yunlan had made a show of not understanding, but of course he understood perfectly well. In writing it out now, he reproduced it exactly. At the end of the row of text, he wrote the word "Kunlun," then underlined it repeatedly.

"I want every book containing this word." He tapped on "Kunlun." "Don't mention it to anyone, not even Wang Zheng. Thanks, bro."

In Sangzan's mind, Zhao Yunlan was halfway to being a savior. Sangzan might have been a self-taught conspirator, but one of the greatest qualities of his people still ran bone-deep: he knew when to love and when to hate. Deadly serious, he said, "Leave it to me, Deeractor Zhao slutterer."

Zhao Yunlan responded with something that could have been a smile. "Okay. And I'll go kick that fatass Daqing for you."

CHAPTER 12

DRAGON CITY'S YAO BANQUET was planned for the 28th day of the year's final lunar month. As it happened, this year the last month once again had only twenty-nine days, so the banquet was being held on the last day before Lunar New Year's Eve.

Early that morning, Zhao Yunlan's invitation to the Yao Market had arrived by sparrow. The cleaning staff had left his office bright and spotless. When the curtains on the room's huge floor-to-ceiling window were open, the room was flooded with winter sunlight. With the heat cranked all the way up, there was no need to wear layers for warmth. The office held two giant taro plants, green and plump, and a tank by the door contained a relaxed, carefree silver arowana.

Leisurely guqin music flowed through the speakers. The office was spacious, and its two occupants had each claimed half. After watering the plants, Shen Wei sat and read a book. He was temporarily serving as Zhao Yunlan's assistant until his injured eyes recovered.

Zhao Yunlan had asked Shen Wei to mix a bowl of cinnabar and was now sitting at the table with the cinnabar and a thick stack of yellow paper, practicing drawing talismans with his eyes closed. The first ones he drew were a mess, but as he slowly got used to drawing blind, the activity went from an idle time-killer to a way to relax and calm his mind.

It wasn't long before he had a row of evil-warding talismans lined up along the edge of his desk. Anyone who walked through the door could feel their warm, abundant energy.

Zhao Yunlan normally lacked the patience for this kind of work, so it always fell to Chu Shuzhi. But right now—perhaps it was due to his blindness, perhaps he was affected by Shen Wei's presence, but currently—he sat quietly and calmly in a rare moment of stillness.

When Zhu Hong knocked and came in, what she saw was two people who brought out the best in each other without getting in the other's way. She paused in the doorway, gripped by the feeling that if she entered, her presence would be completely extraneous. It all seemed so pointless.

She bit her lip and gave Shen Wei a cold nod, then addressed Zhao Yunlan from the threshold. "I need to head out for a bit. The year-end bonus has arrived, so I have to make a trip to the bank for Wang Zheng."

Zhao Yunlan, the broke bastard, immediately perked up. "Okay, sounds good."

Next, Zhu Hong took a form from her document folder. "I also have our estimated budget for the department's New Year's Eve dinner. In addition to food, we'll need to purchase offerings for the gods in advance. I'll read the list to you. If it all sounds good, I'll get your signature and then go and request funds from the finance department."

She read through the list while Zhao Yunlan listened, then he signed where she touched the paper. Once they'd taken care of official business, Zhu Hong finally glanced at Shen Wei before awkwardly asking, "Will you... Will you still bring in the New Year with us this year?"

Zhao Yunlan didn't even look up. "Well, yeah. Where else would I go?"

A hint of happiness finally showed on Zhu Hong's face, only to vanish a moment later when Zhao Yunlan continued, "Not only that, but I'll be bringing the family. Right, wifey?"

Whether because Shen Wei was already used to Zhao Yunlan's flirting or because of Zhu Hong's presence, Shen Wei didn't put up a fight. He simply smiled with a playful "Oh, shut up" in response.

Zhu Hong's expression clouded over. "Okay," she said gloomily. "I'm off, then."

"Oh hey, wait a second," Zhao Yunlan said. He tidied up his finished evil-warding talismans and handed them to her. "There's a little shop at the far end of Antiques Street behind that large pagoda tree. They don't have a sign—it's just an old man by the door. Go in and have him take a look at these. Tell him the price is the same as always—he'll know. But let him know I drew these while blind, so make sure he examines them carefully. If any of them are flawed, you can give him a discount."

Zhu Hong stuffed them into the pocket of her down jacket. "You sell paper talismans?"

"I have to support my family." Zhao Yunlan stretched out his back. "I need to bring in a little extra income. I just bought a house, and now I desperately need money to renovate."

Zhu Hong didn't even wait for him to finish before walking away. She'd intended to ask if he needed her to accompany him to the Yao Market that night, but that was clearly unnecessary. The door slammed behind her.

Shen Wei looked up from his ancient text. "Do you think she, ah, has feelings for..."

"Mmn." Zhao Yunlan spread out a new piece of yellow paper, measuring with his fingers as he spoke. "I hadn't noticed it before. But now that I do know, I should do something about it before it's too late."

Shen Wei sighed, and Zhao Yunlan chuckled.

"What are you sighing for? What future is there for a workplace romance? Besides, humans and yao don't belong together. What's the point in getting involved?"

Zhao Yunlan only meant exactly what he said, but Shen Wei read more into it than he'd intended. There was a brief silence before Shen Wei asked, "Then you and I...as a ghost and a human, shouldn't we stay apart?"

"What?" Zhao Yunlan reflexively reached out, getting cinnabar all over his hand. After a frozen second, he exclaimed, "We're not the same at all! I like you so much."

He said it so casually, as if there were nothing sweet and romantic about the words. It might have been the kind of idle chitchat people exchange while enjoying tea and a lovely fragrance together. As snow blanketed the world outside, such simple words seemed ordinary, yet warm with sincerity.

A hand suddenly pressed against the hand Zhao Yunlan was using to hold a talisman in place. The touch interrupted the movement of the brush, and the spiritual energy leaked out of the talisman. Just like that, it went to waste.

At some point, Shen Wei had closed the distance between them; now he placed his hands on the chair's armrests, trapping Zhao Yunlan with his arms. Almost piously, Shen Wei closed his eyes and leaned in close. He held his breath, and there was the faintest quiver to his eyelashes. Ever so carefully, he kissed the tip of

Zhao Yunlan's nose. Then, even more slowly, he dared to move his mouth lower. This cautious exploration continued until his lips brushed Zhao Yunlan's.

It was incredibly gentle and warm, even as he parted Zhao Yunlan's lips, feeling their slight dryness and dipping so, so softly between them. There was no sense at all that he sought anything more than this.

He was so helplessly in love, yearning for the sweetness of a kiss, for the simple touch of skin on skin.

This man before him was like some sort of deadly poison. Shen Wei had struggled with all his might and still failed to resist. He had only fallen ever deeper.

At that blissful moment, someone came in unannounced and saw a scene they shouldn't have been privy to. They backed right out again while muttering a curse. The sound of the door startled Shen Wei and made him straighten up in a panic. He coughed dryly, as though trying to hide something.

Back outside, Daqing scratched at the door, pretending nothing had happened. "Boss?" he called, dragging it out. "Director Zhao, are you there? Are you busy?"

Zhao Yunlan's expression was murderous. "Get the fuck in here already!"

Daqing eagerly ran in, giving Shen Wei a curious look. He'd never seen such an easily embarrassed human around Zhao Yunlan before. Shen Wei's expression just then wouldn't have been out of place in a photo of a handcuffed sex worker accompanying an article denouncing pornography and illegal activities. His deep blush had crept almost to his neck.

It really did make Shen Wei seem like a beauty among peach blossoms, as if he belonged in a painting where an exquisite countenance and stunning flowers complemented each other flawlessly.

No wonder Zhao Yunlan, the incorrigible pervert, had relentlessly pursued him for over half a year, yet still not managed to take a bite.

Daqing raised his tail, gratified by Zhao Yunlan's misfortunes and the pleasing thought that, no matter how lovely Shen Wei looked right now, Zhao Yunlan was denied the sight of him.

Impatiently, the incorrigible pervert in question snapped, "You have two minutes. If you dare say a single word of bullshit, I'll skin you and turn you into a scarf!"

The black cat perched on the desk. "I wrote to the Flower tribe. You've received an invitation, right? After all, you know plenty of yao. Tonight, after dusk, someone will be waiting for you at the west entrance to Antiques Street. You can head right on over. Don't forget to bring a gift."

This time, the look he gave Shen Wei was a little worried. "Shen-laoshi knows the customs, right?"

Shen Wei nodded. "Don't worry. I'll take care of him."

That was a relief for Daqing, who still believed that humans required some sense of shame to keep them from just endlessly sinking lower. If there was a point past which they wouldn't sink, they could be depended upon. Shen-laoshi certainly looked more dependable than a certain someone.

Zhao Yunlan was about to order their uninvited guest out when his phone rang. He carelessly felt around for it and picked it up. He couldn't see the caller ID, but Daqing could. It read "Empress Dowager."

The cat immediately perked up and paid attention, keen to see Zhao Yunlan make a fool of himself.

Zhao Yunlan answered very officially. "Hello, this is Special Investigations Department Director Zhao—"

His voice suddenly dropped an octave and softened. He was nearly bowing as he said, "Ah, ah, I didn't see just now. I'm so sorry, Mom, truly..."

The change in his posture was like night and day. He went from sitting boldly on his swivel chair, looking powerful and domineering, to shrinking into a ball. Daqing fell over in silent laughter.

"No, I wouldn't dare forget," Zhao Yunlan was saying. "I honestly have something to do tonight, really... I really do." He sighed. "Please stop asking. It's to do with work... No, when have I ever gone out to fool around? Even if I wanted to, where would I even go to have fun on such a cold day?"

Shen Wei stood off to the side, listening to Zhao Yunlan conversing with the person on the other end. Zhao Yunlan's side of the conversation was affectionate, occasionally punctuated by whining.

At first Shen Wei smiled to hear it, but then an involuntary darkness shadowed his eyes. It suddenly struck him more clearly than ever that Zhao Yunlan was a flesh-and-blood human—someone with parents. Unlike Shen Wei, he had countless connections to the Mortal Realm.

Perhaps thinking that the call would dash his handsome, noble image to pieces, Zhao Yunlan got up, felt his way around the table, and shut himself in the inner room.

Daqing cleaned his claws. He and Shen Wei studied each other for a while, and then he asked, "Are you human?"

Shen Wei didn't know how to respond to that.

Daqing hurried to explain. "No, don't misunderstand. That's not an insult. I mean it literally—literally, you understand? As in, are you human or something else...? Something not human, you know?"

The question hit Shen Wei right where it hurt. After a bit more silence, he shook his head.

To his surprise, Daqing let out a sigh of relief. Talking more to himself than Shen Wei, he said, "It's good that you're not human. Not human... Hmm... That little brat has such a punchable face, but he's not a bad person. He really likes you, so don't betray his trust."

Shen Wei said simply, "How could I? As long as he still wants me, I will not betray him in life or death."

Daqing stared up into his eyes, struck by the sheer weight of the sincerity he saw there. Many, many years had passed since he'd seen such sincerity in anyone. For a moment, he was too shocked to move.

He was still lost in thought when Zhao Yunlan came back after finishing his call. Daqing leapt down and twined around his legs. "What did the old lady say? I want to eat her pan-fried little croakers!"

"Eat my ass and fuck off. Don't trip me." Zhao Yunlan extended a leg, trying to push him away.

Daqing was having none of that. With both front paws, he dug firmly into Zhao Yunlan's pant leg. His spherical body swayed in the air as he yelled, "I want to eat! Fried! Little! Fish!"

"I'll take you, all right? I'll take you! My damn cat ancestor." Zhao Yunlan bent down and grabbed Daqing by the scruff of his neck, tossed him aside, and then slapped him on the butt. "I'll take you on the evening of New Year's Day. Oh—actually, my mom mentioned you just now."

Daqing was delighted. "Mentioned me? Did she praise me?"

"She said, 'That cat's lived so many years now, so he probably won't be with us much longer.' She told me to treat you better."

Daqing slumped to his butt on top of Zhao Yunlan's foot, but Zhao Yunlan was ready for him. Quickly pulling his foot away, he turned to Shen Wei, somehow containing his laughter. "I told her to prepare for an extra person. Do you have other plans? Do you want to come home with me?"

Caught completely off guard, Shen Wei froze. It took him some time to find his voice. With difficulty, he said, "Me? No, no, I couldn't. It's the New Year, and I'm an outsider..."

"An outsider?" Zhao Yunlan grabbed his collar. "What, are you planning to have your way with me and toss me aside when you've had your fill?"

"What are you saying?!"

Daqing had no interest in watching them. He slipped out through the door, which was barely open, and deftly closed it behind him with his hind paw.

That evening, Shen Wei drove them to Antiques Street. Zhao Yunlan wore a pair of sunglasses and carried a cane, and Shen Wei somehow managed to spare one hand to guide him while carrying a lacquer box in the other.

There were four layers inside the box. The first held lingzhi mushrooms and rare essences from the mountains, the second held ancient ritual instruments of gold and jade, the third held pearls and dragon's beard from the bottom of the sea, and the fourth held black iron with a golden sheen from under the Huangquan River.

Altogether, Shen Wei was holding hundreds of kilograms in one hand, but so easily that it seemed weightless.

Antiques Street didn't have a western entrance. Its westernmost point stopped at a dead end. The few shops there had long since closed up for the New Year. There was only a red paper lantern hanging on the pagoda tree, casting a rounded light upon the mottled wall.

When the pair walked under the lantern, a shadow flashed before them, and a horse-drawn carriage materialized out of thin air. Someone stepped down from the carriage. They were tall and lanky, wearing a long robe, and their head was that of a fox. From a distance, it would seem like someone wearing a furry mask. The fox's hands were gathered within their sleeves, and their long, thin eyes sneakily lingered on the box Shen Wei held.

They bowed. "Welcome, honored guests. Please come this way."

There were Yao Markets everywhere, like the ones in the olden days where people gathered from different villages to trade. They were usually held once a year. In some places they were spirited occasions; in some they were quieter affairs. Dragon City was too urban, glutted with humans and their lively energy. As the saying goes, "the best place to disappear is in a city," and urban centers might be a melting pot of people of all kinds, but it wasn't actually suitable for cultivation. Ordinary yao, unless they had some connection to mortal life or had come a great way seeking closure on unfinished business, usually did not choose to live in places like this for the sake of their cultivation prospects. As a result, the local Yao Market was on the quieter side.

Ever since Zhao Yunlan's Special Investigations Department had set up shop in Dragon City, countless yao had spied for him and called him "bro," but he had never been to the Yao Market. It was the yao's equivalent of the Lunar New Year's Eve dinner. No matter how good their relationship might be, any outsider with common sense would know not to stick their nose into an occasion like this.

Sitting in the yao's horse-drawn carriage, Zhao Yunlan had a sudden thought. He smiled.

"What is it?" asked Shen Wei.

Shen Wei's hand was still holding his. Zhao Yunlan squeezed it, then lowered his voice, pitching it to blend with the sound of the wheels. "I was just thinking about how traditionally our relationship has progressed. First, we got to know each other, and then we exchanged information about our respective backgrounds. The next step, starting with holding hands, is to go shopping together and go out on dates. If we continue down this road, we'll soon be able to meet the parents and get married."

Aware of foxes' keen hearing, Shen Wei glanced outside. "We can talk about this after we get back tonight," he murmured.

However, Zhao Yunlan's shame was nowhere to be seen. "And just *how* would you like to 'talk,' hmm?"

Shen Wei did not deign to respond.

Zhao Yunlan winked. "Oh, dear gege, I want you so badly I can't stand it. Won't you please give me what I want?"

Angry with embarrassment, Shen Wei shook off Zhao Yunlan's hand. But then, seeing Zhao Yunlan's hand grasping aimlessly in the air, he gave in after a moment's hesitation and subtly took hold of it again.

It wasn't clear whether the fox had heard or not, but the carriage ride was very smooth. After about fifteen minutes, it came to a stop and their fox guide drew open the curtain, inviting them to descend. Cold wind blew inside. Not too far away, there was the sound of a rough duet between a qin and a xiao. The melody was somber, but the players were obliged to conjure a lively atmosphere in spite of it. The overall effect was somewhat unsettling.

To the left and right of the entrance stood two greeters, both human-bodied with the heads of horses. A man with a snake's tail rather than legs stood in wait with them.

This was another tradition of the Yao Market. Everyone in attendance had to display part of their original form so that younger attendees with lower cultivation could see who they were dealing with, thus preventing any unhappy misunderstandings.

The snake-bodied man came up to them. "Guardian, you've arrived."

It was bitterly cold. The Snake tribe, due to their nature, were reluctant to venture out during the winter. Normally, most wouldn't attend these festivities, only sending a couple of representatives to make a brief appearance.

This Snake tribe man was clearly waiting for Zhao Yunlan.

Zhao Yunlan listened carefully. "My eyes aren't working well just now, but if I haven't misheard, you're Fourth Uncle, correct?"

"Thank you, Guardian, for remembering," replied the Snake tribe man. "Come in. Zhu Hong has explained the situation to me. If you need anything, just let me know."

Shen Wei handed the lacquer box to the horse-headed greeters and guided Zhao Yunlan in.

Inside was a pedestrian street about a hundred meters long. Along the sides were roads paved with long stone slabs, and between them was a long, narrow river crossed by a little stone bridge, on which a stage had been assembled.

Crowds bustled on both sides of the river. There were colorful lanterns and streamers everywhere, and most people walking among them were half-human, half-beast. Some yao had set up stalls and were selling their wares to the other tribes before the banquet started.

Fourth Uncle led Zhao Yunlan and Shen Wei directly to the bridge. There was still a light layer of snow on its frigid stone surface, but thin, flowering vines had wrapped around the small posts at each end. Pale yellow flowers grew sparsely along the vines.

Addressing a small flower, Fourth Uncle said, "Miss Winter Jasmine, the Guardian has arrived. Please come out to meet him."

Hearing that, the thin winter jasmine vines suddenly exploded with growth, instantly spreading all over the bridge like a flower carpet. Countless narrow, fresh buds burst into life, blooming everywhere. From among the flowers, a girl rose.

She was human from the waist up, but her bottom half was still made of flowering vines. She looked about fourteen or fifteen, with her hair framing her face in two bunches. Her long, thin eyes sized up Zhao Yunlan before turning to Shen Wei.

For some reason, Winter Jasmine seemed to fear Shen Wei. Her gaze swept across him hastily before she looked back to Zhao Yunlan. All smiles, she said, "Uncle Black Cat said the Guardian is a dreamboat. So, dreamboat gege, why are you wearing such large sunglasses?"

Zhao Yunlan took the sunglasses off and hung them from his collar. "So people will take pity on me. Perhaps if a sweet young lady like you saw that a handsome gege like me is blind, you'd give me a little honey?"

Winter Jasmine giggled as she looked closely at his eyes before asking Fourth Uncle, "What's wrong with the Crow tribe? Why are they going around messing with mortals for no reason?"

Fourth Uncle patted her on the head and didn't answer.

Winter Jasmine surveyed their surroundings, "Did not a single one of the Crow tribe come to the banquet this year?"

"Not here nor to the other Markets," Fourth Uncle said. "But you kids shouldn't worry about such matters. Concentrate on cultivating. When spring comes, bloom properly."

Murmuring in agreement, Winter Jasmine took out a small bottle and placed it in Zhao Yunlan's palm. "The chief of our tribe asked me to bring this to the Guardian, and also told me to relay this message: In the future, if the Guardian needs anything, just let us know. We're all at your disposal."

A little overwhelmed by the unexpected favor, Zhao Yunlan took a moment before replying, "At my disposal? No, no, no, the esteemed chief is showing far too much courtesy..."

Before he finished speaking, a little monkey leaped onto the stage. It was holding a bronze gong, which it forcefully struck once. All the yao immediately quieted down. Along the side of the road, far more stone chairs and tables were quickly set out.

"Aiyou," Winter Jasmine exclaimed. "The banquet's about to start. I have to go on stage. Guardian-gege, I can't talk any longer. Take care."

"Wait—" Zhao Yunlan began.

But Winter Jasmine had already shifted into a tremendous number of vines. She quickly curled up along the entire stone bridge, wrapping each post in flowers. Together with the fine dusting of snow, the bridge seemed to bloom with life.

Zhao Yunlan hadn't even had time to take his other hand out of his pocket, where he was carrying something Daqing had given him. Apparently, it had belonged to the past Guardian...which now seemed to mean it was a treasured belonging from his past life, or his past-past life. It was a tiny luminescent cup carved with moonflowers, indescribably intricate and lovely. The cup was said to be able to store moonlight. For the Flower Yao, it was a valuable object for cultivation.

Zhao Yunlan had intended to exchange it for the Flower Yao's Nectar of a Thousand Essences, but not only had they given him the Nectar, they gave it as though it were an offering. He had no idea what to make of it.

Thinking it over, Zhao Yunlan turned to tell Shen Wei that they should leave. As he moved, he bumped into a stone table. Shen Wei swiftly grabbed him around the waist, turning and holding him close to block the view of the crowd of little yao who were trying to sneak a peek.

Shen Wei addressed Fourth Uncle. "We are outsiders here, and this is the Yao Banquet. We shouldn't impose any further, so we'll take our leave now."

Fourth Uncle took note of Shen Wei's possessive behavior. "Seats have already been prepared for you both. You are our honored guests. At least have a drink and warm up before you go?"

Shen Wei's brow furrowed.

Fourth Uncle continued, "As the coming year is that of the Snake, I am hosting the banquet tonight. Please excuse me."

Without waiting for Shen Wei to object, he slithered away, dragging his floor-length sleeves as he slowly ascended the steps onto the tall stage on the bridge. Music filled the air again, but it was very different from the eerie qin and xiao duet. This was a sacrificial song passed down from the beginning of time.

A woman's voice clearly rang out in the distance. "All under Heaven sprang forth from Buzhou."

The yao all suddenly looked solemn.

Eyes downcast, Fourth Uncle stood respectfully while adjusting his collar. In his deep, resonant voice, he declared, "All that is old is gone; welcome all that is new. At year's end, the yao honor the three sages, the Mountain God of the Great Wild, and those who came before."

All the yao stood up and bowed to the northwest.

The woman picked the song back up, dragging out each syllable.

"In the Great Wild,
atop the clouds,
the cloven peak
bears Heaven's weight.
The Great Lord of Water,
Zhurong's son,
struck it on dragonback,
shifting the stars..."

Very quietly, Zhao Yunlan asked Shen Wei, "Who are they singing about? It sounds like the Water God, Gonggong."

For some reason, Shen Wei's expression was growing darker by the second. "Mnnh," was all he said.

"Is it the part where Gonggong knocked down Buzhou Mountain?"

Shen Wei made another affirmative sound.

Baffled, Zhao Yunlan persisted, "But isn't Gonggong the God of Water? Who's this 'Mountain God of the Great Wild'? God of which mountain? I've never heard of Buzhou also having a Mountain God."

This time Shen Wei took even longer to reply, and his answer was vague. "Maybe it does have one? I don't know the details of things that happened back in those times."

Something in his voice told Zhao Yunlan to stop pressing. He fell silent, idly scratching his fingernail across his palm and occasionally tapping along to the beat of the song.

The song was long, and its lyrics dragged. It waxed on about Zhuanxu[9] and Gonggong's battle, and how Gonggong in a fit of rage had ultimately damaged public property by toppling Buzhou

9 *Zhuanxu (颛顼) was an emperor from Chinese mythology said to be the grandson of the Yellow Emperor.*

Mountain. The song seemed to attribute the current natural order, with the sun rising in the east and setting in the west, entirely to this rude act of vandalism. It gave the strong impression that this story was significant to the origin of the yao, but the lyrics never actually explained the connection.

Plenty of historical records were incomplete, forcing people to read between the lines and deduce that there were "other factors at play"; that was inevitably even more true of ancient and unreliable things like legends and myths from the beginning of time. Zhao Yunlan knew he shouldn't read too much into a few old lyrics, but he couldn't help himself. Some tiny voice in his heart was absolutely insistent that those seemingly unrelated things were actually tremendously significant.

The thing that particularly nagged at him was this "Mountain God of the Great Wild." Zhao Yunlan had never heard of primordial gods fulfilling multiple roles at once, so if Gonggong was the Water God, he obviously couldn't also be this "Mountain God" whom the yao seemed to regard as just one step below the three sages.

In myths, mountain gods were always minor deities on about the same level as the local lords of the land.[10] What kind of random country bumpkin official had managed to leave behind such a lasting legacy?

Zhao Yunlan's tapping fingertip stilled. The crow yao's words sprang to mind, especially one term in particular: Kunlun.

Kunlun Mountain!

After endless, pointless formalities, the yao finally finished their worship and sat back down. Beautiful female yao walked through the crowd, offering tea and drinks. The Yao Banquet had officially begun. Shen Wei refused any alcohol with the excuse

10 *Lords of the land (土地公) are minor deities who oversee a specific area of land.*

that he was driving. He waited until Zhao Yunlan had had a cup before saying, "Shall we take our leave now?"

Zhao Yunlan didn't know why he was in such a rush but also saw no point in staying any longer. He nodded and was about to stand up when there was a sudden commotion among the gathered yao.

He turned to listen. "What's happening?"

Shen Wei glanced at what was unfolding on the stage. "That snake pushed a half-yao man onto the stage. The half-yao's innate yao energy is spilling out of him. He's covered in a black aura and reeks of blood, so he must be riddled with sin. To keep heavenly retribution from affecting others when it strikes him, the yao are probably going to deal with him first, in accordance with tradition."

Had Guo Changcheng been there, he would have recognized this half-yao man as the one he'd nearly run over the other day.

This was an affair that didn't involve them, so Zhao Yunlan lost interest. While Fourth Uncle recited the person's crimes, Zhao Yunlan held out his arm to Shen Wei and allowed himself to be led away.

But then, having finished the litany of crimes, Fourth Uncle's declaration continued. "This half-yao of the Crow tribe has gone astray and caused great harm to many in defiance of the Heavens. In humility, we acknowledge the wrongs of one of our own; humbly do we enact the justice of the Heavens..."

At the words "Crow tribe," Zhao Yunlan and Shen Wei both stopped dead in their tracks.

At the same moment, a painfully hoarse voice rang out and interrupted Fourth Uncle. "Hold it!" Some note in that voice sounded inexplicably ominous.

Shen Wei pulled Zhao Yunlan behind him, gaze growing cold. A line of short, unremarkable-looking people in black robes stood in a neat row across the entrance to the Yao Market. Every one of them had pitch-black wings on their backs.

The Crow tribe had arrived.

CHAPTER 13

"SHEN WEI!" Zhao Yunlan grabbed Shen Wei's wrist. Even blind, there was no missing the piercing-cold killing intent that was suddenly radiating from him.

When Shen Wei spoke, his voice held no trace of his usual refinement. Instead, it was dark and ominous. "How dare the Crow tribe harm you? Wretched, ungrateful things! Even death by a thousand cuts or their total extinction could never make up for—"

Every syllable dripped with bloodlust, but his seething was broken off when Zhao Yunlan wrapped both arms around him. Instinctively, Shen Wei began to struggle fiercely, but then inspiration struck Zhao Yunlan.

"Xiao-Wei!" he exclaimed. Shen Wei went utterly still in his arms.

After a moment, Shen Wei turned and gave Zhao Yunlan a disbelieving look. Voice trembling, he said, "Wh-what did you call me...?"

"Shhh. Listen to me. Don't move." Zhao Yunlan closed his eyes and opened his Heavenly Eye. His perception through it had become a bit blurry, overwhelmed by the Yao Market surrounding them. He tugged Shen Wei slightly back, and the two of them blended into the crowd of yao.

Shen Wei's mind was in complete disarray. In his outburst, a tiny clue had slipped out, clearly unintentionally. But Zhao Yunlan latched onto it at once. *What had he meant by "ungrateful"?*

What connection did he, Zhao Yunlan, have to the Crow tribe—or rather, to all the yao?

An ancient saying sprang to mind: "If misfortune descends from the heavens, the crows are the first to know."

So what had the Black Crow tribe "known first" this time?

Fourth Uncle nodded politely to the group of crows and said calmly, "I thought the Crow tribe wasn't planning to attend."

The Crow tribe elder was a woman. Other than the half-yao man, every member of their tribe was short, with large noses and deeply wrinkled faces. There was no telling young from old or beautiful from ugly. The elder's eyes were a little crooked and made her seem as though she could be looking elsewhere, but her gaze might also have swept unintentionally across Zhao Yunlan, a reserved spark shining from her cloudy eyes.

She slammed her staff against the ground, and when she raised her hand again, the ropes binding the half-yao fell off. "Child, come here."

Fourth Uncle tucked his hands into his sleeves and made no move to stop him. The Yao Market was suddenly full of muttering.

The half-yao man had nearly stumbled off the stage when Fourth Uncle slowly said, "If the elder wishes to take away her own people, it's not my place to stand in her way. But does this indicate that the Crow tribe wishes to part ways with the rest of the yao and stand alone?"

Hoarsely, the Crow tribe elder answered, "That's right!"

A wave of whispers swept across the crowd. The little yao exchanged looks. Even Winter Jasmine peeked out from the vines wrapped around the bridge and peered at the others, completely lost.

Calmly, Fourth Uncle said, "No matter how much rotten flesh you eat, or how many dealings you have with white bone and the dead, the Crows will always be yao. You are neither reapers nor ghost immortals. Words may easily slip through your lips, Elder, but you'd better consider consequences carefully."

The laugh that burst from the Crow tribe elder was harsh and heavy. It was unclear whether it was born of anger or glee, but it was thick with grief, indignation, and ridicule passed down from the dawn of time. "If Lord Fourth didn't hear me clearly, let me repeat myself. We, the Black Crow tribe, are severing ourselves from the throngs of the yao. From this day forward, we are our only family, and we will never look back."

Winter Jasmine cried out in shock. "Crow Elder!"

Fourth Uncle held her back.

With a sweep of her arm, the Crow elder prompted the Crow tribe to leave as they had come: in a single dark mass that moved too swiftly for anyone to react.

The crowd's whispering became an uproar.

Fourth Uncle waved his arm, and the little monkey with the gong banged on it heavily a few times, scolding the chaotic crowd. During the upheaval, Zhao Yunlan pulled Shen Wei out of the crowd of yao and the two of them quickly left the Yao Market.

Following the stone-slab road from the entrance all the way to its end, they found a cloud of mist. They stepped through the mist, and on the other side, they were greeted by the bright neon lights of Dragon City, with its broad streets and small alleyways.

A row of crows had landed on the large pagoda tree at the mouth of Antiques Street. As a taxi swept by, its talkative driver said to his passenger, "Look, even the crows are celebrating Lunar New Year!"

The black cat silently prowled out from a corner, paw pads lightly brushing the ground before he leapt nimbly up onto the wall.

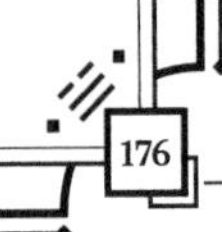

Dozens of crows simultaneously snapped their heads around to peer at him. The rows of tiny scarlet eyes shone like inauspicious light bulbs.

Daqing stopped ten steps away and didn't approach, to show he had no ill intent.

The Crow tribe elder took a step forward and asked bluntly, "To what do we owe the pleasure?"

The black cat's dark green eyes were just like a pair of genuine cat's-eye quartz. Their corners were slightly raised, and their depths held an eerie glimmer. In that moment, he was the epitome of the lazy elegance unique to felines. One could almost forget that he was a furry sphere of a cat.

"If I may be so bold," Daqing said with tremendous courtesy, "I've come seeking an answer, Elder. How did the bell I lost centuries ago come to be in your tribe's hands?"

The Crow tribe elder studied him coldly. "My Black Crow tribe are harbingers of tragedy, never joy. We are never found among the living, only the dead. Why ask such a pointless question? Where do you suppose we might have acquired it other than from one of the dead?"

Daqing's body tensed for a second, but he pressed on. "Where and when did that person die? Of what cause?"

The Crow tribe elder laughed. "Once someone is dead, they're dead. Once he goes through the cycle of reincarnation, his previous life is already over. In this life, who knows? He might be a dog or a pig. Why do you care when and where he died?"

Daqing lowered his head slightly and said nothing.

The Crow tribe elder shared his silence for a moment, then said, with a touch of impatience, "A pavilion ten kilometers outside

Shanhai Pass. Go take a look if you feel so inclined. Don't say I kept things hidden from you. You don't think carrying around a dead person's bell is unlucky?"

At her whistle, the large murder of crows shot skyward, flying toward the ink-dark horizon.

Daqing stood there in the darkness, head down, for some time. He suddenly looked like a desolate stray cat. It wasn't until a car's headlights flashed in his direction that he jumped down silently from the wall and disappeared into the night.

With one blink of the Torch Dragon's eyes, a day and night passed by. In no time at all, it was Lunar New Year's Eve.

On Lunar New Year's Eve, all the lights were on at the Special Investigations Department. The humans feasted while the ghosts savored incense and spirit money. With great joy, lao-Wu from the gatehouse and his daytime colleague with the penchant for carving bones were finally able to be together. Lao-Wu happily toasted lao-Li with a stick of incense, and the other man returned the toast with alcohol in a bone china cup. Lao-Li always seemed to have a nearly unhealthy obsession when it came to bones.

Toward the latter half of the night, after the New Year's bell had already rung, drunk humans and ghosts alike started to run wild. Guo Changcheng flopped down on the table, sobbing loudly for some reason. After he finished crying, he tucked himself into a little corner and ignored everyone, meticulously polishing his work ID over and over with a microfiber cloth. Finally, he rolled under the table and fell into a deep sleep.

Chu Shuzhi, Lin Jing, Zhu Hong, and Daqing were gathered at a mahjong table. Other people's chips automatically became dried fish when they arrived in front of Daqing. The cat's expression was deadly serious. He had no choice but to keep winning, having eaten almost all his chips.

Lao-Li pulled a giant femur from out of nowhere and started pole dancing in front of everyone. Sangzan grabbed Wang Zheng's hand, pulling her unexpectedly into his arms. He held her waist and lifted her up high; she laughed, humming a little tune from a faraway time, and danced a Hanga tribe dance with him.

Zhao Yunlan, having already gone through a round of drinks with everyone, couldn't quite sit steadily. The Flower Yao's Nectar of a Thousand Essences had proved to be as miraculous as he'd hoped. His vision had already started to return, although it was still a bit blurry, as if he were severely nearsighted. Despite being unable to distinguish between six dots and nine dots on the mahjong tiles, he still squinted determinedly and ignored his current disability. With his face pressed close to the table, he was backseat driving Daqing. "Pung, pung, pung!"

Daqing shoved him with a paw. "Pung, your ass! Shen-laoshi, hurry and lead this noisy donkey away—four bamboo!"

"Sorry, I win," said Zhu Hong.

Disappointed, Zhao Yunlan smacked Daqing in the head. "See? If you don't listen to your elders, it comes back to bite you!"

Daqing's heart shattered as he lost custody of his dried fish. Furious, he roared, "Hurry and drag him away!"

Shen Wei obligingly dragged Zhao Yunlan away. In his hands, a full-grown man or a fifty-kilogram lacquer box seemed equally weightless, as easy to carry around as a thin old book.

Despite her best efforts, Zhu Hong didn't manage to be inconspicuous as she dropped her eyes to avoid his gaze.

Shen Wei took a seat and let Zhao Yunlan lie down and use his thigh as a pillow. He gently massaged Zhao Yunlan's temples. "Close your eyes. They haven't fully recovered, so don't strain them trying to see. You'll overwhelm yourself."

Zhao Yunlan shut his eyes, completely blissed out. Voice muffled, he said, "Can you warm me another cup of liquor?"

But Shen Wei was clearly a little distracted and didn't hear.

Zhao Yunlan looked at him again. Through his blurry vision, he saw that Shen Wei was spacing out, gaze drifting to the corner of the table. Astute as he was, Zhao Yunlan understood at once. He reached up and gave Shen Wei's collar a tug. "What, are you nervous about meeting the in-laws?"

Attention returning to the conversation, Shen Wei didn't bother denying it. "All parents want their children to be safe and healthy for their entire lives. They hope their son will be happy and at peace with a *wife* and kids. Bringing me over like this... How can you deny your parents a good New Year?"

Shutting his eyes again, Zhao Yunlan grabbed Shen Wei's hand. Since his eyesight had started returning, his Heavenly Eye seemed to be affected by his physical ones, rendering him unable to see people's merits anymore. But he would always remember the text forming on Shen Wei and being wiped away with the mercilessness of the tides, drowned under a bottomless darkness.

"If I didn't invite you home with me, where would you spend Lunar New Year?"

"New Year or not, what difference does it—"

"Back on that side?" Zhao Yunlan interrupted. "Under the Huangquan, where there isn't even a single ray of light, with maybe a few passing spirits at best for company?"

Shen Wei pursed his lips. No, it was worse than that.

Not that Shen Wei had ever thought anything of it. He had lived thousands of years like that, each day exactly like the one before. But somehow, after hearing Zhao Yunlan put it that way, it suddenly struck him as unfair. He was long since accustomed to passing his days like that, but now a feeling washed over him: the feeling that he couldn't bear a single day more of it.

From the dawn of Chaos, when the spirits of all things came into being, to the present moment, the world had changed countless times and in countless ways. And yet Shen Wei still tenaciously honored the oath that had long since been forgotten by even the person he had sworn it to. His entire existence had been devoted to that single sentence.

Zhao Yunlan silently put Shen Wei's hand on his chest. Perhaps because of the alcohol, Zhao Yunlan's pulse was a little fast. After a while, when Shen Wei thought he was about to fall asleep, Zhao Yunlan quietly asked, "'Wei'... How did you come by that name?"

"It was originally the character Wei that's made up of 'mountain' and 'ghost.'" Shen Wei's gaze dropped, seeming to gaze right through the gleaming floor; there was no knowing how far into the past he was looking. "But someone once said to me that while 'mountain ghost' was fitting, it was perhaps naming me into a corner. He told me that in this world, the mountains and seas are all connected, and lofty peaks stretch out endlessly. He suggested, 'Why don't we add a few more strokes and make it a proper name?'"[11]

Zhao Yunlan touched his nose. This mysterious "someone" had a way of speaking that sounded rather familiar. "Who has the audacity to just randomly rename someone?"

---

11 *Wéi* (嵬) *is formed from the characters mountain* (山) *and ghost* (鬼), *while wēi* (巍) *has the added character wei* (委). Both characters mean large, tall, lofty, but 嵬 has a more uneven, craggy connotation while 巍 is more majestic and dignified.

Shen Wei smiled. "Just someone I met by chance on the road."

The conversation dropped off there. Dawn had just broken, and the entire street was filled with the cacophony of firecrackers. Inside, the mahjong players shouted at each other while little ghosts tried to avoid the light of sunrise.

The lively sight was blinding.

A small snowstorm pulled open the curtains on Dragon City's Lunar New Year. The world was at peace, and the spectacular lights dimmed for the first time this year.

Tens of thousands of families took their first breaths of the year through this auspicious first snow, the air tinged with the smell of gunpowder. The new year had begun and, once again, the Mortal Realm welcomed the countless new joys and griefs that awaited them.

On the first day of the Lunar New Year, the raucous celebration at 4 Bright Avenue finally ended around noon. Everyone bundled up in their coats, leaving one by one in a drunken daze, and lined up at the entrance for taxis.

Lao-Li, however, waited for everyone to leave before washing his face and getting out cleaning supplies from somewhere. Slowly, he began cleaning up the wreckage of the office. Daqing poked his head in, saw that the floor was a mess, and pulled his paws back, afraid of being roped into doing work. Lao-Li hurriedly pulled out a rag, wiped the chairs clean, and lined them up, then respectfully lifted the cat lord up to the chairs. "Walk up here. The chairs are clean."

"You're the only one left again. Kids these days, they're getting more and more disrespectful." Muttering like an old man, Daqing carefully jumped onto the desk from the chair.

"There's one left." Lao-Li pointed to the corner, where Daqing saw Guo Changcheng, who had just gotten up.

"Come here, kid. I was just looking for you." Daqing glared at Guo Changcheng and found a coaster on Zhu Hong's desk. He swiped the coaster away, revealing a red envelope containing gift cards. Picking it up with his teeth, he threw it right into Guo Changcheng's face and huffed, "Lao-Zhao wants you to take that to your second uncle. Tell him Director Zhao said that he won't be dropping by so that your uncle can fully enjoy one of his rare days off during the New Year. It's just a small New Year's gift, so your aunt and cousin can add a few new things to their wardrobes." Daqing spat. "Stupid humans, making me relay such disgusting words."

Guo Changcheng was dizzy with a headache, so it took him half a beat to react. When he finally remembered where he was, he smiled politely, carefully picked up the red envelope, and tucked it away. Then he looked back at lao-Li and saw him holding a mop. Guo Changcheng immediately rolled up his sleeves and headed over. "Li-ge! Let me help you! I'll—"

Mid-sentence, he tripped over a chair leg and fell on his face.

With a *hmph*, Daqing settled in front of a computer and turned it on with a paw. Wielding the mouse with the same paw, he opened a browser. It was no easy task.

When lao-Li saw, he hurried over to help. "What do you need to type?" he asked warmly. "I can help you."

"Shanhai—" Daqing began, but he cut himself short as the "hai" slipped out of his mouth and changed tone, sounding like "he." He clamped his mouth shut and stared expressionlessly at the screen for a while before looking down. "Oh—I mean, I want to go on Weibo."

Zhao Yunlan had said he had some "important business" to take care of and would be back a little later to pick Daqing up, so the cat had decided to pass his time in front of the computer. He logged into the "Lord Meow Number One in the World" account and started idly taking selfies with the webcam and uploading them. Meanwhile, lao-Li and xiao-Guo quietly dealt with the sad state of the office.

Earlier, Daqing had intended to say that he wanted to go to the pavilion about ten kilometers outside Shanhai Pass and see for himself what kind of place it was, but the Crow tribe elder was right. What good would seeing do? A dead person was dead. Ashes to ashes, dust to dust.

With a click of the camera, Daqing uploaded his large pancake face onto the web, captioned it "uniquely handsome meow," and posted it. In no time, cat lovers were littering the post with comments. Some praised the solid, pure color of his fur while others gave such friendly suggestions as, "OP, your cat's too fat. Please adjust its diet and make sure it gets more exercise so it can be healthy."

Daqing deleted the comment at the speed of light. Indignant, he thought, *You're the fat one, stupid human.*

The bell on his neck jostled as he moved, but it didn't make a sound. Now and then, a golden glint would bounce off it onto the snow-white walls. Lao-Li couldn't help raising a hand to block the blinding light. He glanced back at the black cat, who seemed to be in low spirits. He was just about to say something when Chu Shuzhi walked out of the wall.

Normally, Chu Shuzhi was barred from the library, but he was allowed inside once a year, on the first day of the Lunar New Year. However, it didn't look like he had borrowed any books or read anything this time. Furthermore, there was something deeply strange about his expression: he looked a little haggard, but also somehow derisive.

Guo Changcheng perked up at once. "Chu-ge!"

He didn't seem to hear. He picked up his bag with a smile that bordered on icy and headed for the exit. Daqing peeked out from behind the monitor and, seemingly out of nowhere, asked, "How many years has it been?"

Chu Shuzhi's footsteps paused. "Exactly three hundred," he said, voice rough.

"Ah! Then… Hmm, is it time for congratulations?" asked Daqing.

In response, Chu Shuzhi abruptly took out a pitch-black wooden plaque. Without even looking back, he raised his hand and shook the plaque in front of the cat.

Guo Changcheng had to wonder if his eyes were playing tricks on him. It looked for all the world as if text had flashed across Chu Shuzhi's face, right on his cheek, like the tattoos convicts had been forced to bear in ancient times.

Daqing's ears pricked up, and his eyes widened.

Chu Shuzhi held the plaque so fiercely that his fingers turned blue. Prominent veins popped out on the back of his hand. Then, without a word, he stalked out.

Immediately turning to Guo Changcheng, Daqing said, "Xiao-Guo, get a taxi and see your Chu-ge home!"

Guo Changcheng had only the faintest idea of what was going on. Daqing spoke again, even more sternly. "He had too much to drink. Make sure you take him home. You can't come back until you've gotten him home and made sure he's absolutely fine, do you hear me?"

Pulling out a tissue to wipe his hands, Guo Changcheng jogged out after Chu Shuzhi and grabbed his bag from him. It was as though Chu Shuzhi had lost his soul. He just let Guo Changcheng take what was in his hands with absolutely no reaction. From behind, he was extremely skinny—practically just skin and bones.

Shen Wei had only just left with Zhao Yunlan, who was thoroughly drunk, when the beer-bellied supervisor at DCU unexpectedly called to say he needed a file urgently. Shen Wei was somewhat confused, but before he could ask for more details, his supervisor said goodbye and hung up with a speed that suggested his ass was on fire.

With Zhao Yunlan stuck to him like a barnacle, Shen Wei had little choice but to head to his own frigid apartment. They'd barely gotten in the door when his supervisor called yet again to tell Shen Wei to bring the file to the university's west entrance.

Zhao Yunlan rolled around on the soft sofa, then cracked his eyes open. Still a little bleary from the booze, he said, "On the first day of Lunar New Year? What's that fatty's problem?"

Shen Wei was multitasking, looking for the requested file with one hand while cushioning Zhao Yunlan's head with the other to keep him from banging it on the coffee table. File found, he tucked a cushion behind Zhao Yunlan's head. "I'll be back soon. You—"

"I need to take a nap." Zhao Yunlan's voice was nearly as sticky as his eyelids.

Voice low, Shen Wei asked, "Do you want some water?"

"Mm..." Zhao Yunlan turned his head away, batting at his hands. "No."

Zhao Yunlan's eyes seemed to glisten. His lips were a vivid red, and his long brows slanted up toward his hair. With his head slightly raised, the line of his jaw was stretched taut; his unbuttoned shirt showed off a long, impossibly attractive throat.

Shen Wei's breath hitched. He carefully smoothed back the stray hairs on Zhao Yunlan's forehead before pulling a blanket over him.

He gently caressed Zhao Yunlan's lips with his thumb. Despite his reluctance to leave, he finally leaned down and kissed Zhao Yunlan's forehead, then grabbed the file his supervisor wanted as well as his car keys and headed out.

A little while later, Zhao Yunlan heard the sound of the door being carefully opened and shut.

And then Zhao Yunlan, who had been apparently too drunk to walk straight just moments earlier, sat up like a reanimated corpse. He took out his phone and texted "keep him busy for a while," then called a moving company he had already been in touch with.

The mover had never received such a weird job before, and was hesitant. "I—If the owner isn't here, shouldn't we..."

"There's no 'we.' Hurry and get this stuff outta here," Zhao Yunlan commanded. "He's going to end up on my household register sooner or later. Am I supposed to have two addresses in the same household register? Just looking at all his single-use belongings pisses me off. Be here in five minutes, got it?!"

Zhao Yunlan hung up, took a pad of sticky notes from his bag, and quickly started making two lists: the things to be moved and the things he planned to throw out and replace for Shen Wei. Then his pen paused as an incredibly perverted thought took root: *Where does Shen Wei keep his underwear? Especially the ones he's already worn?*

He had recently managed to force Shen Wei to reluctantly stay with him in his tiny apartment, but in the process, he had wound up maintaining the excellent tradition of "starting from affection while restrained by etiquette." During his half month of blindness, despite his ulterior motives, Zhao Yunlan hadn't quite managed to obtain his heart's desire. He spent his days and nights under the same roof as his beloved, but he could neither see nor consume him. It was a heroic feat of cultivation both physically and mentally;

he felt as though he was on the verge of being able to take a monk's ascetic vows.

"You drove me to this." Zhao Yunlan rubbed his hands together and went out on Shen Wei's balcony. It might have been because Shen Wei hadn't stayed there in a long time, but the clothes hangers that were still on the balcony were empty. Zhao Yunlan didn't give up. He opened the huge wardrobe in the living room only to find it contained the shirts and pants Shen Wei normally wore but nothing else. There weren't even any socks.

Zhao Yunlan's eyesight was still recovering, so he didn't see the little storage bin in the wardrobe, covered by a long trench coat. Undeterred, he turned his sights to Shen Wei's bedroom, which was always closed. Upon inspection, the bedroom door didn't have a handle, nor an obvious lock. Zhao Yunlan got out a little flashlight and shone it into the crack of the door but couldn't find a hinge or any hidden locks. It got weirder by the minute.

Trying to figure things out, Zhao Yunlan pressed his palms to the door and looked at it with his Heavenly Eye. Finally, something was revealed: faint patterns on the door. Within the pitch-black wood, some sort of energy seemed to be flowing. It was gentle and just, tight and meticulous; it carried an unspeakable aura of magnificent dignity.

Zhao Yunlan kept feeling around, and then suddenly, there was a surge of familiarity. He found himself mumbling, "The Lock of Kunlun?"

Recently, while keeping it secret from everyone, he had been researching Kunlun with Sangzan's help. But other than the fact that Kunlun Mountain was incredible and ancient, and that some odd schools of thought, concepts, and inventions had named themselves after Kunlun, he hadn't found anything useful.

The Lock of Kunlun was described in a book he'd happened to skim through. According to legend, the Lock was round on top and square on the bottom, with the circle representing the Heavens and the square representing earth. In between were fourteen lock latches representing the six directions and eight compass points.[12] It was so old that it predated the sixty-four hexagrams; there was only the concept of yin and yang, which made it all the more bizarre, unpredictable, and hard to grasp.

What was in Shen Wei's bedroom that needed the Lock of Kunlun?

Or rather...what was the connection between the Soul-Executing Emissary and Kunlun? Why was Shen Wei so familiar with such an ancient seal?

Zhao Yunlan hesitated in front of the door for a moment longer. Then he reached out tentatively, concentrating on his palm and carefully guiding his power, and flicked the Kunlun Lock. The Lock was immediately activated. The fourteen latches rose, one after another, yin and yang coexisting.

At first, it was almost overwhelming. Zhao Yunlan had too many thoughts, messy and unrefined, and sometimes his imagination was too far-ranging. Generally speaking, he didn't share Chu Shuzhi's talent with such detailed things. But for some reason, faced with the Kunlun Lock, he felt an innate familiarity. It was as if he could see every change, as if every shifting latch corresponded precisely to some natural rhythm of his heart.

His fingers danced across the door as though someone were guiding his hand.

---

12 *The eight compass points and six directions (八荒六合) represent all of space. The eight compass points are: north, northeast, east, southeast, south, southwest, west, and northwest. The six directions are: above, below, left, right, forward, and behind.*

The sun and moon rise and fall, thus completing the cycle. Follow the thirty-six pillars until...

With a click, the utterly black door slowly swung inward, just the tiniest crack. The door was open, and the room beyond was completely devoid of light.

Suddenly hesitant, Zhao Yunlan stood at the doorway. He was beginning to regret opening the door at all. But the fact remained that it *was* open, so after a bit of pacing, he turned on his phone's flashlight and carefully ventured inside.

A subtle, ancient fragrance of ink drifted through the room, along with the scent of paper. And the walls were covered in... paintings?

Zhao Yunlan raised his phone, squinting hard at his surroundings, and stood stunned by what he saw.

The paintings covered every inch of the walls. Large and small, depicting anger or laughter, they were all the same person. Zhao Yunlan's hands trembled so violently that his phone nearly fell to the floor. The last trace of tipsiness evaporated.

Eventually, the beam of light made its way to an ancient ink painting on the southern wall. It was huge, nearly occupying the entire wall on its own. The paper was as thin as a cicada's wing, the surface as smooth as snow...and like all the others, it was a painting of a person.

The person was drawn with delicate brows and an almost lifelike expression. His long hair reached the ground, and he wore the simplest green robe imaginable. His head was tilted slightly, lips curved in the faintest hint of a smile. The brushwork was so vivid that it seemed the man might step out of the painting at any moment...and it was clearly none other than Zhao Yunlan himself!

Along the edge of the painting was a small line of text. It wasn't modern simplified or traditional Chinese. In fact, it wasn't any sort of writing he was familiar with. Zhao Yunlan had never laid eyes on it before. And yet, somehow, one quick look told him exactly what it said:

Laying eyes on Kunlun-jun for the first time, in the shades of the grove. A single fleeting glance and the melody of my heart faltered.
By Wei.

Was...was *he*, Zhao Yunlan, the Mountain God of the Great Wild...?

Ten minutes later, the movers knocked on the door of Shen Wei's apartment, and a weird man stepped out.

Without a single word of explanation, he told them that the move wasn't happening. Then he got out his wallet, paid the moving fees anyway, and said to consider it his apology for making them come all that way for nothing.

The moment Shen Wei laid eyes on his supervisor, he knew someone had deliberately lured him out. His heart sank. As soon as the man turned away, Shen Wei struck his shoulder heavily from behind. In an arctic tone, he demanded, "Who told you to summon me?"

The oppressive authority in his voice suppressed his supervisor's soul within his body, rendering him unable to move. The man's eyes went absolutely empty, as if he were nothing but a soulless meat suit. His blank gaze was fixed straight ahead.

Shen Wei added more pressure through his hand. "Speak!" he commanded.

No secrets could be kept when faced with the Soul-Executing Blade, which could discern right from wrong, kindness from evil. Shen Wei watched as his supervisor seemed to slip further away by the second, unable to say anything. He understood that this mortal's memory had been tampered with.

Shen Wei left without a backward glance, anxious fury filling his mind with hundreds of possible scenarios. He was, after all, a gentleman. It could never have crossed his mind that someone might go to such lengths to lure him away just to move his belongings and steal a couple pairs of underwear.

He raced back to his own apartment. When he flung the door open and found no one in the living room, icy dread gripped his heart.

As he stood frozen in the doorway, an uncontrollable desire to kill boiled up inside him. The urge awakened like a vast dragon that had lain dormant for countless years, jarred into wakefulness by an assault on its weak spot. Ever since Zhao Yunlan's eyes had been injured due to Shen Wei's own carelessness, a string in his heart had been stretched taut, and now the sight of the empty living room threatened to snap it.

Shen Wei's eyes grew red, but at that moment, the sound of a voice on the balcony brought him back to himself. With tremendous effort, he just barely managed to snap out of it. Moving faster than the eye could see, he was out on the balcony at once.

Zhao Yunlan was leaning on the windowsill of the enclosed balcony, smoking lazily as he cursed into the phone. "...I don't want stone. Marble is too ugly... I know... What? White marble? I'm not fucking renovating the Forbidden Palace! Listen, just do the job properly and well, and I'll give you whatever rebate you're owed as a bonus—not one cent less, all right? Just don't turn my house into a karaoke bar. But I swear, if you dare fuck with me, you're dead..."

Shen Wei's heart, which had leapt into his throat, thudded heavily back into his chest. That was when he realized he had actually broken out in a cold sweat. Even his palms were clammy.

Zhao Yunlan heard the noise, tilted his head, and saw him. He immediately broke into a big grin. To the person on the other end of the phone, he said, "Enough bickering about all this crap. Just make sure you use nontoxic materials... I still need to live in the place. I don't wanna feel like I'm trudging through a biochemical warzone, with the stink of formaldehyde lingering for hundreds of years—okay, enough talk. I'm hanging up."

He stubbed out his cigarette and leaned against the windowsill, spreading his arms wide. In a smarmy, provocative voice, he said, "C'mere, babe. Come give your husband a hug."

Teasing Shen Wei had already become a habit. Most of the time, Shen Wei ignored it, but this time, he walked over and swept Zhao Yunlan into his arms. Burying his face in the dip of Zhao Yunlan's shoulder, he slipped his arms around Zhao Yunlan's waist, pulling him away from the windowsill and closing the window. "Don't you know it's cold out?"

Zhao Yunlan stretched his shoulders, then contentedly rested his chin on Shen Wei's shoulder. The warmth coming from Shen Wei's body and hands made him close his eyes in satisfaction. A hint of a subtle, peaceful smile spread across his face, like a big cat that had eaten and drunk its fill.

Shen Wei felt that he was acting a little strange. "What's wrong?"

"Nothing." The word seemed to roll around and around in his mouth before he spoke it aloud. He studied Shen Wei's profile, mere centimeters away, then said, expression unchanging,

"I'm overwhelmed and flattered to have gained the favor of a great beauty. Of course, if I'm allowed a taste of these sweet lips, I'll be even more lost."

While Shen Wei was processing that, Zhao Yunlan gave him a quick peck on the lips, then nimbly broke free before Shen Wei could react. "Let me wash my face and sober up. Then we can go pick up Daqing, and I'll take you home."

Zhao Yunlan didn't breathe a word about the Lock of Kunlun or anything else he had seen in that bedroom.

Zhao Yunlan and Daqing had fully intended to go home empty-handed, bringing nothing but their mouths. Shen Wei, on the other hand, wasn't shameless enough to freeload. So Zhao Yunlan, who couldn't stop yawning, found himself dragged out shopping while Shen Wei bought heaps of New Year's gifts.

The closer they got to Zhao Yunlan's family home, the more nervous Shen Wei became. If he weren't a gentleman of his word, he might very well have made his escape long before this point.

Zhao Yunlan's parents lived in a luxury apartment. Its sheer size made it seem a bit cold and lacking in cheer. When they walked in, the pair could only faintly hear the sounds of activity in the kitchen. Two brand-new pairs of slippers were waiting for them just inside the front door.

Daqing jumped down from Zhao Yunlan's arms, padded over to the kitchen door, and gave an adorable meow.

As Zhao Yunlan changed into slippers, he muttered, "You old-ass cat, still putting on a cute act—don't you have any shame?"

Daqing glowered fiercely over his shoulder.

"Oh, is that Daqing?" A woman's gentle voice came from the

kitchen. She came out, dusting the flour off her hands, and scooped the black cat up. "Look how sleek and shiny you are! And how do you keep getting fatter and fatter?"

Daqing, mortally wounded, rested his fat paws on the lady of the house's hands, purring as though he had been wronged.

Zhao Yunlan's mom took good care of herself. Her long hair was pulled back, displaying a long neck. At a glance, Zhao Yunlan didn't resemble her very much, but upon closer inspection, there was a vague shadow of her in his brows. But the lines of her face were gentle and refined, so even when she wasn't smiling, it appeared as though she was. All of this combined with the glasses perched on her nose to make her look like one of those mild, beautiful, well-educated upper-class ladies from ancient times.

Fathers and sons do often have somewhat similar tastes in partners, after all.

But when this "upper-class lady" laid eyes on Zhao Yunlan, her expression transformed. She almost seemed to sprout fangs. "What are you laughing about? Aren't you scared your mouth will spring a leak from laughing so hard? Get your ass in here!"

Zhao Yunlan obediently got his ass in there.

As he moved out of the way, his mother finally got a look at Shen Wei and froze. Recovering quickly, she rinsed the remaining flour off her hands and pushed her glasses up before saying, every bit the gracious hostess, "Ah, you must be xiao-Shen?"

Zhao Yunlan casually put an arm around Shen Wei's shoulders and pushed him toward her. "Didn't I find you a lovely daughter-in-law?"

Shen Wei was too embarrassed to speak.

But given Zhao Yunlan's habit of spewing sheer nonsense, his mom didn't take him seriously at all. When she saw the load Shen

Wei was carrying, she said, "Oh, you sweetheart. When you come to eat at auntie's house, you don't need to bring anything but yourself."

"It was all me!" Zhao Yunlan pointed at his own nose. "Me! I bought that."

His mom grabbed her rolling pin and swung it at him as if by habit. "You? Buying? If you had that kind of awareness, I could have died peacefully ages ago. Go pour some water for our guest and then come roll out dumpling skins for me! All you know to do is come home right at dinnertime, just in time to be fed!"

With his back floured from the rolling pin, Zhao Yunlan dared not say a word of protest. "...Oh."

Shen Wei gingerly took a seat, his spine ramrod straight.

In the kitchen, Zhao Yunlan's lack of skill was earning him whacks from the rolling pin for his uneven and misshapen dumpling skins. He shrugged and bore it, only half trying to dodge, and quietly pleaded, "Can you spare me some dignity in front of him?"

"All you do is eat!" his mother scolded. "You don't do a thing. There are 365 days in a year and you barely come home once. What's the point in raising you? You think you have any dignity? Get out of the way!"

Zhao Yunlan moved out of her way with a smile, but he didn't leave the kitchen. He watched her flit busily about, then stole a look around. "Where's the maid who usually cooks for you? And where's Dad? How come the family beauty's the only one home today?"

"She went home for the New Year, and your dad has a work thing tonight."

"Good." Zhao Yunlan let out a sigh of relief, then lowered his voice. "If Dad knew about this, he'd beat me to death."

She glanced back at him. "What did you do this time?"

"Nothing, really." Zhao Yunlan's gaze drifted sideways toward the chopstick holder. His vision still hadn't fully recovered, so he squinted subconsciously. Keeping a close eye on his mother's expression, he tentatively began, "It's just..." Then he sighed. "Mom, how do you feel about gay people?"

She clearly didn't make the connection. "Their sexuality is becoming more socially accepted these days. Why? We're talking about your treasonous crimes here. Don't change the subject."

"That *is* my treasonous crime," Zhao Yunlan said honestly. "Don't be all technical about it. I wanted to ask what you'd do if one day your son came out of the closet."

"If you want to keep bullshitting, you can—"

"Mom." He cut her off and fixed her with an unusually intent look. "I'm serious. This isn't a joke."

The rolling pin hit the floor as her hands went slack. She stared at him blankly.

Zhao Yunlan sighed again and bent down to retrieve the rolling pin. The tension in his back was faintly visible through his shirt. "I'm afraid Dad won't be able to accept it, so I'm telling you first. I've thought it over, and I can't hide it or put off telling you. You're the only mom I've got."

She still seemed dumbfounded. Finally, stumbling over her words, she said, "Is he... The man you brought with you, is he..."

Zhao Yunlan nodded. He had both hands on the door, as though blocking it with his body. "I, your son, spent over half a year doing everything I could—cajoling and lying, consulting all thirty-six stratagems and seventy-two transformations... I used every trick I know. It would've been easier to start an uprising. And now he's finally, *finally* mine. If you feel like you need to kill or maim someone, come at me, but please don't go out there and ruin all my hard work. It'll break my heart."

To an onlooker, it would've appeared as though her soul had left her body. Her eyes far away, Zhao Yunlan's mother began robotically wrapping dumplings without another word.

"Mom?"

His voice didn't reach her. For a minute or two she was simply in a daze, completely unaware of what she was doing or what she had just heard. She was on autopilot.

Suddenly, after Zhao Yunlan's repeated attempts to talk to her, she snapped out of it. Words began tumbling from her mouth before she could think. "What about your job? Will people gossip about you? What about your future? That's right, I... I think your dad said you bought a house a few days ago. Do you still have money?"

Zhao Yunlan blinked, not at all sure how she'd jumped from him coming out to him not having money. If there was any logic there, he couldn't see it. It seemed like she'd latched on to a few key terms and strung them into random sentences, and they all rushed out at once.

His mother was a highly educated intellectual who had never needed to worry about the mundane, daily necessities. His father had always doted on her so much that she didn't really have any worries or anxieties to deal with. As a result, she'd always been easygoing and accepting. Considering that, Zhao Yunlan's coming-out strategy had been simple and straightforward: if his mom came around and accepted it, his dad would follow suit.

He had imagined many possible ways she might take the news. He'd supposed she might get angry and be unable to accept it at first, but then after calming down, perhaps she'd suggest they take a few hours and have a proper chat. Alternatively, like many other mothers, she might have turned into a census-taker and started asking after Shen Wei's family tree. But Zhao Yunlan hadn't expected this half-panicked, frightened reaction, perhaps because he himself had never been a parent.

He opened his mouth but had no idea what to say.

Eventually, she calmed down a little. Chopsticks in hand, she paused and asked, "Are you fooling around, or have you really thought this through?"

"How could I fool around about something like this? If you got too upset and something were to happen to you, Dad would stew me for dinner."

Lost, she slowly leaned to the side. More time passed before she finally said, very quietly, "Don't... Don't mention it to your father just yet. Let me think about it some more. What kind of person is this man? What does he do?"

Before Zhao Yunlan could respond, she pinched her brow firmly. "Oh, that's right. You already told me he's a professor at Dragon City University. Where's his family from? Is his family okay with this? What's his character like? Does he have a good personality? Does he treat you well? You've had so many girlfriends before, so how come all of a sudden..."

"If we have your blessing, no one under the sun would dare disagree. Dad has to look to you, now, doesn't he? As for what Shen Wei is like..." Zhao Yunlan smiled. "To me, it's like people say: he's like 'the finest polished jade, completely unique.' Once you talk to him, you'll understand. And yes, I've had girlfriends, but I've been with two guys before too. Though for him, I'll kiss every trace of straightness goodbye."

Parents often feel moved as well as delighted when they see someone deeply in love with their child, but when it's the other way around, they have mixed feelings. Zhao Yunlan's mom, currently in the mixed-feelings stage, huffily said, "Oh, please. Like I'd believe that."

Zhao Yunlan's expression didn't change, but his heart started creeping up into his throat...until his mother added, "If he's as great as you say, how could he fall for you? Can he see a thing with those glasses?"

Chapter 14

CHU SHUZHI got into the taxi, gave an address, and leaned back in the seat without another word, eyes firmly closed.

The whole way, Guo Changcheng snuck peeks at him, unable to shake the impression that Chu-ge's face was covered in a layer of gray. Guo Changcheng accompanied him the entire ride, and when they arrived at their destination, it wasn't until Chu Shuzhi had gotten out of the car that Guo Changcheng realized he was still holding Chu Shuzhi's bag. He hurried to catch up. "Chu-ge! Your bag!"

He accepted the bag without even lifting his eyes. "Mmn. You can go now."

Chu Shuzhi's house was in a very deep alleyway that formed a wind tunnel. Bitter wind swept under Chu Shuzhi's collar, inflating his wide jacket until it seemed he might be blown away.

Keeping Daqing's instructions at the front of his mind, Guo Changcheng followed Chu Shuzhi's every step. Chu Shuzhi's brow furrowed. "I said you. Can. *Go*. Did you not understand?"

Nervously, Guo Changcheng said, "Daqing told me to take you home. I can't leave until I'm sure you're safely inside..."

Chu Shuzhi stopped walking. Pinning Guo Changcheng with a vicious glare, in a voice that promised suffering, he said, "You? Take *me* home? Don't you know I'm not human?"

An "ah" escaped Guo Changcheng, as if he were intimidated, but when Chu Shuzhi turned and resumed walking, he once again heard footsteps behind him. Would nothing stop the young idiot?!

Wheeling around, Chu Shuzhi closed the distance between them. He made no effort to conceal his musty, sinister energy, which overwhelmed Guo Changcheng. Two fangs were visible between his narrow lips. "Do you know what human flesh tastes like? It's both smooth and rich on the tongue. The cartilage cracks between your teeth. The organs are pungent, and when you pull them out of the abdomen, they're still steaming hot."

Expression full of malice, he stared straight into Guo Changcheng's horrified face as he swept his tongue over his lips. "Do you know how I know? Because I'm a zombie that eats humans."

Guo Changcheng shuddered. His courage must surely have been cut off at birth along with his umbilical cord. He was afraid of everything, so how could he not fear the unpredictable Chu Shuzhi? But in this secluded, quiet alleyway, even as he looked at Chu Shuzhi's fangs and found it all too easy to picture them stained with blood, the appropriate fear just never came.

In fact, the thought that flashed through his mind was incredibly bizarre: *No wonder Chu-ge doesn't eat peas.*

Sure that he'd finally terrified Guo Changcheng, Chu Shuzhi snorted and resumed walking...yet astonishingly, Guo Changcheng seemed to have finally found his courage and was once again following him!

"What, are you going to follow a zombie into his coffin?" he demanded.

Guo Changcheng stood silent and still.

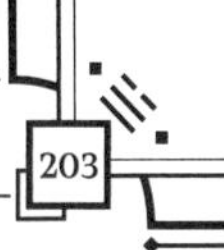

Chu Shuzhi finally ran out of patience. "Fuck off!" he roared.

In a tiny, almost whiny voice, Guo Changcheng said, "Daqing told me to take you home, and we're not there yet—"

Before Guo Changcheng could finish speaking, he was grabbed and pinned up against the wall. Chu Shuzhi's bony hands were like steel, icy cold as they gripped him by the throat. Dangling by his neck with his feet off the ground, Guo Changcheng quickly found himself unable to breathe. He kicked and struggled fruitlessly.

Chu Shuzhi's gaze was frigid. At such close range, Guo Changcheng noticed that there was a slight dullness to his pupils. It wasn't normally obvious, but in direct sunlight, those eyes held a subtle hint of death.

"I don't owe a thing to the Heavens or Earth! My conscience is clean! I've been atoning for my crimes for three hundred years—I paid it all off ages ago. Who the fuck do they think they are? What right do they have to judge me?" Chu Shuzhi squeezed these final words out from between his teeth. "If that's how it is, why shouldn't I actually commit the crimes they're accusing me of?!"

Guo Changcheng's eyes started to water. He really was a snot spirit—quick to cry, with a soft personality and weak spine. As he stared back at Chu Shuzhi, his expression was full of disbelief, pleading, and a little sadness, but not much anger. When he managed to open his mouth, no sound came out. The shape of his lips seemed to be forming "Chu-ge."

Guo Changcheng was a person made of mud. If you were to hit him, he wouldn't make a sound—all you got out of it was a mucky hand. Suddenly, Chu Shuzhi didn't see the point in bothering with him. He let go, dumping Guo Changcheng to the ground, then stood there indifferently as Guo Changcheng coughed up a lung.

The young man was truly a little tail. Every day he carried a little notebook around, following Chu Shuzhi everywhere, taking note of everything, and meticulously writing down every word anyone said, up to and including Daqing calling someone a stupid human. In ancient times, he would have been like a little eunuch keeping records of the emperor's daily life.

A thick layer of glowing merits emanated from Guo Changcheng, who was about to cough his trachea into a bow. The impossibly white light seared Chu Shuzhi's eyes.

The hand that had gripped Guo Changcheng's neck suddenly lifted and came to rest on that messy bird's nest atop his head. Guo Changcheng shivered instinctively. Chu Shuzhi patted the top of the man's head, voice calmer and a bit tired now as he said, "You didn't study properly as a kid, did you? Have you read *The Injustice to Dou E*? It clearly states that 'those who act in kindness often suffer through poverty and live short lives, while those who do evil enjoy riches and long lives.' Do you remember that?"

Guo Changcheng really wasn't wired for studying. At the end of every year, he'd return everything he'd learned that year right back to the teacher, every last bit. So now he just squatted on the ground, looking up at Chu Shuzhi with a blank expression.

Chu Shuzhi tipped Guo Changcheng's chin up and examined him for a while. "Your forehead is somewhat flat and narrow, which means the fate linking you and your parents is shallow. Your ears are thin, which means your youth was full of troubles. The middle third of your nose bridge protrudes a bit, which means you will lose the protection of your elders after you leave middle age, and the latter half of your life will be unpredictable.

"Overall, your face says you'll have a hard life and ultimately won't amount to much. There's no point in collecting so many merits. Donating money and doing good will only make you even poorer. Try to be smarter from now on. Live in comfort like the nepo baby you are. Enjoy what you should and live a few good days while you can."

Guo Changcheng kept looking up at him, confused.

"You really are a bit dense," Chu Shuzhi said. The two of them stared at each other for a while, and then he reached out and pulled Guo Changcheng up. "Go give that cat yao a message for me: What could I possibly do? I'm just a minor character at the mercy of others. Don't worry, I'm not stupid enough to look for trouble, and I won't try to kill myself. I'm taking a few days off to clear my mind, and I'll be back after the fifteenth, once the Lunar New Year is over."

Then, like mist evaporating, he disappeared right in front of Guo Changcheng's eyes.

The empty alleyway held the sulfurous smell of firecracker debris. On the first day of the Lunar New Year, the streets seemed a little bleak and empty. The swirling cold wind lifted a stray strand of hair atop Guo Changcheng's head. Face still tear-stained, he sniffled.

Chu Shuzhi hadn't really seemed like he was trying to convince Guo Changcheng; rather, it had seemed like he was just grumbling about his own circumstances. The thing about grumbling was that there was no rhyme or reason to it. Whether or not someone was blessed by fortune was decided at birth. What did it have to do with what kind of life he chose to lead or what he chose to do?

Guo Changcheng had always thought he was a useless, irredeemable person who had taken advantage of all sorts of resources that someone like him didn't deserve, so he always tried to tread carefully. He worked hard to do what he could, as much as he could, but it really couldn't be considered benevolent or compassionate. He just wanted to feel a little more useful.

He never anticipated getting anything in return.

But despite all that, having someone explain precisely why he was destined not to have a good life still made Guo Changcheng feel a little put out. With that gloom weighing on his heart, he headed home.

After leaving Zhao Yunlan's family home, Shen Wei felt like he'd just endured a huge tribulation. He was exhausted in both heart and mind. While he'd been careful not to reveal anything in front of Zhao Yunlan's mom, her eyes constantly scanned him like X-rays trying to discover his inner secrets. He felt like all that excess radiation was about to part his flesh from his bones.

"Why did your mother keep looking at me like that?" he asked. "Did I unknowingly slip up in some way?"

Daqing, who was flopped belly down on his container of dried fish, responded before Zhao Yunlan could. "Lao-Zhao used to fuck around all over the place and had a bit of a reputation. I think his mom is just a little traumatized."

Shen Wei didn't want to seem unreasonable, but hearing this, he couldn't help his darkening expression.

"Damn fatty, if you keep spouting bullshit, I *will* throw you out of this car," Zhao Yunlan said flatly.

Daqing raised his tail. "Meow—"

Zhao Yunlan glared harshly at the cat in the rearview mirror. "Don't think too much of it. Before—*ahem*, before...I never brought anyone to meet her. And it wasn't you in particular she was being paranoid about. It was because earlier, when we were making dumplings, I accidentally came out to her."

Shen Wei didn't know how to react.

"Oho!" Daqing said. "Brave warrior."

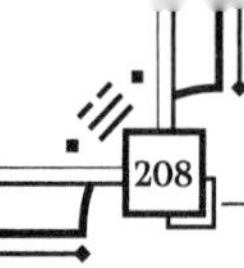

Shen Wei found his voice. "Y-you told your mom..."

"I told her my love for you can stir up a storm and shatter the world. If she gives her blessing, she gets to have a second son from now on—buy one, get one free. That's a phenomenal deal. And if she doesn't, I'll kill myself for love, and she won't have any sons. My mom's smart. She'll do the math. Don't worry."

Daqing tore him down mercilessly. "Dream on! As if you'd ever dare talk to the Empress Dowager like that. Shen-laoshi, there's flour on his pants, right? I bet he prostrated himself in the kitchen." Then he addressed Zhao Yunlan directly. "You even chose a day when the Grand Emperor wouldn't be home. How amazing you are!"

Zhao Yunlan didn't answer.

Lacking the patience to watch them flirt, Daqing changed the subject. "Oh, right. Lao-Zhao, I have something to tell you. Did you know lao-Chu's merit shackles were due to come off today?"

"Today?" It took a second for Zhao Yunlan to react. "Has it already been three hundred years? What did he say? With the shackles off, he'll be free from now on. Is he going to leave the SID?"

"Don't get ahead of yourself," Daqing said. "The Netherworld wouldn't take them off."

"Why?"

"How would I know? Probably some garbage like 'he hasn't collected enough merits.' As if there's even a quota. They never name a target for how many merits someone has to collect, and they're the ones who say whether the target's been hit or not."

"Chu Shuzhi wears merit shackles?" asked Shen Wei.

"Mmn." Daqing nodded. "Sometimes when the Soul-Guarding Order is short-staffed, the Guardian will go to the Netherworld and borrow a convict. I guess it's a kind of labor reform."

Shen Wei understood. "There's nothing we can do, then. Most prisoners the Netherworld manages to catch are small, powerless ghosts—not much use at all. Anyone with real power will usually put up a fight, unless they go willingly for some reason. So when they finally manage to shackle someone with real abilities, of course they have to squeeze every last drop out of him. Prolonging the sentence on the merit shackles seems to be normal practice. Another century or two would be typical."

Zhao Yunlan didn't say anything, but his gaze was a little cold.

Everyone had their own plans and calculations; that was just how things were. Zhao Yunlan wasn't some sheltered, naive fool who didn't know how the world worked. It was one thing if, in the big picture, things were still going in the right direction; people could have their own little games of chess under the table and take advantage of each other. It wasn't a big deal. But recently, signs of the other side secretly dipping their hands in kept cropping up. Whether Zhao Yunlan said anything or not, he was still irritated.

"Why was Chu Shuzhi put in merit shackles? Can you tell me?" asked Shen Wei.

From the backseat, Daqing looked at Shen Wei with his eerie feline eyes. Shen Wei seemed intimately acquainted with the unwritten rules of the Netherworld.

Who exactly *was* he?

Daqing thought it over. Finally, slowly, he said, "Chu Shuzhi's cultivation path is necromancy. Dying, becoming one of the undead, and finding this path was something he basically stumbled into. Most people who dabble in necromancy are giant weirdos, and they're all heretics in their own ways. Chu Shuzhi is more mild-mannered than your average necromancer, so his peers thought *he* was the one on an immoral path. Back then, Chu Shuzhi got into it accidentally. He was a solitary cultivator, so he barely knew the rules and taboos.

"Shen-laoshi's scope and depth of knowledge are as impressive as his efforts to hide them. You presumably know that a person's final resting place is the foundation for the cultivation of their necromancy. If their resting place is destroyed and they aren't powerful enough, their very essence may be damaged. Well, in this case, when someone chased a pet cricket all the way to a burial mound and lost it among all the unmarked graves, he had one grave dug up to look for it—Chu Shuzhi's. When he still couldn't find the cricket, he burned down the entire burial mound in his rage.

"Fortunately, by that point Chu Shuzhi had already ascended through the restraints of the Earthly Gates and was on his way to the Heavenly Pass, so he no longer feared the sun. His actual body wasn't in the grave, so he wasn't severely injured. Cultivation depends on cause and effect, no matter who or what is doing it. Someone wrecked Chu Shuzhi's cultivation for no reason, and you reap what you sow. That's how the world works. Of course he was going to take revenge."

This was Zhao Yunlan's first time hearing the story too. "And then what happened?" he asked.

"Then Chu Shuzhi found him, hung him up to bleed him dry, cured the meat, and ate him," Daqing said. "Trouble was, the person who'd done all that was a child from an influential family. He'd been spoiled rotten his entire life, and when this all happened, he was only a day and a half shy of his seventh birthday."

Zhao Yunlan didn't really understand. "So what if they're not seven yet? Is there some kind of rule?"

Shen Wei explained quietly. "Before a little yao can cultivate a human form, the thing they most fear encountering is a child under seven. Children are young and naive. No matter what a child does, the Heavens won't punish them. If a child catches and kills you, your only choice is to be resigned to that fate. There can be no vengeance. If you insist on pursuing revenge and harm a child, it's a major offense."

By its very nature, cultivation went against the natural order of things. Only one in a million might succeed, and doing so required talent, hard work, and luck—*especially* luck.

If this had happened to Zhao Yunlan, he might have thought the brat was a little bastard, but the worst he could do to them was cause a nightmare and mess with them a bit to scare them. If he didn't die or get badly hurt, there was no need to seriously harm a brat. There was a reason why the Heavens don't punish children with their hair still down:[13] children were naive and couldn't possibly understand their wrongdoings. Cultivating yao could simply avoid them, or perhaps play dead or cast an illusion to get it over with. It wasn't that big a deal.

And if avoiding the encounter proved truly impossible and the little yao had to meet the child directly, it was probably due to something from a previous life, or someone being out to get them. Either way, it just went to show that fate is inescapable.

Unfortunately, necromancer Chu Shuzhi was exactly the kind of proud person to seek revenge over even a small slight, rules be damned.

"Well, no one can push back against the Heavens, but pushing back against the Netherworld is fair game." Zhao Yunlan took his

---

13 *Children traditionally wore specific hairstyles depending on their age. Between the ages of 3 and 7, children would have typically worn their hair down.*

phone from his pocket and tossed it into the backseat. "Call Chu Shuzhi," he ordered.

Daqing deftly tapped away at the screen with his paw pads. On the first attempt, Chu Shuzhi hung up on him.

"Call again," said Zhao Yunlan.

On the third try, Chu Shuzhi turned off his phone.

Zhao Yunlan hit the brakes and parked on the roadside. He took a Soul-Guarding Order from his wallet, pulled out a pen, and quickly scribbled on the yellow paper: *Come see me at 4 Bright Avenue before midnight.*

He folded the Soul-Guarding Order into a paper crane, which flew out the window. In the blink of an eye, it disappeared like a wisp of smoke.

RATHER THAN DRIVING HOME, Zhao Yunlan decided to drop by the place he'd just bought near Dragon City University before it got dark.

It was only one street away from the university campus. The neighborhood was made up of a group of gardened Western-style buildings with a very distinctive architectural style.

Zhao Yunlan pulled out a ring of keys, removed one, and placed it in Shen Wei's hand. "I know you don't actually need a key to get in, so it's mostly symbolic, but it's the spirit of the thing."

It was almost as if the metal of the key burned Shen Wei's fingers. He curled them slightly. "For me...?"

"Of course! The key to our house." Zhao Yunlan led the way as he spoke. "The plumbing, wiring, and interior walls are basically done now. They were working on the floors before the New Year, so it's a little messy inside, but everything should be done in about a month. At that point, you can move your stuff in first, and just keep the stuff you normally use at my place. We can move in properly in the spring, after we air the place out for a while. Come on, the elevator's this way."

Shen Wei felt as though his heart had been submerged in water. It was tender, soft, and swelling in his chest.

The building was four stories high, with one unit occupying each floor. The underground parking area was divided into separate garages for each unit, and each private garage had its own elevator with direct access to their unit. When Shen Wei and Zhao Yunlan reached theirs, they found construction debris still scattered all over the place, but the natural lighting inside was wonderful. Although the sun was currently setting, enough fading light trickled in, gilding the scraps strewn around the floor. The view out the windows on one side was of Dragon City University's Republican-era buildings, hidden by ancient trees. The other side overlooked a man-made creek that wound its way through the neighborhood. Even in the middle of winter, with the water drained, one could look down at it and see the marks the flowing water had carved into the stone.

"They say one should hide their mistress in a golden house, but I don't have the money for that. If I actually built one, I'd get investigated for corruption. So I hope you can be content with this for a while." Zhao Yunlan smiled. "I'll save up slowly until we can upgrade to somewhere better. The master bedroom is the one on the south side with a balcony. Pick which of the others you'd like for your study."

Shen Wei took a long look at him. So much emotion and longing, so agonizingly repressed for thousands of years, and Zhao Yunlan had casually set it all ablaze with absolutely no warning. The intensity was rapidly reaching a breaking point, and with it, an indescribable sadistic urge welled up in Shen Wei's heart. He ached to gather Zhao Yunlan in his arms and smother him there, to crush every bit of flesh and bone to dust and melt it in his palms, preserving this moment for eternity.

The world inside his heart was collapsing, and yet in front of Zhao Yunlan, he couldn't bear to even draw a harsh breath. Only his gaze burned.

Of course, when three's a crowd, someone must be the third wheel. Daqing—possibly to prevent the two of them from simply falling to the debris-littered floor together and rolling around—jumped onto the windowsill and announced loudly, "I want my own bedroom too! And a luxurious cat tower!"

"Oh, fuck off." Angry that the furball had ruined the mood, Zhao Yunlan grumbled, "Cat tower? Even scaffolding wouldn't be able to hold your weight!"

"What did you say, you blind man?!"

Zhao Yunlan didn't bat an eye. "I'm saying you're fat."

Furious, Daqing launched right onto Zhao Yunlan's shoulder and buried his claws in Zhao Yunlan's hair, digging at it chaotically.

And so, a fierce battle between human and cat began.

Shen Wei let out a slow breath, leaning sideways against the window. The warm, fading glow of the sunset brushed his skin, lending a touch of brightness to even his ever-pale complexion. As he quietly watched pandemonium break out in the living room, he couldn't help the small smile that made its way over his face.

But a flicker of a black shadow in his sleeve dragged the corners of Shen Wei's lips back down again. He pinched the shadow between his fingertips, transforming it into a letter. It read: *Black clouds have formed in the thirty-third heaven to the northwest. A sign of vast inauspiciousness. Please return with all haste, my lord.*

Shen Wei crumpled the letter in his fist. "Yunlan."

Zhao Yunlan and Daqing turned toward him in tandem.

"Something urgent has come up," Shen Wei said. "I'll be gone for a while. If you have free time during the holiday, go back home and try to spend more time with your parents. Your eyes still haven't recovered. I'll worry less if they're caring for you."

"What happened?" asked Zhao Yunlan.

"I'm not sure. The puppet delivered a letter from the Netherworld that says black clouds have formed in the thirty-third heaven. I'm afraid it might be serious. I must go investigate." Shen Wei reached out and stroked Zhao Yunlan's creased brow with a fingertip. "Don't frown. No need to worry."

Ordinary clouds couldn't reach up to the thirty-third heaven. Clouds there were generally one of two kinds: the auspicious purple clouds from the east or the inauspicious black clouds that cover everything.

Daqing said, "Black clouds haven't been seen in a long time. As far as I know, it's been eight hundred years since they last appeared."

"What caused them last time?" Zhao Yunlan asked.

Confused, the cat replied, "Why would I know?"

But Shen Wei didn't respond. He reflexively avoided Zhao Yunlan's gaze.

Zhao Yunlan's gift for reading people was well above average—especially when it came to Shen Wei, who wasn't good at hiding his thoughts. Something flashed through Zhao Yunlan's mind. "Does it have something to do with Ghost Face? Was it him the last time too? What exactly is he? How is he so powerful?"

Daqing was even more confused. "Ghost Face? Who's Ghost Face?"

The trace of color that the setting sun had lent Shen Wei's face was long gone. "I'm sorry. I can't say."

Zhao Yunlan deflated, unable to bear seeing him like that. Despite wanting answers, he didn't press further. "You should get going, then. Be careful. I'll keep the door unlocked for you at night. Come back soon."

With Daqing there, Shen Wei didn't say anything. He just gave Zhao Yunlan a deep glance before walking into a cloud of black mist.

Mind heavy, Zhao Yunlan walked to the balcony. He looked up at the slowly darkening sky and lit a cigarette.

Daqing was well and truly worried. He jumped onto the ledge and asked, "Do you really know Shen-laoshi's background?"

When Zhao Yunlan nodded silently, the cat cocked his head. "Then what are you worried about?"

"So many things." Zhao Yunlan blew a smoke ring and squinted in the white smoke. "Daqing, let me ask you something. Why is it that the literary classics discuss and dissect all the gossip about the gods, and yet they're completely silent about one person in particular?"

"Who?"

"Kunlun-jun."

Daqing opened his mouth, but no words came out. Cat and human were silent together for some time. Annoyed, Zhao Yunlan lit another cigarette. "What, you can't tell me either?"

"It's not that," said Daqing. "But plants and animals aren't like humans. We don't have the same type of innate intelligence. We need vast amounts of luck to even set foot upon the path of cultivation. It isn't until we cultivate more that we can begin to understand human issues and principles. Kunlun-jun... Kunlun-jun had long been a deity in the Great Wild before Buzhou Mountain fell. No one's heard tell of him for at least five thousand years. To be honest, until you...my previous master left me, I was just a little cat who could only sleep and eat. You overestimate my cultivation." Daqing curled up on the ledge. A little desolate, he said, "We're different from humans. We're foolish and stupid. Even after thousands of years, we can't cultivate much intelligence. We're only able to recognize our master. I don't know much about anything else."

Zhao Yunlan flicked the ashes from his cigarette. "Actually, I've seen a painting of Kunlun-jun."

Daqing raised his head.

"Little cat," Zhao Yunlan said, and then fell silent, thinking. "How long were you a little cat...? What kind of place would make a small animal like you stop growing?"

Kunlun Mountain's peak was the birthplace of all gods, and also the burial place for countless gods and demons from the era of Chaos. The snow never melted, and some flowers there bloomed only once every thousand years. From the dawn of time to the present, only a handful of rough, stunted, gnarled trees grew there, but each growth ring in their trunks recorded extraordinary stories beyond number.

A heavy unease rose in Daqing's heart. It felt like an invisible hand was pushing everyone toward a predetermined destination. His fur stood on end.

Change is constant with mortals and their affairs, their comings and goings through time make up history,[14] and their ant-like fates were no different than the rise and fall of innumerable gods. In all the Heavens and Earth, nothing could remain on top forever. Did Pangu really split Chaos open? Or did Chaos's form simply change?

Daqing was suddenly consumed with fear. He had few memories of his youth, but some things were buried deep within his very blood and bones—such as how, despite his first master's cycles of reincarnation, Daqing smell him through them all. He could still remember his master's robes, green as the distant mountains, their sleeves scented with new snow and bamboo. The unruly laugh, the warm hand that cradled him close...

---

14 *From the poem Climbing Xian Mountain with Friends (与诸子登岘山) by Tang Dynasty poet Meng Haoran.*

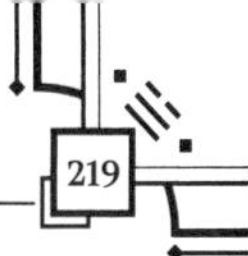

A sudden piercing bird cry came from not far away.

Daqing and Zhao Yunlan turned and looked in unison. A huge murder of crows had all taken flight at once. It was as if all the crows in the city had spread their black wings and covered the sky.

If misfortune descends from the heavens, the crows are the first to know.

Surrounded by the noise of howling wind and cawing crows, Zhao Yunlan abruptly said, "I want to tell you something. Can you keep your mouth shut?"

Daqing faced him and solemnly said, "What you say will enter and never leave. Go ahead."

"Shen Wei is the Soul-Executing Emissary," said Zhao Yunlan. "I'm a little worried about him right now."

Daqing slipped, losing his footing as if he were having a stroke, and fell straight off the ledge.

"HE'S *WHAT*?! Zhao Yunlan, have you no fear at all?!"

Zhao Yunlan, not really listening, made a vague affirmative noise.

Daqing had seen everything the world had to offer, all there was to see—or so he'd believed. Now, for the first time, he truly understood what it meant for someone to be "so deep in lust's grip that they felt brave enough to challenge the sky."

So many tales of emperors' behavior—King Zhou cutting out loyal Bigan's heart for Daji; King You of Zhou lighting the warning beacons just to coax a smile from his concubine; Emperor Xuanzong missing morning court after a night of bliss[15]—all seemed downright reasonable in comparison. Beauty could drive these stupid men to do anything!

So many moments from Zhao Yunlan and "Shen-laoshi's" interactions flashed through Daqing's mind: Shen Wei's knowledge of the Netherworld, how familiar he seemed, how he had appeared whenever they'd dealt with a Hallowed Artifact, his authority when interrogating Wang Xiangyang... Appalled,

15 *Rulers obsessed with their beautiful lovers whose states fell or declined. King Zhou of Shang committed atrocities for his consort, Daji, and tore out the heart of his uncle, Bigan, for trying to stop him. King You, the last Western Zhou ruler, faked an invasion by lighting warning beacons to please his concubine, Baosi. Emperor Xuanzong, whose reign ended the Tang Golden Era, neglected his duties out of lust for his consort, Yang Guifei.*

Daqing realized that this explained everything. There was no choice but to believe it.

"Do you know what exactly the Soul-Executing Emissary is?" he asked.

Zhao Yunlan's expression didn't even flicker. "That's what I wanted to ask you."

Daqing was about to lose his mind. "I am an old, old cat. From back as far as the investiture of the gods, for the most part I can tell you the ins and outs of everything, from gods and Buddhas to all the creatures that walk the earth. But I can't tell you a thing about the Soul-Executing Emissary's origin. Do you understand what that means?"

This wasn't a surprise to Zhao Yunlan, having seen the portrait Shen Wei had painted and read the words "Laying eyes on Kunlun-jun for the first time, in the shades of the grove." If Shen Wei had personally laid eyes on Kunlun-jun, of course he must have been born in truly ancient times. That had been long before Daqing became self-aware, so how could the cat possibly know the Emissary's origin?

"Just tell me what you do know," Zhao Yunlan said.

Daqing anxiously clawed the ledge. "Do you know about Houtu?"

"Mm-hmm." Zhao Yunlan began outlining what he knew. "In *The Classic of Mountains and Seas*, Houtu was said to be born from Gonggong, and was considered a descendant of the Flame Emperor lineage. *The Summons of the Soul* recorded that Houtu was the god who controlled the Netherworld. But later, legends passed down in the Mortal Realm often referred to Houtu along with the 'Imperial Sky,' indicating immense reverence for both. Thanks to that, there are also some legends that claim Houtu is actually Nüwa."

Daqing nodded, so Zhao Yunlan continued. "Back when Gonggong overturned Buzhou Mountain, Nüwa repaired the sky by creating the Stones of Many Hues, which held up the Pillars of Heaven. Then she turned into loess, separating the yin world from the yang. That was the beginning of the Netherworld, and therefore people revered her as 'Houtu,' meaning 'Queen Earth.'"

Having said all that, Zhao Yunlan still wasn't entirely sure what Houtu had to do with anything.

"As for the Soul-Executing Emissary," said Daqing, "it's said that he was born thousands of zhang below the Huangquan. But here's the problem: the Emissary was born before Buzhou Mountain fell. That was before the Netherworld and the Huangquan existed. So where did this 'thousands of zhang below the Huangquan' idea come from?"

"In other words, the Emissary wasn't born from the Netherworld at all."

"Haven't you noticed how the Netherworld fears him?" Daqing said. Zhao Yunlan's cigarette had burned down to almost nothing, but he was oblivious. Daqing sighed. "You... How did you get tangled up with him? Can't you keep it in your pants?"

The real tragedy was that Zhao Yunlan had yet to get it *out* of his pants.

"It's a little late to be saying that now," Zhao Yunlan said, after which he stood by the window silently, the last rays of the sun giving him an almost endless shadow. He smoked cigarette after cigarette, enveloping himself in so much smoke that it seemed like he was at the misty South Heavenly Gate. The ground was littered with cigarette butts and his pockets were empty before he finally motioned for Daqing to jump onto his arm. The two of them headed out.

"Where are we going?" asked Daqing.

"Back to 4 Bright Avenue." Zhao Yunlan's tone was frosty. "I need to see Chu Shuzhi and then make an appointment with a reaper. I won't let anyone else bully those who work for me."

They arrived just after the day shift had finished up, but Chu Shuzhi hadn't arrived yet. Zhao Yunlan set out dried fish and milk for Daqing and then went right into the library. He grabbed a pair of protective glasses by the entrance and had just put them on when he saw Wang Zheng and Sangzan hastily pulling away from each other in the corner.

"Carry on," he said. "Don't mind me."

Wang Zheng scoffed and fled, covering her face.

Sangzan ran his hands through his hair. He had thick skin and wasn't easily embarrassed. He walked over and said, "Kunlun again?"

The glasses made Zhao Yunlan's nose bridge seem a little taller than normal. When he looked up, revealing the sharp lines of his jaw, something about his handsome face seemed colder than usual.

"There's no point. Someone's already wiped all the useful information." Zhao Yunlan ran a finger along the spines of the books on the shelf, searching. "I want any information at all regarding... Nüwa. Nüwa creating humans, Nüwa repairing the sky, the battles between Chiyou and the Flame and Yellow Emperors, the battle between Gonggong and Zhuanxu—I want all of it. They may be able to erase one individual entirely, but I refuse to believe they can hide every trace of that sequence of events."

Zhao Yunlan looked like an illiterate punk, but his appearance was deceiving. He had an impressive knowledge of ancient texts, letting him quickly skim through a book, and he was familiar with several ancient languages. Now he sat cross-legged on the tall metal ladder and got to work. When he finished with a book, he tossed it down. Sangzan didn't bother him and just waited below, reshelving

the books without a word. The only sound in the library was that of pages being turned.

But Zhao Yunlan's vision still wasn't back to a hundred percent. When he got tired, it was like there was a film over his eyes. He had to take periodic breaks and talk to Sangzan.

"Buzhou Mountain is a sacred mountain. Legend says it's the road to the Heavens." Zhao Yunlan gestured as he explained carefully to Sangzan. "Historical records show that Gonggong and Zhuanxu battled for power. In the end, Gonggong lost, and in a rage, he rode the divine dragon and knocked Buzhou Mountain down."

Sangzan still had trouble parsing what people said to him. He reacted slowly, then nodded half a beat later.

"But I don't believe it," Zhao Yunlan said softly. "The two Emperors, Flame and Yellow, battled Chiyou for more years than anyone could count. They fought until the skies divided and the earth was split, sending sand and rock flying everywhere. But even with that, Buzhou Mountain was fine. Even when Pangu separated the sky and earth with his axe, Buzhou Mountain remained unharmed. How could a *ride* knock it over?"

Sangzan had learned to ignore all the adjectives and nouns he didn't understand. After a while, in his unusual accent, he said, "Iv... this is something that's imbossible...but it still habbened—*happened*, thin someone mod...mad...made...it happen."

"Cutting off the road to the Heavens." Zhao Yunlan tapped a finger against the ancient tome. "Who could have done it? Why?"

Sangzan watched as Zhao Yunlan's gaze slowly deepened.

"After Buzhou Mountain fell, Nüwa used huge rocks to plug up the sky. She herself turned into Houtu and her spirit scattered in the Netherworld," Zhao Yunlan continued. "It was like Nüwa held up the sky and earth with her bare hands. Earth... Earth... Mud..." His

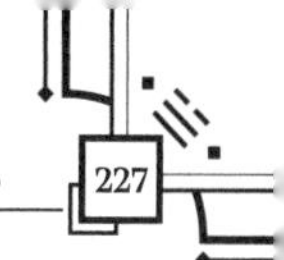

voice got quieter and quieter until he was nearly talking to himself. Then he suddenly said, "Wait—give me the part about Nüwa creating humans again."

Sangzan had just passed him the book when Daqing came in and addressed Zhao Yunlan. "Lao-Chu is here."

Zhao Yunlan immediately tucked the book away and descended the tall ladder. He was about to leave when Sangzan suddenly spoke up behind him. "At thet time, there was...no order, right? Averyone wanted more puw...power. Mountain... The road to Heaven you mentioned, if it bru...broke, parhaps someone wanted to end..."

Unable to find the correct words, he gestured, and Zhao Yunlan immediately understood: *unending battle.*

Zhao Yunlan's brows rose. A new line of thinking had opened up.

At the beginning of Chaos, all gods battled endlessly. The Flame and Yellow Emperors defeated Chiyou, forming a new order, but there kept being more and more humans. When Nüwa breathed life into the first human, a thing called "power" was also born. Humans had joined in the battles. Then...was striking down Buzhou Mountain and cutting off the road to the Heavens an attempt to break the order, end the battle between the gods, and return to the beginning of all creation, when things had been prosperous?

Again, Zhao Yunlan thought of his dream. Who had been talking to him?

Chu Shuzhi had arrived, but not alone. He had a tail: Guo Changcheng, dressed like a cotton ball. Guo Changcheng had two scarves wrapped around his neck, covering half his face. He had packaged himself into a ninja turtle.

After Chu Shuzhi had vanished into thin air, Guo Changcheng had no choice but to head home. But before he even got into a taxi, he changed his mind. He felt bad for letting Daqing down on the first day of the Lunar New Year. So he'd returned to that little alleyway to search for Chu Shuzhi, gritting his teeth and asking for information from everyone he encountered.

After he'd searched in the biting cold for over half an hour, a kindhearted auntie from the neighborhood committee had noticed him and his bright red nose and had brought him right to Chu Shuzhi's door. But once she left him there, Guo Changcheng didn't dare knock or leave. It wasn't until Chu Shuzhi received the Soul-Guarding Order's call and stepped out to go to 4 Bright Avenue that he found this popsicle of a coworker outside his door. What could Chu Shuzhi do but bring him along?

The atmosphere in the office was tense. Chu Shuzhi sat in front of the desk, fidgeting a bit with Zhao Yunlan's lighter. His eyes stayed fixed on the desk, and his expression was somber. Off to the side, Daqing paced in equal silence. The only sound in the entire criminal investigation unit was Guo Changcheng's sniffling.

Chu Shuzhi didn't look up until Zhao Yunlan hurried out from the wall, carrying a book. "Why did you call me here?"

Zhao Yunlan sat across from him, took in his expression, and asked a straightforward question. "Do you intend to leave?" When Chu Shuzhi didn't say anything, Zhao Yunlan icily added, "Take your hand out of your pocket. Don't act like I can't smell that thing's stench!"

Chu Shuzhi's mouth curled in a fake smile. He pulled his hand out to reveal a tiny bone in his palm, illuminated with a dim blue light. The bone was hollow, with four holes: a bone flute, which could be used to control corpses and spirits of the dead. Such profound disrespect for the dead meant that bone flutes had been considered sorcery since ancient times.

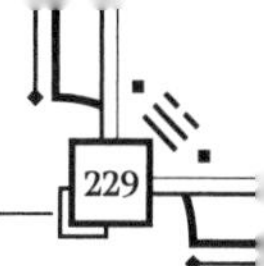

Guo Changcheng sneezed. Chu Shuzhi side-eyed him and slowly said, "I think you should find someone to take the poor kid home first—"

"Xiao-Guo, go with Daqing to the kitchen. Make yourself a bowl of banlangen." Once Guo Changcheng and Daqing had left the room, Zhao Yunlan's expression darkened. Slapping the table, he demanded, "What do you think you're doing, bringing that reeking thing? Do you want to lie back down in the mud and go back to being a shackled Corpse King? Do you want to spend the rest of your days in hiding?"

Chu Shuzhi held his head up high. "Three hundred years ago, I was insolent and didn't understand the rules. I committed a crime and agreed that I should bear the consequences. I *accepted* these three hundred years. If I'd thought I was wronged, what could some puny reapers have done to me? I gave them an inch and now they're fucking taking a mile!"

"Postponing the removal of merit shackles is standard practice. Other people can bear it, so why can't you?"

"Because. I. Am. Not. Other. People! Zhao Yunlan, don't forget. I put on the merit shackles of my own will. I was giving them face! That doesn't mean I think I was wrong..."

"You have the gall to tell me the stupid shit you did wasn't wrong?"

"That's right! I'm not afraid to say it. So what? I don't regret it! If I had it to do all over again, I'd still skin the little brat and tear out his tendons and just sit in jail for another three hundred years! What's this shit about merits and sins, adults and children? To me, there are two types of people: those I can kill, and those I can't. If they're forcing me like this, if my crimes are so unforgivable that three hundred years aren't enough to atone, then why shouldn't I commit the crimes I've been charged for? If I rack up a few more offenses, this transaction would be worth it! From now on, everyone had better keep an eye on their kids, or the bone flute might scatter their souls, never to return!"

He hadn't quite gotten the final word out when Zhao Yunlan slapped him square in the face, fast and precise. The sharp sound filled the room as Chu Shuzhi's head snapped to the side.

Daqing and Guo Changcheng had both come back just in time to witness this. Daqing yowled, tail bristling. He was sure they were about to fight.

At that moment, a gray mist seeped in through the window. It bumped Zhao Yunlan's shoulder and rolled into his arms, where it turned into a letter.

Looking down, Zhao Yunlan saw a hurried note from Shen Wei: *The reaper is already on their way. No matter what they want you to do, under no circumstances should you agree. Wait for me to come home. —Wei*

Zhao Yunlan showed no outward reaction, but the ice in his expression thawed ever so slightly.

Chu Shuzhi glanced at him and stood to leave. Three Soul-Guarding Orders immediately blazed from Zhao Yunlan's hand, spraying sparks everywhere. They struck Chu Shuzhi's back as a ball of flame, forcing him back into the chair, binding him in place.

Though he was angry enough to spit blood, Chu Shuzhi still had a contract with the Soul-Guarding Order. Even if he had all the power in the world, he still had to answer to it.

Zhao Yunlan took a recording pen from a drawer and pressed *play*. Chu Shuzhi's last words filled the room again: *"From now on, everyone had better keep an eye on their kids, or the bone flute might scatter their souls, never to return!"*

In the recording, his voice sounded impossibly cold. Just listening could make someone break out in goosebumps.

"Listen to yourself," Zhao Yunlan said. "Does that sound like something a human being would say?"

Chu Shuzhi's eyes flashed, but he looked away stubbornly. "I'm not human to begin with."

In a truly pathetic whimper, Guo Changcheng said, "Chu-ge, don't say things you don't mean just because you're angry." When Chu Shuzhi gave him a piercing look, Guo Changcheng carefully shifted closer and kept sniveling. "I-I d-don't believe you meant that. I didn't really understand, but Chu-ge is a good person. You wouldn't do something bad for no reason..."

Zhao Yunlan leaned back heavily in his chair, rapped his lighter against the desk twice, and then lit a cigarette. Brimming with impatience, he said, "Do you even understand the concept of finding the crux of the matter before striking? All you do is lash out. The kid has more maturity than you. I'm embarrassed for you."

Chu Shuzhi gave him a ferocious glare.

"What are you looking at? Aren't you embarrassed at all? Anyway, I don't have time for this right now. Xiao-Guo, wheel him into my office, lock the door, and keep an eye on him. There's a side room in there with a single bed. If you're tired, you can lie down."

Kind as always, Guo Changcheng immediately asked, "What about Chu-ge?"

"Him?" Zhao Yunlan's gaze swept over Chu Shuzhi. "Just let him sit there. He might as well do some serious meditation and wake the hell up."

He picked up his teacup, swirling the cold dregs. Still furious, he added, "I really want to throw this in your face. Fuck off."

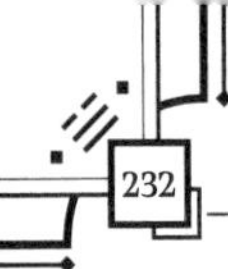

Guo Changcheng obediently fucked off, pushing Chu Shuzhi in the rolling chair out of the room.

Zhao Yunlan propped his long legs up on the table, book against his knees, and started flipping through it.

The legends regarding Nüwa were fragmented and disjointed. This particular book, *Record of Ancient Secrets*, had a chapter specifically dedicated to "Nüwa of the Feng Family." Neither the author nor the original publication info was specified, but it had most likely been written by some Daoist cultivator after the Song Dynasty.

It began by citing *Imperial Readings of the Taiping Era*[16] on its record of Nüwa's creation of humans: "As it is told, when the Earth and Sky were separated, humans did not yet exist. Nüwa formed humans out of the loess, but because it was too much work, she dipped a rope in the mud and flicked it, and humans were formed out of the flung specks of mud."

In a side note, the author went on to add: "Humans have five features on the face, created in Sovereign Wa's own likeness, and are able to speak. Born from the mud, the heavenly wind ignited their three fires, and the turbid soil gave rise to their three worms,[17] not to be extinguished until death. They are intelligent but unclean. From infancy to old age, their lives are as fleeting as the sun moving across the sky. Out of pity for them, Sovereign Wa conceived of marriage and became a matchmaker, allowing them to live on through hundreds of generations."

Zhao Yunlan found a pen and heavily underlined "the heavenly wind ignited their three fires, and the turbid soil gave rise to their three worms." Then he continued flipping until he reached the part lifted from *The Huainanzi* about "mending the sky."

---

16 *A massive encyclopedia compiled by a team of scholars during the Song Dynasty.*

17 *According to some Daoist texts, the three worms are the sources of greed, wrath, and delusion.*

"In the old days, the Four Pillars that held up the sky came to ruin and the Nine Lands split apart. The sky could no longer cover, and the earth could no longer contain; the fire was wild and inextinguishable, and the water was an ocean, vast and unstoppable. Fierce beasts feasted upon good humans; ferocious birds carried off the weak and the old. Nüwa used the Stones of Many Hues to mend the sky, cut off the giant turtle's legs to use as the Four Pillars of Heaven, slaughtered the black dragon to save the land of Ji, and collected reed ash to soak up the flood. Thus was the sky repaired, and the Four Pillars stood once again; the flood waters receded, and the land of Ji was saved; the evil beasts died, and the good humans could live.

"Note: Out of gratitude to the old turtle for giving its legs, Sovereign Wa gifted it a brocade robe to serve as its fin. Since that time, the Four Pillars have guarded the four corners and the sky has tilted toward the northwest. Kunlun spoke, saying, 'Stone that is aged but not yet old, water that is frozen but not yet cold, body that is dead but not yet born, soul that is melted but not yet burned,' and thus were the Pillars sealed.

"These impossibilities would be sealed in the place beyond all reach and named 'the Four Hallowed Artifacts.' So long as the sky does not fall and the earth does not sink, the Four Hallowed Artifacts will not resurface, and peace will reign beneath the sky."

As he read, Zhao Yunlan smoothed a hand over Daqing's fur every now and then. "It says here that humans' six senses are tainted due to the poor quality of the mud they were made from. At the end, Nüwa used the old turtle's legs to hold up the sky and mend it, and Kunlun sealed the Four Pillars with some words—I'm guessing the 'Kunlun' here is probably Kunlun-jun. Also, I've come across these words before."

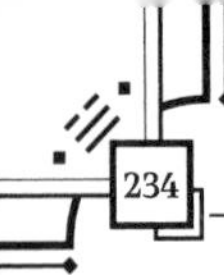

"Where?" asked Daqing.

"At the base of the Mountain-River Awl," Zhao Yunlan said. "If the 'impossibilities' are the Four Hallowed Artifacts, then this means that once someone has acquired them and achieved the impossible, they'll reach the base of the Four Pillars?"

Daqing circled around his hand and mumbled, "What is all this? It's making me dizzy."

Zhao Yunlan ignored him. He seemed to be talking to himself, getting his thoughts in order. "First they talked about using the Stones of Many Hues to repair the sky. Symmetrically speaking, after 'repairing the sky,' the next step should be to 'hold down the earth,' which was likely what those Four Pillars were for. This 'earth' they're referring to is presumably the 'earth' from the time humanity was created, rather than meaning the Houtu that Nüwa turned into... That makes sense. No wonder Ghost Face is so desperate for the Four Hallowed Artifacts. Once he has them, he can find the way to destroy the Four Pillars."

The fragrance of dried fish still lingered on Zhao Yunlan's fingers from when he'd touched some earlier. Daqing sniffed at them and asked, "Who is this 'Ghost Face' you guys keep talking about?"

Zhao Yunlan quickly summarized what had happened with the Mountain-River Awl, and then his face went a little solemn. "Ghost Face wears a mask. But I'm pretty sure I know what he looks like underneath."

"Is it possible..."

"My guess is he looks a lot like Shen Wei," Zhao Yunlan said. "Shen Wei thinks too much. He's kind to everyone but himself. I don't know why he hates himself so much, but I'm really worried that he'll..."

Daqing looked up. "What?"

Zhao Yunlan glanced down and met the black cat's eyes, then suddenly took his legs off the desk and murmured, "Someone's here."

No sooner had he said that than they heard the distant sound of the woodblock. As it approached, the chill and humidity in the air deepened. A bitter wind rattled the windows in their frames. Zhao Yunlan took a small handful of incense from a drawer, lit the sticks, and stuck them into a flowerpot. Next, he took out a ceramic pot and a stack of spirit money, lit the spirit money, and dropped it inside. As the smoke rose, he put away his book and poured himself some hot tea.

This reaper had clearly learned from the last one's mistakes. They stood a short distance from the door and announced loudly, "This uninvited guest from the Netherworld asks to see the Guardian. Will the Guardian honor us with an audience?"

Zhao Yunlan lightened his expression. "Please come in."

The door to the criminal investigation unit creaked open, and their guest could immediately smell the spirit money and incense smoke filling the room. Money, as they say, can make even a ghost willingly push a grinding stone, and it worked its magic now. The newcomer's face relaxed into a smile. He bowed before saying, "The Guardian shows too much courtesy."

For just a moment, Zhao Yunlan went very still when he saw who it was. He stood and said, with some surprise, "What kind of wind blew my lord Magistrate here?"

The Magistrate was his usual smiling, easygoing self. He seemed less like a reaper and more like the god of marriage, Yue Lao, who distributed wealth, offered well-wishes, and brought people together. After entering, the Magistrate exchanged casual pleasantries with Zhao Yunlan, and then the two were sitting across from each other, each with his own agenda.

Daqing jumped into Zhao Yunlan's arms, tail twining around his wrist in absolute silence. Deep green eyes locked grimly onto the Magistrate, signaling the cat's readiness to protect his master.

The Magistrate spent some time sighing pointedly, wanting Zhao Yunlan to be the one to start the conversation, but Zhao Yunlan showed no sign of taking the hint. He just sipped his tea, seemingly oblivious.

Eventually, the Magistrate gave in. "This humble old man would never disturb the Guardian in the middle of the night if it weren't important. I've come to beg the Guardian's aid, for the sake of the world and all who live in it."

"No, please, none of that." Zhao Yunlan waved his hand hurriedly. "There's no need for such flattery. I'm an ordinary mortal citizen who happens to know a few tricks. I'm grateful to be thought of so highly, but I don't dare consider myself anyone of importance. I barely know how to react to your kind words. But of course, if there's anything at all I can help with, just say the word. If it's within my ability to help, I'll do my best."

"I'm sure the Guardian must have noticed the Crow tribe's warning tonight?" the Magistrate began.

Zhao Yunlan's face was the very picture of confusion. "No? I was at my mother's all afternoon watching a rerun of the New Year's Gala. I honestly wasn't paying attention."

The Magistrate didn't know how to respond.

"What's up with the crows?" Zhao Yunlan prompted.

The Magistrate was perfectly aware that Zhao Yunlan was playing dumb. Coming to deal personally with the Guardian had in no way been his own idea. For one thing, the Mountain God's soul was sealed within the Guardian, and the Magistrate neither wanted nor dared to offend such a great god. For another thing, the Guardian was audacious, slippery, and sneaky, and had only ever mastered three talents: shamelessness, leading people in circles, and evasion, any of which was more than enough to keep anyone busy for a while.

"Crows always report the bad, never the good. They've always been a bad omen." The Magistrate's face was bleak. "We've received word that black clouds have risen in the northwest. Someone with no fear of being struck down by lightning has set up a giant array on the peak of Kunlun Mountain, with the intent of extracting a corporeal soul from every living being."

"All living things?" Zhao Yunlan exclaimed. "The global population is exploding! Is this person strong enough to lift it all?"

The Magistrate was once again speechless.

Zhao Yunlan chuckled. "I'm a mortal without much knowledge of the world. If you wish for me to do something, you'll have to explain it to me first."

With another sigh, the Magistrate pulled a wanted notice from his sleeve. Zhao Yunlan glanced at it and saw someone familiar: Ghost Face. Feigning ignorance, he asked, "Who's this?"

"It's a long story. This is a demon king born from the filthiest of places. He is also known as the Chaos King of the Gui. In the era of the great Chaos, when gods and demons were at war, he was sealed thousands of zhang beneath the Huangquan by Nüwa herself. After all these years, Nüwa's seal has begun to loosen, and he managed to escape.

"The Guardian is a smart man. I won't beat around the bush. The truth is, most of his power is still trapped by Nüwa's seal. If we work together, we still have a chance, but were he ever to fully escape..."

Zhao Yunlan listened to this half-fake bullshit and pretended not to understand where the Magistrate was trying to lead him. "An evil being sealed by Nüwa? That must be different from the evil beings we ordinarily discuss, then? Which is more powerful?"

The Magistrate held his tongue.

Displaying keen interest, Zhao Yunlan continued, "And whatever does he want with all those souls?"

The Magistrate finally caught his breath. "His goal is to force the Merit Brush to reappear. Every living person has a corporeal soul connected to the Merit Brush. Every merit and every sin, past and present, is recorded on this soul—merits in red and sins in black. If this individual manages to draw out these corporeal souls and collect them at the peak of Kunlun Mountain, the Merit Brush will appear. We mustn't allow him to get the Merit Brush, or else..."

"Oh, I know about the Merit Brush," Zhao Yunlan interrupted. "Just recently, a little yao from the Crow tribe used what I thought was the Merit Brush to lure me in. He even injured my eyes! I still have double vision from that, so you, my lord, look about twice as wide as you were. And now you're saying the Merit Brush he spoke of was fake, and someone was just trying to start shit with me?"

The Magistrate looked up and met Zhao Yunlan's taunting gaze. A whole slew of grievances flooded his mind. It had been the Magistrate himself who decided to go to extreme measures to wake Kunlun-jun's spirit, which was sealed within Zhao Yunlan. He had instructed his subordinates to force open Zhao Yunlan's Heavenly Eye—by any means necessary—and left them to figure it out.

Unfortunately, some useless underling had gone and asked the Crow tribe for help. The carrion-feeding Crow tribe had always answered to the Netherworld. Having a crow carry out the plan was the same as hanging a neon sign announcing who was actually responsible. Who had been foolish enough to come up with *that* idea?

"The Four Hallowed Artifacts have been adrift in the Mortal Realm for so many years," Zhao Yunlan said. "Those are objects of such immense power, and yet until now the Netherworld paid no attention to them. You never bothered to look for them or tried to take them back, but now that shit's going down, you're telling me it's serious? It sounds to me like you're trying to close the barn door after the horse is already making a break for it. That's not very reasonable of you, is it?"

The Magistrate forced a sorry excuse for a smile. "That is...true, we didn't think things through..."

"Think things through?" Zhao Yunlan arched a brow. "Why do I feel like it's because you guys have something to fall back on?"

The Magistrate felt as though he were sitting on a carpet of needles.

Zhao Yunlan rapped his knuckles against the desk. "My lord, you and I have worked together for many years. Let's speak plainly. What do you want me to do?"

The Magistrate put his hands together in a small bow. "This lowly one humbly asks the Guardian to lead us up Kunlun and destroy the soul-summoning array."

Zhao Yunlan's expression was mild. "How is that supposed to work? I'm a recluse, not a backpacker. I've never even been to Xiangshan Park despite it being right outside the city, and I certainly don't know which way the entrance to Kunlun faces. Why is my lord asking *me* to lead the way?"

This answer, at least, the Magistrate had been able to prepare in advance. He quickly replied, "The Guardian may be unaware that the true Soul-Guarding Order is a piece of wood from the Great Divine Tree on Kunlun Mountain. That tree was planted by Pangu. It is as old as the earth and sky. The mountain's peak has always been

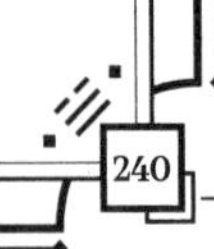

forbidden as a place of the gods. That object is the only thing that can grant access."

"Oh, so you're saying I'm the only one who has a travel pass to Kunlun Mountain?"

"That's correct."

Zhao Yunlan reached out and tapped the face on the Wanted notice. "Okay, then how did this—what did you call him, 'demon king'? How'd he get up there? Does he have secret VIP access? Is he Pangu's brother-in-law?"

"We mustn't blaspheme a god like that." The Magistrate's voice was tinged with fear. "To be honest, this evil being was born below the Huangquan, next to the Ancient Merit Tree. The Ancient Merit Tree was born from the same source as the sacred tree atop Kunlun Mountain, and has a bit of connection to Kunlun, so..."

A hint of a smile seemed to take shape on Zhao Yunlan's lips. "So does making an array on the peak of Kunlun Mountain to call forth the Merit Brush also have something to do with that tree?"

The Magistrate, unsure of where Zhao Yunlan was taking this, didn't dare answer carelessly.

"Beneath the Huangquan, huh...?" Zhao Yunlan sighed. "Why do I have the feeling that that's very close to the Soul-Executing Emissary's manor?"

The Magistrate's eyes flickered. Making a show of hesitance, he said, "One could say that."

"Oh, I see." Zhao Yunlan's smile deepened, but his eyes were like shards of ice. "So the Magistrate is trying to imply that the Emissary and this evil being have some sort of deep connection."

The Magistrate was flummoxed. Was the Guardian really so dense, or was he putting on an act and saying the quiet part aloud? Unsure, he scrutinized Zhao Yunlan's expression. The Netherworld had left

the black book with him. Was he or was he not aware that Shen Wei and the Emissary were one and the same?

A reaper had recently reported that even blindness wasn't enough to stop the Guardian from welcoming someone to his bed. Surely that must indicate that he had no contact with the Emissary? Otherwise, how could the Emissary possibly tolerate...

The Magistrate stroked his beard and hid behind a smile. "How could this lowly one speak of a high immortal behind his back? The Guardian is teasing me."

Zhao Yunlan rummaged in his pockets. "You want to borrow the Soul-Guarding Order, right? Hold on, I'll find it for you."

The Magistrate quickly waved for him to stop. "No, no. How could we touch the Soul-Guarding Order that came from the sacred tree? The only option is to trouble the Guardian to make the journey to Kunlun with us."

Zhao Yunlan paused and looked at him. It was impossible to know what the Guardian's intentions were. His eyes were dark, bright, and unspeakably sharp. The Magistrate gritted his teeth and met Zhao Yunlan's gaze, ruing the thankless job he'd taken on.

Unhurriedly, Zhao Yunlan asked, "Oh, so you guys are afraid to take the Soul-Guarding Order, but not afraid to let me, a mortal, be the Guardian? I may be a world-class bullshitter, but I don't have any real abilities—and not that many brain cells either. See, I'm easily bewitched."

The Magistrate smiled politely. "No, no."

Zhao Yunlan suddenly leaned forward and asked, "It couldn't be that my ancestors also had something to do with Kunlun, could it?" The Magistrate wailed silently, but Zhao Yunlan was far from finished with him. "Look, I haven't managed to catch a break in half a year. First it was the Reincarnation Dial, then the Mountain-River Awl, and now there's a Merit Brush. If another one shows up, they can form the four winds in a mahjong set: North, South, East, and West. Where do the Four Hallowed Artifacts even come from? It looks like the Merit Brush has something to do with Kunlun, and apparently the Reincarnation Dial's base was made from the Three-Life Rock. I hear that when Nüwa created humans, every time she flicked a human into existence, a grain of sand fell. Those grains eventually became a rock that recorded the humans' past, present, and future lives. After the Netherworld came to be, that rock stayed next to the Huangquan and was later named the 'Three-Life Rock.' That links the Reincarnation Dial to Sovereign Nüwa. And then there's the Mountain-River Awl. The great Black Tortoise's element is water, so does the Awl have some connection to Fuxi of the Feng family?"

The Magistrate wiped sweat from his brow.

"Now black clouds have disturbed even the thirty-third heaven, and surely the Netherworld isn't attempting to handle such a huge disturbance alone, yes? Who have you teamed up with? The yao? Cultivation masters from all over? And I'm sure the Emissary wouldn't refuse to help." Zhao Yunlan studied the Magistrate's face. "With such great powers assembling, what do you need me for? I don't know anyone other than the Emissary. Surely my lord isn't specially asking me to lead the way just so that..." He paused and chuckled lightly. The Magistrate's heart was in his throat. "...so that I can greet the Lord Emissary and have a little chitchat?"

For a second, petrified, the Magistrate thought the man had seen right through him.

All smiles, Zhao Yunlan said, "My lord Magistrate, this is exactly how my mother used to go about tricking me into blind dates. What, are you planning on setting me up with the Soul-Executing Emissary?"

A hostile sound came from Daqing's throat. It wasn't remotely like a housecat's meow; it much more closely resembled the roar of a tiger or panther. He stood up on Zhao Yunlan's lap, the bell at his neck swinging as he flashed his sharp claws. Clearly frightened, the Magistrate shrank back in his chair. "The Guardian's little joke has perhaps gone a bit far..."

Zhao Yunlan casually leaned back in his own chair. "It's the Lunar New Year. I'm just a powerless mortal. What if something happens to me after I get sucked into something so dangerous?"

"We guarantee the Guardian's safety, of course—"

Zhao Yunlan snorted. "You guys can't even get into a mountain. What are you guaranteeing my safety with?"

"Well..."

"I want to bring my own people," Zhao Yunlan said.

Not having expected Zhao Yunlan's cooperation, the Magistrate froze. But the look that crossed Zhao Yunlan's face next made his teeth ache.

"The thing is though," Zhao Yunlan continued, "I don't have enough people. Honestly, most of my staff are low-level minions. They're not up for more than running errands. The only really useful personnel are a little snake yao who can't even transform properly, a tiny cat that's barely a foot long, a clueless intern, and a terminally online selfie addict."

The Magistrate had an inkling of where this was headed.

"I finally managed to get a Corpse King with some useful skills, but..." Zhao Yunlan sighed.

It was an olive branch, and the Magistrate immediately took it. "No need to worry on that front. The Corpse King's merit shackles are due to be removed as soon as our side gets through the necessary paperwork. Since the Guardian brought it up, I'll authorize it and have his shackles taken off. Our side will deal with the red tape later."

"So that's why!" Zhao Yunlan exclaimed, only half-genuine. "Here I thought he'd failed to work off his sins and had gone behind my back to misbehave again. Look, he's right in the next room—I locked him up there to reflect on things!"

"It's all a misunderstanding..." the Magistrate began.

"Of course it's a misunderstanding," said Zhao Yunlan. "You guys should really streamline your processes. You're so inefficient sometimes that anyone who didn't know better would assume you were deliberately delaying things."

The Magistrate simply had nothing to say.

Zhao Yunlan picked up the desk phone and called HR. "Wang Zheng, it's me. You saw my message just now, right? Mm-hmm. Okay, print a copy and bring it up to me so our guest here can take a look."

Wang Zheng was very competent. In short order, she came floating in with a long list of names. A group of ghosts followed her, all peering through the crack in the door. Zhao Yunlan pushed the list of names across the desk to the Magistrate. "There sure have been a lot of unjust cases over the last few years—some paperwork delays and some sentences that have just been unreasonably harsh. But today's as good a day as any to deal with them, since you're here and all. Let's seize the opportunity and take care of them right now. And one more thing: when the merit shackles were put on Chu Shuzhi, did some of his old belongings end up in your custody?"

The Magistrate was silent.

"Well?"

Having finally seen firsthand just how difficult Zhao Yunlan could be, the Magistrate squeezed out an answer through clenched teeth. "We will, of course, return those."

Zhao Yunlan was unsatisfied. "How soon will that be? Now you're in a rush to leave, but you need to at least give us time to pack our bags."

By this point, the Magistrate wanted to never see Zhao Yunlan's face again. "Before daybreak." He rolled up the list of names and made a hasty exit.

Zhao Yunlan smiled and lit a cigarette with the embers from the burning spirit money.

Daqing glanced up at him. "Didn't the Emissary say not to agree?"

"Why are you reading my mail?" Zhao Yunlan rolled his eyes at the cat, then got serious. "I have to go."

Under Shen Wei's gentle, polite appearance, he was incredibly stubborn and uncompromising. He was an ancient god! Why was he allowing the Netherworld to suspect and plot against him like this? To Zhao Yunlan, it almost seemed like he was protecting something—carrying out some sort of duty that only he knew about.

But Zhao Yunlan didn't say anything else. He just ruffled the fur on Daqing's head, then evaded the resulting swipe of paws with the ease of experience. "I want the Merit Brush," he said. "I'm going to bring it back as a betrothal gift."

Daqing's fur bristled. "Don't speak nonsense!"

Zhao Yunlan shut up, perhaps realizing that wasn't something he was capable of.

Daqing jumped onto his shoulder. "What about Chu Shuzhi?"

"Who cares? He actually dared challenge me! He can fucking drop dead for all I care. Don't bother me about him until his body's finally cold."

DURING THE MAGISTRATE'S VISIT, Guo Changcheng had been taking care of Chu Shuzhi. Unable to release him from the Soul-Guarding Order, all Guo Changcheng could do was tuck a throw blanket over him and put earphones on him so that he could watch movies and not be too bored.

For a while, Guo Changcheng sat and watched movies too, but eventually he fell asleep. He didn't wake until morning, when Zhao Yunlan called. With a start, he realized that Chu Shuzhi was standing up—and the blanket was covering *him* now.

Chu Shuzhi stood at the window, his expression serious as he gazed out at the pitch-black sky. It was late enough that the streetlights' timers had already automatically shut the lights off...and yet it was still dark outside.

On the other end of the phone, Zhao Yunlan said, "You're about to have a guest there. Keep an eye on your Chu-ge and tell him to remain calm. It's not time to burn bridges yet, but stay confident. There's no need to be overly polite to them, understand?"

Guo Changcheng didn't really follow. "Director Zhao, where are you?"

"Out taking care of some stuff." Zhao Yunlan's signal didn't seem to be very good. The line was crackling with static. "Don't go running off anywhere. Remember to call your family and tell them you're safe. Stay with Chu Shuzhi."

Guo Changcheng had just hung up when he heard the hair-raising sound of the woodblock. His head snapped around as someone knocked lightly on Zhao Yunlan's office door. Chu Shuzhi turned and calmly said, "Come in."

The locked door swung open with a creak, admitting a papier-mâché person in a tall hat. They were carrying a huge package, which they very politely set down in front of Chu Shuzhi. Next, they clasped their hands together, muttering under their breath.

Chu Shuzhi's appearance immediately began to change: tattooed words became visible on his face, and heavy shackles suddenly appeared around his wrists and neck. However, no sooner had those things appeared than they fell to the floor, text and shackles rolling into a small ball that the paper person took possession of.

Guo Changcheng's mouth hung open in shock.

The paper person bowed at him. Guo Changcheng hastily tried to return the gesture, only to accidentally bonk his head into Zhao Yunlan's monitor.

Chu Shuzhi opened the package. Most of its contents were made of bone that glowed with a cold, ominous light. They were all things he hadn't seen in three hundred years.

"Where's our Guardian?" Chu Shuzhi demanded.

But the reaper didn't dare speak. Giving nothing away, they shook their head, bowed at the pair of them, and hurried off as if they couldn't leave fast enough.

By that point, the Soul-Executing Emissary had arrived at the foot of Kunlun Mountain.

The air was thin and cold, carrying within it a desolate weight reminiscent of ancient times. Dawn had come, but the ink-black curtains of the night had no intentions of being drawn. As the wind blew, it sounded like weeping.

The Emissary couldn't help touching the Soul-Severing Blade at his waist.

At the sound of footsteps behind him, he spoke mildly without turning to look. "If everyone is here, let us proceed."

"Wait," said a familiar voice. "Not everyone's here yet. I was worried about flight delays, so I left a little early."

Hearing that, the Emissary whipped around and found himself looking at Zhao Yunlan. He was dressed in hiking gear from head to toe, with a black cat trailing close behind, and carrying a cup of coffee and a burger, which he bit into as he spoke. With a wave, he said, "Have you eaten, my lord? I still have a hash brown."

For a moment, the Soul-Executing Emissary—Shen Wei—wanted nothing more than to pound *him* into a hash brown. The fury that washed over him made even the black mist surrounding him tremble.

Zhao Yunlan found a passably flat rock, took a seat, and drained his cup of coffee. Using his canine teeth, he plucked the cheese slice out of his burger and discarded it. There was no outward sign that he realized he'd made the Soul-Executing Emissary swell into a balloon filled with rage.

Shen Wei moved to shield him from the wind. "What did I tell you?"

Zhao Yunlan wiped his mouth. "Don't agree to anything the Netherworld says and wait for you to come home."

Enunciating so crisply that there was a pause between words, Shen Wei said, "Then what are you doing here?"

After a quick look around to be sure they were alone aside from the black cat, Zhao Yunlan got up and hugged the Emissary. It was like embracing an ice sculpture. "What's wrong? Are you angry?"

Daqing silently turned aside to avoid witnessing the train wreck.

Shen Wei pushed Zhao Yunlan away. "Will nothing satisfy you until I die of anger?"

Zhao Yunlan took Shen Wei's hand and held it for just a moment before letting go. In a small, sincere voice, he said, "When we get back, you can make me kneel on Lego, okay? I really had no choice this time. Just ask Daqing. It's all because that brat Chu Shuzhi gave the Netherworld leverage over me..."

Clearly you *were the one with leverage against the Netherworld! You used it to force them to remove Chu Shuzhi's merit shackles!*

"Besides, I'm already here—too late for me to go back now." Zhao Yunlan spread his arms. "Don't be angry, you know it's bad for you. If anything were to happen to you because you were too angry, it'd break my heart. Shen Wei? A-Wei, xiao-Wei, babe... Come on, don't ignore me. Say something."

Daqing shuddered as if he'd pulled a muscle. Unable to bear hearing another word, he took a few steps further away.

Zhao Yunlan was just about to lean in shamelessly, when he suddenly sensed something. He immediately backed up several paces just as the Magistrate, Ox-Head, Horse-Face, and the Heibai Wuchang[18] arrived with a group of reapers. Trailing behind them was another large group, although it wasn't clear who exactly they were. This second group seemed to include yao and humans, and a few even had the auspicious aura of Buddhist enlightenment.

---

18 *Along with the Heibai Wuchang pair, Ox-Head and Horse-Face (牛头马面) are mythological beings who bring dead souls to the Netherworld. They are often paired as guards of the Netherworld gates.*

He and the Soul-Executing Emissary stood to either side of the people approaching. The Emissary was shrouded within his customary black mist, and Zhao Yunlan wore no expression at all. His face was a little pale, perhaps due to the cold or the high elevation. Even his lips were devoid of color. As he gazed at the new arrivals, his brow seemed to furrow slightly before he gave a dispassionate nod.

Something seemed off between the two of them, but no one could put a finger on why.

Having the Soul-Executing Emissary see Zhao Yunlan alone first had very much been part of the Magistrate's plan. If they were already at the foot of Kunlun Mountain, the Emissary would never allow Zhao Yunlan to head back alone, leaving him no choice but to take Zhao Yunlan up the mountain with them. After all, that was his beloved. Even if the Emissary were entertaining notions of defecting, Zhao Yunlan's presence would give him second thoughts. The Emissary certainly wouldn't dare take action with him there.

But by orchestrating this, the Netherworld had jabbed at the Emissary's tender underbelly, putting themselves solidly in his bad books. The Magistrate anxiously studied the Emissary's silhouette through the thick black mist, unsure if he had made the right move. "Magistrate" sounded like a weighty title, but he served at the pleasure of the Ten Kings of the Yanluo Courts. By the time matters fell in his lap, he didn't have all that much power. The Magistrate himself sometimes felt like his real job was to serve as a scapegoat.

The Magistrate gave a dry laugh. "The Guardian arrived so early." He then turned toward the Emissary, hands clasped, and bowed down nearly to the ground. With the greatest politeness, he began, "This lowly one..."

But before he even finished bowing, the Emissary had already turned and begun walking up the mountain. Withholding even the most basic of courtesies was a clear sign that he was furious. The Magistrate didn't dare object. He could only laugh awkwardly and call to the crowd to keep up.

The sky grew darker as they walked. Lightning and wind crashed together in the heavens. Looking up, one could glimpse a shape like that of a black dragon flickering in and out of sight.

Kunlun Mountain was sealed by ice year-round. It was as tall as thousands of men, majestic and craggy, and reached up into the very clouds. Here there were a thousand mountains among which no birds flew, and ten thousand trails with no sign of human passage.[19]

Zhao Yunlan had never been to Kunlun Mountain before. It had never crossed his mind that he could have any sort of connection with this great, snowy mountain. But after the long journey, in the first moment he set foot on Kunlun, he fully and abruptly understood what it meant to be bound by blood. It was a profoundly peculiar feeling, as though a data cable had reached into the depths of his very soul and connected him to this mountain range.

For a brief instant, everything else left Zhao Yunlan's mind. He forgot all the complicated scheming and plotting in his mind, the mishmash of beings around him, and even Shen Wei, who was still angry. Moving almost purely on instinct, he walked forward. The original Soul-Guarding Order, pressed against his chest, felt searingly hot.

As they continued up the mountain, Daqing, perched on Zhao Yunlan's shoulders, became increasingly nervous, as if he felt something.

"...Guardian? Guardian?"

---

19 *From the poem River Snow (江雪) by the Tang Dynasty poet Liu Zongyuan.*

Startled, Zhao Yunlan came back to himself to find the Magistrate tugging on him. It turned out they had reached a flat patch of ground covered in unbroken, pristine new snow. To one side were huge rocks as tall as a person, arranged into hexagrams in an eight-by-eight grid. Small vortexes intermittently blew through the formation, giving it a tranquil, almost solemn atmosphere.

With some reservation, the Magistrate said, "Past here is the Kunlun Mountain Pass. My apologies, but we must trouble the Guardian to take us up there."

Shen Wei's face was hidden, but the weight of his gaze was palpable. However, when Zhao Yunlan tried to meet his eyes, Shen Wei feigned aloofness and turned away. Zhao Yunlan smiled bitterly and gave Daqing's butt a pat, signaling him to get down. Pulling out the Soul-Guarding Order, he walked to the center of the giant rocks.

The watching crowd couldn't help holding their breaths as Zhao Yunlan took those steps. The moment he reached the center of the rock formation, the harsh wind died down to nothing. The trail of footprints he left behind him seemed lonely yet peaceful.

He stood still in the center and closed his eyes, revealing a profile as quiet as the deepest currents. Listening carefully, he heard an echo coming from the ten thousand great mountains:

North of the crimson waters, earth and sky do meet;
Ninety thousand slopes on which immortals hold their seat.
From lofty peaks that brush the clouds, all creation lies below.
Here was born the universe, where mountains stand and rivers flow...
Kunlun is its name.

Without a word of instruction from anyone, Zhao Yunlan knew exactly what to do. Something akin to a voice in his heart guided him. His eyes snapped open. Wherever he looked, the giant rocks turned in response, obediently rearranging themselves—as mystifying as the path of the stars. It was an overwhelming sight.

In Shen Wei's eyes, there was only one person in the world.

As Zhao Yunlan stood there in his mismatched windbreaker and boots, his short hair whipped into a snarled bird's nest by the wind, another silhouette overlaid him in Shen Wei's vision: that of a man whose green robe brushed the ground, an image from impossibly long ago.

He was unable to contain himself a moment longer. Black mist rose from his sleeve and enveloped Zhao Yunlan, cutting him off from everyone else's view. He was for Shen Wei's eyes only, as though they were the only people left in the world.

Shen Wei laughed bitterly at himself. Thousands of years ago, he would have gladly died in exchange for one more look from that man...and yet, at the same time, he'd felt himself unworthy of sullying those eyes. But now his greed was bottomless. He wanted nothing less than to be his beloved's one and only, and to be the only one who could so much as lay eyes on him.

All without him realizing it, the seed planted in his heart millennia ago had blossomed into a demon—one from which he couldn't break free.

Shen Wei had been fighting both nature and instinct for all he was worth since the day he entered the world. Yet in the end, a single unexpected meeting had been enough to be his undoing.

The earth began to shake. A distant roar came from atop Kunlun Mountain. Then the thick layer of clouds was torn asunder by a flash of divine lightning that struck the ground with all its devastating force. Atop the mountain, a strange mask flickered in and out of sight, as though Ghost Face was standing above them, looking down with eyes of ice.

The massive rock pillars toppled with a tremendous boom. Everyone present was instantaneously transported to the peak of Kunlun Mountain, the forbidden place of the gods.

Before they could find their footing, the black cat let out a howl. Following his gaze, they all saw the Great Divine Tree. It was as old as the very earth and sky, and its gnarled branches were half-withered. Not a single leaf grew; not a single blossom remained. Its aura was one of death.

The black cat struggled out of Zhao Yunlan's arms. The instant his paws hit the ground, his body shifted and elongated, taking human form. Zhao Yunlan, having never had even an inkling that Daqing could transform, stood dumbfounded for a moment.

The person before him had long hair as black as a raven's wing, pulled back in a ponytail, and gemlike, feline eyes. Daqing stared at the half-withered tree, eyes reddening with emotion, and spat, "Who dares make trouble atop Kunlun Mountain?"

In response, innumerous youchu surged up from the ground, as if born out of the ancient tree's roots. A fierce wind rose in the next moment, and Ghost Face's giant head appeared in the thick layers of clouds, spanning thousands of meters and blocking out the sun. An eerie smile adorned his face. His mountain-sized limbs and torso drifted in and out of view among the ever-present clouds and mist atop the mountain.

Forming a symbol with one hand, he reached behind himself with the other. A cauldron dozens of stories tall floated up into the air behind him. It spun furiously, generating a wind so loud and ferocious that it was painful to hear.

There was a shocked cry. "Soul-Tempering Cauldron! The Soul-Tempering Cauldron!"

Ghost Face reached out again with the same hand, now holding a huge axe. He swung it mercilessly downward.

Someone harshly shoved Zhao Yunlan aside. The fierce wind, reeking with blood, blew into his eyes. He was unable to force them open. As a great clang rang out, everyone turned to look and saw that the mountain of an axe had been stopped in its descent by a thick blade three chi and three cun long.

Below the axe, the Soul-Executing Emissary was like an ant holding up a behemoth. Fierce wind ripped at his sleeves, revealing slender, pale hands. There came a small crack as the Emissary twisted his wrist, and a corner of the huge axe chipped off. Then, as he turned to the side, another sharp clang sounded. The axe was driven a meter up in the air, and a thin crack started to spread from the chip through the rest of the weapon. It hit the ground with such force that a gigantic hundred-meter chasm opened at the peak of the snowy mountain. Countless youchu died under their master's axe before they could even crawl out of the earth.

"The Soul-Tempering Cauldron," the Emissary said quietly. "You're crazy."

"I'm not crazy. You've already taken the Mountain-River Awl, so you can have it. Sooner or later, you'll come to me with it. But the Merit Brush will be mine no matter what, and once two of the Four Pillars are broken and half the sky is overturned, nothing in the world will be able to stop me." Ghost Face's dark, heavy gaze swept around. "Why did you bring such an odd bunch with you? Were they afraid you'd jump ship on the spot?"

This was an indiscriminate attack, a slap delivered to almost everyone present in one fell swoop.

Ghost Face's gaze landed on Zhao Yunlan. Somehow, the smile on his face grew even creepier. "Oh, I see the Guardian is here too. No wonder."

Daqing's face went cold, but he only managed a single step before Zhao Yunlan grabbed him by the hair and yanked him back. Holding Daqing's ponytail in one hand, Zhao Yunlan dug out a cigarette with the other.

Daqing might've been in human shape, but he still had the instincts of a cat. Having his hair pulled made him turn and swipe at Zhao Yunlan, but since he no longer had claws, it only left a faint white mark. He realized Zhao Yunlan's hands were as cold as ice.

"Don't make things worse, you damn fatty." Zhao Yunlan rolled the cigarette between his fingers. Voice below even a whisper, he confided, "I'm a little nervous."

Daqing's eyes widened.

Zhao Yunlan glanced to one side. "The Crow tribe's there behind the Netherworld. The rest of the yao form one family, and then there're the Arhats of the West. Who are those people over there? Daoists?"

When the earth-shattering axe had made its descent, the crowd had automatically split into groups.

"They're either well respected or they've ascended to godhood," Daqing said. "But not a single one of them has the right to interfere in a battle between these two. If you hadn't brought them, they wouldn't even have been able to get up here. Other than these two, the only one I've seen who dared cause such a commotion here was a woman with a snake tail."

The one with a human face and snake body, one of the Three Sovereigns: Nüwa.

Snow began drifting down from the darkened sky. The hideous youchu stood opposite the denizens of the Netherworld; the tension between the two groups was ready to erupt at any moment.

Daqing turned to avoid looking at the Great Divine Tree, forcing himself to calm down, and told Zhao Yunlan, "You'd better back up a little."

The snow had extinguished Zhao Yunlan's cigarette. He pulled out a napkin, carefully wrapped the cigarette butt and ashes in it, and stuffed it all back into his pocket—very environmentally conscientious. He backed up outside the field of battle, circled around everyone else to the Great Divine Tree, and placed a hand on its icy, withered trunk.

No one knew how tall the Great Divine Tree was, but the exposed roots alone were level with Zhao Yunlan's chest. It was like a god entrenched in this place.

I don't know anything, he thought. *But you know me, don't you?*

As he thought those words, something brushed his fingers. Zhao Yunlan froze, then realized that a tiny, vivid green leaf had sprouted from the Great Divine Tree's trunk, right between his fingers. It slowly grew into a stalk as thin as a strand of hair and curled gently around his finger.

Zhao Yunlan smiled in surprise and felt for his lightweight hiking bag.

Just then, Ghost Face reached out. The massive Soul-Tempering Cauldron appeared between his huge palms, which seemed as if they could cover the sky. In stark contrast to his deathly pale fingers, wisp after wisp of black gas was surging within the Cauldron.

"The Ancient Merit Tree—the body that is dead but not yet born," said Ghost Face. "Does the Guardian know what exactly the Merit Brush is?"

Zhao Yunlan turned and leaned back against the Great Divine Tree, looking up at Ghost Face from a distance. "Why don't you tell me?"

"Before the Flame and Yellow Emperors famously fought with Chiyou, the gods were already embattled. Two Sovereigns, Fuxi and Nüwa, ascended Kunlun Mountain and asked for a branch from the Great Divine Tree with which to create order. Nüwa, resentful that she had created humans out of mud contaminated by the three worms, acted on her own. She thrust the branch from the Great Divine Tree into the Place of Great Disrespect—"

"Silence!" The Soul-Executing Emissary's shout tore the air.

The Soul-Executing Blade in his hand extended, as limitless as the Monkey King's staff from legends of old. While the hilt remained less than two cun, and thus possible to hold, it bore enormous weight, and the Blade's tip seemed to reach the very edge of the sky, stirring the wind and thunderclouds together. There came a loud *whoosh* as a bolt of lightning lanced downward, as if the very sky had been pierced. Divine thunder flew straight toward the crown of Ghost Face's head.

Ghost Face only laughed. Tilting his head back, he caught the heavenly thunder in his mouth and swallowed it whole. The Soul-Executing Blade followed immediately in its wake, slicing first through the Cauldron in Ghost Face's hands before ripping through, all the way up to his chest. Wherever the blade cut, razor-sharp wind rose up. Fist-sized shards of ice flew everywhere. Hordes of youchu rushed forward and began indiscriminately attacking the crowd on the mountaintop amid all the flying sand and rock.

Meanwhile, Zhao Yunlan sat on the swollen roots of the Great Divine Tree. He had no place in the chaotic battle, and he finally understood the Emissary's awkward position: Ghost Face didn't see him as an enemy, but no one here saw him as an ally either.

The Emissary and Ghost Face were unleashing their true capabilities now. Back under the Mountain-River Awl, if Ghost Face hadn't shown mercy, things definitely wouldn't have ended so easily.

Ghost Face hadn't seemed to want to fight the Emissary seriously at the time.

"The Place of Great Disrespect?" Zhao Yunlan murmured to himself.

In those few sentences, Ghost Face had given clear answers to the questions Zhao Yunlan had been turning over in his mind. Legend said that all people have three worms: greed, wrath, and delusion. In *Record of Ancient Secrets*, it said the three worms came from the dirt. By extension, the "Place of Great Disrespect" might very well be the origin of the so-called "three worms."

Ghost Face soared up into the sky, evading the Soul-Executing Blade. When he landed, the entire mountain trembled along with him.

He showed no sign of shutting up. "The Divine Tree is merciful. It withers first, then grows roots. That branch grew into the legendary Ancient Merit Tree. After the battle between the Flame and Yellow Emperors and Chiyou—"

"Shut up!" The Soul-Executing Blade slashed toward him horizontally. Zhao Yunlan could barely even see where Shen Wei was, much less imagine how he could so easily wield a blade that was nearly a hundred meters long.

The Blade followed Ghost Face's every move. His voice was once again cut off as his body suddenly shrank down. Just as it reached half of its previous size, the Blade swept across the top of his head, barely clearing it. The Soul-Tempering Cauldron hit the ground with a deafening boom.

Another endless wave of youchu began to appear around the Cauldron...but Ghost Face had disappeared.

Zhao Yunlan watched impassively, not turning around even when he felt someone approach from behind. But Daqing wasn't so calm. He sprang down from the tree, holding a short, palm-sized knife that had been hidden in his hand like feline claws. Phantom-like, he flung himself at the approaching person.

Ghost Face raised a hand and took the attack. There was a soft clang as Daqing's blade ricocheted off—was his wrist made of iron? Ghost Face made a grab for Daqing's neck, but even after transforming, Daqing was still impossibly nimble. Two quick backflips and he was back up in the Great Divine Tree's branches, fixing him with a hostile glare.

"Before trying to hit a cat, you should check to see who its owner is." Zhao Yunlan slowly turned to look at Ghost Face. His smile faded, leaving only a steady gaze. "You only managed to sneak your way to the peak of Kunlun Mountain thanks to my soul fire. Did you really think this was *your* territory?"

Those words seemed to hit harder than either lightning or thunder. Ghost Face stopped dead in his tracks, aggression seemingly forgotten. He hung back a good three meters away, not daring to take another step. Shen Wei, who had come rushing over, was equally unprepared to hear those words. He too stood immobilized.

"After the battle between the Flame and Yellow Emperors and Chiyou, the Three Sovereigns couldn't bear to see any more suffering. After seeking guidance from the Heavens, they carved a Merit Brush from the Ancient Merit Tree. Everything has a spirit, and the Merit Brush records all the merits and sins, rights and wrongs, of those living spirits," Zhao Yunlan said evenly. "Later, the Merit Brush became one of the Four Hallowed Artifacts. When Nüwa repaired the sky, it was used to seal the Four Pillars of Heaven. The Reincarnation

Dial fell to the Mortal Realm, the Mountain-River Awl landed below the earth, and the Merit Brush..."

The corner of Zhao Yunlan's mouth curved up as he glanced to the side. "The Merit Brush shattered into countless fragments and fell onto every living being in the world. Isn't that right, Magistrate?"

From his hiding place behind the Great Divine Tree, the Magistrate slowly came forward and prostrated himself. Voice trembling, he said, "This lowly one has concealed much. I truly had no other choice. Kunlun-jun, please let me atone for my crimes."

The Soul-Tempering Cauldron started to shake violently, and the entire mountain with it. Behind Zhao Yunlan, countless new buds burst into life on the Great Divine Tree. The dead branches rustled as sparse, tiny flowers formed.

The man leaning casually against the trunk of the tree said, "Since the Merit Brush belongs to me, Kunlun, why don't you return it to its rightful owner?"

The face on the ghost mask twisted involuntarily.

Zhao Yunlan spared him a glance. "You don't need to act all mysterious with me. I know what you look like."

Feeling Shen Wei stiffen, Zhao Yunlan dropped his voice as though explaining. "All forms are illusory. Do you really think I can't tell two different people apart?"

Before the Emissary could open his mouth, a huge wind picked up on the peak of Kunlun Mountain, even fiercer than it did during the battle between the Emissary and Ghost Face. It nearly blew Daqing straight out of the tree. He promptly transformed back into his cat form, claws digging into the tree for purchase.

Zhao Yunlan, leaning against the tree, avoided being buffeted about, but nobody else was so lucky. The Magistrate fell on his face. Dozens of youchu were flung up into the vortex of wind. The beings

who had taken to the air fell to the ground, rolling with the force of the impact.

Within the vortex, the outline of a massive brush faded in and out of view—the Merit Brush!

The Soul-Tempering Cauldron disintegrated entirely, and the Merit Brush once again appeared in the Mortal Realm.

Zhao Yunlan, Shen Wei, and Ghost Face held each other in check. For a time, no one moved.

Ghost Face spoke first. "Since the Guar—Mountain God is so sure that he'll have the Merit Brush sooner or later, why don't you go ahead?"

Though he could barely stand upright against the fierce wind, Zhao Yunlan successfully maintained his pose like a wise master. "Perhaps someone's waiting to reap the benefits without doing any work."

The Magistrate, who had a huge lump on his head, didn't dare make a sound.

Ghost Face sighed. "We are indebted to the Mountain God for the use of your soul fire. I really wish it didn't have to be this way."

And then he whistled.

Hundreds of youchu burst from beneath the ground and surrounded them. The Emissary immediately took up a position beside Zhao Yunlan, hands on the hilt of his blade.

In the next moment, the Merit Brush started to rapidly shrink and came flying straight toward the Great Divine Tree. Before anyone could react, it flew right into the Tree.

Everyone was caught off guard. Ghost Face flung out a sleeve and sent the Magistrate flying, then began to reach into the Great Divine Tree—only to have his hand blocked by Zhao Yunlan.

Ghost Face's arm was hard and cold. Zhao Yunlan felt as though he'd slammed his wrist against a rock. He didn't need to pull his sleeve back and check to know it was going to bruise.

Fortunately, Ghost Face didn't dare fight him head-on. He slipped past Zhao Yunlan and thrust his claws into the Great Divine Tree, but was rewarded only with a sharp, grating noise that could set anyone's teeth on edge. Ghost Face's hand was mercilessly forced back out of the tree. Two of his metal-hard nails had snapped off entirely.

Ignoring the pain in his wrist, Zhao Yunlan feigned a lack of surprise. All smiles, he said, "I tried to stop you so you wouldn't get hurt, but you really don't know what's good for you, huh?"

Ghost Face ground his teeth hard enough for all to hear. He spun away, transformed into a swirl of black mist, and disappeared. He didn't bother to take the youchu, who were still heading for Zhao Yunlan. Every one of them was cut down by the Soul-Executing Blade without getting within a meter of Zhao Yunlan.

Zhao Yunlan sighed in relief and tentatively touched the Great Divine Tree. Some sort of gravitational pull was trying to draw him inside.

The hood of Shen Wei's cloak had fallen back in the fierce gale when the Merit Brush first appeared. Not much of the black mist remained around him, revealing glimpses of the face Zhao Yunlan knew. His expression was complicated—hopeful and worried, with a hint of cautious nervousness. "Do you remember everything?"

Shaking his wrist, Zhao Yunlan winced. "Remember what? I just guessed and made up more bullshit as I went... What is that brat *made* of? Why is he so hard?"

Shen Wei didn't know how to respond.

"Help me stop them. I think the Great Divine Tree is calling to me," Zhao Yunlan said. He began climbing into the Tree. Once he was halfway in, a thought occurred to him. Turning back, he said to Shen Wei, "Whoever gets home first, remember to leave the door unlocked and the lights on. Love you."

With that, he disappeared into the Great Divine Tree.

BY THE TIME SHEN WEI had dealt with all the youchu on the peak of Kunlun Mountain, the stragglers were also gone, having at least some ability to read the room. Only Ox-Head and Horse-Face remained, supporting the Magistrate between them. They kept their distance from Shen Wei, as if they wanted to say something to him but were too afraid to approach.

Shen Wei extended a hand to Daqing. "Come. I'll take you home."

Daqing hesitated for a moment. His legs were stumpy and so was his courage, but it wouldn't do for a cat to be left alone in all this ice and snow, so his only real choice was to thank Shen Wei timidly and jump onto his shoulder. Shen Wei and Zhao Yunlan were actually built similarly, but somehow Daqing felt uncomfortable enough on this new perch that he had to curl up into a black puff of fur.

The Magistrate finally scraped together enough courage to call out. "My lord—"

Shen Wei put the Blade away without breaking stride. "You should all leave," he said, blank-faced, as he cut the Magistrate off. "Don't force me to be discourteous."

The sky finally brightened as sunlight belatedly streamed down over them.

The Soul-Executing Emissary could cross great distances as if they were mere centimeters and travel thousands of kilometers in a heartbeat. It was barely past noon when he and Daqing returned to Zhao Yunlan's little apartment. All the TV stations were covering the morning's strange phenomenon, and since the mainstream media appeared to have nothing better to talk about, they were inviting all sorts of quack experts to come on air and expound on their wild theories.

Shen Wei waited for a full three or four hours. As the afternoon sun began sliding westward, Shen Wei's phone vibrated a few times on the table. Shen Wei had only a passing familiarity with electronic devices, so he initially didn't react at all. Daqing had to meow delicately and nudge the phone toward him before he even took notice. A jolt ran through him as he seemed to reanimate.

Unlocking his phone, he found three texts that had been sent in rapid succession.

The first read: *Signal at last! Nothing happened. I'll be home soon.*

The second, sent just a minute later: *Upper management's calling on me. There's a dinner I have to attend tonight. I just saw. Don't wait up.*

And the third one followed immediately: *Go to bed early. Be good.*

Daqing circled halfway around the couch, gathering his courage to ask, with the utmost courtesy, "My lord, was that our Guardian?"

"Mnn." Shen Wei nodded. "He said he had some things to take care of and will be back later."

Daqing let out a sigh of relief, hesitated again, and said, "Then... Then I'll take my leave and head over to the office."

Shen Wei lowered his eyes, and Daqing instinctively bowed his head under that gaze. He might have been an entirely different cat from the one who had always comfortably called him "Shen-laoshi."

Shen Wei nodded again. "Safe travels."

Having been granted leave, Daqing sprang to his feet, unlocked the door, and jogged out.

Zhao Yunlan did not, in fact, have some dinner to attend. In reality, he didn't go anywhere in particular. Having texted Shen Wei, he just wandered aimlessly through the streets of Dragon City.

It was a chilly, damp winter with an abundance of snow and fog. The ground was glazed with frosted ice. A few shops along the road had already closed for the day, and not many pedestrians were out and about. It all gave the streets a desolate feeling.

Zhao Yunlan's bloodshot eyes made him seem a little worse for wear. He was still just roaming around when his phone rang. He hesitated when he saw the caller ID but ended up answering the call. "Hey, Dad."

"Mnn," said the voice on the other end of the line. "Why wasn't your phone in service?"

The spot where he'd stopped to take the call was right in the wind. The cold, dry air blowing in his eyes made them even redder. He was half a beat late to react. "Maybe the signal wasn't very good."

"Then where are you now?" asked his dad.

Zhao Yunlan wasn't entirely sure. He hung up and shared his location on his phone, then hunkered down on the side of the road to wait. Twenty minutes or so later, a car pulled up. The driver leaned out and fixed him with a judgmental look. "Why do you look like a panhandler? Get in."

Zhao Yunlan gave a weak roll of his eyes and stood up while stomping his feet to get some feeling back into them. There was an aura of sorrow about him.

Once he was in the car, his dad stepped on the gas and then glanced at him. "Where did you go, dressed up like that?"

"The Tibetan Plateau," Zhao Yunlan said flatly.

"For what?"

"To help capture some poachers."

"Cut the crap," said his father.

Zhao Yunlan answered with silence, and eventually his father was the one who broke it.

"Your mom told me a few days ago. I wasn't sure how to approach you about this, so I didn't come find you right away."

Zhao Yunlan gave him a tired glance. Wasn't a brawl involving all Three Realms enough for one day, never mind the severe physical and emotional trauma he'd been through? Now he had to come out of the closet to his dad? But then, at least he couldn't get any *more* miserable. He let out a half-dead grunt of acknowledgment.

His father kept talking. "When you were little, I was focused on advancing my career. I was too busy to pull my weight with you, but I didn't really think anything of it. Later, after you'd started school, your mom dragged me to the parents' club. On weekends, a bunch of us parents would sit and chat about our kids. That's when I realized you were different from the other children."

He smiled helplessly. "Let's talk about this some other time, okay, Dad? I'm really not up for it today."

"I've already been too easy on you. Remember how I let you indulge your wild fantasies and apply to create some Special Investigations Department? I even pulled some strings for you. But did I ever put my nose in your business? I'm giving you an inch here. Don't take a mile."

Zhao Yunlan leaned back. "Fine. What do you want to know?"

"First, the clichéd question: will you break up with that teacher?"

"Absolutely not."

"Let's discuss this rationally," his dad said. "Tell me, what do you like about him? What's so special about him that he's irreplaceable? What about him is worth facing societal pressure and public opinion, never mind the issue of not having a legal marriage? Why is it that, even with all that stands between you two, it has to be him?"

"Mom's not as pretty as Zhiling-jiejie,[20] so what made you give up on all the fish in the sea just to be with her?" Zhao Yunlan replied, impatience creeping into his tone. "To hell with public opinion. And what's the big deal about legality? I can draw myself a marriage certificate. There're all sorts of official seals sold near University Street carved out of white radishes. They're only five yuan apiece. I can put as many seals on it as I want."

"I'm trying to have a civil conversation here," said his dad. "What's with your attitude?"

Zhao Yunlan lowered his head and gave his brow a firm pinch.

"Have you considered that once you've gotten your kicks and your hormones return to normal you'll regret this decision?" his dad continued steadily. "Passion is a beautiful thing. I know how it is. I was young once too. But if a love faces too many obstacles, I don't condone pursuing it. Do you know why?"

Zhao Yunlan didn't answer.

"Have you read *Anna Karenina*?" The car crawled along the empty road at twenty miles an hour. "Why did Anna die in the end? It was because an unfaithful love is immoral, because a third party gets hurt. And yes, that doesn't apply to you two, but your relationship still has something in common with that one: it's not accepted

---

20 *Lin Chi-Ling, a Taiwanese model and actress, at one point widely considered one of the most desirable female celebrities in the Sinosphere.*

by mainstream society. Love is very resilient, but it's also delicate. In the face of oppression and obstacles, it can become a huge driving force—a love for the ages. There's a reason people have sung about it for all of human history. But remember: it's not the tall mountain in your path that defeats you. It's always the grain of sand in your shoe."

"What's your point?"

His dad sighed. "Sheer strength of will and sacrifice can carry a love past all the huge obstacles, but sooner or later, passion inevitably calms down. Have you thought about what happens then? You'll reach a point where seeing each other won't make you think about the way your hearts used to beat for one another when you first fell in love. Instead, you'll look into his eyes and only remember all the pain and suffering that being together brought you. How will you face him? How will he face you? Have you considered that? It happens to everyone. Don't think you'll be an exception. Do you still remember that ice cream you loved when you were a kid?"

Zhao Yunlan shook his head.

"Your mom never let you have junk food, so you obsessed over it day and night. You even had a hunger strike. Then one time, after I got back from a work trip, I had an idea. I took you to that shop three times a day, and every time, I let you pick whatever you wanted—at least two tubs each time. Even when eating it all gave you an upset stomach, I didn't relent. You had no choice. For an entire month, I forced you to eat it until you started crying if that ice cream store was even mentioned. You clung to the doorframe and refused to go."

"Dad of the Year right there."

Calmly, his father continued. "Now, think it over carefully before you answer. Do you really think you can continue like this with that teacher?"

Zhao Yunlan found and opened a bottle of water and gulped half of it down in one go. His voice still rasped when he spoke. "Shen Wei and I have actually known each other for a long time. When I stop and think about it, I've known him since I first started working. That's several years now. Dad, I hear what you're saying, but there are people in the world where it's not about how great they are, or how it feels like you can't live without them, but rather the feeling that if you do wrong by them, you're lower than scum."

His dad glanced over at him. Zhao Yunlan slumped against the seat, his eyes half-closed. Perhaps it was a lack of sleep, but his unusually heavy double eyelids almost seemed to fold into three layers.

Zhao Yunlan's dad chewed over his answer for a while. Finally, he said, "You're an adult. There are some things I don't have the right to meddle in too much. Sometime when you're both free, you can bring him over for a meal when I'm home."

"Thanks." Zhao Yunlan had managed to defeat the boss, but he didn't look happy at all. His eyebrows were still knitted together lightly. After another stretch of silence, he said, "Dad, would you have a few drinks with me?"

His dad gave him another glance and wordlessly turned the car around. They soon found themselves in a small, relatively quiet restaurant owned by a local. His dad opened the drink menu, pushed it toward Zhao Yunlan, and then ordered a pot of Iron Goddess tea for himself. Father and son sat across from each other, interestingly similar in temperament. Each drank their own drinks without bothering the other.

Drinking alcohol didn't make Zhao Yunlan flush—quite the opposite. The more he drank, the paler he got. Once he'd gone through more than two bottles, his dad stopped him from calling for the server, then asked for a cup of honey water to be brought over.

To Zhao Yunlan, he said, "You can drink a little when you're in a bad mood, but I'm your father. I have to keep an eye on you. I can't let you get alcohol poisoning or rot your gut with the stuff."

After a pause, Zhao Yunlan said, "I haven't eaten yet. Get me a plate of fried rice."

"Can you tell me what happened now? Did you and the teacher have a fight?" his dad asked.

"Oh, please." With some difficulty, Zhao Yunlan managed a smile. "I'm way too old to get in a fight over something stupid."

"Then what happened?"

Zhao Yunlan stared at the marble tabletop as if trying to find a pattern in the irregular swirls. His eyes stayed fixated on it until his water and food came. Then, as if talking to himself, he murmured, "If...you did something, and you don't know if it was right or wrong, what would you do?"

His dad lit a cigarette. "Having lived this long, I feel like there are four things in life you can't be too persistent about figuring out: the idea of eternity, right or wrong, good and evil, and life and death."

Zhao Yunlan looked up at him as his father continued, "First, persistence can be a virtue, but if you're inflexible and insist that something must last forever, you'll fear loss even while you hold that thing in your hands. You won't be able to see your path clearly. Second, of course you should have a sense of justice, but if you're consumed by the idea that something must be right or wrong, it's easy to develop tunnel vision. There aren't that many absolute rights or absolute wrongs in the world.

"Third, while it's important to repent of your mistakes and strive for goodness, being locked into a dichotomy of good and evil will make you rigid and unforgiving. You'll become arrogant and expect the world to conform to your perspective, and you'll always be disappointed. And finally, while life and death are tremendously important, if you live your entire life in terror of death, you'll never really live at all."

Silently, Zhao Yunlan kept listening.

"There are some things that aren't worth that kind of pondering. In my opinion, once you've made a decision, there's no need to be bogged down in thinking about whether it was right or wrong. Instead of torturing yourself with those thoughts, why not think about what you can do about it now? What do you think?"

Zhao Yunlan's heart jolted. A bit of brightness entered his dull gaze. After sitting stiffly for a while, he gulped down all the honey water before calmly saying, "I can't eat another bite. I'm going to go throw up now. After that, will you drive me home?"

As requested, Zhao Yunlan's dad drove him to his apartment but made no move to accompany him inside. "That teacher lives with you, right? He's unprepared, so I won't just show up without warning. Go on in. We can make proper plans at a later date."

Zhao Yunlan waved without looking back and made his way upstairs with the starry night behind him.

Shen Wei was still waiting up. As soon as he heard the key, he got up and opened the door before Zhao Yunlan even got it unlocked. Zhao Yunlan looked sober enough, but he reeked of alcohol and tripped over the threshold as he came inside. Shen Wei quickly steadied him. "How much did you drink?"

"I'm fine." Zhao Yunlan pressed his forehead into Shen Wei's shoulder. "I need a shower first thing. Is there anything to eat?"

Shen Wei didn't know what to say. He had a bone to pick about Zhao Yunlan heading up Kunlun on his own without any warning, but the pitiful way he had a hand pressed to his stomach made it impossible for Shen Wei to speak up. He just sighed. "I'll go warm something up for you."

Zhao Yunlan gave him a quick kiss on the neck, then pulled out a long, narrow wooden box from his own inside pocket. "A gift," he said, pushing the box into Shen Wei's hands before disappearing into the bathroom.

After a moment, Shen Wei opened the nicely wrapped wooden box to find a calligraphy brush inside. The brush's handle was made of wood, and its bristles glistened with gold. There was a transcendent, subtle sheen to it. Despite its ordinary size, it was unmistakably the Merit Brush!

Just then, a loud noise from the bathroom startled Shen Wei. He tucked the Hallowed Artifact away and rushed to the door. "Yunlan? Are you all right?"

The bathroom had a tub with a shower head. Zhao Yunlan might have accidentally turned the water temperature up too high. He'd been only a bit drunk when he got in, but the hot steam sent the alcohol in his system straight to his head. It made him careless, and he slipped and fell heavily against the bottom of the tub, golden stars swimming before his eyes.

Shen Wei waited for a response, but when none came, he pushed open the bathroom door...

...And came face-to-face with a reminder that no one showered with their clothes on.

Zhao Yunlan was dazed from the fall, and the relentless stream of hot water only made the world spin faster around him. He grabbed the edge of the tub with both hands, struggling to get to his feet. The curve of his back showed off his sharp shoulder blades; smooth lines of muscle met at his slim waist. The planes of his body were indescribably beautiful.

A single glance was all it took for Shen Wei to overheat as well.

Panicked, Shen Wei looked away and grabbed a large bath towel, then floundered as he turned off the shower. Still not looking, he extended his arms and flung the towel over Zhao Yunlan. Blushing right to the tips of his ears, with the thick towel between their bodies, he carefully got Zhao Yunlan out of the tub, half helping and half carrying him.

On the upside, Zhao Yunlan's brain was still so sodden that he wasn't making things worse with his smart mouth.

Zhao Yunlan's body heat quickly radiated through the towel, and since the towel wasn't up to the task of covering him completely, Shen Wei had intermittent glimpses of his long legs. Temples pounding, Shen Wei gently eased Zhao Yunlan down onto the bed. Then he yanked his hands back as though electrocuted and simply stood there at a loss.

Seeing damp spots on the pillow finally brought him back to his senses. He draped the blanket over Zhao Yunlan before daring to take hold of a corner of the towel and carefully pull it out from beneath the blanket.

But as he did so, Zhao Yunlan suddenly grabbed his hand.

The drunkard was surprisingly strong, his palms warm and still damp from the shower. His half-open eyes were unfocused, his gaze lost, and his face was bright red.

Shen Wei's throat felt like it was on fire, and his Adam's apple bobbed.

Zhao Yunlan said something too muddled to make out. Shen Wei bent down and nervously leaned toward his mouth. "What was that?"

The hand gripping his tightened. "I'm sorry..." Zhao Yunlan mumbled, as if in a dream. "I'm so sorry..."

Shen Wei froze. Slowly, he sat on the edge of the bed and gathered Zhao Yunlan close, still bundled in the blanket. He patted Zhao Yunlan's back softly. "What is there for you to be sorry for?"

Zhao Yunlan flipped over and wrapped his arms around Shen Wei's waist, exposing the upper half of his own naked body. Shen Wei pulled a hand back but then had nowhere to put it. It hung awkwardly in midair.

Then, belatedly, he realized Zhao Yunlan was shaking all over.

Wanting to raise Zhao Yunlan's head, Shen Wei attempted to break free, but Zhao Yunlan's embrace tightened into a death grip. With a start, Shen Wei felt a trace of wetness on his clothes and lifted Zhao Yunlan's chin. There were no visible tear tracks, but his eyes were all red.

Zhao Yunlan had only been half-drunk to begin with and capable of at least acting like a normal person. But between the alcohol going to his brain and the fall in the tub, his head felt far heavier now. He barely knew what he was saying even as he repeated, over and over, "I'm so sorry."

Shen Wei felt as though his heart had been set ablaze. All the water in the world couldn't have extinguished the flame raging in his chest.

In the dark quiet of the night, his hand finally came to rest on Zhao Yunlan's bare back. Every inch of warm skin tested his nerves. Eyes bottomless as the abyss, Shen Wei brought his mouth closer to Zhao Yunlan's ear. "Every living being under the sun has wronged me," he breathed. "All but you."

Zhao Yunlan shook his head. A droplet hung from his eyelashes; it might have lingered from the shower, or it might have been a tear. He barely had the energy to speak. In all his thirty years of life, he had never felt such a crushing weight on his mind.

Lowering his head, Shen Wei pressed trembling lips to Zhao Yunlan's eyes. He kissed that stray droplet, tasting its faint saltiness and bitterness. Barely audible, he said, "You gave me my life, my eyes. You gave me everything. How have you wronged me?"

"If I'd known..." Zhao Yunlan said in a haze, "If I'd known... I wish I'd killed you back then. I never would've..."

He didn't continue. Shen Wei caught him up in an embrace. By now, the crumpled blanket had fallen away, lying uselessly off to the side. Shen Wei propped himself up with his hands on either side of Zhao Yunlan's body, scarcely able to breathe. His chest heaved. "Kunlun...? Is it you?"

Zhao Yunlan lay face up on the bed, a thread of tears streaming from the corner of his eye. His eyes suddenly closed, as though his heart held more pain than he could endure. Even his brow was tinged red. He didn't answer or respond to the question. Again and again, he repeated, "I'm so sorry."

"Five thousand years beneath the sky on this mortal earth, and that's all you have to say to me?" Shen Wei asked quietly.

He had once told Li Qian that in life, there are only two things worth dying for: to fulfill your duty to your home and country, or to give your life for someone who truly knows you. Throughout history, people have spoken of sacrificing oneself for someone who truly understands them. Shen Wei's willingness to die for Zhao Yunlan also encompassed a willingness to live for him, to give Zhao Yunlan everything he was and savor the resulting pain like honey.

"They all want Kunlun-jun to return. In order to awaken his spirit, they went as far as destroying your vision to pry open your Heavenly Eye and then demanded that you ascend Kunlun Mountain to face the Great Divine Tree," Shen Wei said softly. "I want him back too.

I miss him to the point of madness. But I can't bear you going back to how he was. Kunlun-jun bore the weight of ten thousand mountains and rivers on his shoulders, and more—the natural order of things, the Great Seal, the Reincarnation Cycle... There's no room to breathe. I don't want you to live with that pain. All I want now is for you to be mortal and content."

Voice muffled, Zhao Yunlan said, "You were the one who sealed Daqing's memories and severed the connection between me and the Soul-Guarding Order."

Shen Wei shut his eyes piously.

"So I'll be a content mortal while you shoulder the weight of the Great Seal? Who are you to decide that?" Zhao Yunlan's voice rasped painfully, barely a wisp of sound despite his best efforts. "You accepted me that day because you thought a mortal life lasts barely a hundred years—over in the blink of an eye. Next time I reincarnate, I'll just forget you again, right? Were you going to accompany me on this last stretch and then...then follow in Nüwa's footsteps...?"

Zhao Yunlan dragged Shen Wei down by the collar, fingers trembling almost convulsively. His teeth gritted tightly together. "I'll never allow it! Not even in death!"

Shen Wei let himself be pulled down. Half-crazed, Zhao Yunlan hooked an arm around Shen Wei's neck and took him in his arms, kissing him desperately. He tore two buttons off Shen Wei's shirt, baring an expanse of pale chest. "*Never*, do you hear me?!"

It was the first time their bodies had touched like this, skin on skin. The spark that ignited between them instantly became a wildfire, burning beyond any hope of control. It seamlessly blended with the memory of countless intimate, tender midnight dreams from which Shen Wei had bolted awake; *this* was like a grand dream that upended the Mortal Realm entirely.

Dreaming, Shen Wei had never known when he would wake or when it would fragment around him. Now he found that the dream that could never see the light of day, the dream with the power to split the sky and shatter the earth, had always been born of the thoughts he didn't dare entertain in daylight. It had been the heart that was never able to bare itself; the heart that couldn't be born, couldn't die, couldn't be forgotten, and couldn't be remembered.

At last, Shen Wei's control broke. Reclaiming the upper hand, he turned Zhao Yunlan over beneath himself, pressing him down into the soft pillows. The dam in his heart finally burst, unleashing torrential floods.

The next day, Zhao Yunlan was woken up by sunlight streaming in through the curtains. He was disoriented for a while, thinking he might have eaten his own brain as a drinking snack the night before. It felt like he'd spent the entire night in a daze.

He tried to open his eyes, but the lids were too heavy. The slightest movement made the ceiling spin. He fell back down against the mattress.

Had he been able to look in a mirror, he would have seen that his face was horribly ashen—far more so than the face of someone who just felt a little weak. It was the face of someone worryingly near their deathbed.

Hands carefully helped him sit up, and a bowl was brought to his lips. Whatever the medicine was, Zhao Yunlan didn't recognize it. The smell was incredibly strange—raw and visceral. He instinctively shied back. "Wha..."

"Herbal medicine. I hurt you last night." Shen Wei's tone was very gentle, but his actions were not. He turned Zhao Yunlan's face firmly and all but force-fed the stuff to him.

Zhao Yunlan regained some energy at once. He shoved Shen Wei's hand away, gagging so hard that he dissolved into a coughing fit. The vile taste had him on the edge of throwing up. Then a glass of water touched his mouth. Finally wide awake, he opened his eyes, glanced at Shen Wei, and drank the water silently.

Afterward, he sat up, leaning against the headboard with his elbows on his knees. He gave Shen Wei a dejected look, then lowered his head and reflected. Eventually, after yet another dejected glance, he forced some words out. "I've always topped before. Even if you didn't check with me first, couldn't you have been a little nicer about it?"

Shen Wei flushed red. He looked away and coughed awkwardly. "I'm sorry."

"I..." Zhao Yunlan began, but the soreness at his waist made his expression twist. He gasped faintly, then caught sight of Shen Wei's expression. Shen Wei looked as if Zhao Yunlan had somehow been the one taking advantage, not the other way around! Sure, he'd always dreamed of dying in some beauty's bed, but this was *not* what he'd had in mind. What the fuck?!

Zhao Yunlan's face flushed red, then purple. Then he looked down at the bowl that had held the unfamiliar medicine, and the thought of the flavor made his face twist again. "Bring me another glass of water." Shen Wei got up immediately. Zhao Yunlan couldn't resist adding, "You know, anti-inflammatories would've been fine."

Shen Wei took the bowl from him. "This is effective. I wouldn't harm you."

Stone-faced, Zhao Yunlan said, "I'd prefer if you didn't try to torment me to death."

The gentlemanly Shen-laoshi stood there with the expression of someone who had brought shame upon his family. He looked uncannily like a pitiful wife who had accidentally smashed a bowl.

It infuriated Zhao Yunlan enough to not want to look at him.

Shen Wei timidly approached and helped ease him back down. "You... You should sleep a little more. Do you want to eat anything?"

"Yes, you." Zhao Yunlan said stubbornly. "Lie down and let me ravage you."

Shen Wei lowered his gaze, the tips of his ears burning. He licked his lips awkwardly and asked, "What nonsense are you going on about in broad daylight?"

For fuck's sake, Zhao Yunlan thought.

Shen Wei had treated him without a medical license, but whatever the medicine had been, it seemed like drowsiness was a side effect. Zhao Yunlan's head had barely touched the pillow again and his consciousness was already blurring. But he still held onto Shen Wei's hand, not giving up. "I've already given all of myself to you, so don't try to start any shit, you hear me? The natural order can't stop humans from finding a way. The Great Seal... I have a solution... I have..." His voice weakened with every word.

Shen Wei rested his palm against Zhao Yunlan's forehead, feeling his breathing even out slowly.

Thanks to the "herbal medicine," some color was returning to Zhao Yunlan's gray cheeks. Relieved, Shen Wei stood up quietly and went to the kitchen to wash the bowl.

Zhao Yunlan slept until the evening, dreaming chaotic, fragmented dreams the whole time.

THAT DAY WHEN Zhao Yunlan had walked into the Great Divine Tree, the Merit Brush wasn't the only thing he came back out with.

The Great Divine Tree and Kunlun Mountain were connected at the roots, cradling the full history of five thousand years. As Zhao Yunlan walked inside, he felt as if he'd entered an alternate dimension. When he looked back, there was no sign of where he'd come from, while what lay ahead seemed to stretch out before him in an infinite expanse.

There was no light around him at all, and the air was stagnant. He was in absolute blackness, but he kept squinting into the distance and finally found a dim pinprick of light, small as a firefly. As he approached, he saw it was the Merit Brush, now shrunk to the size of an ordinary calligraphy brush.

He reached out for it. Somewhat to his surprise, he was able to take hold of it with almost no effort. However, as soon as he had it in his hand, he began to feel a pull through the brush, leading him forward.

Logically, Zhao Yunlan knew that, having gotten what he'd come for, he should immediately start finding a way back out. But in that moment, for whatever reason, he couldn't help moving toward whatever was drawing him in deeper.

He couldn't have said how long he walked through the darkness. His phone was unresponsive, his lighter wouldn't even throw a spark—all the light sources he had on him had stopped working. Fortunately, his resolve was firm, and he had no fear of darkness or enclosed spaces.

The darkness surrounding him was unique; being inside it wasn't uncomfortable at all. In fact, he got the sense that he was meant to sleep soundly here. He yawned as he walked, feeling himself grow drowsy.

There came a huge *crack* by his ear. Before he could figure out what had caused it, it was followed by another huge noise. The darkness shattered and cold light poured in. Zhao Yunlan jumped and backed up a dozen or so steps before looking up. He had to immediately close his eyes against the vast swath of light shining down upon him. Cracking his eyes open the tiniest bit, he saw a giant axe.

The axe was what had split the darkness open!

Yet another loud noise sounded. A fissure opened beneath his feet and rapidly widened and lengthened, dividing the ground.

The great axe was brandished by a man: a man of incomparable size, whose head touched the very sky while his feet were planted firmly upon the earth. His hair and beard were untamed. His mouth opened and unleashed an angry roar that quaked the whole world.

It came to pass that Pangu's cleverness surpassed that of the heavens and his strength eclipsed that of the earth. Each day the sky rose higher, the earth grew thicker, and Pangu grew taller. In this way, eighteen thousand years passed. The height of the sky and the depth of the earth attained incredible vastness, and so too did Pangu grow taller still.

When the day came that ninety thousand li lay between the sky and the ground, then too came the Three Sovereigns.[21]

This, then, was Pangu.

Before Zhao Yunlan's eyes, the sky ascended and the ground thickened. He saw Pangu plummet with a mighty crash, his axe breaking in two as it fell. Its long handle became Buzhou Mountain, and its massive head became Kunlun Mountain. The man's own limbs and head became eight great mountains spread across the land, rising steeply from the earth to stand tall and support the sky.

After that came the rivers and lakes, the sun and moon, the mountain creeks and deep valleys.

As the rivers of time flowed into the sea, an unnamed sorrow flowed into Zhao Yunlan's heart. He couldn't help coming closer, wanting another look at this man to whom he was bound by blood. But he only managed to get there in time to bear witness as Pangu soundlessly disappeared in front of his eyes.

Zhao Yunlan spun back around and found that he was already in the endless Great Wild. Tens of thousands of years rushed past him. He heard the blowing wind of Buzhou and also the turbulence stirring deep within the earth, but none of them left even the barest of traces behind.

All these things that lay beneath the earth—whether sincere, brutal, insolent, unrestrained, or wild—were connected to the true bloodline of Kunlun.

Kunlun Mountain was born from the heavens and nurtured by the earth. Over the course of a billion and three thousand years, it developed a soul and was given the title of Kunlun-jun, the Mountain God of the Great Wild.

---

21 *From* Sanwu Liji (三五历记), The Historical Account of the Three Sovereigns and Five Emperors, *attributed to third-century author Xu Zheng.*

In those days, the Three Sovereigns were still young and the Five Emperors had yet to be born. Between the sky and the earth, there were only birds on the wing and beasts that walked upon the ground. There were no humans.

At that point, Zhao Yunlan's memories became jumbled. On the one hand, he knew where he'd come from. He kept a firm grip on the Merit Brush. On the other hand, he now remembered being an unruly brat who had run and frolicked all over the mountains, causing mischief wherever he went.

He had hugged the Great God Fuxi's tail...while peeing on it. The phoenix that had once perched upon the Great Divine Tree had been forced to move because of his antics, and from then on, it only perched atop parasol trees.

Sometime later, Nüwa found a tiny newborn beast from somewhere—a mutant mutt of the White Tiger tribe, covered in black fuzz from the tip of his nose to the tip of his tail. He had yet to gain awareness and had been rejected by his own tribe, so he was placed in Kunlun's care.

The poor little thing was very weak. Surrounded by the eternal ice on Kunlun Mountain, he seemed likely to die at any moment. It was the first time Kunlun-jun had seen such a troublesome little thing. Seeing no other choice, he personally melted some golden sand and crafted a bell to anchor the tiny beast's soul and open his mind. Then he hung the bell around the beast's neck.

All in all, it took an unbelievable amount of effort to be sure the little thing would survive, never mind thrive. As a result, Kunlun no longer had time to cause trouble for anyone else.

It wasn't until the puny beast reached the size of a dumpling and was able to run and jump that Kunlun went down the mountain, bringing the beast along. That was when he came across Nüwa, who was making humans out of mud. With an effortless flick of an immortal branch, countless "people" were born on the ground. They looked no different from the gods and demons themselves. Kunlun-jun had never witnessed such bustle and commotion. For a time, he was utterly enthralled and unwilling to look away.

Nüwa smiled at him. "Kunlun, you've grown so much."

Kunlun walked over carefully. He and the mud person Nüwa had just made stared at each other for some time. He watched as the human grew from a child to a youth in the blink of an eye. The youth worshipped him with reverence and awe, but before they could even rise from their bow, middle age was upon them. Next, they began to shed their head of black hair, which was now frosted white. Finally, they collapsed in abject weariness and rejoined the mud from which they'd come.

It was a life as fleeting as fire and smoke.

An unspeakable envy suddenly bloomed in Kunlun-jun's heart. Perhaps because his own time was beyond measure, he was somewhat jealous of these brilliant lives that burned with the brightness of a meteor. He scooped up some mud in his hands. "What are they called?"

Nüwa said, "These are humans."

Without considering his words, Kunlun replied, "How lovely they are. They carry the scent of mud with them."

Hearing that, Nüwa's expression transformed. For an instant, her features twisted as though she were consumed with shock and panic.

But Kunlun was still young. What did he know beyond rampaging around the Great Divine Tree with his furball cat, causing trouble? How could he have looked at her gaze and grasped that in that moment, she had perceived that innumerous trials and calamities lay ahead?

Humans were born from mud, through which the Chaotic evil beneath the ground was able to enter them and become the three worms. By the time Nüwa realized what had happened, humans had already started living together happily like monkeys. They had even followed her rules by separating into men and women, forging marital ties, and perpetuating their bloodlines. These people of mud were already roaming across all the mountains and lands, and even into the rivers and sea on the edge of the Great Wild. Countless days and months turned into years. Several generations passed.

Nüwa looked back and saw how the human world bustled with life, the smoke of communal fires rising through the air. Men and women were clad in animal furs and children played in groups. They were a happy, cheerful people with features no different from those of the gods and demons.

What was done was done. The only possible way to reverse it would be to utterly annihilate humanity.

The Heavens had already blessed Nüwa with great merits for her creation. She suddenly looked up at the sky with its disorderly swirls of stars and felt as if she had caught the first glimpse of something—something cold, restraining her from every direction. It was like an invisible, unstoppable hand pushing all humans and gods forward.

Nüwa covered her face and sobbed. Kunlun and the little beast stood helplessly aside.

Later, Nüwa sought help from the Great God Fuxi, borrowing three thousand stars from the Milky Way. Together, the two of them spent thirty-three days weaving a great seal that covered the entire ground.

Kunlun sat and watched, hugging his tiny furball. He had never supposed that so much magma lay below the land, erupting forth with a roar from the deepest places underground. The two onlookers had only the faintest idea of what they were seeing, unaware that

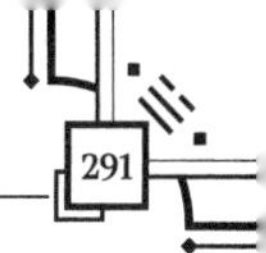

they had experienced a battle fiercer than even the Great War of Gods and Demons or the Battle of the Creation of Gods, which were yet to come.

Finally, Fuxi made a Bagua and forced the Great Seal down. In doing so, both he and the Chaotic evil underground suffered greatly, but the Great Seal was formed. Once it was accomplished, Kunlun never saw Fuxi again.

Nüwa borrowed a branch of the Great Divine Tree from Kunlun and planted it at the entrance of the Great Seal, thus demoting all that lay beneath it as the "Place of Great Disrespect."

When the Great Seal was first established, Kunlun felt a pang of emptiness in his heart. The brutality and evil of the now-sealed Chaos were like a tiny flame, scorching and dangerous. Given the slightest chance, it would bring about calamitous disaster. But it also burned hot and free, and Kunlun found himself yearning for it, ever so slightly. The young Kunlun couldn't say exactly what he was feeling, but he shed a string of inexplicable tears from which the Yangtze River later sprang.

Fuxi had disappeared, leaving Nüwa alone. She wandered the Great Wild Earth on her own, watching the people who rose with the sun and rested as it set, struggling to survive. The worry on her face only deepened.

In the end, Nüwa went into seclusion and would see no one. Kunlun-jun, in turn, returned to his Kunlun Mountain. During the turning of a hundred years, he passed by the Place of Great Disrespect several times and looked at that withered branch of the Great Divine Tree. As time passed, he grew to understand many more things; gradually, he realized what was locked behind the Great Seal and understood, if only vaguely, the intentions of the sages who had come before.

But although curiosity burned within him, Kunlun never indulged it. He never took a single step inside. He remembered the deep red heart's blood that Fuxi had vomited up when the Bagua first settled and would never do anything that might undermine that sacrifice.

But the seeds of the three worms had already been planted.

Time passed. The Human Sovereign[22] rose to the level of sage. Shennong's lineage declined. Xuanyuan, the Yellow Emperor, reigned over the humans while the wu and yao worshipped the ancient war god Chiyou. Xuanyuan and Chiyou engaged in battle so fierce that it dragged in the gods and demons, who were already diminishing, and the wu and yao, who had not come into their own. The entirety of the Three Realms was ensnared by this great catastrophe.

With the Three Sovereigns either defeated or vanished, the land that had been all but deserted was suddenly swarming with activity. The happy little mud people Kunlun remembered had become something he could barely fathom. They were pious and strong, warm and joyful, and yet they would fight and kill in the name of survival and power.

Humans contained qualities of both gods and demons, which enabled them—more than any other kind of living being—to form emotions of all kinds: jealousy, animosity, obsession, restraint...and unparalleled love and hatred.

It was then, finally, that Kunlun understood why Nüwa had been so fearful and panicked despite the merits rained down on her by the Heavens for her creation of humans.

---

22 *The Human Sovereign (人皇) is the third of the Three Sovereigns in some myths, after the Heavenly and Earthly Sovereigns. Other sources give this title to Fuxi, Nüwa, and Shennong, with some other variations.*

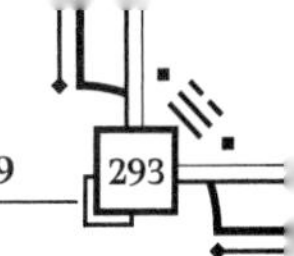

The Chaos that Pangu had torn asunder had never truly disappeared. Rather, it had infused itself into everything that existed in the world, and there it was still, ever-changing.

It came to pass that the fires of war spread across the Three Realms. Even the Heavens quaked with the impact, and the Kun-Peng[23] traveled west, never to return. Kunlun watched coldly from the sidelines as the first Great War of Gods and Demons raged. Seemingly influenced by the roiling malevolence, his heart, which had been pristine for all those thousands of years, came to harbor uncontrollable sorrow and frustration and unquenchable loneliness.

It seemed that Chiyou had foreseen his own defeat. His divine spirit left his body and came to the foot of Kunlun Mountain only for Kunlun-jun to close his doors and refuse to see him. Thus, the three-headed, six-armed war god climbed all the way up the mountain on his own two feet. His clothes were tattered, and he left a trail of blood in his wake, which would later become the galsang flowers that bloomed despite the harsh, frozen ground beneath the glaciers. Chiyou begged Kunlun-jun to look after the wu and yao, on the grounds that they had been born in these mountains.

When Kunlun-jun again refused to see him, Chiyou knelt just outside the boundary, kowtowing again and again.

Kunlun had lived a long, long time in this frozen land. His heart was colder and harder than the frozen stone of the mountain's peak. But his furball companion had been born a yao and so couldn't help being drawn to the ancestor of the yao. The little cat crept out and licked the blood from the wound that had

---

23 *Kun-Peng (鲲鹏) is a mythological creature that can transform between its fish form Kun (鲲) and its bird form Peng (鹏).*

opened on Chiyou's forehead after so much kowtowing against the ground.

By the time Kunlun-jun noticed, the wheels of fate had been set in motion. At long last, the Mountain God of the Great Wild, like Nüwa before him, was forced onto the path he had so desperately tried and failed to avoid: the path that would carry him to his predestined end.

Chiyou died in battle and became the Blood Maple Forest. Xuanyuan, the Yellow Emperor, admired his courage and fierceness and gave him the title of War God. To repay Chiyou, Kunlun-jun took the wu and yao under his wing. From that day on, all wu and yao belonged to Kunlun and were sheltered by the mountains.

Kunlun-jun never once left the mountain. He continued to wait. He had watched Fuxi fall, seen Nüwa go into seclusion, and witnessed Shennong lose his divine powers and subsequently disappear, and he had been waiting ever since. When he saw Xuanyuan pick up Chiyou's head, he said nothing. He was waiting for someone—*anyone*—to return peace to the world. Anyone at all. He was waiting for the Yellow Emperor to unify the land and for the fighting to finally cease.

But that never happened.

Even after the Great War of Gods and Demons, peace never came.

Xuanyuan's entire life was one of battle. When things finally took a turn for the better, he quietly departed the Mortal Realm. Following his death, the descendants of the Flame and Yellow Emperors became locked in a struggle for power.

The east was no more peaceful. Chiyou's descendant, Houyi, happened across the great bow Fuxi had left behind. He gave himself the title "Emperor Jun" and traveled into the depths of the Great Wild, unifying all the tribes to the east and making allies of the wu of the Great Wild.

Kunlun remembered that year, when all the crows were silent. Conflict arose again between Shennong's descendants, who had lain low for many years, the Water God Gonggong, and Zhuanxu, the descendant of Xuanyuan. As Gonggong commanded water, the Dragon tribe, spirits of the water, were the first to take sides.

Consequently, countless yao were drawn into the conflict. Although Houyi wasn't involved in that battle of the Central Plains, the wu and the yao, both under the protection of the Mountain God, had already started showing signs of going separate ways.

Innumerable yao died in that battle. So much blood was shed that it formed rivers atop which shields could float. Tumult gripped the entire continent. The souls of the yao trapped on the Earth's surface cried in despair, day in and day out; the ground was covered in scorched dirt. In death, Chiyou had gained the respect of his greatest enemy, but the descendants for whom he worried until his final breath burned down his War God Temple.

Slowly, the humans, the wu, and the yao all forgot about this ancestor and the brutal but brave inheritance he had left in their blood. Chiyou was slowly recast as an evil god with twisted features in mortal legends.

Kunlun finally lost hope.

He finally came to understand that when Nüwa had first created humans, she had already foreseen this foulness overtaking the Three Realms. With no way to prevent it, she had spent thousands of years, each day like the last, refusing to hear or inquire about the issue.

Kunlun-jun ruled ten thousand great mountains in the Mortal Realm, and in accordance with his vow to Chiyou he had cared for the wu and yao who lived off the mountains for many years. He had watched as they grew up, cultivated, and entered the world. And now they were dying in batches, like worthless weeds tossed into an open fire.

If *this* was the will of the Heavens...

Later, Gonggong was defeated and made his escape astride the divine dragon, preparing to rise once again when the stars aligned. The Dragon tribe had always been precious to Kunlun-jun's heart, but when they reached the Northwestern Abyss he still mercilessly blinded the divine dragon. Gonggong and the divine dragon both ran into Buzhou Mountain, knocking a vast hole in the Great Fuxi Seal below. The Place of Great Disrespect shook as tens of thousands of gui cried out as one, and tremendous evil erupted into the very sky.

The gui, like the god born atop the mountain peak, were wholly without fear. They swept across Buzhou Mountain, whistling like the wind. Aiding them with the soul fire on his left shoulder, Kunlun-jun woke the silent underworld in its entirety. He broke apart the Pillars of Heaven, and thus the sky fell and the earth sank.

To what is the axis of the sky tied? How far and to where do the sky's edges extend? Where are the Eight Pillars that hold up the sky? Why is the southeast sunken?[24]

Atop the peak of Kunlun, the lofty Mountain God of the Great Wild finally set foot upon a path in no way akin to the path of the gods who had come before him. Nüwa finally resurfaced after her long absence to find that her old friend had changed

24 From the poem "Heavenly Questions" (天问), by Warring States era poet Qu Yuan.

almost beyond recognition. Kunlun's green robes billowed in the great winds atop the mountain, and his gaze was sharp and fierce—vaguely reminiscent of the axe that had once split the sky from the earth.

Kunlun-jun had sent his little furball, who had been at his side for so long, to the world below. As the Pillars of Heaven collapsed with a thunderous roar, he glanced back, hands folded behind him. His face betrayed no shock upon seeing Nüwa there. He simply said, "I've done what you couldn't bear to—what you feared to do back then. I've done it for you."

Pangu used every scrap of his life to separate the earth and the sky, shattering the dark nothingness. In the end, driven by Heaven's Will, he died of exhaustion.

But the gods in the Great Wild, who fed on wind and slept on dew—why should they bend the knee to something as imaginary as "Heaven's Will"?

Why should they be controlled by it?

Why should they have to bow to fate?

"I want Zhuanxu's people to die along with my innocent lands of the Great Wild," Kunlun said. "I want every connection between the heaven and earth to be severed, that the so-called gods above can no longer spy upon us. I want the Path to Heaven to be broken. All living things in the world will support each other through yin and yang, like the Fuxi Bagua. Everything that exists will be shaped according to its own will. I...don't want anyone to control my fate anymore. Let there be no one who can judge my merits and sins. I wish to turn the withered divine tree at the Place of Great Disrespect into a brush, with which every living being can inscribe their own merits and sins, their rights and wrongs. I want a clean slate."

Nüwa was unable to speak.

"Let all who remain come at me. Pangu and Fuxi are gone. Only you and I are left. You're biding your time, but I refuse to accept this." The sound of Kunlun-jun's sudden laugh was so broken that it might not have been a voice at all. He pointed skyward. "Let them send thunder down upon me if they can. Let them blast Kunlun Mountain open; let them strike me down and kill me. Nothing else will make me accept their will."

With every sentence he spoke, a flash of divine lightning struck. The air at the mountain's peak was filled with flying ice and snow, blinding Nüwa to the point of tears. And through it all, she heard only Kunlun-jun's laughter.

Thunder crashed down for an entire night; relentless rain fell for several days. The gui terrorized everything. The next day, there was no sign of Kunlun-jun's raiment, and every part of him was charred black, but he sat naked in the same spot. After a while, he got to his feet. His blackened flesh sloughed off like a molting snake, leaving only new skin behind.

He reached out, and a leaf from the Great Divine Tree fell into his hand. He curled it upon himself, and it became fresh green robes. Kunlun-jun gathered his loose hair back and straightened his spine. He coughed up a mouthful of blood, then looked up at Nüwa with an arrogant smile, lips still stained with the blood he didn't bother wiping away. "See? What can they do to me?"

That smile, at least, was the same as always. It held a kind of careless innocence.

Nüwa finally found her voice. "Kunlun, the sky is broken. Come help me find the rocks to repair it. Don't be stubborn."

Kunlun-jun only laughed quietly. He walked down the mountain without a backward glance.

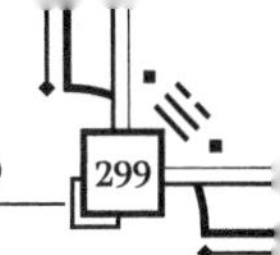

Pangu had died of exhaustion, leaving behind the power to create worlds and birth gods.

Then "the Heavens" had used Nüwa to create humans, planting countless seeds of omens. Fuxi said nothing directly but left a hint with the Bagua; in the end, he was also unable to escape the will of the Heavens. Shennong's people had waned, gradually becoming ordinary. Only Nüwa, overly cautious, had remained.

The Heavens seemed disinclined to let the power to create worlds remain in the Mortal Realm, and thus, one by one, the gods born from Pangu's powers fell. One day, it would be Kunlun-jun's turn. He already felt his death looming.

But why? In this world, were only the weak and unenlightened permitted to eke out bare survival, living lives no longer than a day?

Then he, the Mountain God of the Great Wild, would be the first to go against the Heavens.

Kunlun-jun descended from the mountain and found the world full of the evil beings that had been released from the Place of Great Disrespect. Those were the true ghosts, creatures born not from living souls but from the deep, deep evil sealed within the Place of Great Disrespect.

The laughable truth was that even these wretched things had a hierarchy. The lowest of them bore no resemblance at all to humans. They were like muck, rolling across the ground and feeding on rotten corpses.

Above those in the hierarchy were gui who had heads and bipedal bodies, giving them the approximate shape of humans. But they were covered from head to toe with pustules, and their features were twisted. Their nature was one of brutality. These were known as "youchu."

The higher-ranked any individual gui was, the closer they seemed to human. At the top were the Kings of the Gui: ethereally lovely, like flowers blooming in blood. The more blood-tainted they were, the greater their beauty.

Legend told that two such kings had existed beneath the Great Seal, peerless and unique. Considered in a certain light, the pair of them were even more precious than the Three Sovereigns in the Mortal Realm. What a coincidence, then, that when Kunlun-jun passed through the forest where Kuafu[25] was buried, he encountered one.

This was a boy with black hair and impossibly dark eyes. He sat with appalling posture atop a huge rock, with his unbound hair flowing freely around him. He was the picture of impropriety, barefoot and clad in a coarse hemp garment that someone had given him.

Kunlun-jun's unexpected appearance in the woods evidently gave him a terrible shock. He slipped and tumbled down from the rock, landing in the little creek below. There he sat, sopping wet.

Even as Kunlun-jun stood there trying not to laugh, a youchu climbed up from beneath the earth and clamped its jaws on the boy's slender, delicate neck. The young king's hand came flying up out of the water at a strange angle, closing over the youchu's mouth and shoving its head under the water. He pressed down on it with such force that half of the youchu's head shattered, spraying blood across the king's clean face like red plum blossoms unfurling in the snow.

The young king peeked at Kunlun-jun, then looked at the blood all over himself. Somewhat embarrassed, he carefully squatted down and rinsed his face and hands in the creek. That done, he pulled

---

25 *Kuafu (夸父) is a mythological giant whose attempt to catch the sun is a metaphor for optimism and willingness to face challenges for a goal. When he died, his club became a peach forest. Meeting in a peach forest is a traditional image for lovers in Chinese media.*

the youchu's body closer and opened his mouth, revealing his sharp fangs. He started to gnaw at the most delicate part, the neck.

The beautiful boy sat in the bloody water, daintily feeding on the youchu's corpse. Noticing that Kunlun-jun was still watching, he couldn't help eating more slowly, carefully chewing with his mouth closed and not letting blood dribble out. Then he licked his lips lightly, as though hoping to lick away every trace of blood and appear a bit more refined.

It was true that Kunlun-jun had lent his soul fire to the gui, but his intention had been only to break the Path to Heaven. He didn't deign to interact with these primitive, low-level things; he didn't particularly care for them. But somehow, seeing this young gui, he found himself stepping closer. "Aren't you one of the Kings of the Gui, child? Why aren't you with the others? Why are you pretending to be human?"

The young king lowered his head silently for a while before quietly saying, "They're filthy."

Kunlun-jun's interest was piqued. "You think your fellow gui are filthy?"

The boy didn't dare look directly at him. Instead, he stared at Kunlun-jun's reflection on the water's surface. With intense sincerity, he said, "What do they know other than killing and eating? I don't want to be with them."

"That's just how the gui are," said Kunlun-jun.

Darkness flooded the boy's gaze, but when he looked up at Kunlun-jun, he successfully restrained his innate brutality. It seemed like something he did often. "Must I act as they do, just because we are the same?" he asked earnestly.

Kunlun-jun stood frozen. There was still a bit of youchu blood at the corner of the young king's eye, but his gaze was as clear as autumn water. The boy stood up in the creek. It seemed he might have lost his appetite because he hauled the youchu's corpse out of the water and threw it aside. Then he leaned over and wrung the water out of his coarse clothing before climbing onto the bank of the creek.

He glanced at Kunlun-jun again. His eyes were like a crow's feather fallen on clean, pure snow—a perfect stark contrast of black and white. "I don't want to live like that," he said. "If I must, then I might as well not live at all. I would rather die than live in a way not of my own choosing."

The little king sat down casually by the water's edge, leaving his wet feet to dry. He stared into the distance, taking in the mountains beyond the grove, the mist and snow, and the endless torrential rain falling from the lightning-torn sky.

Kunlun-jun couldn't help asking, "What are you looking at?"

The boy pointed in the direction he was looking. "It's pretty."

"The rain? What's pretty about the rain?" As Kunlun-jun spoke, he sat down next to him and leaned against the huge rock. "You should see the peak of Kunlun Mountain under a clear sky. When the golden sunlight streams down and caresses the snow, it looks like flowers blooming on all that white. There are expanses of craggy rocks under the layer of ice, and in the summer when the snow thins, you can glimpse them here and there. A fine grass grows there, and all sorts of nameless little flowers—all flowers of that sort are called galsang flowers."

Enraptured by his words, the boy stared at him attentively.

Kunlun-jun's description suddenly broke off. "Mmnn—you can't see them now, though."

"Why not?"

"In order to release you and your brethren, I poked a hole in the sky." Kunlun-jun impulsively reached out and patted the young king's head and found that his hair was as soft as it looked. The boy held his neck stiffly, but he didn't move, docilely allowing Kunlun-jun to pet him. It was almost impossible to imagine that he had only just been gnawing on a youchu's neck, even with traces of gore still around his mouth.

Kunlun-jun was suddenly reminded of the little furball he had raised.

"Why...did you poke a hole in the sky?"

"You wouldn't understand, child." Kunlun-jun pressed gently down on his head.

But the young king looked up at him with a tremendously earnest expression. "I *do* understand. I used to be trapped under the Great Seal with no idea what was outside. If I'd known how beautiful it is out here, I would have poked a hole through the seal myself years ago."

Kunlun-jun shook his head, laughing quietly. "'I would rather die than live in a way not of my own choosing,' hmm? Imagine that—you do understand me."

Up in the air, Nüwa flickered in and out of view as she rushed around trying to collect the Stones of Many Hues that could mend the sky. Creatures all throughout the land had been plunged into turmoil, but Kunlun felt a peculiar satisfaction. He stood up to leave, and the young King of the Gui did the same, following close behind.

Kunlun-jun didn't stop him. He raised a hand sharply, and a tall mountain rumbled up out of the ground in the southeast, in the land of Penglai. He beckoned to the wu and the yao, signaling them to go to Penglai to shelter from the disasters.

At that time, the days of heavy rain finally resulted in a great flood. From the highlands to the northwest, water surged eastward, advancing relentlessly. Waves crashed over thousands of miles of

arid land. Devastated, the living wept while Zhuanxu knelt and kowtowed, pleading with the Heavens.

But the Heavens didn't care.

The water kept coming. Houyi led the wu up Penglai, kowtowing after each step. There were young children in the crowd who didn't know what was going on. They cried and fussed until the adults, terrified and panicked, feared that the children's cries would disturb the gods and bring calamity upon them all. So they covered up the children's mouths, and along the way some children were smothered to death.

Halfway up the mountain, the flood caught up to them. Half of the people still struggling to climb up were swept away. On the mountain's highest peak, the coldhearted god closed his eyes.

Then from the west there came a bedraggled crowd carrying all their possessions on their backs. At the front of the group was a very old man carrying a medicine basket leading them toward Penglai. The Northern Emperor, Zhuanxu, trailed deferentially behind him.

Watching from the peak, Kunlun-jun saw a familiar face. "Shennong," he murmured.

Down among the people, Shennong looked up. A flash of divine lightning seemed to be reflected in his murky eyes.

Kunlun didn't stop him. All along, his fight had been only against Heaven's will. He had never wanted or deigned to kill these living beings himself. He watched Shennong lead the surviving humans from the Central Plains up the difficult slope of Penglai. Zhuanxu bowed and kowtowed to the statue of Kunlun-jun, expressing his gratitude for the Mountain God's protection.

It wasn't until the humans had dispersed that Kunlun finally appeared before Shennong. The white-haired old man slapped him cleanly across the face, and Kunlun allowed it.

The young King of the Gui at Kunlun-jun's side was another story. He bared his beastly claws and roared, but before he could pounce at Shennong, the Mountain God reached out and stopped him. Looking at the age-stricken Shennong, Kunlun-jun said quietly, "You're no longer a god. You're about to die."

Shennong's murky eyes rested on him. "I'll die a worthy death. It's nothing I didn't bring upon myself. And you—you were born from the great mountains, innately connected to the evil of the Chaos, not to mention the three ethereal souls you absorbed from the axe of Pangu that opened the sky. Long, long ago I said that your very existence was a terrible omen and that you would one day usher in great ruin. That's why I had drifting snow cover Kunlun Mountain's peak year-round, so that it might hone your spirit. And yet, here you are anyway. You can't let go of eternity, you're unable to see through right and wrong, you can't differentiate between good and evil, and you don't understand life and death! How dare you try to go against the will of the Heavens? You..." And then Shennong sighed.

His words were a dark premonition of what was to come.

On the third day, the night sky fell into disarray. The gui walked the land.

On the fourth day, the floodwaters rose, and all living creatures continued their migration up the mountains. With the wu and the yao in such close proximity, the long-simmering conflict between them finally exploded.

On the seventh day, the wu and yao continued to fight. Half of their population was dead or wounded. The Flame and Yellow Emperors' descendants and Chiyou's descendants formed an alliance as they tried desperately to survive.

On the twelfth day, Nüwa finally repaired the ever-raining sky.

She used the great turtle's legs as the new Pillars of Heaven, leaving her completely exhausted.

On the thirteenth day, the conflict between wu and yao came to a head. The natural order collapsed. The gui swept across the continent, the Four Pillars shook, and the northwestern sky swayed, on the verge of caving in.

The sky and earth were about to become one again. The gui were going to consume everything. All would return to Chaos.

"Nüwa asked me to pass along the word. She has already enforced the Four Pillars and now intends to turn herself into Houtu, in order to secure the Great Fuxi Seal," Shennong said wearily. "You weren't wrong, Kunlun. Pangu wasn't wrong. None of us were wrong. However, the thousands of trials and tribulations of the Mortal Realm, and all the wars and disasters of the living, they are all predetermined. Fuxi was silent in life, and so he died in silence. Recalcitrant as you are, your death will be the same. As for me, I'm dying like a mortal. My body is giving out. All of this was written in the stars. No one can fight it. If anything is to blame, it's that you know too much."

Out of nowhere, Kunlun said, "Chiyou once entrusted both the wu and yao to me. Now the two groups are at odds, unwilling to coexist even on the tiny shelter of Penglai. It seems that Heaven's will is that I must choose which will survive, lest they all die together. Is that right?"

Shennong looked at him in silence.

After what seemed an eternity, Kunlun finally murmured, "Then let the yao remain."

Shennong gave a great sigh, knowing Kunlun had reached the end of his rope. No choice remained but to bow to Heaven's will.

The great floods finally calmed. Nüwa had dealt a heavy blow to the King of the Gui who wielded a giant axe in imitation of Pangu.

She became Houtu and filled the gap in the Great Seal, forcing the gui back under the Four Pillars. But repairing the sky had used up too much of her energy even before the grave injury she had sustained from the King of the Gui's axe. The Great Fuxi Seal had been patched over, but only barely. It still seemed ready to rupture at any moment.

Shennong sat in the great hall of Kunlun-jun's palace in silence.

"I expected to die from the piercing lightning," said Kunlun suddenly. "I didn't imagine that my grave was prepared from the moment I blinded the divine dragon and toppled Buzhou Mountain."

Shennong raised his aged eyes to look upon the very last of the Four Sages of the Great Wild. He couldn't speak. Perhaps Kunlun-jun could leave; perhaps he could use his matchless powers as the Mountain God of the Great Wild to cut Kunlun Mountain off from the world. Even if heaven and earth once again returned to Chaos, no one could intervene.

But Kunlun's three ethereal souls had arisen from the axe that sundered the earth and sky. He alone would never go against Pangu's wishes.

Kunlun himself was Pangu's will.

"I wish...I could see my little furball one more time."

Shennong, medicine basket on his back, walked slowly into the deep mountains. By this time, Nüwa's silhouette was nearly impossible to discern.

Everything seemed to be headed toward a dead end. Returning to his cold, desolate hall, Kunlun-jun looked back and realized that the only one still by his side was the black-haired, black-eyed King of the Gui, who looked so soft and thin.

Very quietly, the young King of the Gui asked, "Are you going to put me back behind the Great Seal?"

"No. Everything else is out of my hands, but at least…at least I can keep you safe." Kunlun-jun laughed quietly. A brief, vicious spasm racked his body, and an imperceptible tremor entered his voice. "Since you don't want to be a gui, I'll give you what you want."

Shocked, the boy grabbed for Kunlun-jun's shoulder, but Kunlun's body was already translucent, his face as pale as snow. The Mountain God raised a hand. His vast sleeves stirred a fresh breeze, and a flame as resplendent as stardust gathered in his palm. "Take it."

The boy accepted it with both hands.

"This is the soul fire from my left shoulder." Sweat beaded Kunlun-jun's forehead, but still he smiled. "And I… I'll give you something else."

As he spoke, his body began to shake violently. He pulled a long, silver tendon from his body; in doing so, he endured a pain more excruciating than any in the world. He seemed not to see the boy's red-rimmed eyes.

"Take my divine tendon," he said. "From this day forward…you can be free of…the Place of Great Disrespect, and rank among the gods… Guard…guard over the Four Pillars for me. With Nüwa's Reincarnation Dial, Fuxi's Mountain-River Awl…the brush from the Ancient Merit Tree…and I'll give you one last…"

"Kunlun!"

Kunlun-jun touched a thumb to the young boy's face, lifting it. Softly, he said, "Stone that is aged but not yet old; water that is frozen but not yet cold; body that is dead but not yet born; soul that is melted but not yet burned… Since Shennong was willing to set aside his divine status to become a mortal, I'll add one more thing to his pile of good deeds…and let him sympathize with humans until the end…"

With those words, he coughed up his heart's blood into his hand, where it became a dark red wick. The Mountain God of the Great

Wild became increasingly transparent, weaker by the second. Finally, he disappeared completely, leaving behind a snow-white oil lamp. There were two words engraved in the corner: Soul Guardian.

Soul that is melted but not yet burned: the Soul-Guarding Lamp.

At last, the pillars stood once again. The Four Hallowed Artifacts were assembled, the Mountain God had faded into thin air, and the Three Sovereigns were gone without a trace. The responsibility for the Four Pillars that held up the sky had, by chance, fallen to the young King of the Gui, who had divinity forced upon him. All that weight lay on his shoulders. It was Kunlun-jun's last taunt to the Heavens.

Once he took up that burden, he faced millions of years with no end in sight.

Zhao Yunlan felt as though there'd been an explosion in his skull. It was as if he had once again endured the excruciating pain of having a tendon pulled out of him, compounded with the agony of ten thousand mountains resting upon his shoulders and the suffering of being driven beyond what he could bear by the Heavens—of being bound with no hope of escape.

Millennia swam before his eyes. A timeless sigh came from the depths of the Great Divine Tree. A low voice said, "Why did you have to do all this..."

"Pan...gu..."

White light flared before Zhao Yunlan's eyes. His head was suddenly heavy, and his feet were light. By the time he opened his eyes again, he was back in Dragon City, with festive Lunar New Year cheer filling the air. All the lights at 4 Bright Avenue had already been turned off. The canopy of the evergreen pines in the courtyard covered the sky.

Feeling something cold on his face, Zhao Yunlan pressed a hand to his cheek and found it wet with tears.

THE STORY CONTINUES IN

Guardian

VOLUME 3

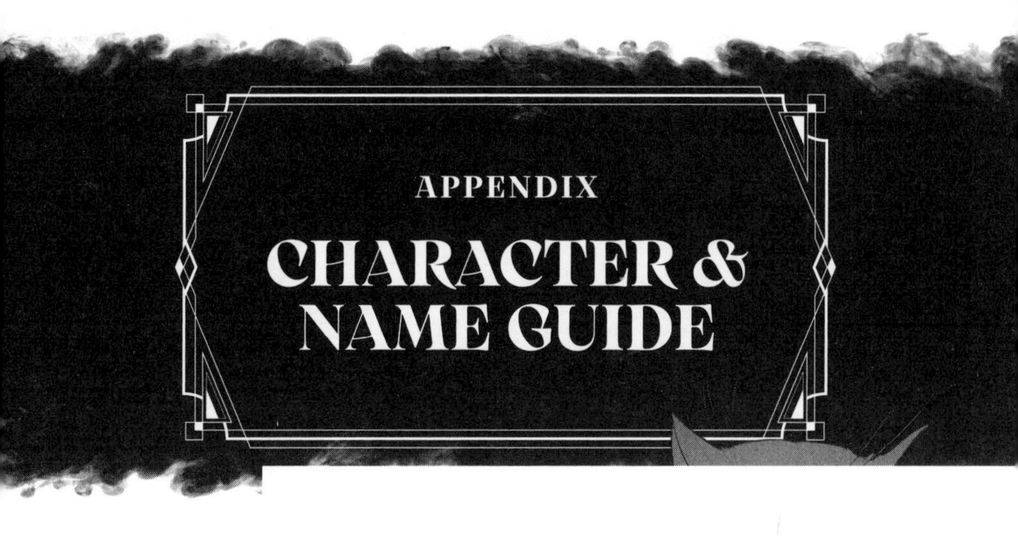

APPENDIX

CHARACTER & NAME GUIDE

CHARACTERS AND ASSOCIATED FACTIONS

The identity of certain characters may be a spoiler; use this guide with caution on your first read of the novel.

SPECIAL INVESTIGATIONS DEPARTMENT (SID)

A police department under the Ministry of Public Security that investigates supernatural crimes in the Mortal Realm. It works with local law enforcement but is not under their jurisdiction.

Zhao Yunlan 赵云澜

TITLES: Director of the Special Investigations Department, Guardian to the Soul-Guarding Order 镇魂令主, Mountain God of the Great Wild 大荒山圣, Kunlun-jun 昆仑君

WEAPONS: Dagger, whip, paper talismans, gun

Zhao Yunlan was born with his third eye open, naturally able to see ghosts and supernatural creatures within the Mortal Realm. When he was ten years old, a black cat, Daqing, brought him the Soul-Guarding Order, which is how he became the Guardian. Later, with the help of his father at the Ministry of Public Security, he became the Director of the Special Investigations Department.

He wears a watch named Clarity (明鉴) which has the ability to reflect supernatural presences even when they can't be seen with the naked eye. The name "Clarity" comes from its mirror-like quality and ability to show the truth.

Chu Shuzhi 楚恕之

A mysterious, stoic man of few words. His grim demeanor intimidates Guo Changcheng.

Daqing 大庆

A talking, fat black cat, and the SID's mascot. Daqing has lived for thousands of years and is very knowledgeable about supernatural and mythological matters. He was the one who brought Zhao Yunlan the Soul-Guarding Order.

Guo Changcheng 郭长城

The new intern at the Special Investigations Department. An orphan brought up by extended family, his uncle was the one who secured him this job. A recent graduate from college, Guo Changcheng has a great fear of people and often finds it hard to interact with others, especially those in positions of authority, such as his boss. Despite this, he has a heart of gold and often donates his time and money to charities and to help those in need.

Lin Jing 林静

A Buddhist monk who doesn't always abide by the strict rules of his religion.

Wang Zheng 汪徵

An employee of the HR Department at the Special Investigations Department. As a ghost, she cannot come in contact with sunlight.

Zhu Hong 祝红

A dependable member of the Special Investigations Department. Zhu Hong is half human and half snake and can transform into her python form at will, except during a certain period each month when her tail is always visible.

SOUL-GUARDING ORDER

In addition to being head of the Special Investigations Department, Zhao Yunlan is also the Guardian, leader of the Soul-Guarding Order. This is an organization that has existed since ancient times and is responsible for overseeing supernatural matters in the Mortal Realm. The Guardian has authority over those who choose to enter the Order and possesses three special talismans with the words "Soul-Guarding" written on them.

DRAGON CITY UNIVERSITY

Shen Wei 沈巍

A professor at Dragon City University. Well-mannered and gentle, he seems to have a mysterious connection to Zhao Yunlan.

Li Qian 李茜

A graduate student at Dragon City University and a person of interest at the center of the Reincarnation Dial case. Neglected by her parents growing up, she lives in a small apartment off campus with her grandma, who raised her.

NETHERWORLD

Soul-Executing Emissary 斩魂使

WEAPON: Soul-Executing Blade

The Soul-Executing Emissary is a mysterious, powerful figure, feared by Netherworld creatures and members of the SID alike. Zhao Yunlan, who has met him occasionally in the past through his work, is one of the only people who doesn't find him intimidating.

Ten Kings of the Yanluo Courts (Yanluo Kings) 十殿阎罗

The highest-ranking officials of the Netherworld, the Ten Kings are final arbiters who decide the fate of each soul based on their previous life's merits and sins. Each presides over a different Hell; these Hells are differentiated by types of crime.

The Magistrate 判官

A high-ranking official of the Netherworld who carries out the Yanluo Kings' orders and manages the reapers.

Reapers 阴差

Low-level Netherworld workers. They are essentially Netherworld law enforcement officers sent out on tasks and errands, including retrieving newly deceased souls and guiding them to the Netherworld.

OTHER

Ghost-Faced Figure 鬼面人

A mysterious masked figure who seems to be an enemy of the Soul-Executing Emissary.

LOCATIONS

DRAGON CITY: A fictional metropolis where most of the story takes place. It is home to Dragon City University and the Special Investigations Department.

THE NETHERWORLD 地府: Where the deceased go after death. Common Chinese folklore believes that when people die, their souls are collected by **reapers** (阴差) who lead them through the **Gates of the Netherworld** (鬼门关) and down the **Huangquan Road** (黄泉路). The souls then arrive at the **The Ten Courts of the Yanluo Kings** (十殿阎王), where they are judged for their merits and sins. If they committed too many sins, they are sent to the **Eighteen Levels of Hell** (十八层地狱), but if they have accumulated enough good deeds in life, they may move on to reincarnation. In order to reincarnate, these souls first have to walk the **Naihe Bridge** (奈何桥), which crosses over the **Wangchuan River** (忘川河), and drink the **Mengpo Soup** (孟婆汤). After drinking the soup, the soul forgets everything from its past life and is ready to move on to the next one.

HUANGQUAN 黄泉: Literally "Yellow Spring." In Chinese mythology, "Huangquan" is a word that can be used to describe the underworld itself, but can sometimes describe a part of the underworld or a literal, extremely deep body of water souls reach after death. In *Guardian*, it is used as a term for both the road to the underworld and a body of water within the underworld.

NAME GUIDE

DIMINUTIVES, NICKNAMES, AND NAME TAGS

A-: Friendly diminutive. Always a prefix. Usually for monosyllabic names, or one syllable out of a two-syllable name. Example: a-Lan

DA-: A prefix meaning "eldest." Not always used literally—can be added to a name or other diminutive as a way to add respect. Example: dage

XIAO-: A prefix meaning "small" or "youngest." When added to a name, it expresses affection. Example: xiao-Guo

LAO-: A prefix meaning "old." Usually added to a surname and used in informal contexts. Example: lao-Wu

GE: Older brother or older male friend. Usually used to refer to a close but respected man older than the speaker. Can be attached to a name as a suffix. Example: Chu-ge

JIE: Older sister or older female friend. Usually used to refer to a close but respected woman older than the speaker. Can be attached to a name as a suffix. Example: Zhu Hong-jie, jiejie

TONGXUE: A general term used to address a student by someone who is not close to them. Used in contexts where calling them by their full name would sound too blunt. Can also be attached to someone's name as a suffix. Example: Zhao-tongxue.

LAOSHI: A term used to refer to any educator, often in deference. Can also be attached to someone's name as a suffix. Example: Shen-laoshi.

These affixes can also be combined. Combinations include but are not limited to:

DAGE: Literally means eldest brother, but when used outside family, it is an informal address to insinuate respect and closeness with a male friend older than the speaker.

LAOGE: Literally means elderly brother. In common usage, it's similar to dage but even less formal and suggests a closer relationship. Usually refers to a significantly older man.

PRONUNCIATION GUIDE

Mandarin Chinese is the official state language of mainland China, and pinyin is the official system of romanization in which it is written. As Mandarin is a tonal language, pinyin uses diacritical marks (e.g., ā, á, ǎ, à) to indicate these tonal inflections. Most words use one of four tones, though some are a neutral tone. Furthermore, regional variance can change the way native Chinese speakers pronounce the same word. For those reasons and more, please consider the guide below a simplified introduction to pronunciation of select character names and sounds from the world of *Guardian*.

More resources are available at sevenseasdanmei.com

NOTE ON SPELLING: Romanized Mandarin Chinese words with identical spelling in pinyin—and even pronunciation—may well have different meanings. These words are more easily differentiated in written Chinese, which uses characters.

Zhènhún

zh as in **j**ohn.
en as in **un**derstand.
h as in **h**orse.
un as in **when**.
(juhn hwen)

Zhào Yúnlán

zhao as in **jou**st.
y as in **y**ou.
un as in b**oon**.
lan as in **l**eaf.
an as in r**un**.
(jow yoon lahn)

Shěn Wēi

shen as in **shun**.
wei as in **way**.
(shun way)

Guō Chángchéng

guo as in **Go**rdon.
ch as in **ch**allenge.
ang as in t**ongue**.
ch as in **ch**allenge.
eng as in **uh+ng**.
(gwo chahng chuhng)
NOTE: The difference between ang and eng is that chang leans more toward ah-ng and eng leans more toward uh-ng.

Dàqìng

da as in **da**rling.
q as in **ch**eap.
ing as in **Eng**lish.
(da ching)

Zhù Hóng

zh as in **j**ohn.
u as in f**oo**l.
ho as in **ho**me.
ng as in lo**ng**.
(joo hohng)

Lín Jìng

lin as in **lean**.
jing as in **jing**le.
(leen jing)

Wāng Zhēng

wa as in **wa**nt.
ng as in lo**ng**.
zh as in **j**ohn.
eng as in **uh+ng**.
(wahng juhng)

Sāngzàn

sang as in **sung**.
z as in regar**ds**.
an as in r**un**.
(sung zun)

APPENDIX

GLOSSARY

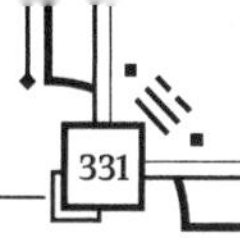

GLOSSARY

While not required reading, this glossary is intended to offer further context to the many concepts and terms utilized throughout this novel and provide a starting point for learning more about the rich Chinese culture from which these stories were written.

China is home to dozens of cultures, and its history spans thousands of years. The provided definitions are not strictly universal across all these cultural groups, and this simplified overview is meant for new readers unfamiliar with the concepts. This glossary should not be considered a definitive source, especially for more complex ideas.

GENRES

Danmei

Danmei (耽美 / "indulgence in beauty") is a Chinese fiction genre focused on romanticized tales of love and attraction between men. It is analogous to the BL (boys' love) genre in Japanese media. The majority of well-known danmei writers are women writing for women, although all genders produce and enjoy the genre.

Webnovels

Webnovels are novels serialized by chapter online, and the websites that host them are considered spaces for indie and amateur writers. Many novels, dramas, comics, and animated shows produced in China are based on popular webnovels.

Guardian was first serialized on the website JJWXC.

FOLKLORE, MYTHOLOGY, AND RELIGION

In Chinese culture, lines between superstitious and folk beliefs may be blurred. Throughout history as different religions drift in and out of popularity, the people have adapted aspects of various religions into practices that better fit their local culture, sometimes mixing elements from several faiths to create something very different from the original religion. The lore in *Guardian* includes elements from Buddhism, Daoism, other folk religions, and local beliefs, and this is a good reflection on the belief system in China. It's quite common for someone to not be religious but still visit temples on special occasions or to pray for good luck. As such, though all definitions and explanations provided in this glossary may not be the only version out there, we've done our best to provide the most commonly accepted version that pertains to *Guardian*.

BI FANG 毕方: A mythological one-legged bird depicted in *The Classic of Mountains and Seas*. It's often described as holding a flame in its beak and known in some folk legends as being the herald of fire.

THE BOOK OF LIFE AND DEATH 生死簿: A book that keeps record of all living beings, how long they live, and all details of their lives. The Netherworld uses it to keep track of all souls and to know when it's time to collect a soul from the Mortal Realm.

BUDDHISM: The central belief of Buddhism is that life is a cycle of suffering and rebirth, only to be escaped by reaching enlightenment (nirvana). Buddhists believe in karma, that a person's actions will influence their fortune in this life and future lives. The teachings of

the Buddha are known as The Middle Way and emphasize a practice that is neither extreme asceticism nor extreme indulgence.

CHAOS 混沌: The original state of all matter, which was shaped like an egg before Pangu hacked it open with his axe from the inside and created the world as we know it.

GHOSTS 鬼: The spirits of deceased sentient creatures. Ghosts emit yin energy. They come in a variety of types: they can be malevolent or helpful, can retain their former personalities or be fully mindless, and can actively try to interact with the living world to achieve a goal or be little more than a remnant shadow of their former lives.

- **HUNGER GHOSTS 饿死鬼:** Ghosts who are punished with an insatiable hunger no matter how much they eat.
- **VIOLENT GHOSTS 厉鬼:** Ghosts with intense spiteful and malicious energy, usually resulting from a violent death or suicide. They tend to roam locations where they died or places that are meaningful to them. They cannot move on unless their source of anger is resolved.
- **EARTHBOUND SPIRITS 地缚灵:** Spirits that, due to resentment or unfulfilled wishes, are bound to a limited area or building, usually related to their death. They are bound there until their wish is fulfilled.

THE HEAVENS: In Chinese culture, the Heavens are a generic yet supreme power, universal and formless, that enforce order upon all matter, often manifesting as forces of nature. This power is not a place or a god, but even presides over gods.

MERITS 功德: Merits are "points" a person accumulates throughout their lifetime that determine their karma. The more good things one does, the more merits they accumulate. The more merits they have, the better their karma. In the end, their karma decides what they are reincarnated as in the next life.

PANGU 盘古: A primordial god who separated the clear from the turbid, forming Heaven and Earth out of the Chaos, thus creating the world.

SIX PATHS OF REINCARNATION/REINCARNATION CYCLE 六道轮回: The Six Paths of Reincarnation are six different realms of existence a soul may be reborn into: gods, demi-gods, humans, animals, wandering spirits, and hell. The previous life's karma determines which realm they reincarnate into in the next life.

THIRD EYE 阴阳眼: An innate ability a person is naturally born with that allows them to see ghosts and other supernatural things in the Mortal Realm. This is sometimes described as one's third eye being open.

THREE ETHEREAL SOULS AND SEVEN CORPOREAL SOULS 三魂七魄: In traditional Chinese belief, humans possess two kinds of souls: ethereal souls (魂) represent the spirit and intellect and leave the body after death, whereas corporeal souls (魄) are earthbound and remain with the body of the deceased. Different traditions claim there are different numbers of each, but three ethereal souls and seven corporeal souls is common in Daoism.

THREE-LIFE ROCK 三生石: It's said that on the shore of the Wangchuan River, there is a large rock with two long markings going through it that divide the rock into three parts, representing the past life, the present life, and the future life.

THE THREE REALMS: Traditionally, the universe is divided into three realms: the Heavenly Realm, the Mortal Realm, and the Netherworld. The Heavenly Realm is where gods reside and rule, the Mortal Realm refers to the realm of the living, and the Netherworld refers to the realm of the dead. However, in *Guardian*, the gods do not live in the Heavenly Realm; they live in the Mortal Realm.

THE THREE SOVEREIGNS 三皇五帝

- **FUXI 伏羲:** One of the Three Sovereigns of ancient mythology, said to have the head of a human and the body of a snake. According to legend, Fuxi is Nüwa's brother or spouse (or both), as well as the ancestor to the humans who came after.
- **NÜWA 女娲:** One of the Three Sovereigns of ancient mythology, with the head of a human and the body of a snake. She is best known for patching up the hole in the sky and for creating humans out of mud; therefore, she is known as the ancestor to all humans.
- **SHENNONG 神农:** One of the Three Sovereigns of ancient mythology, known in folk legends as the inventor of agriculture and herbal medicine.

True Flames of Samadhi 三昧真火: A concept of both Daoist and Buddhist origin. In *Guardian*, it refers to both a special fire that Zhao Yunlan manages to obtain from the Bi Fang bird, as well as the three soul fires every person possesses: one located on the top of their head and another on each shoulder.

GENERAL CHINESE CULTURE

BIRTH CHART 生辰八字: A series of eight characters assigned to a person based on the Sexagenary Cycle (Tian Gan Di Zhi/Heavenly Stems, Earthly Branches). Two characters each are assigned according to their birth year, month, day, and hour, forming eight characters in total. It's thought that one's fate can be told from their birth chart. Usually, when one's birth chart is "too light," it means they have a hard life ahead, perhaps suffering illnesses or other traumatic events. And when one's birth chart is "too hard," one might cause other people who have "lighter" birth charts to die.

CHINESE CALENDAR: The traditional Chinese calendar is a combination of the lunar and solar calendars. Nowadays, it is more common to use the Gregorian calendar to keep track of dates. The Chinese calendar is more often used for traditional holidays (Lunar New Year, Mid-Autumn, etc.), and occasionally, people will keep track of their Chinese calendar birthday. Using the Chinese calendar is considered a little unusual—though perhaps more common with older people.

CINNABAR 朱砂: A red mineral pigment used for drawing paper talismans. A form of mercury sulfide, it's traditionally thought to have mind-calming effects and is effective for dispelling evil.

DAGENG 打更: In the times before clocks, this was the traditional system for telling time at night. A night watchman would walk around town with a gong or a woodblock, striking five times throughout the night, once every geng, or roughly every 2.4 hours.

DEATH RITUALS: After a person dies, their family will lay out food, burn incense, spirit money, and paper renditions of objects to help the dead in the Netherworld. There are specialty funeral stores that will sell various papier-mâché objects specifically for funerals. These offerings, especially spirit money, incense, and food, will be continuously offered after the deceased has died to pay respects.

FENG SHUI 风水: Literally translates to wind-water. Refers to the natural laws believed to govern the flow of qi in the arrangement of the natural environment and man-made structures. Favorable feng shui and good qi flow have various beneficial effects to everyday life and the practice of cultivation, while the opposite is true for unfavorable feng shui and bad qi flow.

GHOST FESTIVAL 中元节/七月半: A traditional festival that falls on the 15th night of the seventh lunar month. During this festival, the living pay homage to their ancestors. It is when the dead are believed to pay a visit to the Mortal Realm.

MOURNING BIRDS 报丧鸟: Large crows that are said to announce the arrival of a calamity.

TOUQI 头七: The first seven days after a person's death. It is believed that a new ghost will visit their family on the seventh day after their death to take one last look before they move on. The family will serve food and lock themselves in their rooms so the ghost won't become attached and refuse to move on.

YIN/YANG ENERGY 阴/阳气: Yin and yang is a concept in Chinese philosophy that describes the complementary interdependence of opposite/contrary forces. It can be applied to all forms of change and differences. Yang represents the sun, masculinity, and the living, while yin represents the shadows, femininity, and the dead, including spirits and ghosts. In fiction, imbalances between yin and yang energy in a person's body can act as the driving force for malevolent spirits that are seeking to replenish themselves of whichever they lack. Those with strong yang energy (e.g., men) are considered effective at warding off yin-natured supernatural beings (e.g., ghosts).

BOOKS REFERENCED IN GUARDIAN

The text of *Guardian* mentions many real-life books and stories, in addition to the many fictional tales that only exist within the novel. This is a list of the real books referenced within the text for your further research if desired.

- *The Injustice to Dou E (play) by Guan Hanqing* - 窦娥冤
- *Classics of Mountains and Sea by* 山海经
- *The Summons of the Soul (poem) by* 招魂
- *Imperial Readings of the Taiping Era by* 太平御览
- *Huainanzi by Huainanzi by* 淮南子
- *Anna Karenina by Leo Tolstoy*

MEASUREMENTS

Measurements have changed during different periods of Chinese history, but these are what they are generally accepted as today. They are often only used as approximations and not to be taken literally. For example, something described as "thousands of zhang" is just very large.

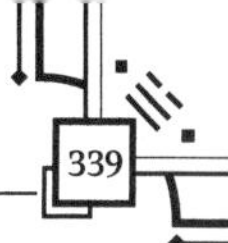

- Cun 寸 - roughly 3 centimeters
- Chi 尺 - roughly ⅓ meter
- Zhang 丈 - roughly 3⅓ meters
- 10 cun = 1 chi
- 10 chi = 1 zhang
- Li 里 = 1,800 cun

GUARDIAN-SPECIFIC TERMINOLOGY

FOUR HALLOWED ARTIFACTS OF THE NETHERWORLD 幽冥四圣器: Within the fictional world of *Guardian*, these are four sacred artifacts that are said to be passed down since primordial times, related to a seal that affects the balance between yin and yang, reincarnation, and life and death. They include:

REINCARNATION DIAL 轮回晷: Made from pieces of the Three-Life Rock, with scales from a black fish from the Wangchuan River. One can use the Reincarnation Dial to give a portion of their life to an older person, thus shortening their own life.

MOUNTAIN-RIVER AWL 山河锥: A large, octagonal pillar that pierces into the ground in the sacred place of the Hanga Tribe. Formed from the spirits of tens of thousands of mountains and rivers, it can absorb and imprison spirits of the dead.

MERIT BRUSH 功德笔: A calligraphy brush made from a branch of the Ancient Merit Tree. It writes in both red and black ink. The red records merits and the black records sins. Using it, anyone is able to rewrite their merits and sins.

SOUL-GUARDING LAMP 镇魂灯: The wick was made of the blood from Kunlun-jun's heart, the lamp itself was made from Kunlun-jun's body.

RECORD OF MERITS 功德录: A record that tracks the merits one has earned throughout their different lives.

GREAT DIVINE TREE 大神木: The ancient tree that grows at the peak of Kunlun Mountain.

ANCIENT MERIT TREE 功德古木: A tree that grew out of a branch of the Great Divine Tree that had been planted in the Place of Great Disrespect. It has no leaves, no flowers, and bears no fruit.

PLACE OF GREAT DISRESPECT 大不敬之地: Thousands of zhang below the Huangquan River, where the gui are imprisoned. It holds all the impurities in the ground left behind from when the earth was first formed.

RACES

WU 巫族: A race of beings that existed around the time of creation.

YAO 妖族: Animals or plants that have gained spiritual consciousness after years of absorbing the essences of Heaven and Earth from their surroundings. Especially high-level or long-lived yao are able to take on a human form after diligent cultivation. This concept is comparable to Japanese yokai, which is a loanword from the Chinese yao. Yao are not evil by nature but often come into conflict with humans for various reasons, one being that the modern world is not conducive to cultivating.

HUMANS 人族: Beings created by Nüwa in the likeness of the gods. For the most part, humans rarely successfully achieve anything from cultivation.

GUI 鬼族: Beings of great evil imprisoned in the Place of Great Disrespect. The more humanlike and beautiful they are, the more powerful. The two most powerful gui are Shen Wei and Ghost Face, the Kings of the Gui. Youchu, appearing in vaguely humanoid forms with festering pustules, are the lowest type of gui.

GODS 神: Powerful deities that existed before humans.

YOUCHU 幽畜: Monstrous creatures born from the Chaos. They come in all shapes and sizes. These are fictional monsters within the world of *Guardian*, not taken directly from any real-world religion or mythology.

▪ priest ▪

An internationally renowned author who writes for the novel serialization website, JJWXC, priest's books have inspired multimedia adaptations and been published in numerous languages around the world. priest is known for writing compelling drama that incorporates humor and creativity, and a grand sense of style that infuses her worldbuilding. Her works include *Stars of Chaos: Sha Po Lang*, *Guardian: Zhen Hun*, *Liu Yao: The Revitalization of Fuyao Sect*, *Mo Du (Silent Reading)*, and *Can Ci Pin (The Defective)*, among others.